Brashieel flinched as the waiting fortresses exploded with power. The terrible energy weapons which had slain so many of Vindicator's brothers in ship-to-ship combat were as nothing beside this! They smote full upon the warships' shields, and as they smote, those ships died. One, two, seven — still they died! Nothing could withstand that fury. Nothing!

❖   ❖   ❖

"All right!" Andrew Samson shouted. Six of the invaders already, and more going! He picked a target whose shields wavered under fire from three different ODCs and popped a gravitonic warhead neatly through them. His victim perished, and this time there was no question who'd made the kill.

❖   ❖   ❖

"Withdraw."

The Order went out, and Brashieel sighed with gratitude. Lord of Thought, Mosharg must have learned what they had come to learn. They could leave.

Assuming they could get away alive.

❖   ❖   ❖

"They're withdrawing!" someone shouted and Gerald Hatcher nodded. Yes, they were, but they'd cost too much before they went. Two missiles had actually gotten through the planetary shield despite all that Vassily and the PDCs could do, and thank God those bastards didn't have gravitonic warheads.

BAEN BOOKS by DAVID WEBER

Honor Harrington:
On Basilisk Station
The Honor of the Queen
The Short Victorious War
Field of Dishonor
Flag in Exile
Honor Among Enemies
In Enemy Hands
Echoes of Honor
Ashes of Victory
War of Honor

edited by David Weber:
More than Honor
Worlds of Honor
Changer of Worlds
The Service of the Sword

Empire From the Ashes *(omnibus)*
Mutineers' Moon
The Armageddon Inheritance
Heirs of Empire

Path of the Fury

The Apocalypse Troll

The Excalibur Alternative

Oath of Swords
The War God's Own

with Steve White:
Insurrection
Crusade
In Death Ground
The Shiva Option

with John Ringo:
March Upcountry
March to the Sea
March to the Stars

with Eric Flint
1633

THE ARMAGEDDON INHERITANCE

DAVID WEBER

THE ARMAGEDDON INHERITANCE

This is a work of fiction. All the characters and events
portrayed in this book are fictional, and any resemblance to
real people or incidents is purely coincidental.

A Baen Books Original

Baen Publishing Enterprises
P.O. Box 1403
Riverdale, NY 10471
www.baen.com

ISBN: 0-671-72197-6

Cover art by David Mattingly

First printing, December 1993
Fifth printing, February 2003

Distributed by Simon & Schuster
1230 Avenue of the Americas
New York, NY 10020

Printed in the United States of America

Book One

Book One

The sensor array was the size of a very large asteroid or a very small moon, and it had orbited the G6 star for a very, very long time, yet it was not remarkable to look upon. Its hull, filmed with dust except where the electro-static fields kept the solar panels clear, was a sphere of bronze-gold alloy, marred only by a few smoothly rounded protrusions, with none of the aerials or receiver dishes which might have been expected by a radio-age civilization. But then, the people who built it hadn't used anything as crude as radio for several millennia prior to its construction.

The Fourth Imperium had left it here fifty-two thousand one hundred and eighty-six Terran years ago, its electronic senses fueled only by a trickle of power, yet the lonely guardian was not dead. It only slept, and now fresh sparkles of current flickered through kilometers of molecular circuitry.

Internal stasis fields spun down, and a computer roused from millennia of sleep. Stronger flows of power pulsed as *testing programs reported, and Comp Cent noted that seven-point-three percent of its primary systems had failed. Had it been interested in such things, it might have reflected that such a low failure rate was near miraculous, but this computer lacked even the most rudimentary of awarenesses. It simply activated the appropriate secondaries, and a new set of programs blinked to life.*

It wasn't the first time the sensor array had awakened, though more than forty millennia had passed since last it was commanded to do so. But this time, Comp Cent observed, the signal which had roused it was no demand from its builders for a systems test. This signal came from another sensor array over seven hundred light-years to galactic east, and it was a death cry.

Comp Cent's hypercom relayed the signal another thousand light-years, to a communications center which had been ancient before Cro-Magnon first trod the Earth, and awaited a response. But there was no response. Comp Cent was on its unimaginative own, and that awakened still more autonomous programs. The signal to its silent commanders was replaced by a series of far shorter-ranged transmissions, and other sensor arrays stirred and roused and muttered sleepily back to it.

Comp Cent noted the gaping holes time had torn in what once had been an intricately interlocking network, but those holes were none of its concern, and it turned to the things which were. More power plants came on line, bringing the array fully alive, and the installation became a brilliant beacon, emitting in every conceivable portion of the electromagnetic and gravitonic spectra with more power than many a populated world of the Imperium. It was a signpost, a billboard proclaiming its presence to anyone who might glance in its direction.

And then it waited once more.

Months passed, and years, and Comp Cent did not care. Just over seven years passed before Comp Cent received a fresh signal, announcing the death of yet another sensor array. This one was less than four hundred light-years distant. Whatever was destroying its lonely sisters was coming closer, and Comp Cent reported to its builders once again. Still no one answered. No one issued new orders or directives. And so it continued to perform the function it had been programmed to perform, revealing itself to the silent stars like a man shouting in a darkened room. And then, one day, just over fifteen years after it had awakened, the stars responded.

Comp Cent's sensitive instruments detected the incoming hyper wake weeks before it arrived. Once more it reported its findings to its commanders, and once more they did not respond. Comp Cent considered the silence, for this was a report its programming told it must be answered. Yet its designers had allowed for the remote possibility that it might not be received by its intended addressees. And so Comp Cent consulted its menus, selected the appropriate command file, and reconfigured its hypercom to omni-directional broadcast. The GHQ signal vanished, replaced by an all-ships warning addressed to any unit of Battle Fleet.

Still there was no answer, but this time no backup program told Comp Cent to do anything else, for its builders had never considered that possibility, and so it continued its warning broadcasts, unconcerned by the lack of response.

The hyper wake came closer, and Comp Cent analyzed its pattern and its speed, adding the new data to the warning no one acknowledged, watching incuriously as the wake suddenly terminated eighteen light-minutes from the star it orbited. It observed new energy sources approaching, now at sublight speeds, and added its analysis of their patterns to its broadcast.

The drive fields closed upon the sensor array, wrapped about cylindrical hulls twenty kilometers in length. They were not Imperial hulls, but Comp Cent recognized them and added their identity to its transmission.

The starships came closer still at twenty-eight percent of light-speed, approaching the sensor array whose emissions had attracted their attention, and Comp Cent sang to them, and beckoned to them, and trolled them in while passive instrumentation probed and pried, stealing all the data from them that it could. They entered attack range and locked their targeting systems upon the sensor array, but no one fired, and impulses tumbled through fresh logic trees as Comp Cent filed that fact away, as well.

The starships approached within five hundred kilometers, and a tractor beam — a rather crude one, but nonetheless effective, Comp Cent noted — reached out to the sensor array. And as it did, Comp Cent activated the instructions stored deep within its heart for this specific contingency.

Matter met antimatter, and the sensor array vanished in a boil of light brighter than the star it orbited. The detonation was too terrible to call an "explosion," and it reduced the half-dozen closest starships to stripped atoms, ripped a dozen more to incandescent splinters, damaged others, and — just as its long-dead masters had intended — deprived the survivors of any opportunity to evaluate the technology which had built it.

Comp Cent had performed its final function, and it neither knew nor cared why no one had ever answered its warning that, after sixty thousand years, the Achuultani had returned.

Chapter One

It was raining in the captain's quarters.

More precisely, it was raining in the three-acre atrium inside the captain's quarters. Senior Fleet Captain Colin MacIntyre, self-proclaimed Governor of Earth and latest commanding officer of the Imperial planetoid *Dahak*, sat on his balcony and soaked his feet in his hottub, but Fleet Captain Jiltanith, his tall, slender executive officer, had chosen to soak her entire person. Her neatly folded, midnight-blue uniform lay to one side as she leaned back, and her long sable mane floated about her shoulders.

Black-bottomed holographic thunderheads crowded overhead, distant thunder rumbled, and lightning flickered on the "horizon," yet Colin's gaze was remote as he watched rain bounce off the balcony's shimmering force field roof. His attention was elsewhere, focused on the data being relayed through his neural feeds by his ship's central command computer.

His face was hard as the report played itself out behind his eyes, from the moment the Achuultani starships emerged from hyper to the instant of the sensor array's

7

self-immolation. It ended, and he shook himself and looked down at Jiltanith for her reaction. Her mouth was tight, her ebon eyes cold, and for just a moment he saw not a lovely woman but the lethal killing machine which was his executive officer at war.

"That's it, then, Dahak?" he asked.

"It is certainly the end of the transmission, sir," a deep, mellow voice replied from the empty air. Thunder growled again behind the words in grimly appropriate counterpoint, and the voice continued calmly. "This unit was in the tertiary scanner phalanx, located approximately one hundred ten light-years to galactic east of Sol. There are no more between it and Earth."

"Crap," Colin muttered, then sighed. Life had been so much simpler as a NASA command pilot. "Well, at least we got some new data from it."

"Aye," Jiltanith agreed, "yet to what end, my Colin? 'Tis little enow, when all's said, yet not even that little may we send home, sin Earth hath no hypercom."

"I suppose we could turn back and deliver it in person," Colin thought aloud. "We're only two weeks out. . . ."

"Nay," Jiltanith disagreed. "Should we turn about 'twill set us back full six weeks, for we must needs give up the time we've but now spent, as well."

"Fleet Captain Jiltanith is correct, Captain," Dahak seconded, "and while these data are undoubtedly useful, they offer no fundamental insights necessary to Earth's defense."

"Huh!" Colin tugged at his nose, then sighed. "I guess you're right. It'd be different if they'd actually attacked and given us a peek at their hardware, but as it is —" He shrugged. "I wish to hell they *had*, though. God knows we could use some idea of what they're armed with!"

"True," Dahak agreed. "Yet the readings the sensor array did obtain indicate no major advances in the Achuultani's general technology, which suggests their weaponry also has not advanced significantly."

"I almost wish there *were* signs of advances," Colin

fretted. "I just can't accept that they haven't got *something* new after sixty thousand years!"

"It is, indeed, abnormal by human standards, sir, but entirely consistent with surviving evidence from previous incursions."

"Aye," Jiltanith agreed, sliding deeper into the hot water with a frown, "yet still 'tis scarce credible, Dahak. How may any race spend such time 'pon war and killing and bring no new weapons to their task?"

"Unknown," the computer replied so calmly Colin grimaced. Despite Dahak's self-awareness, he had yet to develop a human-sized imagination.

"Okay, so what *do* we know?"

"The data included in the transmission confirm reports from the arrays previously destroyed. In addition, while no tactical information was obtained, sensor readings indicate that the Achuultani's maximum attainable sublight velocity is scarcely half as great as that of this vessel, which suggests at least one major tactical advantage for our own units, regardless of comparative weaponry. Further, we have re-confirmed their relatively low speed in hyper, as well. At their present rate of advance, they will reach Sol in two-point-three years, as originally projected."

"True, but I'm not too happy about the way they came in. Do we know if they tried to examine any of the other sensor arrays?"

"Negative, Captain. A hypercom of the power mounted by these arrays has a maximum omni-directional range of less than three hundred light-years. The reports of all pre-viously destroyed sensor arrays were relayed via the tertiary phalanx arrays and consisted solely of confirmation that they had been destroyed by Achuultani vessels. This is the first direct transmission we have received and contains far more observational data."

"Yeah." Colin pondered a moment. "But it doesn't match very well with what little we know about their operational patterns, now does it?"

"It does not, sir. According to the records, normal

Achuultani tactics should have been to destroy the array immediately upon detection."

"That's what I mean. We were dead lucky any of the arrays were still around to tell us they're coming, but I can't help thinking the Imperium was a bit too clever in the way it set these things up. Sucking them in close for better readings is all very well, but *these* guys were after information of their own. What if they change tactics or speed up on us because they figure someone's waiting for them?"

"Methinks thy concern may be over great," Jiltanith said after a moment. "Certes, they needs must know some power did place sentinels to ward its borders, yet what knowledge else have they gained? How shall they guess where those borders truly lie or when their ships may cross them? Given so little, still must they search each star they pass."

Colin tugged on his nose some more, then nodded a bit unhappily. It made sense, and there wasn't anything he could do about it even if Jiltanith were wrong, but it was his job to worry. Not that he'd asked for it.

"I guess you're right." He sighed. "Thanks for the report, Dahak."

"You are welcome, Captain," the starship said, and Colin shook himself, then grinned at Jiltanith.

"Looking forward to sickbay, 'Tanni?" He put an edge of malicious humor into his voice as an anodyne against their worries.

"Hast an uncommon low sense of humor, Colin," she said darkly, accepting the change of subject with a smile of her own. "So long as I do recall have I awaited this day — yea, and seldom with true hope mine eyes might see it. Yet now 'tis close upon me, and if truth be known, there lies some shadow of fear within my heart. 'Tis most unmeet in thee so to tease me over it."

"I know," he admitted wickedly, "but it's too much fun to stop."

She snorted and shook a dripping fist at him, yet there

was empathy as well as laughter in his green eyes. Jiltanith had been a child, her muscles and skeleton too immature for the full bioenhancement Battle Fleet's personnel enjoyed, when the mutiny organized by Fleet Captain (Engineering) Anu marooned *Dahak* in Earth orbit and the starship's crew on Earth. The millennia-long struggle her father had led against Anu had kept her from receiving it since, for the medical facilities aboard the sublight parasite battleship *Nergal* had been unable to provide it. Jiltanith had received the neural computer feeds, sensory boosters, and regenerative treatments before the mutiny, but those were the easy parts, and Colin was fresh enough from his own enhancement to understand her anxieties perfectly . . . and tease her to ease them.

"Bawcock, thou'lt crow too loud one day."

"Nope. I'm the captain, and rank —"

"— hath its privileges," she broke in, shaking her head ominously. "That phrase shall haunt thee."

"I don't doubt it." He smiled down at her, tempted to shuck off his own uniform and join her . . . if he hadn't been a bit afraid of where it might lead. Not that he had any objection to where it *could* lead, but there was plenty of time (assuming they lived beyond the next two years), and that was one complication neither of them needed right now.

"Well, gotta get back to the office," he said instead. "And you, Madam XO, should get back to your own quarters and catch some sleep. Trust me — Dahak's idea of a slow convalescence from enhancement isn't exactly the same as yours or mine."

"Of thine, mayhap," she said sweetly.

"I'll remember that when you start moaning for sympathy." He drew his toes from the tub and activated a small portion of his own biotechnics. The water floated off his feet on the skin of a repellent force field, and he shook the drops away and pulled on his socks and gleaming boots.

"Seriously, 'Tanni, get some rest. You'll need it."

"In truth, I doubt thee not," she sighed, wiggling in the

hottub, "yet still doth this seem heaven's foretaste. I'll tarry yet a while, methinks."

"Go ahead," he said with another smile, and stepped off the edge of the balcony onto a waiting presser. It floated him gently to the atrium floor, and his implant force fields were an invisible umbrella as he splashed through the rain to the door/hatch on the far side of his private park.

It opened at his approach, and he stepped through it into a yawning, brightly lit void over a thousand kilometers deep. He'd braced himself for it, yet he knew he appeared less calm than he would have liked — and felt even less calm than he managed to look as he plunged downward at an instantly attained velocity of just over twenty thousand kilometers per hour.

Dahak had stepped his transit shafts' speed down out of deference to his captain and Terra-born crew, though Colin knew the computer truly didn't comprehend why they felt such terror. It was bad enough aboard the starship's sublight parasites, yet the biggest of those warships massed scarcely eighty thousand tons. In something that tiny, there was barely time to feel afraid before the journey was over, but even at this speed it would take almost ten minutes to cross *Dahak*'s titanic hull, and the lack of any subjective sense of movement made it almost worse.

Yet the captain's quarters were scarcely a hundred kilometers from Command One — a mere nothing aboard *Dahak* — and the entire journey took only eighteen seconds. Which was no more than seventeen seconds too long, Colin reflected as he came to a sudden halt. He stepped shakily into a carpeted corridor, glad none of his crew were present to note the slight give in his knees as he approached Command One's massive hatch.

The three-headed dragon of *Dahak*'s bas relief crest looked back from it across the starburst cradled in its raised forepaws. Its eyes transfixed him for a moment, fierce with the fidelity which had outlasted millennia, and then the hatch — fifteen centimeters of Imperial battle steel thick — slid open, and another dozen hatches opened and closed in succession as he passed through them to Command One's vast, dim sphere.

The command consoles seemed to float in interstellar space, surrounded by the breathtaking perfection of *Dahak*'s holographic projections. The nearest stars moved visibly, but the artificiality of the projection was all too apparent if one thought about it. *Dahak* was tearing through space under maximum Enchanach Drive; at seven hundred and twenty times light-speed, direct observation of the cosmos would have been distorted, to say the very least.

"The Captain is on the bridge," Dahak intoned, and Colin winced. He was going to *have* to do something about this mania Dahak had developed for protecting his commander's precious dignity!

The half-dozen members of Colin's skeleton bridge watch, Imperials all, began to stand, but he waved them back and crossed to the captain's console. Trackless stars drifted beneath his boots, and Fleet Commander Tamman, his Tactical officer and third in command, rose from the couch before it.

"Captain," he said as formally as Dahak, and Colin gave up for the moment.

"I have the con, Commander." He slipped into the vacated couch, and it squirmed under him as it adjusted to the contours of his body. There was no need for Tamman to give him a status report; his own neural feed to the console was already doing that.

He watched the tactical officer retire to his own station with a small, fond smile. Tamman was Jiltanith's contemporary, one of the fourteen Imperial "children" from *Nergal*'s crew to survive the desperate assault on Anu's enclave. All of them had joined Colin in *Dahak*, and he was damned thankful they had. Unlike his Terra-born, they could tie directly into their computers and run them the way the Imperium had intended, providing a small, reliable core of enhanced officers to ride herd on the hundred pardoned mutineers who formed the nub of his current crew. In time, Dahak would enhance and educate his Terra-born to the same standard, but with a complement of over a hundred thousand, it was going to take even *his* facilities a while to finish the task.

Colin MacIntyre reclined in his comfortable command couch, and his small smile faded as he watched the stars sweep towards him and the sleek, deadly shapes of Achuultani starships floated behind his eyes once more. The report from the sensor array replayed itself again and again, like some endless recording loop, and it filled him with dread. He'd known they were coming; now he'd "seen" them for himself. They were real, now, and so was the horrific task he and his people faced.

Dahak was more than twenty-seven light-years from Earth, but the nearest Imperial Fleet base had been over two-hundred light-years from Sol when *Dahak* arrived to orbit Earth. The Imperium proper lay far beyond that, yet despite the distances and the threat sweeping steadily towards his home world, they'd had no choice but to come, for only the Imperium might offer the aid they desperately needed to save that home world from those oncoming starships.

But *Dahak* had been unable to communicate with the Imperium for over fifty thousand years. What if there no longer *was* an Imperium?

It was a grim question they seldom discussed, one Colin tried hard not to ask even of himself, yet it beat in his brain incessantly, for Dahak had repaired his hypercom once the spares he needed had been reclaimed from the mutineers' Antarctic enclave. He'd been calling for help from the moment those repairs were made — indeed, he was calling even now.

And, like the sensor arrays, he had received no reply at all.

Chapter Two

Lieutenant Governor Horus, late captain of the mutinous sublight battleship *Nergal* and current viceroy of Earth, muttered a heartfelt curse as he sucked his wounded thumb.

He lowered his hand and regarded the wreckage sourly. He'd worked with Terran equipment for centuries, and he knew how fragile it was. Unfortunately, Imperial technology was becoming available again, and he'd forgotten the intercom on his desk was Terran-made.

His office door opened, and General Gerald Hatcher, head of the Chiefs of Staff of Planet Earth (assuming they ever got the organization set up), poked his head in and eyed the splintered intercom panel.

"If you want to attract my attention, Governor, it's simpler to buzz me than to use sirens."

"Sirens?"

"Well, that's what I thought I heard when my intercom screamed. Did that panel *do* something, or were you just pissed off?"

"Terran humans," Horus said feelingly, "are pretty damned smart-mouthed, aren't they?"

15

"One of our more endearing traits." Hatcher smiled at Jiltanith's father and sat down. "I take it you did want to see me?"

"Yes." Horus waved a stack of printout. "You've seen these?"

"What are — ?" Horus stopped waving, and Hatcher craned his neck to read the header. He nodded. "Yep. What about them?"

"According to these, the military amalgamation is a month behind schedule, that's what," Horus began, then paused and studied Hatcher's expression. "Why don't you look surprised or embarrassed or something, General?"

"Because we're ahead of where I expected to be," Hatcher said, and Horus sat back with a resigned sigh as he saw the twinkle in his eye. Gerald Hatcher, he sometimes thought, had adapted entirely too well to the presence of extra-terrestrials on his world.

"I suppose," the general continued unabashedly, "that I should've told you we've deliberately set a schedule no one could make. That way we've got an excuse to scream at people, however well they're doing." He shrugged. "It's not nice, but when a four or five-star general screams at you, you usually discover a few gears you weren't using. Wonderful thing, screaming."

"I see." Horus regarded him with a measuring eye. "You're right — you should've told me. Unless you're planning on screaming at me?"

"Perish the thought," Hatcher murmured.

"I'm relieved," Horus said dryly. "But should I take it you're actually satisfied, then?"

"Given that we're trying to merge military command structures which, however closely allied, were never really designed for it, Frederick, Vassily and I are pleased at how quickly it's moving, but time's mighty short."

Horus nodded. Sir Frederick Amesbury, Vassily Chernikov, and Hatcher formed what Vassily was fond of calling Horus's military *troika*, and they were working like demons at their all but impossible task, but they had barely two years before the first Achuultani scout forces could be expected.

"What's the worst bottleneck?" he asked.

"The Asian Alliance, of course." Hatcher made a wry face. "Our deadline hasn't quite run out, and they still haven't gotten off the fence and decided whether to fight us or join us. It's irritating as hell, but not surprising. I don't think Marshal Tsien's decided to oppose us actively, but he's certainly dragging his feet, and none of the other Alliance military types will make a move until he commits himself."

"Why not demand that the Alliance remove him, then?" It was a question, but it didn't really sound like one.

"Because we can't. He's not just their top man; he's also the best they have. They know it, too, and so much of their political leadership was in Anu's pocket — and got killed when you took out the enclave — that he's the only man the Alliance military still trusts. And however much he may hate us, he hates us less than a lot of his juniors do." Hatcher shrugged. "We've asked him to meet us face-to-face, and at least he's accepted. We'll just have to do our best with him, and he's smart, Horus. He'll come around once he gets past the idea that the West has somehow conquered him."

Horus nodded again. All three of his senior generals were "Westerners" as far as Tsien and his people were concerned. The fact that Anu and his mutineers had manipulated Terran governments and terrorist groups to play the First and Third Worlds off against one another was just beginning to percolate through *Western* brains; it would be a while yet before the other side could accept it on an emotional basis. Some groups, like the religious crackpots who had run places like Iran and Syria, never would, and their militaries had simply been disarmed . . . not, unhappily, without casualties.

"Besides," Hatcher went on, "Tsien *is* their senior commander, and we'll need him. If we're going to make this work, we don't have any choice but to integrate our people and their people — no, scratch that. We have to integrate all of *Earth's* military people into a single command structure. We can't impose non-Asian officers on the Alliance and expect it to work."

"All right." Horus tossed the printout back into his "IN" basket. "I'll make myself available to see him if you think it'll help; otherwise, I'll stay out of it and let you handle it. I've got enough other headaches."

"Don't I know it. Frankly, I wouldn't trade jobs with you on a bet."

"Your selflessness overwhelms me," Horus murmured, and Hatcher smiled again.

"How's the rest of it going?"

"As well as can be expected." Horus shrugged. "I wish we had about a thousand times as much Imperial equipment, but the situation's improving now that the orbital industrial units *Dahak* left behind are hitting their stride.

"A lot of their capacity's still going into replicating themselves, and I've diverted some of their weapons-manufacturing tonnage to planetary construction equipment, but we should be all right. It's a geometric progression, you know; that's one of the opportunities of automated units that don't need niggling little things like food or rest.

"We're just about on schedule setting up the tech base Anu brought down with him, and the part *Dahak* landed directly is up and running. We're hitting a few snags, but that's predictable when you set about building a whole new industrial infrastructure. Actually, it's the planetary defense centers that worry me most, but Geb's on that."

Geb, once *Nergal's* Chief Engineer and currently a senior member of the thirty-man (and woman) Planetary Council helping Horus run the planet, was working nineteen-hour days as Earth's chief construction boss. Hatcher didn't envy his exhausting task. There were all too few Imperials available to run the construction equipment they already had, and if purely Terran equipment was taking up a lot of the slack, that was rather like using coolie labor in light of their monumental task.

Geb and Horus had rejected the idea of reconfiguring Imperial equipment — or building new — to permit operation by unenhanced Terra-born. Imperial machinery was designed for operators whose implants let them interface directly with it, and altering it would degrade its efficiency. More to the point, by the time they could adapt any sizable amount of equipment, they should be producing enhanced Terra-born in sufficient numbers to make it unnecessary.

Which reminded Horus of another point.

"We're ready to start enhancing nonmilitary people, too."

"You are?" Hatcher brightened. "That's good news."

"Yes, but it only makes another problem worse. Everyone we enhance is going to be out of action for at least a month — more probably two or three — while they get the hang of their implants. So every time we enhance one of our top people, we lose him for that long."

"Tell me about it," Hatcher said sourly. "Do you realize — well, of course you do. But it's sort of embarrassing for the brass to be such wimps compared to their personnel. Remember my aide, Allen Germaine?" Horus nodded. "I dropped by the Walter Reed enhancement center to see him yesterday. There he was, happily tying knots in quarter-inch steel rods for practice, and there I sat in my middle-aged body, feeling incredibly flabby. I used to think I was pretty fit for my age, too, damn it! And he'll be back in the office in another few weeks. That's going to be even more depressing."

"I know." Horus's eyes twinkled. "But you're just going to have to put up with it. I can't spare any of my chiefs of staff for enhancement until you get this show firmly on the road."

"Now *there's* an efficiency motivater!"

"Isn't it just?" Horus murmured wickedly. "And speaking of getting things on the road, how do you feel about the defensive installations I've proposed?"

"From what I understand of the technology, it looks

pretty good, but I'd feel better if we had more depth to our orbital defenses. I've been reading over the operational data *Dahak* downloaded — and that's another thing I want: a neural link of my own — and I'm not happy about how much the Achuultani seem to like kinetic weapons. Can we really stop something the size of, say, Ceres, if they put shields on it before they throw it at us?"

"Geb says so, but it could take a lot of warheads. That's why we need so many launchers."

"Fine, but if they settle in for a methodical attack, they'll start by picking off our peripheral weapons first. That's classic siege strategy with any weaponry, and it's also why I want more depth, to allow for attrition of the orbital forts."

"Agreed. But we have to put the inner defenses into position first, which is why *I'm* sweating the PDC construction rates. They're what's going to produce the planetary shield, and we need their missile batteries just as badly. Not even Imperial energy weapons can punch through atmosphere very efficiently, and when they do, they play merry hell with little things like jet streams and the ozone layer. That's one reason it's easier to defend nice, airless moons and asteroids."

"Um-hum." Hatcher plucked at his lip. "I'm afraid I've been too buried in troop movements and command structures to spend as much time as I'd like boning up on hardware. Vassily's our nuts-and-bolts man. But am I correct in assuming your problems're in the hyper launchers?"

"Right the first time. Since we can't rely on beams, we need missiles, but missiles have problems of their own. As Colin is overly fond of pointing out, there are always trade-offs.

"Sublight missiles can be fired from anywhere, but they're vulnerable to interception, especially over interplanetary ranges. Hyper missiles can't be intercepted, but they can't be launched from atmosphere, either. Even air has mass, and the exact mass a hyper missile takes into hyper with it is critical to where it reenters normal space.

That's why warships preposition their hyper missiles just inside their shields before they launch."

Hatcher leaned forward, listening carefully. Horus had been a missile specialist before the mutiny; anything he had to say on this subject was something the general wanted to hear.

"We can't do that from a planet. Oh, we could, but planetary shields aren't like warship shields. Not on habitable planets, anyway. Shield density is a function of shield area; after a point, you can't make it any denser, no matter how much power you put into it. To maintain sufficient density to stop really large kinetic weapons, our shield is going to have to contract well into the mesosphere. We can stop most smaller weapons from outside atmosphere, but not the big bastards, and we can't count on avoiding heavy kinetic attack. In fact, that's exactly what we're likely to be under if we do need to launch from planetary bases."

"And if the shield contracts, the missiles would be outside it where the Achuultani could pick them off," Hatcher mused.

"Exactly. So we have to plan on going hyper straight from launch, and that means we need launchers big enough to contain the entire hyper field — just over three times the size of the missiles — or else their drives will take chunks out of the defense center when they depart." Horus shrugged. "Since a heavy hyper missile's about forty meters long and the launcher has to be airtight with provision for high-speed evacuation of atmosphere, we're talking some pretty serious engineering just to build the damned things."

"I see." Hatcher frowned thoughtfully. "How far behind schedule are you, Horus? We're going to need those batteries to cover our orbital defenses whatever happens."

"Oh, we're not really in trouble yet. Geb allowed for some slippage in his original plans, and he thinks he can make it up once he gets more Imperial equipment on line. Give us another six months and we should be back on schedule. By *Dahak's* least favorable estimate, we've got two years before the Achuultani arrive, and we should only be looking at a thousand or so scouts in the first wave. If we can hurt them badly enough, we'll have another year or so to extend the defenses before the main fleet gets here. Hopefully, we'll have more warships of our own by then, too."

"Hopefully," Hatcher agreed. He tried to radiate confidence, but he and Horus both knew. They had an excellent chance of beating off the Achuultani scouts, but unless Colin found the help they needed, Earth had no hope at all against the main incursion.

The cold winter wind and dark, cloudy sky over T'ai-yuan's concrete runways struck Marshal Tsien Tao-ling as an appropriate mirror for his own mood. Impassive and bulky in his uniform greatcoat, Tsien had headed the military machine of the Asian Alliance for twelve tumultuous years, and he had earned that post through decisiveness, dedication, and sheer ability. His authority had been virtually absolute, a rare thing in this day and age. Now that same authority was like a chain of iron, dragging him remorselessly towards a decision he did not want to make.

In less than fifty years, his nation had unified all of Asia that mattered — aside from the Japanese and Filipinos, and they scarcely counted as Asians any longer. The task had been neither cheap nor easy, nor had it been bloodless, but the Alliance had built a military machine even the West was forced to respect. Much of that building had been his own work, the fruit of his sworn oath to defend his people, the Party, and the State, and now his own decision might well bring all that effort, all that sacrifice, to nothing.

Oh, yes, he thought, lengthening his stride, these are the proper skies for me.

General Quang scurried after him, his high-pitched voice fighting a losing battle with the wind. Tsien was a huge man, almost two meters in his bare feet, and a native of Yunnan Province. Quang was both diminutive and

Vietnamese, and all rhetoric about Asian Solidarity notwithstanding, there was very little love lost between the Southern Chinese and their Vietnamese "brothers." Thousands of years of mutual hostility could not be forgotten that easily, nor could Vietnam's years as a Soviet proxy be easily forgiven, and the fact that Quang was a merely marginally competent whiner with powerful Party connections only made it worse.

Quang broke off, puffing with exertion, and the marshal smiled inwardly. He knew the smaller man resented how ridiculous he looked trying to match his own long-legged stride, which was why he took pains to emphasize it whenever they met. Yet what bothered him most just now, he admitted, was hearing a fool like Quang say so many things he had thought himself.

And what of me? Tsien frowned at his own thoughts. I am a servant of the Party, sworn to protect the State, yet what am I to do when half the Central Committee has vanished? Can it be true so many of them were traitors — not just to the State but to all humanity? Yet where else have they gone? And how am I to choose when my own decision has suddenly become so all important?

He looked up at the sleek vehicle waiting on the taxi way. Its bronze-sheened alloy gleamed dully in the cloudy afternoon, and the olive-brown-skinned woman beside its open hatch was not quite Oriental-looking. The sight touched him with something he seldom felt: uncertainty. Which made him think again of what Quang had been saying. He sighed and paused, keeping his face utterly impassive with the ease of long practice

"General, your words are not new. They have been considered, by your government and mine" — what remains of them, idiot — "and the decision has been made. Unless his terms are utterly beyond reason, we will comply with the demands of this Planetary Governor." For now, at least.

"The Party has not been well-advised," Quang muttered. "It is a trick."

"A trick, Comrade General?" Tsien's small smile was wintry as the wind. "You have, perhaps, noticed that there is no longer a moon in our night skies? It has, perhaps, occurred to you that anyone with a warship of that size and power has no need of trickery? If it has not, reflect upon this, Comrade General." He nodded in the direction of the waiting Imperial cutter. "That vehicle could reduce this entire base to rubble, and nothing we have could even *find* it, much less stop it. Do you truly believe that the West, with hundreds of even more powerful weapons now at its disposal, could not disarm us by force as they already have those maniacs in Southwest Asia?"

"But —"

"Spare me your comments, Comrade General," Tsien said heavily. Especially since they are so close to my own doubts. I have a job to do, and you make it no easier. "We have two choices: comply, or be deprived of the poor weapons we still possess. It is possible they are honest, that this danger they speak of is real. If that is true, resistance would spell far worse for all of us than disarmament and occupation. If they are lying, then at least we may have the opportunity to observe their technology at first hand, possibly even to gain access to it ourselves."

"But —"

"I will not repeat myself, Comrade General." Tsien's voice was suddenly soft, and Quang paled. "It is bad enough when junior officers question orders; I will not tolerate it in general officers. Is that clear, Comrade General?"

"I-It is," Quang managed, and Tsien raised an eyebrow over one arctic eye. Quang swallowed. "Comrade Marshal," he added quickly.

"I am relieved to hear it," Tsien said more pleasantly, and walked towards the cutter once more. Quang followed silently, but the marshal could feel the man's resentment and resistance. Quang and those like him, particularly those with a base in the Party, were dangerous. They were quite capable of doing something utterly stupid, and the marshal made a mental note to have Quang quietly reassigned to some less sensitive duty. Command of the air patrols and SAM bases covering the Sea of Japan, perhaps. That once prestigious post had become utterly meaningless, but it might take Quang a few months to realize it.

And in the meantime, Tsien could get on with what mattered. He did not know the American Hatcher who spoke for the . . . beings who had seized control of Earth, but he had met Chernikov. He was a Russian, and so, by definition, not to be trusted, but his professionalism had impressed Tsien almost against his will, and he seemed to respect Hatcher and the Englishman, Amesbury. Perhaps Hatcher was truly sincere. Perhaps his offer of cooperation, of an equal share in this new, planet-wide military organization, was genuine. There had, after all, been fewer outrageous demands by his political masters in the "Planetary Council" than Tsien had feared. Perhaps that was a good sign.

It had better be. All he had said to Quang was correct; the military position made resistance hopeless. Yet that had been true before in Asia's history, and if these Westerners meant to make effective use of Asia's vast manpower, some of their new military technology must fall into Asian hands.

Tsien had used that argument with dozens of frightened, angry juniors, yet he was not certain he believed it, and it irritated him to be unsure whether his own doubts were rational or emotional. After so many years of enmity, it was difficult to think with cold logic about any proposal from the West, yet in his heart of hearts, he could not believe they were lying. The scope of their present advantage was too overwhelming. They were too anxious, too concerned over the approach of these "Achuultani," for the threat to be an invention.

His waiting pilot saluted and allowed him to precede her into the cutter, then settled behind her controls. The small, silent vehicle bulleted upward, then darted away, springing instantly forward at eight times the speed of sound. There was no sense of acceleration, yet Tsien felt another weight — the weight of inevitability — pressing down upon his soul. The wind of change was blowing, sweeping over all this world like a typhoon, and resistance would be a wall of straw before it. Whatever Quang and his ilk feared, whatever he himself thought, they must ride that wind or perish.

And at least China's culture was ancient and there were two billion Chinese. If the promises of this Planetary Council were genuine, if all citizens were to enjoy equal access to wealth and opportunity, that fact alone would give his people tremendous influence.

He smiled to himself. Perhaps these glib Westerners had forgotten that China knew how to conquer invaders it could not defeat.

Chapter Three

Gerald Hatcher and his fellows rose courteously as Marshal Tsien entered the conference room, his shoulders straight and his face impassive. He was a big bastard for a Chinese, Hatcher reflected, taller even than Vassily, and broad enough to make two of Hatcher himself.

"Marshal," he said, holding out his hand. Tsien took it with the briefest of hesitations, but his grip was firm. "Thank you for coming. Won't you sit down, please?"

Tsien waited deliberately for his "hosts" to find seats first, then sat and laid his briefcase neatly on the table. Hatcher knew Frederick and Vassily were right in insisting that he, as the sole charter member of Earth's new Supreme Chiefs of Staff with no prior connection to the Imperials, must serve as their chief, but he wished he could disagree. This hard-faced, silent man was the most powerful single serving military officer on the planet, critical to their success, and he did not — to say the least — look cheerful.

"Marshal," Hatcher said finally, "we asked you to meet us so that we could speak without the . . . pressure of a civilian presence — yours or ours. We won't ask you to strike any 'deals' behind your leaders' backs, but there are certain pragmatic realities we must all face. In that regard, we appreciate the difficulties of your position. We hope —" he looked levelly into the dark, unreadable eyes "— that you appreciate ours, as well."

"I appreciate," Tsien said, "that my government and others which it is pledged to defend have been issued an ultimatum."

Hatcher hid a wince. The marshal's precise, accentless English made his almost toneless words even more unpromising, but they also showed him one possible approach, and he reached for it before prudence could change his mind.

"Very well, Marshal Tsien, I'll accept your terminology. In fact, I *agree* with your interpretation." He thought he saw a flicker of surprise and continued evenly. "But we're military men. We know what can happen if that ultimatum is rejected, and, I hope, we're also all realists enough to accept the truth, however unpalatable, and do our best to live with it."

"Your pardon, General Hatcher," Tsien said, "but your countries' truth seems somewhat more palatable than that which you offer mine or our allies. Our *Asian* allies. I see here an American, a ConEuropean, a Russian — I do not see a Chinese, a Korean, an Indian, a Thai, a Cambodian, a Malaysian. I do not even see one of your own Japanese." He shrugged eloquently.

"No, you don't — yet," Hatcher said quietly, and Tsien's eyes sharpened. "However, General Tama, Chief of the Imperial Japanese Staff, will be joining us as soon as he can hand over his present duties. So will Vice Admiral Hawter of the Royal Australian Navy. It is our hope that you, too, will join us, and that you will nominate three additional members of this body."

"Three?" Tsien frowned slightly. This was more than he had expected. It would mean four members from the Alliance against only five from the Western powers. But was it enough? He rubbed the table top with a thoughtful finger. "That is scarcely an equitable distribution in light of the populations involved, and yet . . . ."

His voice trailed off, and Hatcher edged into the possible opening.

"If you will consider the nations the men I mentioned represent, I believe you'll be forced to admit that the representation is not inequitable in light of the actual balance of military power." He met Tsien's eyes again, hoping the other could see the sincerity in his own. The marshal didn't agree, but neither did he disagree, and Hatcher went on deliberately.

"I might also remind you, Marshal Tsien, that you do not and will not see any representative of the extreme Islamic blocs here, nor any First World hard-liners. You say we represent Western Powers, and so, by birth, we do. But we sit here as representatives of Fleet Captain Horus in his capacity as the Lieutenant Governor of Earth, and of the five men I've named, only Marshal Chernikov and General Tama — both of whom have long-standing personal and family connections with the Imperials — were among the chiefs of staff of their nations. We face a danger such as this planet has never known, and our only purpose is to respond to that danger. Towards this end, we have stepped outside traditional chains of command in making our selections. You are the most senior officer we've asked to join us, and I might point out that we've asked you to *join* us. If we must, we will — as you are well aware we can — compel your obedience, but what we want is your *alliance*."

"Perhaps," Tsien said, but his voice was thoughtful.

"Marshal, the world as we have known it no longer exists," the American said softly. "We may regret that or applaud it, but it is a fact. I won't lie to you. We've asked you to join us because we need you. We need your people and your resources, as allies, not vassals, and you're the one man who may be able to convince your governments, your officers, and your men of that fact. We offer you a full and equal partnership, and we're prepared to guarantee equal access to Imperial technology, military and civilian, and complete local autonomy. Which, I might add, is no more than our own governments have been guaranteed by Governor MacIntyre and Lieutenant Governor Horus."

"And what of the past, General Hatcher?" Tsien asked levelly. "Are we to forget five centuries of Western imperialism? Are we to forget the unfair distribution of the world's wealth? Are we, as some have," his eyes shifted slightly in Chernikov's direction, "to forget our commitment to the Revolution in order to accept the authority of a government not even of our own world?"

"Yes, Marshal," Hatcher said equally levelly, "that's precisely what you are to forget. We won't pretend those things never happened, yet you're known as a student of history. You know how China's neighbors have suffered at Chinese hands over the centuries. We can no more undo the past than your own people could, but we can offer you an equal share in building the future, assuming this planet has one to build. And that, Marshal Tsien, is the crux: if we do not join together, there will be no future for any of us."

"So. Yet you have said nothing of how this . . . body will be organized. Nine members. They are to hold co-equal authority, at least in theory?" Hatcher nodded, and the marshal rubbed his chin, the gesture oddly delicate in so large a man. "That seems overly large, Comrade General. Could it be that you intend to — I believe the term is 'pad' — it to present the appearance of equality while holding the true power in your own hands?"

"It could be, but it isn't. Lieutenant Governor Horus has a far more extensive military background than any of us and will act as his own minister of defense. The function of this body will be to serve as his advisors and assistants. Each of us will have specific duties and operational responsibilities — there will be more than enough of those to go around, I assure you — and the position of Chief of Staff will rotate."

"I see." Tsien laid his hands on his briefcase and studied

his knuckles, then looked back up. "How much freedom will I have in making my nominations?"

"Complete freedom." Hatcher very carefully kept his hope out of his voice. "The Lieutenant Governor alone will decide upon their acceptability. If any of your nominees are rejected, you'll be free to make fresh nominations until candidates mutually acceptable to the Asian Alliance and the Lieutenant Governor are selected. It is my understanding that his sole criterion will be those officers' willingness to work as part of his own command team, and that he will evaluate that willingness on the basis of their affirmation of loyalty under an Imperial lie detector." He saw a spark of anger in Tsien's eyes and went on unhurriedly. "I may add that all of us will be required to demonstrate our own loyalty in precisely the same fashion and in the presence of all of our fellows, including yourself and your nominees."

The anger in Tsien's hooded gaze faded, and he nodded slowly.

"Very well, General Hatcher, I am empowered to accept your offer, and I will do so. I caution you that I do not agree without reservations, and that it will be difficult to convince many of my own officers to accept my decision. It goes against the grain to surrender all we have fought for, whether it is to Western powers or to powers from beyond the stars, yet you are at least partly correct. The world we have known has ended. We will join your efforts to save this planet and build anew. Not without doubts and not without suspicion — you would not believe otherwise, unless you were fools — but because we must. Yet remember this: more than half this world's population is *Asian*, gentlemen."

"We understand, Marshal," Hatcher said softly.

"I believe you do, Comrade General," Tsien said with the first, faint ghost of a smile. "I believe you do."

Life Councilor Geb brushed stone dust from his thick, white hair as yet another explosive charge bellowed behind him. It was a futile gesture. The air was thin, but the damnable dust made it seem a lot thicker, and his scalp was coated in fresh grit almost before he lowered his hand.

He watched another of the sublight parasites *Dahak* had left for Earth's defense — the destroyer *Ardat*, he thought — hover above the seething dust, her eight-thousand-ton hull dwarfed by the gaping hole which would, when finished, contain control systems, magazines, shield generators, and all the other complex support systems. Her tractors plucked up multi-ton slabs of a mountain's bones, and then the ship lifted away into the west, bearing yet another load of refuse to a watery grave in the Pacific. Even before *Ardat* was out of sight, the Terra-born work crews swarmed over the newly-exposed surface of the excavation in their breath masks, drills screaming as they prepared the next series of charges.

Geb viewed the activity with mixed pride and distaste. This absolutely flat surface of raw stone had once been the top of Ecuador's Mount Chimborazo, but that was before its selection to house Planetary Defense Center *Escorpion* had sealed the mountain's fate. The sublight battleships *Shirhan* and *Escal* arrived two days later, and while *Escal* hovered over the towering peak, *Shirhan* activated her main energy batteries and slabbed off the top three hundred meters of earth and stone. *Escal* caught the megaton chunks of wreckage in her tractors while *Shirhan* worked, lifting them for her pressers to toss out of the way into the ocean. It had taken the two battleships a total of twenty-three minutes to produce a level stone mesa just under six thousand meters high, and then they'd departed to mutilate the next mountain on their list.

The construction crews had moved in in their wake, and they had labored mightily ever since. Imperial technology had held the ecological effects of their labors to a minimum impossible for purely Terran resources, but Geb had seen Chimborazo before his henchmen arrived. The esthetic desecration of their labors revolted him; what they had accomplished produced his pride.

PDC *Escorpion,* one of forty-six such bases going up across the surface of the planet, each a project gargantuan enough to daunt the Pharaohs, and each with a completion deadline of exactly eighteen months. It was an impossible task . . . and they were doing it anyway.

He stepped aside as the whine of a gravitonic drive approached from one side. The stocky, olive-brown Imperial at the power bore's controls nodded to him, but despite his rank, he was only one more rubber-necker in her way, and he backed further as she positioned her tremendous machine. She checked the coordinates in her inertial guidance systems against the engineers' plat of the base to be with care, and an eye-searing dazzle flickered as she powered up the cutting head and brought it to bear.

The power bore floated a rock-steady half-meter off the ground, and Geb's implants tingled with the torrent of focused energy. A hot wind billowed back from the rapidly sinking shaft, blowing a thick plume of powdered rock to join the choking pall hanging over the site, and he stepped still further back. Another thunderous explosion burst in on him, and he shook his head, marveling at the demonic energy loosed upon this hapless mountain. Every safety regulation in the book — Imperial and Terran alike — had been relaxed to the brink of insanity, and the furious labor went on day and night, rain and sun, twenty-four hours a day. It might stop for a hurricane; nothing less would be permitted to interfere.

It was bad enough for his Imperials, he thought, watching the dust-caked woman concentrate, but at least they had their biotechnics to support them. The Terra-born did not, and their primitive equipment required far more of pure muscle to begin with. But Horus had less than five thousand Imperials; barely three thousand of them could be released to construction projects, and the PDCs were only one of the clamorous needs Geb and his assistants had to meet somehow. With enhanced personnel and their machinery spread so thin, he had no choice but to call upon the primitive substitutes Earth could provide. At least he could lift in equipment, materials, and fuel on tractors as needed.

A one-man grav scooter grounded beside him. Tegran, the senior Imperial on the *Escorpion* site, climbed off it to slog through the blowing dust to Geb's side and pushed up his goggles to watch the power bore at work.

Tegran was much younger, biologically, at least, than Geb, but his face was gaunt, and he'd lost weight since coming out of stasis. Geb wasn't surprised. Tegran had never personally offended against the people of Earth, but like most of the Imperials freed from Anu's stasis facilities, he was driving himself until he dropped to wash away the stigma of his past.

The cutting head died, and the power bore operator backed away from the vertical shaft. A Terra-born, Imperial-equipped survey team scurried forward, instruments probing and measuring, and its leader lifted a hand, thumb raised in approval. The dust-covered woman responded with the same gesture and moved away, heading for the next site, and Geb turned to Tegran.

"Nice," he said. "I make that a bit under twenty minutes to drill a hundred-fifty-meter shaft. Not bad at all."

"Um," Tegran said. He walked over to the edge of the fifty-meter-wide hole which would one day house a hyper missile launcher and stood peering down at its glassy walls. "It's better, but I can squeeze another four or five percent efficiency out of the bores if I tweak the software a bit more."

"Wait a minute, Tegran — you've already cut the margins mighty close!"

"You worry too much, Geb." Tegran grinned tightly. "There's a hefty safety factor built into the components. If I drop the designed lifetime to, say, three years instead of twenty, I can goose the equipment without risking personnel. And since we've only got *two* years to get dug in —" He shrugged.

"All right," Geb said after a moment's thought, "but get me the figures before you make any more modifications.

And I want a copy of the software. If you can pull it off, I'll want all the sites to be able to follow suit."

"Fine," Tegran agreed, walking back to his scooter. Geb followed him, and the project boss paused as he remounted. "What's this I hear about nonmilitary enhancement?" he asked, his tone elaborately casual.

Geb eyed him thoughtfully. A few other Imperials had muttered darkly over the notion, for the Fourth Imperium had been an ancient civilization by Terran standards. Despite supralight travel, over-crowding on its central planets had led to a policy restricting full enhancement (and the multi-century lifespans which went with it) solely to military personnel and colonists. Which, Geb reflected, had been one reason the Fleet never had trouble finding recruits even with minimum hitches of a century and a half . . . and why Horus's policy of providing full enhancement to every adult Terran, for all intents and purposes, offended the sensibilities of the purists among his Imperials.

Yet Geb hadn't expected Tegran to be one of them, for the project head knew better than most that enhancing every single human on the planet, even if there had been time for it, would leave them with far too few people to stand off an Achuultani incursion.

"We started this week," he said finally. "Why?"

"Welllll . . ." Tegran looked back at the departing power bore, then waved expressively about the site. "I just wanted to get my bid for them in first. I've got a hell of a job to do here, and —"

"Don't worry," Geb cut in, hiding his relief. "We need them everywhere, but the PDCs have a high priority. I don't want anybody with implants standing idle, but I'll try to match the supply of operators to the equipment you actually have on hand."

"Good!" Tegran readjusted his goggles and lifted his scooter a meter off the ground, then grinned broadly at his boss. "These Terrans are great, Geb. They work till they drop, then get back up and start all over again. Enhance me enough of them, and I'll damned well build you another *Dahak!*"

He waved and vanished into the bedlam, and Geb smiled after him.

He was getting too old for this, Horus thought for no more than the three millionth time. He yawned, then stretched and rose from behind his desk and collected his iced tea from the coaster. Caffeine dependency wasn't something the Imperium had gone in for, but he'd been barely sixty when he arrived here. A lifetime of acculturation had taken its toll.

He walked over to the windowed wall of his office atop White Tower and stared out over the bustling nocturnal activity of Shepherd Center. The rocket plumes of the Terran space effort were a thing of the past, but the huge field was almost too small for the Imperial auxiliaries and bigger sublight ships — destroyers, cruisers, battleships, and transports — which thronged it now. And this was only one of the major bases. The largest, admittedly, but only one.

The first enhanced Terra-born crewmen were training in the simulators now. Within a month, he'd have skeleton crews for most of the major units *Dahak* had left behind. In another six, he'd have crews for the smaller ships and pilots for the fighters. They'd be short on experience, but they'd be there, and they'd pick up experience quickly. Maybe even quickly enough.

He sighed and took himself to task. Anxiety was acceptable; depression was not, but it was hard to avoid when he remembered the heedless, youthful passion which had pitted him in rebellion against the Imperium.

The Fourth Imperium had arisen from the sole planet of the Third which the Achuultani had missed. It had dedicated itself to the destruction of the next incursion with a militancy which dwarfed Terran comprehension, but that had been seven millennia before Horus's birth, and the Achuultani had never come. And so, perhaps, there *were* no Achuultani. Heresy. Unthinkable to say it aloud. Yet the suspicion had gnawed at their brains, and they'd come to resent the endless demands of their long, regimented preparation. Which explained, if it did not excuse, why the discontented of *Dahak's* crew had lent themselves to the mutiny which brought them to Earth.

And so here they were, Horus thought, sipping iced tea and watching the moonless sky of the world which had become his own, with the resources of this single, primitive planet and whatever of Imperial technology they could build and improvise in the time they had, face-to-face with the bogey man they'd decided no longer existed.

Six billion people. Like the clutter of ships below his window, it seemed a lot . . . until he compared it to the immensity of the foe sweeping towards them from beyond those distant stars.

He straightened his shoulders and stared up at the cold, clear chips of light. So be it. He had once betrayed the Fleet uniform he wore, but now, at last, he faced his race's ancient enemy. He faced it ill-prepared and ill-equipped, yet the human race had survived two previous incursions. By the skin of their racial teeth and the Maker's grace, perhaps, but they'd *survived*, which was more than any of their prehistoric predecessors could say.

He drew a deep breath, his thoughts reaching out across the light-years to his daughter and Colin MacIntyre. They depended upon him to defend their world while they sought the assistance Earth needed, and when they returned — not if — there would be a planet here to greet them. He threw that to the uncaring stars like a solemn vow and then turned his back upon them. He sat back down at his desk and bent over the endless reams of reports once more.

Alheer va-Chanak's forehead crinkled in disgust as a fresh sneeze threatened. He wiggled on his command pedestal, fighting the involuntary reflex, and heard the high-pitched buzz of his copilot's amusement — buried in the explosive eruption of the despised sneeze.

"Kreegor seize all colds!" va-Chanak grunted, mopping his broad breathing slits with a tissue. Roghar's laughter buzzed in his ear as he lost the last vestige of control, and va-Chanak swiveled his sensory cluster to bend a stern gaze upon him. "All very well for you, you unhatched grub!" he snarled. "You'd probably think it was hilarious if it happened inside a vac suit!"

"Certainly not," Roghar managed to return with a semblance of decent self-control. "Of course, I did warn you not to spend so long soaking just before a departure."

Va-Chanak suppressed an ignoble desire to throttle his copilot. The fact that Roghar was absolutely right only made the temptation stronger, but these four- and five-month missions could be pure torment for the amphibious

Mersakah. And, he grumbled to himself, especially for a fully-active sire like himself. Four thousand years of civilization was a frail shield against the spawning urges of all pre-history, but where was he to find a compliant school of dams in an asteroid extraction operation? Nowhere, that was bloody well where, and if he chose to spend a few extra day parts soaking in the habitat's swamp sections, that should have been his own affair.

And would have been, he thought gloomily, if he hadn't brought this damned cold with him. Ah, well! It would wear itself out, and a few more tours would give him a credit balance fit to attract the finest dam. Not to mention the glamour which clung to spacefarers in groundlings' eyes, and —

An alarm squealed, and Alheer va-Chanak's sensory cluster snapped back to his instruments. All three eyes irised wide in disbelief as the impossible readings registered.

"*Kreegor* take it, look at that!" Roghar gasped beside him, but va-Chanak was already stabbing at the communications console.

More of the immense ships — ninety *dihar* long if they were a *har* — appeared out of nowhere, materializing like fen fey from the nothingness of space. Scores of them — hundreds!

Roghar babbled away about first-contacts and alien life forms beside him, but even as he gabbled, the copilot was spinning the extractor ship and aligning the main engines to kill velocity for rendezvous. Va-Chanak left him to it, and his own mind burned with conflicting impulses. Disbelief. Awe. Wonder and delight that the *Mersakah* were not alone. Horror that it had been left to him to play ambassador to the future which had suddenly arrived. Concern lest their visitors misinterpret his fumbling efforts. Visions of immortality — and how the dams would react to this — !

He was still punching up his communications gear when the closest Achuultani starship blew his vessel out of existence.

The shattered wreckage tumbled away, and the Achuul-tani settled into their formation. Normal-space drives woke, and the mammoth cylinders swept in-system, arrowing towards the planet of Mers at twenty-eight per-cent of light-speed while their missile sections prepped their weapons.

The faint, muted roar of Command One and the distant howl of the core tap grew louder as they fell behind him, and the astonished engineer turned slowly to regard the room once more. In that moment, he wished he knew far more about the men and machines which had created their own tomb.

Chapter Four

The endless, twenty-meter-wide column of lightning fascinated him. It wasn't really lightning, but that was how Vlad Chernikov thought of it, though the center of any Terran lightning bolt would be a dead zone beside its titanic density. The force field which channeled it also silenced it and muted its terrible brilliance, but Vlad had received his implants. His sensors felt it, like a tide race of fire, even through the field, and it awed him.

He turned away, folding his hands behind him as he crossed the huge chamber at *Dahak's* heart. Only Command One and Two were as well protected, for this was the source of *Dahak's* magic. The starship boasted three hundred and twelve fusion power plants, but though he could move and fight upon the wings of their power, he required more than that to outspeed light itself.

This howling chain of power was that more. It was *Dahak's* core tap, a tremendous, immaterial funnel that reached deep into hyper space, connecting the ship to a dimension of vastly higher energy states. It dragged that limitless power in, focused and refined it, and directed it into the megaton mass of his Enchanach Drive.

And with it, the drive worked its sorcery and created the perfectly opposed, converging gravity masses which forced *Dahak* out of normal space in a series of instantaneous transpositions. It took a measurable length of time to build those masses between transpositions, but that interval was perceptible only to one such as *Dahak*. A tiny, imperfect flaw the time stream of the cosmos never noticed.

Which was as well. Should *Dahak* dwell in normal space any longer than that, catastrophe would be the lot of any star system he crossed. As those fields converged upon his hull, he became ever so briefly more massive than the most massive star. Which was why ships of his ilk did not use supralight speed within a system, for the initial activation and final deactivation of the Enchanach Drive took much longer, a time measured in microseconds, not femtoseconds. Anu had induced a drive failure to divert the starship from its original mission for "emergency repairs," and a tiny error in *Dahak's* crippled return to sublight speeds explained the irregularity of Pluto's orbit which had puzzled Terran astronomers for so long. Had it occurred deep enough in Sol's gravity well, the star might well have gone nova.

Chernikov plugged his neural feed back into the engineering subsection of *Dahak's* computer net, and the computers answered him with a joyousness he was still getting used to. It was odd how alive, how aware, those electronic brains seemed, and Baltan, his ex-mutineer assistant, insisted they had been far less so before the mutiny.

Chernikov believed him, and he believed he understood the happiness which suffused the computer net. *Dahak* had a crew once more — understrength, perhaps, by Imperial standards, but a crew — and that was as it should be. Not just because he had been lonely, but because he needed them to provide that critical element in any warship: redundancy. It was dangerous for so powerful a unit to be utterly dependent upon its central computer, especially when battle damage might cut Comp Cent off from essential components of its tremendous hull.

So it was good that men had returned to *Dahak* at last. Especially now, when the very survival of their species depended upon him.

"Attention on deck," *Dahak* intoned as Colin entered the conference room, and he winced almost imperceptibly as his command team rose with punctilious formality. He smoothed his expression and crossed impassively to the head of the crystalline conference table, making yet another mental note to have a heart-to-diode talk with the computer.

Dozens of faces looked back at him from around the table, but at least he'd gotten used to facing so many eyes. *Dahak* was technically a single ship, but one with a full-strength crew a quarter-million strong, a normal sublight parasite strength of two hundred warships, and the firepower to shatter planets. His commander might be called a captain, yet for all intents and purposes he was an admiral, charged with the direction of more destructiveness than Terra's humanity had ever dreamed was possible, and the size of Colin's staff reflected that.

There were a lot of "Fleet Captains" on it, though *Dahak*'s new protocol demanded that they be addressed in Colin's presence either as "Commander" or simply by the department they headed, since he was the only "Senior Fleet Captain" and there could be but one captain aboard a warship. The Imperium had used any officer's full rank and branch, which Colin and his Terra-born found too cumbersome, but *Dahak* had obstinately resisted Colin's suggestion that he might be called "Commodore" to ease the problem.

Colin let his eyes sweep over them as he sat and they followed suit. Jiltanith was at his right, as befitted his second-in-command and the officer charged with the organization and day-to-day management of *Dahak*'s operation. Hector MacMahan sat at his left, as impeccable in the space-black of the Imperial Marines as he had ever been in the uniform of the United States. Beyond them, rows of officers, each department head flanked by his or her senior assistants, ran down the sides of the table to meet at its foot, where he faced Vlad Chernikov, the man who had inherited the shipboard authority which had once been Anu's.

"Thank you all for coming," Colin said. "As you know, we'll be leaving supralight to approach the Sheskar System in approximately twenty-one hours. With luck, that means we'll soon reestablish contact with the Imperium, but we can't count on that. We're going into a totally unknown situation, and I want final readiness estimates from all of my senior department heads — and for all of you to hear them — before we do."

Heads nodded, and he turned to Jiltanith.

"Would you care to begin with a general overview, XO?" he asked.

"Certes, Captain," Jiltanith said, and turned confident eyes to her fellows. "Our Dahak hath been a teacher most astute — aye, and a taskmaster of the sternest!" That won a mutter of laughter, for Dahak had driven his new crew so hard ten percent of even his capacity had been committed full-time to their training and neural-feed education. "While 'tis true I would be better pleased with some small time more of practice, yet have our folk learned their duties well, and I say with confidence our officers and crew will do all mortal man may do if called."

"Thank you," Colin said. It was scarcely a detailed report, but he hadn't asked for that, and he turned to Hector MacMahan.

"Ground Forces?"

"The ground forces are better organized than we could reasonably expect," the hawk-faced Marine replied, "if not yet quite as well as I'd like.

"We have four separate nationalities in our major formations, and we'll need a few more months to really shake down properly. For the moment, we've adopted Imperial organization and ranks but confined them to our original unit structures. Our USFC and SAS people are our recon/special forces component; the Second Marines have been designated as our assault component; the German First Armored will operate our ground combat vehicles; and the Sendai Division and the Nineteenth Guards Parachute Division are our main ground force.

"There's been a bit of rivalry over who got the choicest assignment, but it hasn't gotten physical . . . not very often, anyway." He shrugged. "These are all elite formations, and until we can integrate them fully, a continued sense of identity is inevitable, but they've settled in and mastered their new weapons quite well. I'm confident we can handle anything we have to handle."

"Thank you," Colin said again. He turned to General Georgi Treshnikov, late of the Russian Air Force and now commander of the three hundred Imperial fighters *Dahak* had retained for self-defense. "Parasite Command?"

"As Hector, we are ready," Treshnikov said. "We have even more nationalities, but less difficulty in integration, for we did not embark complete national formations to crew our fighters."

"Thank you. Intelligence, Commander Ninhursag?"

"We've done all we can with the non-data Dahak has been able to give us, Captain. You've all seen our reports." The stocky, pleasantly plain Imperial who had been *Nergal's* spy within Anu's camp shrugged. "Until we have some hard facts to plug into our analyses, we're only marking time."

"I understand. Biosciences?"

"Bioscience is weary but ready, Captain," Fleet Captain (B) Cohanna replied. Fifty thousand years in stasis hadn't blunted her confidence . . . or her sense of humor. "We finished the last enhancement procedures last month, and we're a little short on biotechnic hardware at the moment —" that won a fresh mutter of laughter "— but other than that, we're in excellent shape."

"Thank you. Maintenance?"

"We're looking good, Captain." Fleet Captain (M) Geran was another of *Nergal*'s "children," but aside from his eyes, he looked more like a Terran, with dark auburn hair, unusually light skin for an Imperial, and a mobile mouth that smiled easily. "Dahak's repair systems did a bang-up job, and he slapped anything he wasn't using into stasis. I'd like more practice on damage control, but —" He raised his right hand, palm upward, and Colin nodded.

"Understood. Hopefully you'll have lots of time to go *on* practicing. We'll try to keep it that way. Tactical?"

"We're in good shape, sir," Tamman said. "Battle Comp's doing well with simulators and training problems. Our Terra-born aren't as comfortable with their neural feeds as I'd like yet, but that's only a matter of practice."

"Logistics?"

"Buttoned up, sir," Fleet Commander (L) Caitrin O'Rourke said confidently. "We've got facilities for three times the people we've actually got aboard, and all park and hydroponic areas have been fully reactivated, so provisions and life support are no sweat. Magazines are at better than ninety-eight percent — closer to ninety-nine — and we're in excellent shape for spares."

"Engineering?"

"Engineering looks good, sir," Chernikov replied. "Our Imperials and Terra-born have shaken down extremely well together. I am confident."

"Good. Very good." Colin leaned back and smiled at his officers, glad none of them had tried to gloss over any small concerns they still had. Not that he'd expected them to.

"In that case, I think we can conclude, unless there are any questions?" As he'd expected, there were none. In a very real sense, this meeting had been almost ceremonial, a chance for them to show their confidence to one another.

"Very well." He rose and nodded to them all. "We shall adjourn." He started for the door, and a mellow voice spoke again.

"Attention on deck," it repeated, and Colin swallowed a resigned sigh as his solemn-faced officers stood once more.

"Carry on, ladies and gentlemen," he said, and stepped out the hatch.

"Supralight shutdown in two minutes," Dahak remarked calmly.

Colin took great pains to project a matching calm, but his own relaxation was all too artificial, and he saw the same strain, hidden with greater or lesser success, in all of his bridge officers. *Dahak* was at battle stations, and a matching team under Jiltanith manned Command Two on the far side of the core hull. The holographic images of Command Two's counterparts sat beside each of his officers, which made his bridge seem a bit more crowded but meant everyone knew exactly what was happening . . . and that he got to sit beside Jiltanith's image on duty.

A score of officers were physically present at their consoles on the starlit command deck. In an emergency, Colin could have run the ship without any of them, something which would have been impossible with the semi-aware Comp Cent of yore. But even though Dahak was now capable of assessing intent and exercising discretion, there were limits to the details Colin's human brain could handle. Each of his highly trained officers took his or her own portion of the burden off of him, and he was devoutly thankful for their presence.

"Sublight in one minute," Dahak intoned, and Colin felt the beginnings of shutdown flowing through his interface with Chernikov's engineering computers. The measured sequence of commands moved like clockwork, and a tiny, almost imperceptible vibration shook *Dahak*'s gargantuan bulk.

"Sublight . . . now," Dahak reported, and the stars moving across the visual display were abruptly still.

A G3 star floated directly "ahead" of Colin in the projection. It was the brightest single object in view, and it abruptly began to grow as Sarah Meir, his astrogator, engaged the sublight drive.

"Core tap shutdown," Dahak announced.

"Enhance image on the star system, Dahak," Colin requested, and the star swelled while a three-dimensional schematic of the Sheskar System's planetary orbits flicked to life about it. Only the outermost planet was visible even to Dahak at their present range, but tiny circles on each orbit trace indicated the position each planet should hold.

"Any artificial radiation?"

"Negative, Captain," Dahak replied, and Colin bit his lip. Sheskar was — or had been — the Imperium's forward bastion on the traditional Achuultani approach vector. Perimeter Security should have detected and challenged them almost instantly.

"Captain," Dahak broke the silence which had fallen, "I have detected discrepancies in the system."

The visual display altered as he spoke. Oddly clumped necklaces of far smaller dots replaced the circles representing Sheskar's central trio of planets, spreading ominously about the central star, and Colin swallowed.

Dahak had gone sublight at the closest possible safe distance from Sheskar, but that was still eleven light-hours out. Even at his maximum sublight velocity, it would have taken almost twenty-four hours to reach the primary, yet it had become depressingly clear that there was no reason to travel that deep into the system, and Colin had stopped five light-hours out to save time when they left.

At the moment, he, Jiltanith, Hector MacMahan, and Ninhursag sat in Conference One, watching a scaled-down holo of the star system while they tried to decide where to leave to.

"I have completed preliminary scans, Captain," Dahak announced.

"Well? Was it the Achuultani?"

"It is, of course, impossible to be certain, but I would estimate that it was not. Had it been an incursion, it would, of necessity, have followed a path other than that traditionally employed by the Achuultani, else the scanner arrays which reported this incursion had already been destroyed. Since they were not, I conclude that it was not the Achuultani who accomplished this."

"Just what we needed," Hector said quietly. "Somebody *else* who goes around blowing away entire planets."

"Unfortunately, that would appear to be precisely what has happened, General MacMahan. It would not, however, appear to be of immediate concern. My scans indicate that this destruction occurred on the close order of forty-eight thousand years ago."

"How close?" Colin demanded.

"Plus or minus five percent, Captain."

"Shit." Colin looked up apologetically as the expletive escaped him, but no one seemed to have noticed. He drew a deep breath. "All right, Dahak, cut to the chase. What do you think happened?"

"Analysis rules out the employment of kinetic weaponry," Dahak said precisely, "distribution of the planetary rubble is not consistent with impact patterns. Rather, it would appear that the planetary bodies suffered implosive destruction consistent with the use of gravitonic warheads, a weapon, so far as is known to the Imperium's data base, the Achuultani have never employed."

"Gravitonic?" Colin tugged on his prominent nose, and his green eyes narrowed. "I don't like the sound of that."

"Nor I," Jiltanith said quietly. "If 'twas not the Achuultani, then must it have been another, and such weapons lie even now within our magazines."

"Exactly," Colin said. He shuddered at the thought. A heavy gravitonic warhead produced a nice, neat little black hole. Not very long-lived, and not big enough to damage most suns, but big enough, and a hyper-capable missile with the right targeting could put the damned thing almost inside a planet.

"That is true," Dahak observed, then hesitated briefly, as if he faced a conclusion he wanted to reject. "I regret to say, Captain, that the destruction matches that which would be associated with our own Mark Tens. In point of fact, and after making due allowance for the time which has passed, it corresponds almost exactly to the results produced by those weapons."

"Hector? Ninhursag?"

"Dahak's dancing around the point, Colin." MacMahan's face was grim. "There's a very simple and likely explanation."

"I agree," Ninhursag said in a small voice. "I never would have believed it could happen, but it's got all the earmarks of a civil war."

A brief silence followed the words someone had finally said. Then Colin cleared his throat.

"Response, Dahak?"

"I . . . am forced to concur." Dahak's mellow voice sounded sad. "Sheskar Four, in particular, was very heavily defended. Based upon available data and the fact that no advanced alien race other than the Achuultani had been encountered by the Imperium prior to the mutiny, I must conclude that only the Imperium itself possessed the power to do what has been done."

"What about someone they ran into after the mutiny?"

"Possible, but unlikely, Captain. Due in no small part to previous incursions, there are very few — indeed, effectively no — habitable worlds between Sol and Sheskar. Logic thus suggests that any hostile aliens would have been required to fight their way across a substantial portion of the Imperium even to reach Sheskar. Assuming technical capabilities on a par with those of this ship — a conclusion suggested, though not proven, by my analysis of the weaponry employed — that would require a hostile imperium whose military potential equaled or exceeded that of the Imperium itself. While it is not impossible that such an entity might have been encountered, I would rate the probability as no greater than that of an Achuultani attack."

Colin looked around the table again, then back at the silent holo display. "This isn't good."

"Hast a gift for understatement, my Colin." Jiltanith shook her head. "Good Dahak, what likelihood wouldst thou assign to decision by the Imperium 'gainst fortifying Sheskar anew?"

"Slight," Dahak said.

"Why?" Colin asked. "There's nothing left *to* fortify."

"Inaccurate, Captain. No Earthlike planets remain, but Sheskar was selected for a Fleet base because of its location, not its planets, and it now possesses abundant large asteroids for installation sites. Indeed, the absence of atmosphere would make those installations more defensible, not less."

"In other words," MacMahan murmured, "they would have come back if they were interested in reestablishing their prewar frontiers."

"Precisely, General."

Another, longer silence fell, and Colin drew a deep breath.

"All right, let's look at it. We have a destroyed base in a vital location. It appears to have been taken out with Imperial weapons, implying a civil war as a probable cause. It wasn't rebuilt. What does *that* imply?"

"Naught we wish to discover." Jiltanith managed a small smile. "'Twould seem the Imperium hath fallen 'pon hard times."

"True," MacMahan said. "I see two probabilities, Colin." Colin raised an eyebrow, inviting him to continue.

"First, they wiped each other out. That would explain the failure to rebuild, and it would also mean our entire mission is pointless." A shiver ran through his human audience, but he continued unflinchingly.

"On the other hand, I don't believe anything the size of the Imperium wiped itself out completely. The Imperium is — or was, or whatever — huge. Even assuming anyone could have been insane enough to embark on destruction on that scale, I don't see how they could *do* it. Their infrastructure would erode out from under them as they took out industrialized systems, and it seems unlikely anyone would follow leaders mad enough to try."

"Yet 'twas done to Sheskar," Jiltanith pointed out.

"True, but Sheskar was primarily a military base, 'Tanni, not a civilian system. The decision to attack it would be evaluated purely in terms of military expedience, like nuking a well-armed island base in the middle of an ocean. It's a lot easier to decide to hit a target like that."

"All right." Colin nodded. "But if they didn't wipe themselves out, why didn't they come back?"

"That's probability two," MacMahan said flatly. "They did so much damage they backslid. They could have done a fair job of smashing themselves without actually destroying all their planets. It's hard for me to visualize a high-tech planet which *wasn't* nuked — or something like it — decivilizing completely, but I can accept that more easily than the idea that all their planets look like this." He gestured at the holo display.

"Besides, they might have damaged themselves in other ways. Suppose they fought their war and found themselves faced with massive reconstruction closer to the heart of the Imperium? Sheskar is — was — a hell of a long way from their next nearest inhabited system, and as Dahak has pointed out, this area isn't exactly prime real estate. If they had heavily damaged areas closer to home, they could've decided to deal with those first. Afterward, the area on the far side of the Imperium, where damage from the Achuultani hadn't wrecked so many planets to begin with, would have been a natural magnet for future expansion."

"Mayhap, yet that leaveth still a question. Whyfor, if Sheskar was so vital, rebuild it not?"

"I'm afraid I can answer that," Ninhursag said unhappily. "Maybe Anu wasn't as crazy — or quite as unique in his craziness — as we thought." She shrugged as all eyes turned to her. "What I'm trying to say is that if things got so bad the Imperium actually fought a civil war, they weren't *Imperials* anymore. I'm the only person in this room who was an adult at the time of the mutiny, and I know how *I* would've reacted to the thought of wiping out a Fleet base. Even those of us who didn't really believe in the Achuultani —

even the 'atheists,' I suppose you might call them, who violently rejected their existence — would have hesitated to do that. That's why Anu lied to us about his own intent to attack the Imperium."

She looked unhappily at the holo for a moment, and none of the others intruded upon her silence.

"None of you were ever Imperial citizens, so you may not understand what I'm trying to say, but preparing to fight the Achuultani was something we'd societized into ourselves on an almost instinctual level. Even those who most resented the regimentation, the discipline, wouldn't have destroyed our defenses. It would be like . . . like Holland blowing up its dikes because of one dry summer, for Maker's sake!"

"You're saying that disbelief in the Achuultani must have become general?" Colin said. "That if it hadn't, the Fleet would never have let itself be caught up in something like a civil war in the first place?"

"Exactly. And if that's true, why rebuild Sheskar as a base against an enemy that doesn't exist?" Ninhursag gave a short, ugly laugh. "Maybe we were the wave of the future instead of just a bunch of murderous traitors!"

"Easy, 'Hursag." MacMahan touched her shoulder, and she inhaled sharply.

"Sorry." Her voice was a bit husky. "It's just that I don't really want to believe what I'm saying — especially not now that I know how wrong we were!"

"Maybe not, but it makes sense," Colin said slowly.

"Agreed, Captain," Dahak said. "Indeed, there is another point. For Fleet vessels to have participated in this action would require massive changes in core programming by at least one faction. Without that, Fleet Central Alpha Priority imperatives would have precluded any warfare which dissipated resources and so weakened Battle Fleet's ability to resist an incursion. This would appear to support Fleet Commander Ninhursag's analysis."

"All right. But even if it's not the Imperium we came to find, there may still be *an* Imperium somewhere up ahead of us." Colin tried to project more optimism than he felt. "Dahak, what was the nearest piece of prime real estate? The closest star system which wasn't purely a military base?"

"Defram," Dahak replied without hesitation. "A G2-K5 binary system with two inhabited planets. As of the last Imperial census in my data base, the system population was six-point-seven-one-seven billion. Main industries —"

"That's enough," Colin interrupted. "How far away is it?"

"One hundred thirty-three-point-four light-years, Captain."

"Um . . . bit over two months at max. That means a round trip of just over eleven months before we could get back to Earth."

"Approximately eleven-point-three-two months, Captain."

"All right, people." Colin sighed. "I don't see we have too much choice. Let's go to Defram and see what we can see."

"Aye," Jiltanith agreed. "'Twould seem therein our best hope doth lie."

"I agree," MacMahan said, and Ninhursag nodded silently.

"Okay. I want to sit here and think a little more. Take the watch, please, 'Tanni. Dismiss from battle stations, then have Sarah get us underway on sublight. I'll join you in Command One when I finish here." Jiltanith rose with a silent nod, and he turned to the others.

"Hector, you and 'Hursag sit down and build me models of as many scenarios as you can. I know you don't have any hard data, but put your heads together with our other adult Imperials and Dahak and extrapolate trends."

"Yes, sir," MacMahan said quietly, and Colin propped his chin in his hands, elbows on the table, and stared sadly at the holo as the others filed out the hatch. He expected no sudden inspiration, for there was nothing here to offer it. He only knew that he needed to be alone with his thoughts for a while, and, unlike his subordinates, he had the authority to be that way.

Chapter Five

"Well, Marshal Tsien?"

Tsien regarded Gerald Hatcher levelly as they strode down the hall. It was the first time either had spoken since leaving the Lieutenant Governor's office, and Tsien crooked an eyebrow, inviting amplification. The American only smiled, declining to make his question more specific, but Tsien understood and, in all honesty, appreciated his tact.

"I am . . . impressed, Comrade General," he said. "The Lieutenant Governor is a *formidable* man." His answer meant more than the words said, but he had already seen enough of this American to know he would understand.

"He's all of that," Hatcher agreed, opening a door and waving Tsien into his own office. "He's had to be," he added in a grimmer voice.

Tsien nodded as they crossed the deserted office. It was raining again, he noted, watching the water roll down the windows. Hatcher gestured to an armchair facing the desk as he circled to reach his own swiveled chair.

"So I have understood," Tsien replied, sitting carefully.

"Yet he seems unaware of it. He does not strike one as so . . . so —"

"Grand? Self-important?" Hatcher suggested with a grin, and Tsien chuckled despite himself.

"Both of those things, I suppose. Forgive me, but you in the West have always seemed to me to be overly taken with personal pomp and ceremony. With us, the office or occasion, not the individual, deserves such accolades. Do not mistake me, Comrade General; we have our own methods of deification, but we have learned from past mistakes. Those we deify now are — for the most part — safely dead. My country would understand your governor. *Our* governor, I suppose I must say. If your purpose is to win my admission that I am impressed by him, you have succeeded, General Hatcher."

"Good." Hatcher frowned thoughtfully, his face somehow both tighter and more open. "Do you also accept that we're being honest with you, Marshal?"

Tsien regarded him for a moment, then dipped his head in a tiny nod.

"Yes. All of my nominees were confirmed, and the Governor's demonstration of his biotechnics —" Tsien hesitated briefly on the still unfamiliar word "— and those other items of Imperial technology were also convincing. I believe — indeed, I have no choice but to believe — your warnings of the Achuultani, and that you and your fellows are making every effort to achieve success. In light of all those things, I have no choice but to join your effort. I do not say it will be easy, General Hatcher, but we shall certainly make the attempt. And, I believe, succeed."

"Good," Hatcher said again, then leaned back with a smile. "In that case, Marshal, we're ready to run the first thousand personnel of your selection through enhancement as soon as your people in Beijing can put a list together."

"Ah?" Tsien sat a bit straighter. This was moving with speed, indeed! He had not expected these Westerners — He stopped and corrected himself. He had not expected these *people* to offer such things so soon. Surely there would be a period of testing and evaluation of sincerity first!

But when he looked across at the American, the slight, ironic twinkle in Hatcher's eyes told him his host knew precisely what he was thinking, and the realization made him feel just a bit ashamed.

"Comrade General," he said finally, "I appreciate your generosity, but —"

"Not generosity, Marshal. We've been enhancing our personnel ever since *Dahak* left, which means the Alliance has fallen far behind. We need to make up the difference, and we'll be sending transports with enhancement capability to Beijing and any other three cities you select. Planetary facilities under your direct control will follow as quickly as we can build them."

Tsien blinked, and Hatcher smiled.

"Marshal Tsien, we are fellow officers serving the same commander-in-chief. If we don't act accordingly, some will doubt our claims of solidarity are genuine. They are genuine. We will proceed on that basis."

He leaned back and raised both hands shoulder-high, open palms uppermost, and Tsien nodded slowly.

"You are correct. Generous nonetheless, but correct. And perhaps I am discovering that more than our governor are formidable men, Comrade General."

"Gerald, please. Or just 'Ger,' if you're comfortable with it."

Tsien began a polite refusal, then paused. He had never been comfortable with easy familiarity between serving officers, even among his fellow Asians, yet there was something charming about this American. Not boyish (though he understood Westerners prized that quality for some peculiar reason), but charming. Hatcher's competence and hard-headed, forthright honesty compelled respect, but this was something else. Charisma? No, that was close, but not quite the proper word. The word was . . . openness. Or friendship, perhaps.

Friendship. Now was that not a strange thing to feel for a Western general after so many years? And yet . . . Yes, "and yet," indeed.

"Very well . . . Gerald," he said.

"I know it's like pulling teeth, Marshal." Hatcher's almost gentle smile robbed his words of any offense. "We've been too busy thinking of ways to kill each other for too long for it to be any other way, more's the pity. Do you know, in a weird sort of way, I'm almost grateful to the Achuultani."

"Grateful?" Tsien cocked his head for a moment, then nodded. "I see. I had not previously thought of it in that light, Comr — Gerald, but it *is* a relief to face an alien menace rather than the possibility of blowing up our world ourselves."

"Exactly." Hatcher extracted a bottle of brandy and two snifters from a desk drawer. He set them on the blotter and poured, then offered one to his guest and raised his own. "May I say, Marshal Tsien, that it is a greater pleasure than I ever anticipated to have you as an ally?"

"You may." Tsien allowed a smile to cross his own habitually immobile face. It was hardly proper, but there was no getting around it. For all their differences, he and this American were too much alike to be enemies.

"And, as you would say, Gerald, my name is Tao-ling," he murmured, and crystal sang gently as their glasses touched.

Out of deference to the still unenhanced Terra-born Council members, Horus had the news footage played directly rather than relayed through his neural feed. Not that it made it any better.

The report ended and the Terran tri-vid unit sank back into the wall amid the silence. The thirty men and women in his conference room looked at one another, but he noted that none of them looked directly at *him*.

"What I want to know, ladies and gentlemen," he said finally, his voice shattering the hush, "is how that was allowed to happen?"

One or two Councilors flinched, though he hadn't raised his voice. He hadn't had to. The screams and thunder of automatic weapons as the armored vehicles moved in had made his point for him.

"It was not 'allowed,'" a voice said finally. "It was inevitable."

Horus's cocked head encouraged the speaker to continue, and Sophia Pariani leaned forward to meet his eyes. Her Italian accent was more than usually pronounced, but there was no apology in her expression.

"There is no doubt that the situation was clumsily handled, but there will be more 'situations,' Governor, and not merely in Africa. Already the world economy has been disrupted by the changes we have effected; as the further and greater changes which lie ahead become evident, more and more of the common men and women of the world will react as those people did."

"Sophia's right, Horus." This time it was Sarhantha, one of his ten fellow survivors from *Nergal's* crew. "We ought to've seen it coming. In fact, we *did*; we just didn't expect it so soon because we'd forgotten how many people are crammed into this world. Hard and fast as we're working, only a small minority are actively involved in the defense projects or the military. All the majority see is that their governments have been supplanted, their planet is threatened by a menace they don't truly comprehend and are none too sure they believe in, and their economies are in the process of catastrophic disruption. This particular riot was touched off by a combination of hunger, inflation, and unemployment — regional factors that pre-date our involvement but have grown only worse since we assumed power — and the realization that even those with skilled trades will soon find their skills obsolete."

"But there'll be other factors soon enough." Councilor Abner Johnson spoke with a sharp New England twang despite his matte-black complexion. "People're people, Governor. The vested interests are going to object — strenuously — once they get reorganized. Their economic and political power's about to go belly-up, and some of them're stupid enough to fight. And don't forget the religious aspect. We're sitting on a powder keg in Iran and Syria, but we've got our own nuts, and you people represent a pretty unappetizing affront to their comfortable little preconceptions." He smiled humorlessly.

" 'Mycos? *Birhat?* You don't really think God created planets with names like *that*, do you?' If you could at least've come from a planet named 'Eden' it might've helped, but as it is — !" Johnson shrugged. "Once *they* get organized, we'll have a real lunatic fringe!"

"Comrade Johnson is correct, Comrade Governor." Commissar Hsu Yin's British-educated accent was almost musical after Johnson's flat twang. "We may debate the causes of Third World poverty —" she eyed her capitalist fellows calmly "— but it exists. Ignorance and fear will be greatest there, violence more quickly acceptable, yet this is only the beginning. When the First World realizes that it is in precisely the same situation, the violence may grow even worse. We may as well prepare for the worst . . . and whatever we anticipate will most assuredly fall short of what will actually happen."

"Granted. But this violent suppression —"

"Was the work of the local authorities," Geb put in. "And before you condemn them, what else could they do? There were almost ten thousand people in that mob, and if a lot of them were unarmed women and children, a lot were neither female, young, nor unarmed. At least they had the sense to call us in as soon as they'd restored order, even if it was under martial law. I've diverted a dozen *Shirut*-class atmospheric conveyers to haul in foodstuffs from North America. That should take the worst edge off the situation, but if the local authorities hadn't 'suppressed' the disturbances, however they did it, simply feeding them wouldn't even begin to help, and you know it."

There were mutters of agreement, and Horus noted that the Terra-born were considerably more vehement than the Imperials. Were they right? It was their planet, and Maker knew the disruptions were only beginning. He knew they were sanctioning expediency, but wasn't that another way to describe pragmatism? And in a situation like the present one . . .

"All right," he sighed finally, "I don't like it, but you may be right." He turned to Gustav van Gelder, Councilor for Planetary Security. "Gus, I want you and Geb to increase the priority for getting stun guns into the hands of local authorities. And I want more of our enhancement capacity diverted to police personnel. Isis, you and Myko deal with that."

Doctor Isis Tudor, his own Terra-born daughter and now Councilor for Biosciences, glanced at her ex-mutineer assistant with a sort of resigned desperation. Isis was over eighty; even enhancement could only slow her gradual decay and eliminate aches and pains, but her mind was quick and clear. Now she nodded, and he knew she'd find the capacity . . . somehow.

"Until we can get local peace-keepers enhanced," Horus went on, "I'll have General Hatcher set up mixed-nationality response teams out of his military personnel. I don't like it — the situation's going to be bad enough without 'aliens' popping up to quell resistance to our 'tyrannical' ways — but a dozen troopers in combat armor could have stopped this business with a tenth the casualties, especially if they'd had stun guns."

Heads nodded, and he suppressed a sigh. Problems, problems! Why hadn't he made sufficient allowance for what would happen once Imperial technology came to Terra in earnest? Now he felt altogether too much like a warden rather than a governor, but whatever happened, he had to hold things together — by main force, if necessary — until the Achuultani had been stopped. *If* they could be —

He chopped off that thought automatically and turned to Christine Redhorse, Councilor for Agriculture.

"All right. On to the next problem. Christine, I'd like you to share your report on the wheat harvest with us, and then . . ."

❖   ❖   ❖

Most of Horus's council had departed, leaving him alone with his defense planners and engineers. Whatever else happened, theirs was the absolutely critical responsibility, and they were doing better than Horus had hoped. They were actually ahead of schedule on almost a fifth of the PDCs, although the fortifications slated for the Asian Alliance were only now getting underway.

One by one, the remaining Councilors completed their business and left. In the end, only Geb remained, and Horus smiled wearily at his oldest living friend as the two of them leaned back and propped their heels on the conference table almost in unison.

"Maker!" Horus groaned. "It was easier fighting Anu!"

"Easier, but not as satisfying." Geb sipped his coffee, then made a face. It was barely warm, and he rose and circled the table, shaking each insulated carafe until he found one that was still partly full and returned to his chair.

"True, true," Horus agreed. "At least this time we think we've got a *chance* of winning. That makes a pleasant change."

"From your lips to the Maker's ears," Geb responded fervently, and Horus laughed. He reached out a long arm for Geb's carafe and poured more coffee into his own cup.

"Watch it," he advised his friend. "Remember Abner's religious fanatics."

"They won't care what I say or how I say it. Just being what I am is going to offend them."

"Probably." Horus sipped, then frowned. "By the way, there was something I've been meaning to ask you."

"And what might that be, O dauntless leader?"

"I found an anomaly in the data base the other day." Geb raised an eyebrow, and Horus shrugged. "Probably nothing, but I hit a priority suppression code I can't understand."

"Oh?" If Geb's voice was just a shade too level Horus didn't notice.

"I was running through the data we pulled out of Anu's

enclave computers, and Colin's imposed a lock-out on some of the visual records."

"He has?"

"Yep. It piqued my interest, so I ran an analysis. He's put every visual image of Inanna under a security lock only he can release. Or, no, not all of them; only for the last century or so."

"He must have had a reason," Geb suggested.

"I don't doubt it, but I was hoping you might have some idea what it was. You were Chief Prosecutor — did he say anything to you about why he did it?"

"Even if he had, I wouldn't be free to talk about it, but I probably wouldn't have worried. It couldn't have had much bearing on the trials, whatever his reasoning. *She* wasn't around to be tried, after all."

"I know, I know, but it bothers me, Geb." Horus drummed gently on the table. "She was Anu's number two, the one who did all those hideous brain transplants for him. Maker only knows how many Terra-born and Imperials she personally slaughtered along the way! It just seems . . . odd."

"If it bothers you, ask him about it when he gets back," Geb suggested. He finished his coffee and rose. "For now, though, I've got to saddle back up, my friend. I'm due to inspect the work at Minya Konka this afternoon."

He waved a cheerful farewell and strode down the hall to the elevator whistling, but the merry little tune died the instant the doors closed. The old Imperial seemed to sag around his bioenhanced bones, and he leaned his forehead against the mirrored surface of the inner doors.

Maker of Man and Mercy, he prayed silently, don't let him ask Colin. *Please* don't let him ask Colin!

Tears burned, and he wiped them angrily, but he couldn't wipe away the memory which had driven him to Colin before the courts martial to beg him to suppress the visuals on Inanna. He'd been ready to go down on his knees, but he hadn't needed to. If anything, Colin's horror had surpassed his own.

Against his will, Geb relived those moments on deck ninety of the sublight battleship *Osir*, the very heart of Anu's enclave. Those terrible moments after Colin and 'Tanni had gone up the crawlway to face Anu, leaving behind a mangled body 'Tanni's energy gun had cut almost in half. A body which had been Commander Inanna's, but only because its brain had been ripped away, its original owner murdered and its flesh stolen to make a new, young host for the mutinous medical officer.

Geb had used his own energy gun to obliterate every trace of that body, for once it had belonged to one of his closest friends, to a beautiful woman named Tanisis . . . Horus's wife . . . and Jiltanith's own mother.

Chapter Six

Fifty Chinese paratroopers in Imperial black snapped to attention as the band struck up, and Marshal Tsien Tao-ling, Vice Chief of Staff for Operations to the Lieutenant Governor of Earth, watched them with an anxiety he had not wasted upon ceremonial in decades. This was his superior's first official visit to China in the five months since the Asian Alliance had surrendered to the inevitable, and he wanted — demanded — all to go flawlessly.

It did. General Gerald Hatcher appeared in the hatch of his cutter and started down the ramp, followed by his personal aide and a very small staff.

"Preeee-sent *arms!*"

Energy guns snapped up. The honor guard, drawn from the first batch of Asian personnel to be bioenhanced, handled their massive weapons with panache, and Tsien noted the perfection of their drill without a smile as he and Hatcher exchanged salutes. The twinkle in the American's brown eyes betrayed his own amused tolerance for ceremonial only to those who knew him very well, and it still surprised Tsien just a bit that he had become one of those few people.

"Good to see you, Tao-ling," Hatcher said under cover of the martial music, and Tsien responded with a millimetric smile before the brief moment of privacy disappeared into the waiting tide of military protocol.

Gerald Hatcher placed his cap in his lap and leaned back as the city of Ch'engtu fell away astern. The cutter headed for Minya Konka, the mountain which had been ripped apart to hold PDC Huan-Ti, and he grimaced as he ran a finger around the tight collar of his tunic.

He lowered his hand, wondering once again if it had been wise to adopt Imperial uniform. While it had the decided advantage of not belonging to any of the rival militaries they were trying to merge, it looked disturbingly like the uniform of the SS. Not surprisingly, considering. He'd done what he could to lessen the similarities — exaggerating the size of the starbursts the Nazis had replaced with skulls, restoring the serrated *hisanth* leaves to the lapels, adopting the authorized variation of gold braid in place of silver — but the overall impact still bothered him.

He put the thought aside — again — and turned to Tsien.

"It looks like your people've done a great job, Tao-ling. I wish you didn't have to spend so much time in Beijing to do it, but I'm impressed."

"I spend too little time here as it is, Gerald." Tsien gave a very slight shrug. "It is even worse than it was while you and I were enemies. There are at least eight too few hours in every day."

"Tell me about it!" Hatcher laughed. "If we work like dogs for another six months, you and I may finally be able to hand it over to someone else long enough to get our own biotechnics."

"True. I must confess, however, that the speed with which we are moving almost frightens me. There is too little time for proper coordination. Too many projects require attention, and I have no time to *know* my officers."

"I know. We're better off than you are because of how

Nergal's people infiltrated our militaries before we even knew about them. I don't envy your having to start from scratch."

"We will manage," Tsien said, and Hatcher took him at his word. The huge Chinese officer had lost at least five kilos since their first meeting, yet it only made him even more fearsome, as if he were being worn down to elemental gristle and bone. And whatever else came of the fusion with the Asian Alliance, Hatcher was almost prayerfully grateful that it had brought him Tsien Tao-ling.

The cutter dropped toward the dust-spewing wound which had once been a mountaintop, and Hatcher checked his breathing mask. He hated using it, but the dust alone would make it welcome, and the fact that PDC Huan-Ti was located at an altitude of almost seventy-five hundred meters made it necessary. He felt a bit better when he saw Tsien reaching for his own mask . . . and suppressed a spurt of envy as Major Allen Germaine ignored his. It must be nice, he thought sourly as he regarded his bioenhanced aide.

They grounded and thin, cold air, bitter with dust, swirled through the hatch. Hatcher hastily clipped on his mask, and his uniform's collar was a suddenly minor consideration as the Imperial fabric adjusted to maintain a comfortable body temperature and he led the way out into the ear-splitting, dust-spouting, eye-bewildering bedlam of yet another of Geb's mighty projects.

Tsien Tao-ling followed Hatcher, hiding his impatience. He hated inspection tours, and only the fact that Hatcher hated them just as badly let him face this time-consuming parade with a semblance of inner peace. That and the fact that, time-consuming or no, it also played its part. Morale, the motivation of their human material, was all important, and nothing better convinced people of the importance of their tasks than to see their commanders inspecting their work.

Yet despite his impatience, Tsien was deeply impressed.

Enough Imperial equipment was becoming available to strain the enhancement centers' ability to provide operators, and the result was amazing for someone who had grown up with purely Terran technology. The main excavation was almost finished — indeed, the central control rooms were structurally complete, awaiting installation of the computer core — and the shield generators were already being built. Incredible.

He bent to listen to an engineer, and movement caught the corner of his eye as a breath-masked officer disappeared behind a heap of building material, waving one hand as he spoke to another officer at his side. There was something familiar about the small figure, but the engineer was still talking, and Tsien returned his attention to him.

"I'm impressed, Geban," Hatcher said, and Huan-Ti's chief engineer grinned. The burly ex-mutineer was barely a hundred and fifty centimeters tall, but he looked as if he could have picked up a hover jeep one-handed — before enhancement.

"Really impressed," Hatcher repeated as the control room door closed off the cacophony beyond. "You're — what, four weeks ahead of schedule?"

"Almost five, General," Geban replied with simple pride. "With just a little luck, I'm going to bring this job in at least two months early."

"Outstanding!" Hatcher slapped Geban's shoulder, and Tsien hid a smile. He would never understand how Hatcher's informality with subordinates could work so well, yet it did. Not simply with Westerners who might be accustomed to such things, either. Tsien had seen exactly the same broad smile on the faces of Chinese and Thai peasants.

"In that case," Hatcher said, turning to the marshal, "I think we —"

A thunderous concussion drowned his words and threw him from his feet.

✧ ✧ ✧

Diego McMurphy was a Mexican-Irish explosives genius from Texas. Off-shore oil rigs and dams, vertol terminals and apartment complexes — he'd seen them all, but this was the most damnable, bone-breaking, challenging, *wonderful* project he'd ever been involved with, and the fact that he was buying his right to a full set of biotechnic implants was only icing on the cake. Which is why he was happy as he waved his crew forward to set the charges on the unfinished western face of Magazine Twelve.

He died a happy man, and six hundred and eighty-six other men and women died with him. They died because one of McMurphy's men activated his rock drill, and that man didn't know someone had wired his controls to eleven hundred kilos of Imperial blasting compound.

The explosion rivaled a three-kiloton nuclear bomb.

Gerald Hatcher bounced off Tsien Tao-ling, but the marshal's powerful arm caught him before he could fall. Alarms whooped, sirens screamed, and Geban went paper-white. The door barely had time to open before he reached it; if it hadn't, he would have torn it loose with his bare hands.

Hatcher shook his head, trying to understand what had happened as he followed Tsien to the open door. A huge mushroom cloud filled the western horizon, and even as he watched, a five-man gravitonic conveyer with a full load of structural steel turned turtle in midair. It had been caught by the fringes of the explosion, and the pilot had almost pulled it out. Almost, but not quite. Its standard commercial drive had never been designed for such abuse, and it impacted nose-first at six hundred kilometers per hour.

A fresh fireball spewed up, and the death toll was suddenly six hundred and ninety-one.

"My God!" Hatcher murmured.

Tsien nodded in silent, shocked agreement. Whatever the cause, this was disaster, and he despised himself for thinking of lost time first and lost lives second. He turned toward the control block ramps in the vanished Geban's wake, then stopped as a knot of men headed towards him. They were armed, and there was something familiar about the small officer at their head —

"*Quang!*" he bellowed.

The fury in Tsien's voice jerked Hatcher's eyes away from the smoke. He started to speak, then gasped as the marshal whirled around and hit him in a diving tackle. The two of them crashed back into the control room, hard enough to crack ribs, as the first burst of automatic fire raked the open doorway.

"Forward!" General Quang Do Chinh screamed. "Kill them! Kill them *now!*"

His troopers advanced at the run, closing on the unfinished control block, and Quang's heart flamed with triumph. Yes, kill the traitors! And especially the arch-traitor who had tried to shunt him aside! What a triumph to begin their war against the invaders!

As he and his men sprinted forward, construction workers raced to drag dead and wounded away from the explosion site, and six other carefully infiltrated assault teams produced automatic weapons and grenades. They concentrated on picking out Imperials, but any target would do.

"What the hell is happening?!" Gerald Hatcher's voice was muffled by his breath mask, but it would have been hoarse anyway — a hundred kilos of charging Chinese field marshal had seen to that. He shoved up onto his knees, reaching instinctively for his holstered automatic.

"I do not know," Tsien replied tersely, checking his own weapon's magazine. "But the Vietnamese leading his men this way is named Quang. He was one of those most opposed to joining our forces to yours."

Another burst of fire raked the open doorway, ricochets whining nastily, and Hatcher rose higher on his knees to hit the door button. The hatch slammed instantly, but it was only lightweight Terran steel; the next burst punched right through it.

"Shit!" Hatcher scurried across the control room on hands and knees. Major Germaine already stood with his back to the wall on the left side of the door, and his grav gun had materialized in his right hand like magic.

"What the fuck do they think they're going to accomplish?!"

"I do not know, Gerald. This is pointless. It simply invites reprisals. But their ultimate objective is immaterial — to us, at least."

"True." Hatcher flattened himself against the wall as another row of holes appeared in the door. "Al?"

"I already put out the word, sir." Unlike his boss, Germaine had a built-in communicator. "But I don't know how much good it's going to do. More of the bastards are shooting up the rescue crews. Geban's down — hurt bad — and he's not the only Imperial."

"God*damn* them!" Hatcher hissed, and fought to think as the half-forgotten terror and adrenalin rush of combat flooded him. Continuous firing raked the panel now, and he gritted his teeth as bullets and bits of door whined about his ears. This room was a deathtrap. He tried to estimate where their attackers had been when Tao-ling tackled him. On the ground to the south. That meant they had to climb at least three ramps. So whoever was firing at the door was covering them until they could get here . . . probably with a demolition charge that would turn them all to hamburger.

"We've got to get ourselves a field of fire," he grated. His automatic was a toy compared to what was coming at them, but it was better than nothing. And anything was better than dying without fighting back.

"I agree," Tsien said flatly.

"All right. Tao-ling, you pop the hatch. Al, I think they're coming up from the south. You can cover the head of the ramp from where you are. Tao-ling, you get over here with me. We'll try to slow 'em down if they come the other way, but Al's got our only real firepower."

"Yes, sir," Germaine said, and Tsien nodded agreement.

"Then do it — now!"

Tsien hit the button and rolled across the floor, coming up on his knees beside Hatcher. They both flattened against the wall as yet another burst screamed into the room, and Hatcher cursed as a ricochet creased his cheek.

"Can you get that sniper without getting yourself killed, Al?"

"A pleasure, sir," Germaine said coldly. His eyes were unfocused as his implants sought the source of the fire, then he crouched and took one step to the side. He moved with the blinding speed of his biotechnics, and the grav gun hissed out a brief burst, spitting three-millimeter explosive darts at fifty-two hundred meters per second.

Quang swore as his covering fire died. So, they had at least one of the cursed grav guns. That was bad, but he still had twenty-five men, and they were all heavily armed.

He had no idea how the rest of the attack was going, but Tsien's reactions had been only too revealing, and the only man who could identify him must die.

His men pounded up the ramp ahead of him.

Her name was Litanil, and, disregarding time spent in stasis, she was thirty-six. It took her precious moments to realize what was happening, and a few more to believe it when she had, but then cold fury filled her.

Litanil hadn't thought very deeply when Anu's people recruited her, for she'd been both young and bored. Now she knew she'd also been criminally stupid, and, like her fellows, she'd labored with the Breaker's own demons on her heels in an effort to atone. Along the way, she'd come to like and admire the Terra-born she worked with, and now hundreds of them lay dead, butchered by the animals responsible for this carnage. She didn't worry about why. She didn't even consider the monstrous treason to her race the attack implied. She thought only of dead friends, and something snarled inside her.

She turned her power bore towards the fighting, and her neural feeds sought out the safety interlocks. It was supposed to be impossible for any accident to get around them — but Litanil was no accident.

Allen Germaine went down on one knee, bracing his grav gun over his left forearm, as the first three raiders hurled themselves over the lip of the topmost ramp, assault rifles on full automatic.

They got off one long burst each before their bodies blew apart in a hurricane of explosive darts.

Litanil goosed her power bore to max, snarling across the stony plain at almost two hundred kilometers per hour. Not even a gravitonic drive could hold the massive bore steady at that speed, but she rode it like a bucking horse, her implant scanners reaching out, and her face was a mask of fury as she raised the cutting head chest-high.

Private Pak Chung of the Army of Korea heard nothing, but some instinct made him turn his head. His eyes widened in horror as he saw the huge machine screaming towards him. Rock dust and smoke billowed behind it like a curdled wake, and the . . . the *thing* at its front was aimed straight at *him*!

The last thing Private Pak ever saw was a terrible brilliance in the millisecond before he exploded in a flash of super-heated body fluids.

General Quang cursed as his three lead men died, but it had not been entirely unexpected. It must be the American's African aide, yet there was only one of him, bioenhanced or not, and the ramp was not the only way up.

"They're spreading out," Germaine reported. "I can't get a good implant reading through the ramp, but some of them are swinging round front."

"There is a scaffold below the edge of the platform," Tsien said.

"Damn! Remind me to detail armed guards to each construction site when we get home, Al."

"Yes, sir."

Litanil wiped out Private Pak's team and raged off after fresh targets. Ahead of her, half a dozen bioenhanced Terra-born construction workers armed with steel reinforcing rods and Imperial blasting compound began working their way around the flank of a second assault group.

Quang poked his head up. This was taking too long. But there would still be time. His men were in position at last, and he barked an order.

"Down!" Germaine shouted, and Hatcher and Tsien dropped instantly as the stubby grenade launchers coughed. Two grenades hit short or exploded against the outer wall; the third headed straight into the door, and Germaine's left hand struck it like a handball. The explosion ripped his hand apart, and shrapnel tore into his chest and shoulder.

Agony stabbed him, but his implants stopped the flow of blood to his shredded hand and flooded his system with a super-charged blast of adrenalin. The first wave came up the ramp after the grenades, and he cut them down like bloody wheat.

Hatcher fired as a head rose over the edge of the scaffolding. His first shot missed; his second hit just above the left eye. Beside him, Tsien was flat on his belly, firing two-handed. Another attacker dropped.

A sudden burst of explosions ripped the dusty smoke as the construction workers tossed their makeshift bombs. The attack squad faltered as three of their number were blown apart. A fourth emptied a full magazine into a charging man. He killed his assailant, but he never knew; the steel rod his victim had carried impaled him like a spear.

His six surviving comrades broke and ran — directly in front of Litanil's power bore.

Eight more of Quang's men died, but a ninth slammed a heart-rupturing burst into Allen Germaine. Major Germaine was a dead man, but he was a bioenhanced corpse. He stayed on his feet long enough to aim very carefully before he squeezed the trigger.

Gerald Hatcher swore viciously as his aide toppled without a sound, grav gun bouncing from his remaining hand. Bastards! *Bastards!* He squeezed off another shot, hitting his target in the torso, then dropped him with a second.

It wasn't enough, and he knew it.

Quang's number four attack squad had a good position between two huge earth-movers, but there were no more targets in their field of fire. It was time to go, and they began to filter back in pairs, each halting in turn to provide covering fire for their fellows. It was a textbook maneuver.

As the first pair reached the ends of their shielding earth-movers, a pair of bioenhanced hands reached out from either side. Fingers ten times stronger than their own closed, and two tracheas crushed. The twitching bodies were tossed aside, and the crouching ambushers waited patiently for their next victims.

Quang popped his head up and saw the grav gun lying two meters beyond the door. Now! He clutched his assault rifle and rose, waving his surviving men forward, and followed up the ramp in their wake.

A last attacker crouched on the scaffolding. He'd seen what happened when his fellows exposed themselves, and he poked just the muzzle of his rifle over the edge. It was a sound idea, but in his excitement he rose just too high. The crown of his head showed, and Gerald Hatcher put a pistol bullet through it in the instant before the automatic fire shattered both of his own legs.

Litanil swung her power bore again and knew they were winning.

The attackers had achieved the surprise they sought, but they hadn't realized what they were attacking. Most of the site personnel were unenhanced Terra-born, but a significant percentage were not, and those who were enhanced had full Fleet packages, modified at Colin MacIntyre's order to incorporate fold-space coms. They might be unarmed, but they were strong, tough, fast, and in unbroken communication.

And, as Litanil herself had proved, a construction site abounded in improvisational weapons.

Tsien Tao-ling was no longer a field marshal. He was a warrior alone and betrayed, and Quang was still out there. Whatever happened, Quang must not be allowed to live.

Tsien tossed aside his empty pistol, his mind cold and clear, and rose on his hands and toes, like a runner in the blocks.

General Quang blinked as Tsien exploded from the control room. He would never have believed the huge man could move that quickly! But what did he hope to gain? He could not outrun bullets!

Then he saw Tsien drop and snatch up the grav gun as he rolled towards the scaffolding. *No!*

Assault rifles barked, but the men behind them had been as surprised as Quang. They were late, and they tried to compensate by leading their target. They would catch him as he rolled over the edge of the scaffolding into cover.

Tsien threw out one leg, grunting as a kneecap shattered on concrete, but it had the desired effect. He stopped dead, clutching Germaine's grav gun, and the bullets which should have killed him went wide. He raised the muzzle, not trying to rise from where he lay.

Quang screamed in frustration as Tsien opened fire. Three of his remaining men were down. Then four. Five! He raised his own weapon, firing at the marshal, but fury betrayed his aim.

Tsien grunted again as a slug ripped through his right biceps. A second shattered his shoulder, but he held down the grav gun's trigger, and his fire swept the ramp like a broom.

Quang's last trooper was down, and sudden terror filled him. Quang threw away his rifle and tried to drop down the ramp, but he was too late. His last memory on Earth was the cold, bitter hatred in Tsien Tao-ling's pitiless eyes.

Gerald Hatcher groaned, then bit his lip against a scream as someone moved his left leg. He shuddered and managed to raise his eyelids, wondering for a moment why he felt so weak, why there was so much pain.

Tao-ling bent over him, and he bit off most of another scream as the marshal tightened something on his right leg. A tourniquet, Hatcher realized dizzily . . . and then he remembered.

His expression twisted with more than pain as he saw Allen Germaine's dead face close beside him, but his mind was working once more. Poorly, slowly, with frustrating dark patches, but working. The firing seemed to have stopped, and if there was no more shooting and Tao-ling was working on him, they must have won, mustn't they? He was rather pleased by his ability to work that out.

Tsien crawled up beside him. One shoulder was swollen by a makeshift, blood-soaked bandage, and his left leg dragged uselessly, but his good hand clutched Allen's grav gun as he lowered himself between Hatcher and the door with a groan.

"T-Tao-ling?" the general managed.

"You are awake?" Tsien's voice was hoarse with pain. "You have the constitution of a bull, Gerald."

"Th-thanks. What . . . what kind of shape are we . . . ?"

"I believe we have beaten off the attack. I do not know how. I am afraid you are badly hurt, my friend."

"I'll . . . live. . . ."

"Yes, I think you will," Tsien said so judiciously Hatcher grinned tightly despite his agony. His brain was fluttering and it would be a relief to give in, but there was something he had to say first. Ah!

"Tao-ling —"

"Be quiet, Gerald," the marshal said austerely. "You are wounded."

"You're . . . not? Looks like . . . I get my . . . implants first."

"Americans! Always you must be first."

"T-Tell Horus I said . . . you take over. . . ."

"I?" Tsien looked at him, his face as twisted with shame as pain. "It was my people who did this thing!"

"H-Horse shit. But that's . . . why it's important . . . you take over. Tell Horus!" Hatcher squeezed his friend's forearm with all his fading strength. It was Tsien's right arm, but he didn't even wince.

"Tell him!" Hatcher commanded, clinging to awareness through the shrieking pain.

"Very well, Gerald," Tsien said gently. "I will."

"Good man," Hatcher whispered, and let go at last.

"Thanks."

"Yes, I think you will. Vlad and I've nicknamed Her-ther general might despise his sprite His brain was faltering and it would be a relief to give in, but there was something he had to say first. All
too long—

"Be quiet, Gerald," the marshal said instantly. "You are wounded?"

"You're ... not Lorris like ... I got my ... implants first."

Another chill! Always we must be true.

"Tell Horus, I told ... you take over.

"I'm ... Istoo botered him, his face as twisted with shame
as pain. "It was my responsibility did this thing."

"Be Horus shut. Tell Horus ... why it's important ... you
take over. Tell Horus," Hacker squeezed his friend's limp
arm with his feeble strength. It was Tsien's right arm
broke didn't even wince.

"Tell him," Hacker commanded, clinging to awareness
through the shadowing pain.

"Very well, Gerald," Tsien said gently, "I will."

"Good man," Hacker whispered, and let go at last.

The city echoed with song and dance as the People of Riahn celebrated. Twelve seasons of war against Tur had ended at last, and not simply in victory. The royal houses of Riahn and Tur had brought the endless skirmishes and open battle over possession of the Fithan copper mines to a halt with greater wisdom than they had shown in far too long, for the Daughter of Tur would wed the Son of Riahn, and henceforth the two Peoples would be one.

It was good. It was very, very good, for Riahn-Tur would be the greatest of all the city-states of T'Yir. Their swords and spears would no longer turn upon one another but ward both from their neighbors, and the copper of Fithan would bring them wealth and prosperity. The ships of Riahn were already the swiftest ever to swim — with Fithan copper to sheath their hulls against worms and weed, they would own the seas of T'Yir!

Great was the rejoicing of Riahn, and none of the People knew of the vast Achuultani starships which had reached their system while the war still raged. None knew they had

*come almost by accident, unaware of the People until they
actually entered the system, or how they had paused
among the system's asteroids. Indeed, none of the People
knew even what an asteroid was, much less what would
happen if the largest of them were sent falling inward
toward T'Yir.*

*And because they did not know such things, none knew
their world had barely seven months to live.*

Chapter Seven

Colin MacIntyre was not afraid, for "afraid" was too weak a word.

He sat with his back to the conference room hatch as the others filed in, and he felt their own fear against his spine. He waited until all were seated, then swung his chair to meet their eyes. Their faces looked even worse than he'd expected.

"All right," he said at last. "We've got to decide what to do next."

Their steady regard threw his lie back at him, even Jiltanith's, and he wanted to scream at them. *We* didn't have to decide; *he* did, and he wished with all his soul that he had never heard of a starship named *Dahak*.

He stopped himself and drew a deep breath, closing his eyes. When he opened them again, the shadows within them had retreated just a bit.

"Dahak," he said quietly, "have you got anything more for us?"

"Negative, Captain. I have examined all known Imperial weapons and research. Nothing in my data base can account for the observational data."

Colin managed not to spit a curse. *Observational data.* What a neat, concise way to describe two once-inhabited planets with no life whatever. Not a tree, not a shrub, nothing. There were no plains of volcanic glass and lingering radioactivity, no indications of warfare — just bare, terribly-eroded earth and stone and a few pathetic clusters of buildings sagging into wind and storm-threshed ruin. Even their precarious existence said much for the durability of Imperial building materials, for Dahak estimated there had been no living hand to tend them in almost forty-five thousand years.

No birds, he thought. No animals. Not even an insect. Just . . . nothing. The only movement was the wind. Weather had flensed the denuded planet until its stony bones gaped through like the teeth of a skull, bared in a horrible, grinning rictus of desecration and death.

"Hector?" he said finally. "Do you have any ideas?"

"None." MacMahan's normally controlled face was even more impassive than usual, and he seemed to hunker down in his chair.

"Cohanna?"

"I can't add much, sir, but I'd have to say it was a bioweapon of some sort. Some unimaginable sort." Cohanna shivered. "I've landed unmanned probes for spot analyses, but I don't dare send teams down."

Colin nodded.

"I can't imagine how it was done," the biosciences officer continued. "What kind of weapon *could* produce this? If they'd irradiated the place. . . . But there's simply nothing to go on, Captain. Nothing at all."

"All right." Colin inhaled deeply. "'Tanni, what can you tell us?"

"Scarce more than 'Hanna. We have found some three score orbital vessels and installations; all lie abandoned to the dead. As with the planets, we durst not look too close, yet our probes have scanned them well. In all our servos have attended lie naught save bones."

"Dahak? Any luck accessing their computers?"

"Very little, Captain. I have been unable to carry out detailed study of the equipment, but there are major differences between it and the technology with which I am familiar. In particular, the computer nets appear to have been connected with fold-space links, which would provide a substantial increase in speed over my own molecular circuitry, and these computers operated on a radically different principle, maintaining data flow in semi-permanent force fields rather than in physical storage units. Their power supplies failed long ago, and without continuous energization —" The computer's voice paused in the electronic equivalent of a shrug.

"The only instance in which partial data retrieval has been possible is artifact seventeen, the Fleet vessel *Cordan*," Dahak continued. "Unfortunately, the data core was of limited capacity, as the unit itself was merely a three-man sublight utility boat, and had suffered from failed fold-space units. Most data in memory are encoded in a multi-level Fleet code I have not yet been able to break, though I believe I might succeed if a larger sample could be obtained. The recoverable data consist primarily of routine operational records and astrogational material.

"I was able to date the catastrophe by consulting the last entry made by *Cordan*'s captain. It contains no indication of alarm, nor, unfortunately, was she loquacious. The last entry simply records an invitation for her and her crew to dine at the planetary governor's residence on Defram-A III."

"Nothing more?" Ninhursag asked quietly.

"No, Commander. There undoubtedly was additional data, but only *Cordan*'s command computer utilized hard storage techniques, and it is sadly decayed. I have located twelve additional auxiliary and special-function computer nets, but none contain recoverable data."

"Vlad?" Colin turned to his engineer.

"I wish I could tell you something. The fact that we dare not go over and experiment leaves us with little hard data, but the remotes indicate that their technology was substantially more advanced than *Dahak's*. On the other hand, we have seen little real evidence of fundamental breakthroughs — it is more like a highly sophisticated refinement of what we already have."

"How now, Vlad?" Jiltanith asked. "Hath not our Dahak but now said their computers are scarce like unto himself?"

"True enough, 'Tanni, but the differences are incremental." Vlad frowned. "What he is actually saying is that they moved much further into energy-state engineering than before. I cannot say certainly without something to take apart and put back together, but those force field memories probably manifested as solid surfaces when powered up. The Imperium was moving in that direction even before the mutiny — our own shield is exactly the same thing on a gross scale. What they discovered was a way to do the same sorts of things on a scale which makes even molycircs big and clumsy, but it was theoretically possible from the beginning. You see? *Incremental* advances."

Jiltanith nodded slowly, and Colin leaned his elbows on the table.

"Bearing that in mind, Dahak, what are the chances of recovering useful data from any other computers we encounter?"

"Assuming they are of the variety Fleet Captain (Engineering) Chernikov has been discussing and that they have been left unattended without power, nil. Please note, however, that *Cordan's* command computer was not of that type."

"Meaning?"

"Meaning, Captain, that it is highly probable Fleet units retained solid data storage for critical systems precisely because energy data storage was susceptible to loss in the event of power failure. If that is indeed the case, any large sublight unit should provide quite considerable amounts of data. Any supralight Fleet combatant would, in all probability, retain a hard storage backup of its complete data core."

"I see." Colin leaned back and rubbed his eyes.

"All right. We're five and a half months from Terra, and so far all we've found is one completely destroyed Fleet base and two totally dead planets. If Dahak's wrong about the Fleet retaining hard storage for its central computers, we can't even hope to find out what happened, much less find help, from any system where this disaster spilled over.

"If we turn back right now, we'll reach Sol over a year before the Achuultani scouts, which would at least permit us to help Earth stand them off. By the same token, it would be impossible for us to do that and then return to the Imperium — or, at least, to move any deeper into it — and still get back to Sol before the main incursion arrives. So the big question is do we go on in the hope of finding *something*, or do we turn back now?"

He studied their faces and found only mirrors of his own uncertainty.

"I don't think we can give up just yet," he said finally. "We know we can't win without help, and we *don't* know there isn't still some help available. In all honesty, I'm not very optimistic, but I can't see that we have any choice but to ride it out and pray."

Jiltanith and MacMahan nodded slightly. The others were silent, then Chernikov raised his head.

"A point, sir."

"Yes?"

"Assuming Dahak is right that Fleet units are a more likely source of information, perhaps we should concentrate on Fleet bases and ignore civilian systems for the moment."

"My own thought exactly," Colin agreed.

"Yet 'twould be but prudent to assay a few systems more ere we leave this space entire," Jiltanith mused. "Methinks there doth lie another world scarce fifteen light-years hence. 'Twas not a Fleet base, yet was it not a richly peopled world, Dahak?"

"Correct, ma'am," Dahak replied. "The Kano System lies fourteen-point-six-six-one light-years from Defram, very nearly on a direct heading to Birhat. The last census data in my records indicates a system population of some nine-point-eight-three billion."

Colin thought. At maximum speed, the trip to Kano would require little more than a week. . . .

"All right, 'Tanni," he agreed. "But if we don't find anything there, we're in the same boat. Assuming we don't get answers at Kano, I'm beginning to think we may have to move on to Fleet Central at Birhat itself."

He understood the ripple of shock that ran through his officers. Birhat lay almost eight hundred light-years from Sol. If they ventured that far, even *Dahak's* speed could not possibly return them to Earth before the Achuultani scouts had arrived.

Oh, yes, he understood. Quite possibly, *Dahak* alone could stop the Achuultani scouts, particularly if backed by whatever Earth had produced. But if Colin continued to Birhat, *Dahak* wouldn't be available to try . . . and the decision was his to make. His alone.

"I recognize the risks," he said softly, "but our options are closing in, and time's too short to scurry around from star to star. Unless we find a definite answer at Kano, it may run out on us entirely. If we're going to Birhat at all, we can't afford to deviate or we'll never get back before the main incursion arrives. If we make a straight run for it from Kano, we should have some months to look around Fleet Central and still beat the real incursion home. Even assuming a worst-case scenario, assuming the entire Imperium is like Defram, we may at least find out what happened and where — if anywhere — a functional portion of the Imperium remains. I'm not definitely committing us to Birhat; I'm only saying we may not have another choice."

He fell silent, letting them examine his logic for flaws, almost praying they would find some, but instead they nodded one by one.

"All right. Dahak, have Sarah set course for Kano immediately. We'll go take a look before we commit to anything else."

"Yes, Captain."

"I think that's everything," Colin said heavily, and rose. "If any of you need me, I'll be on the bridge."

He walked out. This time Dahak did not call the others to attention, as if he sensed his captain's mood . . . but they rose anyway.

"Detection at twelve light minutes," Dahak announced, and Colin's eyes widened with sudden hope. The F5 star called Kano blazed in *Dahak's* display, the planet Kano-III a penny-bright dot, and they'd been detected. Detected! There was a high-tech presence in the system!

But Dahak's next words cut his elation short.

"Hostile launch," the computer said calmly. "Multiple hostile launches. Sublight missiles closing at point-seven-eight light-speed."

Missiles?

"Tactical, Red One!" Colin snapped, and Tamman's acknowledgment flowed back through his neural feed. The tractor web snapped alive, sealing him in his couch, and *Dahak's* mighty weapons came on-line as raucous audio and implant alarms summoned his crew to battle.

"No offensive action!" Colin ordered harshly.

"Acknowledged." Tamman's toneless voice was that of a man intimately wedded to his computers. *Dahak's* shield snapped up, antimissile defenses came alive, and Colin fell silent as others fought his ship.

Sarah Meir was part of Tamman's tactical net, and she took *Dahak* instantly to maximum sublight speed. Evasive action began, and the starfield swooped crazily about them. Crimson dots appeared in the holographic display, flashing towards *Dahak* like a shoal of sharks, tracking despite his attempts to evade.

His jammers filled space and fold-space alike with interference, and blue dots flashed out from the center of the display, each a five-hundred-ton decoy mimicking *Dahak's* electronic and gravitonic signature. More than half the red dots wavered, swinging to track the decoys or simply lost in the jamming, but at least fifty continued straight for them.

They were moving at almost eighty percent of light-speed, but so great was the range they seemed to crawl. And why were they moving sublight at all? Why weren't they hyper missiles? Why —

"Second salvo launch detected," *Dahak* announced, and Colin cursed.

Active defenses engaged the attackers. Hyper missiles were useless, for they could not home on evading targets, so sublight counter-missiles raced to meet them, blossoming in megaton bursts as proximity fuses activated. Eye-searing flashes pocked the holographic display, and red dots began to die.

"They mount quite capable defenses of their own, Captain," Dahak observed, and Colin felt them through his feed. ECM systems lured *Dahak's* fire wide and on-board maneuvering systems sent the red dots into wild gyrations, and they were faster than the counter-missiles chasing them.

"Where are they coming from, Dahak?"

"Scanners have detected twenty-four identical structures orbiting Kano-III," Dahak replied as his close-range energy defenses opened fire and killed another dozen missiles. At least twenty were still coming. "I have detected launches from only four of them."

Only four? Colin puzzled over that as the last dozen missiles broke past Dahak's active defenses. He found himself gripping his couch's armrests; there was nothing else he could do.

Dahak's display blanked in the instant of detonation, shielding his bridge crew's optic nerves from the fury unleashed upon him. Antimatter warheads, their yields measured in thousands of megatons, gouged at his final defenses, but *Dahak* was built to face things like that, and plasma clouds blew past him, divided by his shield as by the prow of a ship. Yet mixed with the antimatter explosions were the true shipkillers of the Imperium: gravitonic warheads.

The ancient starship lurched. For all its unimaginable mass, despite the unthinkable power of its drive, it *lurched* like a broken-masted galleon, and Colin's stomach heaved despite the internal gravity field. His mind refused to contemplate the terrible fury which could produce that effect as gravitonic shield components screamed in protest, but they, too, had been engineered to meet this test. Somehow they held.

The display flashed back on, spalled by fading clouds of gas and heat, and a damage signal pulsed in Colin's neural feed. A schematic of *Dahak's* hull appeared above his console, its frontal hemisphere marred by two wedge-shaped glares of red over a kilometer deep.

"Minor damage in quadrants Alpha-One and Three," *Dahak* reported. "No casualties. Capability not impaired. Second salvo entering interdiction range. Third enemy salvo detected."

More counter-missiles flashed out, and Colin reached a decision.

"Tactical, take out the actively attacking installations!"

"Acknowledged," Tamman said, and the display bloomed with amber sighting circles. Each enclosed a single missile platform, too tiny with distance for even *Dahak* to display visually, and Colin swallowed. Unlike their attackers, Tamman was using hyper missiles.

"Missiles away," *Dahak* said. And then, almost without pause, "Targets destroyed."

Bright, savage pinpricks blossomed in the amber circles, but the two salvos already fired were still coming. Yet Dahak had gained a great deal of data from the first attack, and he was a very fast thinker. Battle Comp was using his predicted target responses well, concentrating his counter-missiles to thwart them, alert now for their speed and the tricks of defensive ECM, killing the incoming missiles with inexorable precision. Energy weapons added their efforts as the range dropped, killing still more. Only three of the second salvo got through, and they were all antimatter warheads. The final missile of the last salvo died ten light-seconds short of the shield.

Colin sagged in his couch.

"Dahak? Any more?" he asked hoarsely.

"Negative, sir. I detect active targeting systems aboard seven remaining installations, but no additional missiles have been launched."

"Any communication attempts?"

"Negative, Captain. Nor have they responded to my hails."

"Damn."

Colin's brain began to work again, but it made no sense. Why refuse all contact and attack on sight? For that matter, how had *Dahak* gotten so deep in-system before being detected? And if attack they must, why use only a sixth of their defensive bases? The four Tamman had destroyed had certainly gone all out, but if they meant to mount a defense at all, why hold anything back? Especially now, when *Dahak* had riposted so savagely?

"Well," he said finally, very softly, "let's find out what that was all about. Sarah, take us in at half speed. Tamman, hold us on Red One."

Acknowledgments flowed back to him, and *Dahak* started cautiously forward once more at twenty-eight percent of light speed. Colin watched the display for a moment, then made himself lean back.

"Dahak, give me an all-hands channel."

"All-hands channel open, sir."

"All right, people," Colin said to every ear aboard the massive ship, "that was closer than we'd like, but we seem to've come through intact. If anyone's interested in exactly what happened —" he paused and smiled; to his surprise, it felt almost natural "— you can get the details from Dahak later. But for your immediate information, no one's shooting at us just now, so we're going on in for a closer look. They're not talking to us, either, so it doesn't look like they're too friendly, but we'll know more shortly. Hang loose."

He started to order Dahak to close the channel, then stopped.

"Oh, one more thing. Well done, all of you. You did us proud. Out.

"Close channel, Dahak."

"Acknowledged, Captain. Channel closed."

"Thank you," Colin said softly, and his tone referred to far more than communications channels and the starship's courtesy. "Thank you very much."

Chapter Eight

The holo of what had once been a pleasant, blue-white world called Keerah hung in Command One's visual display like a leprous, ocher curse. Once-green continents were wind and water-carved ruins, grooved like a harridan's face and pocked with occasional sprawls where the works of Man had been founded upon solid bedrock and so still stood, sentinels to a vanished population.

Colin stared at it, heartsick as even Defram had not left him. He'd hoped so hard. The missiles which had greeted them had seemed to confirm that hope, and so he had almost welcomed them even as they sought to kill him. But dead Keerah mocked him.

He turned away, shifting his attention to the orbiting ring of orbital forts. Only seven remained even partially operational, and the nearest loomed in *Dahak*'s display, gleaming dully in the funeral watch light of Kano. The clumsy-looking base was over eight kilometers in diameter, and a shiver ran down Colin's spine as he looked at it.

Even now, its targeting systems were locked on *Dahak*, its age-crippled computers sending firing signals to its weapons. He shuddered as he pictured the ancient launchers swinging through their firing sequences again and again, dry-firing because their magazines were empty. It was bad enough to know the long-abandoned war machine was trying to kill him; it was worse to wonder how many other vessels must have died under its fire to exhaust its ammunition.

And if Dahak and Hector were right, most of those vessels had been killed not for attacking Keerah, but for trying to escape it.

"Probe One is reporting, Captain." Dahak's mellow voice wrenched Colin away from his frightening, empty thoughts to more immediate matters.

"Very well. What's their status?"

"External scans completed, sir. Fleet Captain (Engineering) Chernikov requests permission to board."

Colin turned to the holo image beside his console. "Recommendations?"

"My *first* recommendation is to get Vlad out of there," Cohanna said flatly. "I'd rather not risk our Chief Engineer on the miserable excuse for an opinion I can give you."

"I tend to agree, but I made the mistake of asking for volunteers."

"In that case," Cohanna leaned back behind her desk in sickbay, a thousand kilometers from Command One, and rubbed her forehead, "we might as well let them board."

"Are you sure about that?"

"Of course I'm not!" she snapped, and Colin's hand rose in quick apology.

"Sorry, 'Hanna. What I really wanted was a run-down on your reasoning."

"It hasn't changed." Her almost normal tone was an unstated acceptance of his apology. "The other bases are as dead as Keerah, but there are at least two live hydroponics farms aboard that hulk — how I don't know, after all this time — and there may be more; we can't tell from exterior bio-scans even at this range. But that thing's entire atmosphere must've circulated through both of them a couple of million times by now and the plants are still alive. It's possible they represent a mutant strain that happened to be immune to whatever killed everything on Keerah, but I doubt it. Whatever the agent was, it doesn't seem to have missed *anything* down there, so I *think* it's unlikely it ever contaminated the battle station." She shrugged.

"I know that's a mouthful of qualifiers, but it's all I can tell you."

"But there's no other sign of life," Colin said quietly.

"None." Cohanna's holographic face was grim. "There couldn't be, unless they were in stasis. Genetic drift would've seen to it long ago on something as small as that."

"All right," Colin said after a moment. "Thank you." He looked down at his hands an instant longer, then nodded to himself.

"Dahak, give me a direct link to Vlad."

"Link open, Captain."

"Vlad?"

"Yes, Captain?" There was no holo image — Chernikov's bare-bones utility boat had strictly limited com facilities — but his calm voice was right beside Colin's ear.

"I'm going to let you take a closer look, Vlad, but watch your ass. One man goes in first — and *not* you, Mister. Full bio-protection and total decon before he comes back aboard, too."

"With all respect, Captain, I think —"

"I know what you think," Colin said harshly. "The answer is no."

"Very well." Chernikov sounded resigned, and Colin sympathized. He would vastly have preferred to take the risk himself, but he was *Dahak*'s captain. He couldn't gamble with the chain of command . . . and neither could Vlad.

Vlad Chernikov looked at the engineer he had selected for the task. Jehru Chandra had come many light-years to risk his life, but he looked eager as he double-checked the seals on his suit. Not cheerful or unafraid, but eager.

"Be cautious in there, Jehru."

"Yes, sir."

"Keep your suit scanners open. We will relay to Dahak."

"I understand, sir." Chernikov grinned wryly at Chandra's manifestly patient reply. Did he really sound that nervous?

"On your way, then," he said, and the engineer stepped into the airlock.

As per Cohanna's insistence, there was no contact between Chernikov's workboat and the battle station, but Chernikov studied the looming hull yet again as Chandra floated across the kilometer-wide gap on his suit propulsors. This ancient structure was thousands of years younger than *Dahak*, but the warship had been hidden under eighty kilometers of solid rock for most of its vast lifespan. The battle station had not. The once bright battle steel was dulled by the film of dust which had collected on its age-sick surface and pitted by micro-meteor impacts, and its condition made Chernikov chillingly aware of its age as *Dahak*'s shining perfection never had.

Chandra touched down neatly beside a small personnel lock, and his implants probed at the controls.

"Hmmmmm. . . ." The tension in his voice was smoothed by concentration. "Dahak was right, Commander. I've got live computers here, but damned if I recognize the machine language. Whups! Wait a minute, I've got something —"

His voice broke off for an agonizing moment, then came back with a most unexpected sound: a chuckle.

"I'll be damned, sir. The thing recognized my effort to access and brought in some kind of translating software. The hatch's opening now."

He stepped through it and it closed once more.

"Pressure in the lock," he reported, his fold-space com working as well through battle steel as through vacuum. "On the low side — 'bout point-six-nine atmospheres. My sensors read breathable."

"Forget it right now, Jehru."

"Never even considered it, sir. Honest. Okay, inner lock opening now." There was a brief pause. "I'm in. Inner hatch closed. The main lighting's out, but about half the emergency lights're up."

"Is the main net live, or just the lock computers?"

"Looks like the auxiliary net's up. Just a sec. Yes, sir. Power level's weak, though. Can't find the main net, yet."

"Understood. Give me a reading on the auxiliary. Then I want you to head up-ship. Keep an eye out for . . ."

Colin rested in his couch, eyes closed, concentrating on his neural feed as Chandra penetrated the half-dead hulk, gaining in confidence with every meter. It showed even in the technicalities of his conversation with Vlad.

Colin only hoped they could ever dare to let him come home again.

" . . . and that's about the size of it," Cohanna said, deactivating her personal memo computer. "We hit Chandra's suit with every decon system we had. As near as Dahak and I can tell, it was a hundred percent sterile before we let him unsuit, but we've got him in total isolation. I *think* he's clean, but I'm not letting him out of there until I'm certain."

"Agreed. Dahak? Anything to add?"

"I am still conversing with *Omega Three*'s core computers, Captain. More precisely, I am attempting to converse with them. We do not speak the same language, and their data transmission speed is appreciably higher than my own. Unfortunately, they also appear to be quite stupid." Colin hid a smile at the peeved note in Dahak's voice. Among the human qualities the vast computer had internalized was one he no doubt wished he could have avoided: impatience.

"How stupid?" he asked after a moment.

"Extremely so. In fairness, they were never intended for even rudimentary self-awareness, and their age is also a factor. *Omega Three*'s self-repair capability was never up to

Fleet standards, and it has suffered progressive failure, largely, I suspect, through lack of spares. Approximately forty percent of *Omega Three*'s data net is inoperable. The main computers remain more nearly functional than the auxiliary systems, but there are failures in the core programming itself. In human terms, they are senile."

"I see. Are you getting anything at all?"

"Affirmative, sir. In fact, I am now prepared to provide a hypothetical reconstruction of events leading to *Omega Three*'s emplacement."

"You are?" Colin sat straighter, and others at the table did the same.

"Affirmative. Be advised, however, that much of it is speculative. There are serious gaps in the available data."

"Understood. Let's hear it."

"Acknowledged. In essence, sir, Fleet Captain (Biosciences) Cohanna was correct in her original hypothesis at Defram. The destruction of all life on the planets we have so far encountered was due to a bio-weapon."

"What *kind* of bio-weapon?" Cohanna demanded, leaning forward as if to will the answer out of the computer.

"Unknown at this time. It was the belief of the system governor, however, that it was of Imperial origin."

"Sweet Jesu," Jiltanith breathed. "In so much at least wert thou correct, my Hector. 'Twas no enemy wreaked their destruction; 'twas themselves."

"That is essentially correct," Dahak said. "As I have stated, the data are fragmentary, but I have recovered portions of memoranda from the governor. I hope to recover more, but those I have already perused point in that direction. She did not know how the weapon was originally released, but apparently there had been rumors of such a weapon for some time."

"The fools," Cohanna whispered. "Oh, the *fools*! Why would they build something like this? It violates every medical ethic the Imperium ever had!"

"I fear my data sample is too small to answer that, yet I have discovered a most interesting point. It was not the

Fourth Imperium which devised this weapon but an entity called the Fourth *Empire*."

For just a moment, Colin failed to grasp the significance. Dahak had used Imperial Universal, and in Universal, the differentiation was only slightly greater than in English. "Imperium" was *umsuvah*, with the emphasis on the last syllable; "empire" was *umsuvaht*, with the emphasis upon the second.

"What?" Cohanna blinked in consternation.

"Precisely. I have not yet established the full significance of the altered terminology, yet it suggests many possibilities. In particular, the Imperial Senate appears to have been superseded in authority by an emperor — specifically, by Emperor Herdan XXIV as of Year Thirteen-One-Seven-Five."

"Herdan the *Twenty-fourth*?" Colin repeated.

"The title would seem significant," Dahak agreed, "suggesting as it does an extremely long period of personal rule. In addition, the date of his accession appears to confirm our dating of the Defram disaster."

"Agreed," Colin said. "But you don't have any more data?"

"Not of a political or societal nature, Captain. It may be that *Omega Three* will disgorge additional information, assuming I can locate the proper portion of its data core and that the relevant entries have not decayed beyond recovery. I would not place the probability as very high. *Omega Three* and its companions were constructed in great haste by local authorities, not by Battle Fleet. Beyond the programming essential for their design function, their data bases appear to be singularly uninformed."

Despite his shock, Colin grinned at the computer's sour tone.

"All right," he said after a moment. "What can you tell us about the effects of this bio-weapon and the reason the fortifications were built?"

"The data are not rich, Captain, but they do contain the essentials. The bio-weapon appears to have been designed to mount a broad-spectrum attack upon a wide range of life-forms. If the rumors recorded by Governor Yirthana are correct, it was, in fact, intended to destroy *any* life-form. In mammals, it functioned as a neurotoxin, rendering the chemical compounds of the nervous system inert so that the organism died."

"But that wouldn't kill trees and grasses," Cohanna objected.

"That is true, Commander. Unfortunately, the designers of this weapon appear to have been extremely ingenious. Obviously we do not have a specimen of the weapon itself, but I have retrieved very limited data from Governor Yirthana's own bio-staff. It would appear that the designers had hit upon a simple observation: all known forms of life depend upon chemical reactions. Those reactions may vary from life-form to life-form, but their presence is a constant. This weapon was designed to invade and neutralize the critical chemical functions of any host."

"Impossible," Cohanna said flatly, then flushed.

"By the standards of my own data base, you are correct, ma'am. Nonetheless, Keerah is devoid of life. Empirical evidence thus suggests that it was, indeed, possible to the Fourth Empire."

"Agreed," the biosciences head muttered.

"Governor Yirthana's bio-staff hypothesized that the weapon had been designed to modify itself at a very high rate of speed, attacking the chemical structures of its victims in turn until a lethal combination was reached. An elegant theoretical solution, although, I suspect, actually producing the weapon would be far from simple."

"*Simple!* I'm still having trouble believing it was *possible!*"

"As for *Omega Three* and its companions," Dahak continued, "they were intended to enforce a strict quarantine of Keerah. Governor Yirthana obviously was aware of the contamination of her planet and took steps to prevent its spread. There is also a reference I do not yet fully understand to something called a mat-trans system, which she ordered disabled."

"'Mat-trans'?" Colin asked.

"Yes, sir. As I say, I do not presently fully understand the reference, but it would appear that this mat-trans was a device for the movement of personnel over interstellar distances without recourse to starships."

"What?!" Colin jerked bolt upright in his chair.

"Current information suggests a system limited to loads of only a few tons but capable of transmitting them hundreds — possibly even several thousands — of light-years almost instantaneously, Captain. Apparently this system had become the preferred mode for personal travel. The energy cost appears to have been high, however, which presumably explains the low upper mass limit. Starships remained in use for bulk cargoes, and the Fleet and certain government agencies retained courier vessels for transportation of highly classified data."

"Jesus!" Colin muttered. Then his eyes narrowed. "Why didn't you mention that before?"

"You did not ask, Captain. Nor was I aware of it. Please recall that I am continuing to query *Omega Three's* memory even as we speak."

"All right, all right. But matter transmission? *Teleportation?"* Colin looked at Chernikov. "Is that possible?"

"As Dahak would say, empirical data suggests it is, but if you are asking *how,* I have no idea. Dahak's data base contains some journal articles about focused hyper fields linked with fold-space technology, but the research had achieved nothing as of the mutiny. Beyond that — ?" He shrugged.

"Maker!" Cohanna's soft voice drew all eyes back to her. She was deathly pale. "If they could —" She broke off, staring down at her hands and thinking furiously as she conferred with Dahak through her neural feed. Her expression changed slowly to one of utter horror, and when her attention returned to her fellows, her eyes glistened with sorrow.

"That's it." Her voice was dull. "That's how they did it to themselves."

"Explain," Colin said gently.

"I wondered . . . I wondered how it could go this far." She gave herself a little shake. "You see, Hector's right — only maniacs would deliberately dust whole planets with a weapon like this. But it wasn't that way at all."

They looked at her, most blankly, but a glimmer of understanding tightened Jiltanith's mouth. She nodded almost imperceptibly, and Cohanna's eyes swiveled to her face.

"Exactly," the biosciences officer said grimly. "The Imperium could have delivered it only via starships. They'd've been forced to transport the bug — the agent, whatever you want to call it — from system to system, intentionally. Some of that could have happened accidentally, but the Imperium was huge. By the time a significant portion of its planets were infected, the contaminating vector would have been recognized. If it wasn't a deliberate military operation, quarantine should have contained the damage.

"But the Empire wasn't like that. They had this damned 'mat-trans' thing. Assuming an incubation period of any length, all they needed was a single source of contamination — just one — they didn't know about. By the time they realized what was happening, it could've spread throughout the entire Imperium, and just stopping starships wouldn't do a damned thing to slow it down!"

Colin stared at her as her logic sank home. With something like the "mat-trans" Dahak had described, the Imperium's worlds would no longer have been weeks or months of travel apart. They would have become a tightly integrated, interconnecting unit. Time and distance, the greatest barriers to holding an interstellar civilization together, would no longer apply. What a triumph of technology! And what a deadly, deadly triumph it had proven.

"Then I was wrong," MacMahan murmured. "They *could* wipe themselves out."

"Could and did." Ninhursag's clenched fist struck the table gently, for an Imperial, and her voice was thick with anguish. "Not even on purpose — by accident. By *accident*, Breaker curse them!"

"Wait." Colin raised a hand for silence. "Assume you're right, Cohanna. Do you really think *every* planet would have been contaminated?"

"Probably not, but the vast majority certainly could have been. From the limited information Dahak and I have on this monster of theirs — and remember all our data is third- or fourth-hand speculation, by way of Governor Yirthana — the incubation time *was* quite lengthy. Moreover, Yirthana's information indicates it was capable of surviving very long periods, possibly several centuries, in viable condition even without hosts.

"That suggests a strategic rather than a tactical weapon. The long incubation period was supposed to bury it and give it time to spread before it manifested itself. That it in fact did so is also suggested by the fact that Yirthana had time to build her bases before it wiped out Keerah. Its long-term lethality would mean no one dared contact any infected planet for a very, very long period. Ideal, if the object was to cripple an interstellar enemy.

"But look what that means. Thanks to the incubation period, there probably wasn't any way to know it was loose until people started dying. Which means the central, most heavily-visited planets would've been the first to go.

"People being people, the public reaction was — *must* have been — panic. And a panicked person's first response is to flee." Cohanna shrugged. "The result might well have been an explosion of contamination.

"On the other hand, they had the hypercom. Warnings could be spread at supralight speeds without using their mat-trans, and presumably *some* planets must have been able to go into quarantine before they were affected. That's where the 'dwell time' comes in. They couldn't know how long they had to *stay* quarantined. No one would dare risk contact with any other planet as long as the smallest possibility of contamination by something like this existed."

She paused, and Colin nodded.

"So they would have abandoned space," he said.

"I can't be certain, but it seems probable. Even if any of their planets did survive, their 'Empire' still could have self-destructed out of all too reasonable fear. Which means —" she met Colin's eyes squarely "— that in all probability, there's no Imperium for us to contact."

Vladimir Chernikov bent over the work bench, studying the disassembled riflelike weapon. His enhanced eyes were set for microscopic vision, and he manipulated his exquisitely sensitive instruments with care. The back of his mind knew he was trying to lose himself and escape the numbing depression which had settled over *Dahak's* crew, but his fascination was genuine. The engineer in his soul rejoiced at the beauty of the work before him. Now if he could only figure out what it did.

There was the capacitor, and a real brute it was, despite its tininess. Eight or nine times a regular energy gun's charge. And these were rheostats. One obviously regulated the power of whatever the thing emitted, but what did the second . . . ?

Hmmmmm. Fascinating. There's no sign of a standard disrupter head in here. But then — aha! What do we have here?

He bent closer, bending sensor implants as well as vision upon it, then froze. He looked a moment longer, then raised his head and gestured to Baltan.

"Take a look at this," he said quietly. His assistant bent over and followed Chernikov's indicating test probe to the component in question, then pursed his lips in a silent whistle.

"A hyper generator," he said. "It has to be. But the *size* of the thing."

"Precisely." Chernikov wiped his spotless fingers on a handkerchief, drying their sudden clamminess. "Dahak," he said.

"Yes, sir?"

"What do you make of this?"

"A moment," the computer said. There was a brief period of silence, then the mellow voice spoke again. "Fleet Commander (Engineering) Baltan is correct, sir. It is a hyper generator. I have never encountered one of such small size or advanced design, but the basic function is evident. Please note, however, that the generator cavity's walls are composed of a substance unknown to me, and that they extend the full length of the barrel."

"Explanations?"

"It would appear to be a shielding housing around the generator, sir — one impervious to warp radiation. Fascinating. Such a material would have obvious applications in such devices as atmospheric hyper missile launchers."

"True. But am I right in assuming the muzzle end of the housing is open?"

"You are, sir. In essence, this appears to be a highly advanced adaptation of the warp grenade. When activated, this weapon would project a focused field — in effect, a beam — of multi-dimensional translation which would project its target into hyper space."

"And leave it there," Chernikov said flatly.

"Of course," Dahak agreed. "A most ingenious weapon."

"Ingenious," Chernikov repeated with a shudder.

"Correct. Yet I perceive certain limitations. The hyper suppression fields already developed to counteract warp grenades would also counteract this device's effect, at least within the area of such a field. I cannot be certain without field-testing the weapon, but I suspect that it might be fired *out* of or *across* such a suppression field. Much would depend upon the nature of the focusing force fields. But observe the small devices on both sides of the barrel. They appear to be extremely compact Ranhar generators. If so, they presumably create a tube of force to extend the generator housing and contain the hyper field, thus controlling its area of effect and also tending, quite possibly, to offset the effect of a suppression field."

"Maker, and I always hated warp *grenades*," Baltan said fervently.

"I, too," Chernikov said. He straightened from the bench slowly, looking at the next innocent-seeming device he'd abstracted from *Omega Three* once Cohanna had decided her painstaking search confirmed the original suggestion of the functional hydroponic farms. There was no trace of anything which could possibly be the bio-weapon aboard the battle station, and Chernikov had gathered up every specimen of technology he could find. He'd been looking forward to taking all of them apart.

Now he was almost afraid to.

Chapter Nine

Colin MacIntyre sat in Conference One once more. He'd grown to hate this room, he thought, bending his gaze upon the tabletop. Hate it.

Silence fell as the last person found a seat, and he looked up.

"Ladies and gentlemen," he said, "for the past month I've resisted all arguments to move on because I believe Keerah represents a microcosm of what probably happened to the entire Imperium. I now believe we've learned all we can here. But —" he drew out the slight pause behind the word "— that still leaves the question of what we do next. Before turning to that, however, I would like to review our findings, beginning with our Chief Engineer."

He sat back and nodded to Chernikov, who cleared his throat quietly, as if organizing his thoughts, then began.

"We have examined many artifacts recovered from *Omega Three*. On the basis of what we have discovered to date, I have reached a few conclusions about the technical base of the Imperium — that is to say, the Empire.

"They had, as we would have expected, made major

108

advances, yet not so many as we might have anticipated. Please bear in mind that I am speaking only of nonbiological technology; neither Cohanna nor I are in a position to say what they had achieved in the life sciences. The weapon which destroyed them certainly appears to evidence a very high level of bioengineering.

"With that reservation, our initial estimate, that their technology was essentially a vastly refined version of our own, seems to have been correct. With the probable exception of their mat-trans — on which, I regret to say, we have been unable as yet to obtain data — we have encountered nothing Engineering and Dahak could not puzzle out. This is not to say they had advanced to a point far beyond our current reach, but the underlying principles of their advances are readily apparent to us. In effect, they appear to have reached a plateau of fully mature technology and, I believe, may very well have been on the brink of fundamental breakthroughs into a new order of achievement, but they had not yet made them.

"In general, their progress may be thought of as coupling miniaturization with vast increases in power. A warship of *Dahak's* mass, for example, built with the technology we have so far encountered — which, I ask you to bear in mind, represents an essentially *civilian* attempt to create a military unit — would possess something on the order of twenty times his combat capability."

He paused for emphasis, and there were signs of awe on more than one face.

"Yet certain countervailing design philosophies and trends, particularly in the areas of computer science and cybernetics, also have become apparent to us. Specifically, the *hardware* of their computer systems is extremely advanced compared to our own; their *software* is not. Assuming that *Omega Three* is a representative sample of their computer technology, their computers had an even lower degree of self-awareness than that of Comp Cent prior to the mutiny. The data storage capacity of *Omega Three's* Comp Cent, whose mass is approximately thirty percent that of Dahak's central memory core, exceeded his capacity, including all subordinate systems, by a factor of fifty. The *ability* of *Omega Three*, on the other hand, despite a computational speed many times higher than his, did not approach even that of Comp Cent prior to the mutiny.

"Clearly, this indicates a deliberate degradation of performance to meet some philosophical constraint. My best guess — and I stress that it is only a guess — is that it results from the period of civil warfare which apparently converted the Imperium into the Empire. Fleet computers would have resisted firing on other Fleet units, and while this could have been compensated for by altering their Alpha Priority core programming, the combatants may have balked at allowing semi-aware computers to decide whether or not to fire on other humans. This is only a hypothesis, but it is certainly one possibility.

"In addition, we have confirmed one other important point. While *Omega Three's* computers did use energy-state technology, they also incorporated non-energy backups, which appears to reflect standard Imperial military practice. This means a deactivated Fleet computer would not experience a complete core loss as did the civilian units discovered at Defram. If powered up once more, thus restoring its energy-state circuitry, it should remain fully functional.

"Further, even civilian installations which have been continuously powered could remain completely operational. *Omega Three's* capabilities, for example, suffered not because it relied upon energy-state components, but because it was left unattended for so long that *solid*-state components failed. Had the battle station's computers possessed adequate self-repair capability and spares, *Omega Three* would be fully functional today."

He paused, as if rechecking his thoughts, then glanced at Colin.

"That concludes my report, sir. Detailed information is in the data base for anyone who cares to peruse it."

"Thank you." Colin pursed his lips for a moment, inviting questions, but there were none. They were waiting for the other shoe, he thought dourly.

"Commander Cohanna?" he said finally.

"We still don't know how they did it," Cohanna replied, "but we're pretty sure *what* they did. I'm not certain I can accept Dahak's explanation just yet, but it fits the observed data, assuming they had the ability to implement it.

"For all practical purposes, we can think of their weapon as a disease lethal to any living organism. Obviously, it was a monster in every sense of the word. We may never learn how it was released, but the effect of its release was the inevitable destruction of all life in its path. Any contaminated planet is *dead*, ladies and gentlemen.

"On the other hand —" as Colin had, she drew out the pause for emphasis "— we've also determined that the weapon had a finite lifespan. And whatever that lifespan was, it was less than the time which has passed. We've established test habitats with plants and livestock from our own hydroponic and recreational areas, using water and soil collected by remotes from all areas of Keerah's surface. From Governor Yirthana's records, we know the weapon took approximately thirty Terran months to incubate in mammals, and we've employed the techniques used in accelerated healing to take our sample habitats through a forty-five-month cycle with no evidence of the weapon. While I certainly don't propose to return those test subjects to *Dahak*'s life-support systems, I believe the evidence is very nearly conclusive. The bioweapon itself has died, at least on Keerah and, by extension, upon any planet which was contaminated an equivalent length of time ago.

"That concludes my report, Captain."

"Thank you." Colin squared his shoulders and spoke very quietly as the full weight of his responsibility descended upon him. "On the basis of these reports, I intend to proceed immediately to Birhat and Fleet Central."

Someone drew a sharply audible breath, and his face tightened.

"What we've discovered here makes it extremely unlikely Birhat survived, but that, unfortunately, changes nothing.

"I don't know what we'll find there, but I do know three things. One, if we return with no aid for Earth, we lose. Two, the best command facilities at the Imperium's — or Empire's — disposal would be at Fleet Central. Three, logic suggests the bio-weapon there will be as dead as it is here. Based on those suppositions, our best chance of finding usable hardware is at Birhat, and it's likely we can safely reactivate any we find. At the very least, it will be our best opportunity to discover the full extent of this catastrophe.

"We will depart Keerah in twelve hours. In the meantime, please carry on about your duties. I'll be in my quarters if I'm needed."

He stood, catching the surprise on more than one face when his audience realized he did not intend to debate the point.

"Attention on deck," Dahak intoned quietly, and the officers rose.

Colin walked out in silence, wondering if those he'd surprised realized why he'd foreclosed all debate.

The answer was as simple as it was bitter. In the end, the decision was his, but if he allowed them to debate it they must share in it, however indirectly, and he would not permit them to do so.

He couldn't know if *Dahak's* presence was required to stand off the Achuultani scouts, but he hoped desperately that it was not, for he, Colin MacIntyre, had elected to chase a tattered hope rather than defend his home world. If he'd guessed wrong about Horus's progress, he had also doomed that home world — a world which it had become increasingly obvious might well be the only planet of humanity which still existed — whatever he found at Birhat.

And the fact that logic compelled him to Birhat meant nothing against his fear that he had guessed wrong. Against his ignorance of Horus's progress. His agonizing suspicion that if Fleet Central still existed, it might be another *Omega Three*, senile and crippled with age . . . the paralyzing terror of bearing responsibility for the death of his own species.

He would not — could not — share that responsibility with another soul. It was his alone, and as he stepped into the transit shaft, Senior Fleet Captain Colin MacIntyre tasted the full, terrible burden of his authority at last.

The moss was soft and slightly damp as he lay on his back, staring up at the projected sky. He was coming to understand why the Imperium had provided its captains with this greenery and freshness. He could have found true spaciousness on one of the park decks, where breezes whipped across square kilometers of "open" land, but this was his. This small, private corner of creation belonged to him, offering its soothing aliveness and quiet bird song when the weight of responsibility crushed down upon him.

He closed his eyes, breathing deeply, extending his enhanced senses. The splash of the fountains caressed him, and a gentle breeze stroked his skin, yet the sensations only eased his pain; they did not banish it.

He hadn't noted the time when he stretched out upon the moss, and so he had no idea how long he'd been there when his neural feed tingled.

Someone was at the hatch, and he was tempted to deny access, for his awareness of what he'd done was too fresh and aching. But that thought frightened him suddenly. It would be so easy to withdraw into a tortured, hermitlike existence, and it was over six months to Birhat. A man alone could go mad too easily in that much time.

He opened the hatch, and his visitor stepped inside. She came around the end of a thicket of azaleas and laurel, and he opened his eyes slowly.

"Art troubled, my Colin," she said softly.

He started to explain, but then he saw it in her eyes. She knew. One, at least, of his officers knew exactly why he'd refused to discuss his decision.

"May I sit with thee?" she asked gently, and he nodded.

She crossed the carpet of moss with the poised, catlike grace which was always so much a part of her, straight and slim in her midnight-blue uniform, tall for an Imperial, yet delicate, her gleaming black hair held back by the same jeweled clasp she'd worn the day they met. The day when he'd seen the hate in her eyes. The hate for what he'd done, for the clumsy, cocksure fumbling which had cost the lives of a grandnephew and great-nieces she loved, but even more for what he was. For the threat of punishment he posed to her mutineer-father. For the fullness of his enhancement while she had but bits and pieces. And for the fact that he, who had never known of *Dahak*'s existence, never suspected her own people's lonely, hopeless fight against Anu, had inherited command of the starship from which she had been exiled for a crime others had committed.

There was a killer in Jiltanith. He'd seen it then, known it from the first. The mutiny had cost her her mother and the freedom of the stars, and the endless stealth of her people's shadowy battle on Earth had been slivered glass in her throat, for she was a fighter, a warrior who believed in open battle. Those long, agonizing years had left dark, still places within her. Far more than he could ever hope to be, she was capable of death and destruction, incapable of asking or offering quarter.

But there was no hate in her eyes now. They were soft and gentle under the atrium's sun, their black depths jewel-like and still. Colin had grown accustomed to the appearance of the full Imperials, yet in this moment the subtle alienness of her beauty smote him like a fist. She had been born before his first Terran ancestor crawled into a cave to hide from the weather, yet she was young. Twice his age and more, yet they were both but children against the lifespan of their enhanced bodies. Her youthfulness lay upon her, made still more precious and perfect by the endless years behind her, and his eyes burned.

This, he thought. This girl-woman, who had known and

suffered so much more than he, was what this all was about. She was the symbol of humankind, the avatar of all its frailties and the iron core of all its strength, and he wanted to reach out and touch her. But she was the mythic warrior-maid, the emblem, and the weight of his decision was upon him. He was unclean.

"Oh, my Colin," she whispered, looking deep into his own weary, tormented eyes, "what hast thou taken upon thyself?"

He clenched his hands at his sides, gripping the moss, and refused to answer, but a sob wrenched at the base of his throat.

She came closer slowly, carefully, like a hunter approaching some wild, snared thing, and sank to her knees beside him. One delicate hand, slender and fine-boned, deceiving the eye into forgetting its power, touched his shoulder.

"Once," she said, "in a life I scarce recall, I envied thee. Yea, envied and hated thee, for thou hadst received all unasked for the one treasure in all the universe I hungered most to hold. I would have slain thee, could I but have taken that treasure from thee. Didst thou know that?"

He nodded jerkily, and she smiled.

"Yet knowing, thou didst name me thy successor in command, for thine eyes saw more clear than mine own. 'Twas chance, mayhap, sent thee to *Dahak*'s bridge, yet well hast thou proven thy right to stand upon it. And never more than thou hast done this day."

Her hand stroked gently from his shoulder to his chest, covering the slow, strong beating of his bioenhanced heart, and he trembled like a frightened child. But her fingers moved, gentling his strange terror.

"Yet thou art not battle steel, my Colin," she said softly. "Art flesh and blood for all thy biotechnics, whate'er thy duty may demand of thee."

She bent slowly, laying her head atop her hand, and the fine texture of her hair brushed his cheek, its silken caress almost agony to his enhanced senses. Tears brimmed in the corners of his eyes, and part of him cursed his weakness while another blessed her for proving it to him. The sob he had fought broke free, and she made a soft, soothing sound.

"Yea, art flesh and blood, though captain to us all. Forget that not, for thou art not Dahak, and thy humanity is thy curse, the sword by which thou canst be wounded." She raised her head, and his blurred eyes saw the tears in her own. One moss-stained hand rose, stroking her raven's-wing hair, and she smiled.

"Yet wounds may be healed, my Colin, and I am likewise flesh, likewise blood," she murmured. She bent over him, and her mouth tasted of the salt of their mingled tears. His other hand lifted, drawing her down beside him on the moss, and he rose on an elbow as she smiled up at him.

"Thou wert my salvation," she whispered, caressing his unruly sandy hair. "Now let me be thine, for *I* am thine and thou art mine. Forget it never, my dearest dear, for 'tis true now and ever shall be."

And she drew him down to kiss her once again.

The computer named Dahak closed down the sensors in the captain's quarters with profound but slightly wistful gratitude. He had made great strides in understanding these short-lived, infuriatingly illogical, occasionally inept, endlessly inventive, and stubbornly dauntless descendants of his long-dead builders. More than any other of his kind, he had learned to understand human emotions, for he had learned to share many of them. Respect. Friendship. Hope. Even, in his own way, love. He knew his presence would embarrass Colin and Jiltanith if it occurred to them to check for it, and while he did not fully understand the reason, they were his friends, and so he left them alone.

He gave the electronic equivalent of a sigh, knowing that he could never comprehend the gentle mysteries which had enfolded them. But he did not need to comprehend to know how important they were, and to feel deeply grateful to his new friend 'Tanni for understanding and loving his first friend Colin.

And now, he thought, while they were occupied, he might add that tiny portion of his attention which constantly attended his captain's needs and desires to another problem. Those encoded dispatches from the courier *Cordan* still intrigued him.

His latest algorithm had failed miserably, though he had finally managed to crack the scramble and reduce the messages to symbol sets. Unfortunately, the symbols were meaningless. Perhaps a new value-substitution subprogram was in order? Yet pattern analysis suggested that the substitution was virtually random. Interesting. That implied a tremendous symbol set, or else there was a method to generate the values which only appeared random. . . .

The computer worried happily away at the fascinating problem with a fragment of his capacity while every tiny corner of his vast starship body pulsed and quivered with his awareness.

All the tiny corners save one, where two very special people enjoyed a priceless gift of privacy made all the more priceless because they did not even know it had been given.

patent understood illegal. Time for understanding and living his few spare hours.

And now, he thought, while they were occupied he might add that any portion of his attention which remained vanished the culture-track and desire to analyze problem. Those revelation shape themselves the curiosities will succeed him.

His latest algorithm had not substantially brought he just finally managed to crack the scramble and reduce that messages to symbol acts. Unfortunately, the symbol was meaningless. Perhaps a new value-absorption subroutine was in order. Yet patient analysis suggested that the substitution was probably random addressing. That implies whenever the symbol say, or else there was a need had to retrieve the values which once appropriate for stop.

The computer waited happy away at the fascinating problem with a fragment of its capacity, while over fifty others of its vast starship body picked and pursued with his awareness.

All the daydreams sans one, where two very special people enjoyed a greatness all of perhaps made all the more priceless because they did not even hope it had been given.

The last crude spacecraft died, and the asteroid battered through their wreckage at three hundred kilometers per second. Bits of debris struck its frontal arc, vanishing in brief, spiteful spits of flame against its uncaring nickel-iron bow. Heat-oozing wounds bit deep where the largest fragments had struck, and the asteroid swept onward, warded by the defenders' executioners.

Six Achuultani starships rode in formation about the huge projectile as it charged down upon the blue and white world which was its target. They had been detached to guard their weapon against the pygmy efforts of that cloud-swirled sapphire's inhabitants, and their task was all but done.

They spread out, distancing themselves from the asteroid, energy weapons ready as the first missiles broke atmosphere. The clumsy chemical-fueled rockets sped outward, tipped with their pathetic nuclear warheads, and the starships picked them off with effortless ease. The doomed planet flung its every weapon against its killers in despair and desperation . . . and achieved nothing.

The asteroid hurtled onward, an energy state hungry for immolation, and the starships wheeled up and away as it tasted air at last and changed. For one fleeting instant it was no longer a thing of ice-bound rock and metal. It was alive, a glorious, screaming incandescence pregnant with death.

It struck, spewing its flame back into the heavens, stripping away atmosphere in a cataclysm of fire, and the Achuultani starships hovered a moment longer, watching, as the planetary crust split and fissured. Magma exploded from the gaping wounds, and they spread and grew, racing like cracks in ice, until the geologically unstable planet itself blew apart.

The starships lingered no longer. They turned their bows from the ruin they had wrought and raced outward. Twenty-one light-minutes from the primary they crossed the hyper threshold and vanished like soap bubbles, hastening to seek their fellows at the next rendezvous.

Chapter Ten

Horus stood on the command deck of the battleship *Nergal*, almost unrecognizable in its refurbished state, and watched her captain take her smoothly out of atmosphere. A year ago, Adrienne Robbins, one of the US Navy's very few female attack submarine skippers, had never heard of the Fourth Imperium; now she performed her duties with a competence which gave him the same pleasure he took from a violin virtuoso and a Mozart concerto. She was good, he decided, watching her smooth her gunmetal hair. Better than he'd ever been, and she had the confident, almost sleepy smile of a hungry tiger.

He turned from the bridge crew to the holo display as *Nergal* slid into orbit. Marshal Tsien, Acting Chief of the Supreme Chiefs of Staff, towered over his right shoulder, and Vassily Chernikov stood to Horus's left. All three watched intently as *Nergal* leisurely overtook the half-finished bulk of Orbital Defense Center Two, and Horus suddenly snapped his fingers and turned to Tsien.

"Oh, Marshal Tsien," he said, "I meant to tell you that I spoke with General Hatcher just before you arrived, and he expects to return to us within the next four or five weeks."

Relief lit both officers' eyes, for it had been touch and go for Gerald Hatcher. Though Tsien's first aid had saved his life, he would have lost both legs without Imperial medical technology, assuming he'd lived at all, yet that same technology had nearly killed him.

Hatcher was one of those very rare individuals, less than one tenth of a percent of the human race, who were allergic to the standard quick-heal drugs, but the carnage at Minya Konka had offered no time for proper medical workups, and the medic who first treated him guessed wrong. The general's reaction had been quick and savage, and only the fact that that same medic had recognized the symptoms so quickly had prevented it from being fatal.

Even so, it had taken months to repair his legs to a point which permitted bioenhancement, for if the alternate therapies were just as effective, they were also far slower. Which also meant his recuperation from enhancement itself was taking far longer than normal, so it was a vast relief to all his colleagues and friends to know he would soon return to them.

And, Horus thought, remembering how Hatcher had chuckled over Tsien's remark at Minya Konka, as the *first* enhanced member of the Chiefs of Staff.

"I am relieved to hear it, Governor," Tsien said now. "And I am certain you will be relieved to have him back."

"I will, but I'd also like to congratulate you on a job very well done these past months. I might add that Gerald shares my satisfaction."

"Thank you, Governor." Tsien didn't smile — Horus didn't think he'd ever seen the big man smile — but his eyes showed his pleasure.

"You deserve all the thanks *we* can give *you*, Marshal," he said quietly.

In a sense, Hatcher's injuries had been very much to their advantage. If any other member of the chiefs of staff was his equal in every way, it was Tsien. They were very different; Tsien lacked Hatcher's ease with people and the flair which made exquisitely choreographed operations seem effortless, but he was tireless, analytical, eternally self-possessed, and as inexorable as a Juggernaut yet flexibly pragmatic. He'd streamlined their organization, moved their construction and training schedules ahead by almost a month, and — most importantly of all — stamped out the abortive guerrilla war in Asia with a ruthlessness Hatcher himself probably could not have displayed.

Horus had been more than a little horrified at the way Tsien went about it. He hadn't worried about taking armed resisters prisoner, and those he'd taken had been summarily court-martialed and executed, usually within twenty-four hours. His reaction teams had been everywhere, filling Horus with the fear that Hatcher had made a rare and terrible error in recommending him as his replacement. There'd been an elemental implacability about the huge Chinese, one that made Horus wonder if he even cared who was innocent and who guilty.

Yet he'd made himself wait, and time had proved the wisdom of his decision. Ruthless and implacable, yes, and also a man tormented by shame; Tsien had been those things, for it had been his officers who had betrayed their trust. But he'd been just as ruthlessly just. Every individual caught in his nets had been sorted out under an Imperial lie detector, and the innocent were freed as quickly as they had been apprehended. Nor had he permitted any unnecessary brutality to taint his actions or those of his men.

Even more importantly, perhaps, he was no "Westerner" punishing patriots who had struck back against occupation but their own commander-in-chief, acting with the full support of Party and government, and no one could accuse Tsien Tao-ling of being anyone's puppet. His reputation, and the fact that *he* had been selected to replace the wounded Hatcher, had done more to cement Asian support of the new government and military than anything else ever could have.

Within two weeks, all attacks had ended. Within a

month, there was no more guerrilla movement. Every one
of its leaders had been apprehended and executed; none
were imprisoned.

Nor had the chilling message been lost upon the rest of
the world. Horus had agonized over the brutal suppression
of the African riots, but Tsien's lesson had gone home.
There was still unrest, but the world's news channels had
carried live coverage of the trials and executions, and out-
bursts of open violence had ended almost overnight.

Tsien bobbed his head slightly in acknowledgment of
the compliment, and Horus smiled, turning back to the
display as ODC Two grew within it.

The eye-searing fireflies of robotic welders crawled
over the vast structure while suited humans floated nearby
or swung through their hard-working mechanical minions
with apparently suicidal disregard for life and limb. Shuttles of components from the orbital smelters arrived with
the precision of a well-run Terran railroad, disgorging their
loads and wheeling away to return with more. Construction ships, raw and naked-looking in their open
girder-work, seized structural members and frame units
on tractors, placing them for the swarm of welders to tack
into place and then backing away for the next. Conduits of
Terran cable for communication nets, crystalline icicles of
Imperial molycircs for computer cores and fire control,
the huge, glittering blocks of prefabricated shield generators, Terran lighting and plumbing fixtures, and the
truncated, hollow stubs of missile launchers — all vanished into the seeming confusion as they watched, and
always there were more awaiting the frantically laboring
robots and their masters.

It was impressive, Horus thought. Even to him — or,
possibly, *especially* to him. Geb had shared Tegran's
remarks about the Terra-born with him, and Horus could
only agree. Unlike these fiercely determined people, he'd
known their task was all but impossible. They hadn't
accepted that, and they were making liars of his own fears.

He and the generals watched the seething construction

work for several minutes, then Horus turned away with a sigh, followed by his subordinates. They stepped into the transit shaft with him, and he hid a smile at Tsien's uneasy expression. Interesting that this should bother him when facing a totally unexpected ambush by traitors within his own military hadn't even fazed him.

They arrived at the conference room Captain Robbins had placed at their disposal, and he waved them towards the table as he seated himself at its head and crossed his legs comfortably.

"I'm impressed, gentlemen," he said. "I had to see that in person before I could quite believe it, I'm afraid. You people are producing miracles."

He saw the pleasure in their eyes. Flattery, he knew, was anathema to these men, however much of it they'd heard during their careers, but knowing their competence was appreciated — and, even more importantly, recognized for what it was — was something else.

"Now," he said, planting his forearms on the table and looking at Tsien, "suppose you tell me what other miracles you plan on working."

"With your permission, Governor, I shall begin by presenting a brief overview," the marshal replied, and Horus nodded approval.

"In general," Tsien continued, "we are now only one week behind General Hatcher's original timetable. The resistance in Asia has delayed completion of certain of our projects — in particular, PDCs Huan-Ti and Shiva suffered severe damage which has not yet been made entirely good — but we are from one month to seven weeks ahead of schedule on our non-Asian PDCs. Certain unanticipated problems have arisen, and I will ask Marshal Chernikov to expand upon them in a moment, but the overall rate of progress is most encouraging.

"Officially, the merger of all existing command structures has been completed. In fact, disputes over seniority have continued to drag on. They are now being brought to an end."

Tsien's policy was simple, Horus reflected; officers who objected to the distribution of assignments were simply relieved. It might have cost them some capable people, but the marshal *did* have a way of getting his points across.

"Enhancement is, perhaps, the brightest spot of all. Councilor Tudor and her people have, indeed, worked miracles in this area. We are now two months ahead of schedule for military enhancement and almost five weeks ahead for nonmilitary enhancement, despite the inclusion of additional occupational groups. We now have sufficient personnel to man all existing warships and fighters. Within another five months, we will have enhanced staffs for all PDCs and ODCs. Once that has been achieved, we will be able to begin enhancement of crews for the warships now under construction. With good management and a very little good fortune, we should be able to crew each unit as it commissions."

"That *is* good news! You make me feel we may pull this off, Marshal."

"We shall certainly attempt to, Governor," Tsien said calmly. "The balance between weapons fabrication and continued industrial expansion remains our worst production difficulty, but resource allocation is proving more than adequate. I believe Marshal Chernikov's current plans will overcome our remaining problems in this area.

"General Chiang faces some difficulties in his civil defense command, but the situation is improving. In terms of organization and training, he is two months ahead of schedule; it is construction of the inland shelters which poses the greatest difficulty, then food collection."

Horus nodded. Chiang Chien-su, one of Tsien's nominees to the Supreme Chiefs of Staff, was a short, rotund martinet with the mind of a computer. He smiled a lot, but the granite behind the smile was evident. Less evident but no less real was his deep respect for human life, an inner gentleness which, conversely, made him absolutely ruthless where saving lives was concerned.

"How far behind is shelter construction running?"

"Over three months," Tsien admitted. "We anticipate that some of that will be made up once PDC construction is complete. I must point out, however, that our original schedules already allowed for increases in building capacity after our fortification projects were completed. I do not believe we will be able to compensate completely for the time we have lost. This means that a greater proportion of our coastal populations will be forced to remain closer to their homes."

Horus frowned. Given the ratio of seas to land, anything that broke through the planetary shield was three times more likely to be an ocean strike than to hit land. That meant tsunamis, flooding, salt rains . . . and heavy loss of life in coastal areas.

"I want that program expedited, Marshal Tsien," he said quietly.

"Governor," Tsien said, equally quietly, "I have already diverted eighty percent of our emergency reserve capacity to the project. Every expedient is being pursued, but the project is immense and there is more civilian opposition to the attendant disruptions than your Council anticipated. The situation also is exacerbated by the food program. Collection of surpluses even in First World areas places severe strains on available transport; in Third World areas hoarding is common and armed resistance is not unknown. All of this diverts manpower and transport from population relocation efforts, yet the diversion is necessary. There is little point saving lives from bombardment only to lose them to starvation."

"Are you saying we won't make it?"

"No, Governor, I do not say we will fail. I only caution you that despite the most strenuous exertions, it is unlikely that we will succeed entirely."

Their eyes held for a moment, then Horus nodded. If they were no more than three months behind, they were still working miracles. And the marshal's integrity was absolute; if he said every effort would be made, then every effort would be made.

"On a more cheerful note," Tsien resumed after a moment, "Admiral Hawter and General Singhman are doing very well with their training commands. It is unfortunate that so much training must be restricted to simulators, but I am entirely satisfied with their progress — indeed, they are accomplishing more than I had hoped for. General Tama and General Amesbury are performing equally well in the management of our logistics. There remain some personnel problems, principally in terms of manpower allocation, but I have reviewed General Ki's solutions to them and feel confident they will succeed.

"In my own opinion, our greatest unmet training needs lie in the operational area. With your permission, I will expand upon this point following Marshal Chernikov's report."

"Of course," Horus said.

"Then, if I may, I will ask Marshal Chernikov to begin."

"Certainly." Horus turned his bright old eyes to Chernikov, and the Russian rubbed a fingertip thoughtfully over the table as he spoke.

"Essentially, Horus, we are well ahead of schedule on our PDC programs. We have managed this through allocation of additional manufacturing capacity to construction equipment and the extraordinary efforts of our personnel.

"We are not so advanced on our orbital work, but Geb and I agree that we should be on schedule by the end of next month, though it is unlikely we will complete the projects very much ahead of schedule. Nonetheless, we believe we will at least make our target dates in all cases.

"Despite this, two problems concern me. One is the planetary power grid; the other is the relative priority of munitions and infrastructure. Allow me to take them in turn.

"First, power." Chernikov folded his arms across his broad chest, his blue eyes thoughtful. "As you know, our planning has always envisioned the use of existing Terran generator capacity, but I fear that our estimates of that capacity were overly optimistic. Even with our PDCs' fusion plants, we will be hard put to provide sufficient power for maximum shield strength, and the situation for our ODCs is even worse."

"Excuse me, Vassily, but you said you were on schedule," Horus observed.

"We are, but, as you know, our ODC designs rely upon fold-space power transmission from Earth. This design decision was effectively forced upon us by the impossibility of building full-scale plants for the ODCs in the time available. Without additional power from Earth, the stations will not be able to operate all systems at peak efficiency."

"And you're afraid the power won't be there," Horus said softly. "I see."

"Perhaps you do not quite. I am not *afraid* it will not be available; I *know* it will not. And without it —" He shrugged slightly, and Horus nodded.

Without that power net, the ODCs would lose more than half their defensive strength and almost as much of their offensive punch. Their missile launchers would be unaffected, but energy weapons were another matter entirely.

"All right, Vassily, you're not the sort to dump a problem on me until you think you've got an answer. So what rabbit's coming out of the hat this time?"

"A core tap," Chernikov said levelly, and Horus jerked in his chair.

"*Are you out of your — ?!* No. Wait." He waved a hand and made himself sit back. "Of course you're not. But you do recognize the risks?"

"I do. But we *must* have that power, and Earth cannot provide it."

Maker, tell me what to do, Horus thought fervently. A *core* tap on a *planet*? Madness! If they lose control of it, even for an instant — !

He shuddered as he pictured that demon of power, roused and furious as it turned upon the insignificant mites who sought to master it. A smoldering wasteland, scoured of life, and raging storm fronts, hurricanes of out-raged atmosphere which would rip across the face of the planet. . . .

"There's no other choice?" His tone was almost plead-ing. "None?"

"None that my staff have been able to discover," Chernikov said flatly.

"Where —" Horus paused and cleared his throat. "Where would you put it?"

"Antarctica," Chernikov replied.

There's a fitting irony in that, Horus thought. Anu's enclave hid there for millennia. But a polar position? So close to the Indian Ocean biosystem? Yet where would I prefer it? New York? Moscow? Beijing?

"Have you calculated what happens if you lose control?" he asked finally.

"As well as we can. In a worst-case scenario, we will lose approximately fifty-three percent of the Antarctic surface. Damage to the local ecosystem will be effectively total. Damage to the Indian Ocean biosystem will be severe but, according to the projections, not irrecoverable. Sea level worldwide will rise, with consequent coastal flooding, and some global temperature drop may be anticipated. Esti-mated direct loss of life: approximately six-point-five million. Indirect deaths and the total who will be rendered homeless are impossible to calculate. We had considered an arctic position, but greater populations would lie in relative proximity, the flooding would be at least as severe, and the contamination of salt rains would be still worse when the sea water under the ice sheet vaporized."

"Maker!" Horus whispered. "Have you discussed this with Geb?"

"I have. It is only fair to tell you he was utterly opposed, yet after we had discussed it at some length, he modified his position somewhat. He will not actively oppose a core tap, but he cannot in good conscience recommend it. On the other hand —" the gaze from agate-hard blue eyes stabbed at Horus "— this is his planet only by adoption. I do not say that in any derogatory sense, Horus, yet it is true. Worse, he continues to feel — as, I believe, do you — a guilt which produces a certain protective paternalism within him. If he could refute the logic of my arguments, he would oppose them; his inability to support them suggests to me that his own logic is unable to overrule his emotions. Perhaps," the hard eyes softened slightly, "because he is so good a man."

"And despite that, you want to go ahead."

"I see no option. We risk seven million dead and severe damage to our world if we proceed; we run a far greater risk of the total destruction of the planet if we do not."

"Marshal Tsien?"

"I am less conversant with the figures than Marshal Chernikov, but I trust his calculations and judgment. I endorse his recommendation unreservedly, Governor. I will do so in writing if you wish."

"That won't be necessary." Horus sighed. His shoulders slumped, but he shook his head wryly. "You Terra-born are something else, Vassily!"

"If so, we have had good teachers," Chernikov replied, eyes warming with true affection. "Thanks to you, we have a possibility of saving ourselves. We will not throw away the chance you have given us."

Horus felt his face heat and turned quickly to another point.

"Maker! I hope you didn't plan on discussing your concerns in order of severity. If your munitions problem is worse — !"

"No, no!" Chernikov laughed. "No, this is not quite so grave. Indeed, one might almost call it planning for the future."

"Well *that* has a cheerful ring."

"Russians are not always melancholy, Horus. Generally, but not always. No, my major concern stems from the high probability that our planetary shield will be forced back into atmosphere. Our ODCs will be fairly capable of self-defense, although we anticipate high losses among them if

the planetary shield *is* forced back, but our orbital industrial capacity will, unfortunately, also be exposed. Nor will
it be practical to withdraw it to the planetary surface."

That was true enough, Horus reflected. They'd
accepted that from the beginning, but by building purely
for a weightless environment they'd been able to produce
more than twice the capacity in half the time.

"What do you have in mind?"

"I am about to become gloomy again," the Russian
warned, and Horus chuckled. "Let us assume we have succeeded in driving off the scouts but that *Dahak* has not
returned when the main incursion arrives. I realize that
our chances of survival in such an eventuality are slight, yet
it is not in me to say there are none. Perhaps it is unrealistic
of me, but I admire the American John Paul Jones and
respect his advice. Both the more famous quote, and another: It seems a law inflexible unto itself that he who will
not risk cannot win. I may not have it quite correct, but I
believe the spirit comes through."

"This is heading somewhere?" Horus asked quizzically.

"It is. If we lose our orbital industry, we lose eighty percent of our total capacity. This will leave us much weaker
when we confront the main incursion. Even if we beat off
the scouts quickly and with minimal losses — a happy state
of affairs on which we certainly cannot depend — we will
be hard-pressed to rebuild even to our current capacity
out of our present Imperial planetary industry. I therefore
propose that we should place greater emphasis on increasing our planetary industrial infrastructure."

"I agree it's desirable, but where do you plan to get the
capacity?"

"With your permission, I will discontinue the production of mines."

"Ah?"

"I have studied their capabilities, and while they are
impressive, I feel they will be less useful against the scouts
than an increase in planetary industrial capacity will be to
our defense against the main incursion."

"Why?"

"Essentially, the mines are simply advanced hunter-killer satellites. Certainly their ability to attack vessels as they emerge from hyper is useful, yet they will be required in tremendous numbers to effectively cover the volume of space we must protect. Their attack radius is no more than ninety thousand kilometers, and mass attacks will be required to overpower the defenses of any alert target. Because of these limitations, I doubt our ability to produce adequate numbers in the time available to us. I would prefer to do without them in order to safeguard our future industrial potential."

"I see." Horus pursed his lips, then nodded. "All right, I agree."

"Thank you."

"Now, Marshal," Horus turned to Tsien, "you mentioned something about operational problems?"

"Yes, Governor. General Amesbury's Scanner Command is well prepared to detect the enemy's approach, but we do not know whether we would be better advised to send our units out to meet them as they move in-system after leaving hyper or to concentrate closer to Earth for sorties from within the shield after they have closed with the planet. The question also, of course, is complicated by the possibility that the Achuultani might attempt a pincer attack, using one group of scouts to draw our sublight units out of position and then micro-jumping across the system to attack from another direction."

"And you want to finalize operational doctrine?"

"Not precisely. I realize that this almost certainly will not be possible for some time and that much ultimately will depend upon the differences between Achuultani technology and our own. For the moment, however, I would like to grant Admiral Hawter's request to deploy our existing units for operational training and war games in the trans-asteroidal area. It will give the crews valuable experience with their weapons, and, more importantly, I believe, give our command personnel greater confidence in themselves."

"I agree entirely," Horus said firmly. "And it'll also let us use some of the larger asteroids for target practice — which means the Achuultani *won't* be able to use them for target practice on us! Proceed with it immediately, by all means, Marshal Tsien. Vassily, I'll take your recommendations to the Council. Unless someone there can give me an overpowering counterargument, they'll be approved within forty-eight hours. Is that good enough?"

"Eminently, Governor."

"Good. In that case, gentlemen, let's get into our suits. I want to see ODC Two firsthand."

The Achuultani scouts gathered their strength once more, merging into a single huge formation about their flagship. A brilliant F5 star lay barely five light-years distant, but it held no interest for them. Their instruments probed and peered, listening for the electromagnetic voices they had come so far to find. The universe was vast. Not even such accomplished killers as they could sweep it of all life, and so worlds such as T'Yir were safe unless the scouts literally stumbled across them.

But other worlds were not, and the sensor crews caught the faint signals they had sought. Directional antennae turned and quested, and the scouts reoriented themselves. A small, G2 star called to them, and they went to silence it forever.

Chapter Eleven

"Barbarian!" Tamman shook his head mournfully as he took a fresh glass of lemonade from his wife and buried his sorrows in its depths.

"And why might that be, you effete, over-civilized, not to say decadent, epicure?" Colin demanded.

"That ought to be obvious. *Mesquite* charcoal? How . . . how *Texan!*"

Colin stuck out his tongue, and meat juices hissed as he turned steaks. A fragrant cloud of smoke rose on the heat shimmer of the grill, pushed out over the lake by the park deck's cool breezes, and the volleyball tournament was in full cry. He glanced up in time to see Colonel Tama Matsuo, Tamman's grandson, launch a vicious spike. One of the German team's forwards tried to get under it, but not even an enhanced human could have returned *that* shot.

"*Banzai!*" the Sendai Division's team screamed, and the Germans muttered darkly. Jiltanith applauded, and Matsuo bowed to her, then prepared to serve. His hand struck the ball like a hammer, and Colin winced as it bulleted across the net.

"Now, Tamman, don't be so harsh," his critic's wife chimed in. "After all, Colin's doing the best he knows how."

"Oh, *thank* you, kind lady! Thank you! Just remember — your wonderful husband is the one who courted bad luck by broiling *tai* in *miso* last week."

Recon Captain Amanda Givens laughed, her cafe-au-lait face wreathed in a lovely smile, and Tamman pulled her down beside him to kiss her ear.

"Nonsense," he said airily. "Just doing my bit to root out superstition. Anyway, I was out of salt."

Amanda snuggled closer to him, and Colin grinned. *Dahak*'s sickbay had regenerated the leg she'd lost in the La Paz raid in time for her wedding, and the sheer joy she and Tamman took in one another warmed Colin's heart, even though their marriage had caused a few unanticipated problems.

Dahak had always seemed a bit pettish over the Terran insistence that one name wasn't good enough. He'd accepted it — grumpily — but only until he got to attend the first wedding on his decks in fifty thousand years. In some ways, he'd seemed even more delighted than the happy couple, and he'd hardly been able to wait for Colin to log the event officially.

That was when the trouble started, for Imperial conventions designating marital status sounded ridiculous applied to Terran names, and Dahak had persisted in trying to make them work. Colin usually wound up giving in when Dahak felt moved to true intransigence — talking the computer out of something was akin to parting the Red Sea, only harder — but he'd refused pointblank to let Dahak inflict a name like Amandacollettegivens-Tam on a friend. The thought of hearing *that* every time Dahak spoke to or of Amanda had been too much, and if Tamman had originally insisted (when he finally stopped laughing) that it was a lovely name which fell trippingly from the tongue, his tune quickly changed when he found out what Dahak intended to call *him*. Tamman-Amcolgiv was shorter; that was about all you could say for it.

"Methinks it little matters what thou sayst, Tamman," Jiltanith's mournful observation drew Colin back to the present as she opened another bottle of beer. "Our Colin departeth not from his fell intent to poison one and all with his noxious smokes and fumes."

"Listen, all of you," Colin retorted, propping his fists on his hips, "I'm captain of this tub, and we'll fix food *my* way!"

"Didst'a hear thy captain speak of thee, Dahak, my tub?" Jiltanith caroled, and Colin shook a fist at her.

"I believe the proper response is 'Sticks and stones may break my bones, but words will never hurt me,'" a mellow voice replied, and Colin groaned.

"What idiot encouraged him to learn cliches?"

"Nay, Colin, acquit us all. 'Tis simply that we *dis*couraged him not."

"Well you should have."

"Stop complaining and let the man cook." Vlad Chernikov lay flat on his back in the shade of a young oak. Now he propped one eye open. "If you do not care for his cuisine, you need not eat it, Tamman."

"Fat chance!" Colin snorted, and stole Jiltanith's beer.

He swallowed, enjoying the "sun" on his shoulders, and decided 'Tanni had been right to talk him into the party. The anniversary of the fall of Anu's enclave deserved to be celebrated as a reminder of some of the "impossible" things they'd already accomplished, even if uncertainty over what waited at Birhat continued to gnaw at everyone. Or possibly *because* it did.

He looked out over the happy, laughing knots of his off-watch crewmen. Some of them, anyway. There was a null-grav basketball tournament underway on Deck 2460, and General Treshnikov had organized a "Top Gun" contest on the simulator deck for the non-fighter pilots of the crew. Then there was the regatta out on the thirty-kilometer-wide park deck's lake.

He glanced around the shaded picnic tables. Cohanna and Ninhursag sat at one, annihilating one another in a game of Imperial battle chess with a bloodthirsty disregard for losses that would turn a line officer gray, and Caitrin O'Rourke and Geran had embarked on a drinking contest — in which Caitrin's Aussie ancestry appeared to be a decided advantage — at another. General von Grau and General Tsukuba were wagering on the outcome of the volleyball tournament, and Hector wore a dreamy look as he and Dahak pursued a discussion, complete with neural-feed visual aids, of Hannibal's Italian tactics. Sarah Meir sat with him, listening in and reaching down occasionally to scratch the ears of Hector's huge half-lab, half-rottweiler bitch Tinker Bell as she drowsed at her master's feet.

Colin returned Jiltanith's beer, and his smile grew warmer as her eyes gleamed at him. Yes, she'd been right — just as she'd been right to insist they make their own "surprise" announcement at the close of the festivities. And thank God he'd been firm with Dahak! He didn't know how she would have reacted to Jiltanith-Colfranmac, but he knew how *he* would have felt over Colinfrancis-macintyre-Jil!

"Supralight shutdown in ten minutes," Dahak announced into the fiery tension of Command One's starlit dimness, and Colin smiled tightly at Jiltanith's holo image, trying to wish she were not far away in Command Two.

He inhaled deeply and concentrated on the reports and commands flowing through his neural feed. Not even the Terra-born among *Dahak*'s well-drilled crew needed to think through their commands these days. Which might be just as well. There had been no hails or challenges, but they'd been thoroughly scanned by someone (or something) while still a full day short of Birhat.

Colin would have felt immeasurably better to know what had been on the other end of those scanners . . . and how whatever it was meant to react. One thing they'd learned at Kano: the Fourth Empire's weaponry had been, quite simply, better than *Dahak*'s best. Vlad and Dahak had done all they could to upgrade their defenses, but if an active Fleet Central was feeling belligerent, they might very well die in the next few hours.

"Sublight in three minutes."

"Stand by, Tactical," Colin said softly.

"Standing by, Captain."

The last minutes raced even as they trickled agonizingly slowly. Then Colin felt the start of supralight shutdown in his implants, and suddenly the stars were still.

"Core tap shutdown," Dahak reported, and then, almost instantly, "Detection at ten light-minutes. Detection at thirty light-minutes. Detection at five light-hours."

"Display system," Colin snapped, and the sun Bia, Birhat's G0 primary, still twelve light-hours away, was suddenly ringed with a system schematic.

"God's Teeth!"

Jiltanith's whisper summed up Colin's sentiments admirably. Even at this range, the display was crowded, and more and more light codes sprang into view with mechanical precision as Sarah took them in at half the speed of light. Dahak's scanners reached ahead, adding contact after contact, until the display gleamed with a thick, incredible dusting of symbols.

"Any response to our presence, Dahak?"

"None beyond detection, sir. I have received no challenges, nor has anyone yet responded to my hails."

Colin nodded. It was a disappointment, for he'd felt a spurt of hope when he saw all those light codes, but it was a relief, as well. At least no one was shooting at them.

"What the hell are all those things?" he demanded.

"Unknown, sir. Passive scanners detect very few active power sources, and even with fold-space scanners, the range remains very long for active systems, but I would estimate that many of them are weapon systems. In fact —"

The computer paused suddenly, and Colin quirked an eyebrow. It was unusual, to say the least, for Dahak to break off in the middle of a sentence.

"Sir," the computer said after a moment, "I have determined the function of certain installations."

An arc of light codes blinked green. They formed a ring forty light-minutes from Bia — no, not a ring. As he watched, new codes, each indicating an installation much smaller than the giants in the original ring, began to appear, precisely distanced from the circle, curving away from *Dahak* as if to embrace the entire inner system. And there — there were two more rings of larger symbols, perpendicular to the first but offset by thirty degrees. There were thousands — millions — of the things! And more were still appearing as they came into scanner range, reaching out about Bia in a sphere.

"Well? What are they?"

"They appear, sir," Dahak said, "to be shield generators."

"They're *what*?" Colin blurted, and he felt Vlad Chernikov's shock echoing through the engineering subnet.

"Shield generators," Dahak repeated, "which, if activated, would enclose the entire inner system. The larger stations are approximately ten times as massive as the smaller ones and appear to be the primary generators."

Colin fought a sense of incredulity. Nobody could build a shield with that much surface area! Yet if Dahak said they were shield generators, shield generators they were . . . but the *scope* of such a project . . . !

"Whatever else it was, the Empire was no piker," he muttered.

"As thou sayst," Jiltanith agreed. "Yet methinks —"

"Status change," Dahak said suddenly, and a bright red ring circled a massive installation in distant orbit about Birhat itself. "Core tap activation detected."

"Maker!" Tamman muttered, for the power source which had waked to sudden life was many times as powerful as *Dahak*'s own.

"New detection at nine-point-eight light-hours. I have a challenge."

"Nature?" Colin snapped.

"Query for identification only, sir, but it carries a Fleet Central imperative. It is repeating."

"Respond."

"Acknowledged." There was another brief silence, and then Dahak spoke again, sounding — for once — a bit puzzled. "Sir, the challenge has terminated."

"What do you mean? How did they respond?"

"They did not, sir, beyond terminating the challenge."

Colin raised an eyebrow at Jiltanith's holo-image, and she shrugged.

"Ask me not, my Colin. Thou knowest as much as I."

"Yeah, and neither of us knows a whole hell of a lot," he muttered. Then he drew a deep breath. "Dahak, give me an all-hands link."

"Acknowledged. Link open."

"People," Colin told his crew, "we've just responded to a challenge — apparently from Fleet Central itself — and no one's shooting at us. That's the good news. The bad news is no one's talking to us, either. We're moving in. We'll keep you informed. But at least there's *something* here. Hang loose.

"Close link, Dahak."

"Link closed, sir."

"Thank you," Colin said, and leaned back, rubbing his hands up and down the armrests of his couch as he stared at the crowded, enigmatic display. More light codes were still appearing as *Dahak* moved deeper in-system, and the active core tap's crimson beacon pulsed at their center like a heart.

"Well, we found it," Colin said, rising from the captain's couch to stretch hugely, "but God knows what it is."

"Aye." Jiltanith once more manned her own console in Command Two, but her hologram sat up and swung its legs over the side of her couch. "I know not what chanced here, my Colin, but glad am I Geb is not here to see it."

"Amen," Colin said. He'd once wondered why Geb was the only Imperial with a single-syllable name. Now, thanks to Jiltanith and Dahak's files, he knew. It was the custom of his planet, for Geb had been one of those very rare beings in Battle Fleet: a native-born son of Birhat. It was a proud distinction, but one Geb no longer boasted of; his part in the mutiny had been something like George Washington's grandson proclaiming himself king of the United States.

"But whate'er hath chanced, these newest facts do seem stranger still than aught else we have encountered." Jiltanith coiled a lock of hair about her index finger and stared at Command Two's visual display, her eyes perplexed.

With good reason, Colin thought. In the last thirty-two hours, they'd threaded deeper into the Bia System's incredible clutter of deep-space and orbital installations until, at last, they'd reached Birhat itself. There should have been plenty of room, but the Bia System had not escaped unscathed. Twice they passed within less than ten thousand kilometers of drifting derelicts, and that was much closer than any astrogator cared to come.

Yet despite that evidence of ruin, Colin had felt hopeful as Birhat herself came into sight, for the ancient capital world of the Imperium was alive, a white-swirled sapphire whose land masses were rich and green.

But with the wrong kind of green.

Colin sat back down, scratching his head. Birhat lay just over a light-minute further from Bia than Terra did from Sol, and its axial tilt was about five degrees greater, making for more extreme seasons, but it had been a nice enough place. It still was, but there'd been a few changes.

According to the records, Birhat's trees should be mostly evergreens, but while there were trees, they appeared exclusively deciduous, and there were other things: leafy, fernlike things and strange, kilometer-long creepers with cypress-knee rhizomes and upstanding plumes of foliage. Nothing like *that* was supposed to grow on Birhat, and the local fauna was even worse.

Like Earth, Birhat had belonged to the mammals, and there *were* mammals down there, if not the right ones. Unfortunately, there were other things, too, especially in the equatorial belt. One was nearly a dead ringer for an under-sized Stegosaurus, and another one (a big, nasty looking son-of-a-bitch) seemed to combine the more objectionable aspects of Tyrannosaurus and a four-horned Triceratops. Then there were the birds. None of them seemed quite right, and he *knew* the big Pterodactyl-like raptors shouldn't be here.

It was, he thought, the most god-awful, scrambled excuse for a biosystem he'd ever heard of, and none of it — not a single plant, animal, saurian, or bird they'd yet examined — *belonged* here.

If it puzzled him, it was driving Cohanna batty. The senior biosciences officer was buried in her office with Dahak, trying to make sense of her instrument readings and snarling at any soul incautious enough to disturb her.

At least the sadly-eroded mountains and seas were where they were supposed to be, loosely speaking, and there were still some clusters of buildings. They were weather-battered ruins (not surprisingly given the worn-away look of the mountain ranges) liberally coated in greenery, but they were there. Not that it helped; most were as badly wrecked as Keerah's had been, and there was nothing — absolutely *nothing* — where Fleet Central was supposed to be.

Yet some of the Bia System's puzzles offered Colin hope. One of them floated a few thousand kilometers from *Dahak*, serenely orbiting the improbability which had once been the Imperium's capital, and he turned his head to study it anew, tugging at the end of his nose to help himself think.

The enigmatic structure was even bigger than *Dahak*, which was a sobering thought, for a quarter of *Dahak*'s colossal tonnage was committed to propulsion. This thing — whatever it was — clearly wasn't intended to move, which made all of its mass available for other things. Like the weapon systems *Dahak*'s scanners had picked up. *Lots* of weapon systems. Missile launchers, energy weapons, and launch bays for fighters and sublight parasites *Nergal*'s size or bigger. Yet for all its gargantuan firepower, much of its tonnage was obviously committed to something else . . . but what?

Worse, it was also the source of the core tap *Dahak* had detected. Even now, that energy sink roared away within it, sucking in all that tremendous power. Presumably it meant to do something with it, but as yet it had shown no signs of exactly what that was. It hadn't even spoken to Dahak, despite his polite queries for information. It just sat there, *being* there.

"Captain?"

"Yes, Dahak?"

"I believe I have determined the function of that installation."

"Well?"

"I believe, sir, that *it* is Fleet Central."

"I thought Fleet Central was on the planet!"

"So it was, fifty-one thousand years ago. I have, however, been carrying out systematic scans, and I have located the installation's core computer. It is, indeed, a combination of energy-state and solid-state engineering. It is also approximately three-hundred-fifty-point-two kilometers in diameter."

"Eeep!" Colin whipped around to stare at Jiltanith, but for once she looked as stunned as he felt. Dear God, he thought faintly. Dear, sweet God. If Vlad and Dahak's projections about the capabilities of energy-state computer science were correct, that thing was . . . it was . . .

"I beg your pardon, sir?" Dahak said courteously.

"Uh . . . never mind. Continue your report."

"There is very little more to report. The size of its computer core, coupled with its obvious defensive capability, indicates that it must, at the very least, have been the central command complex for the Bia System. Given that Birhat remained the capital of the Empire as it had been of the Imperium, this certainly suggests that it was also Fleet Central."

"I . . . see. And it still isn't responding to your hails?"

"It is not. And even the Empire's computers should have noticed us by now."

"Could it have done so and chosen to ignore us?"

"The possibility exists, but while it is probable Fleet procedures have changed, we were challenged and we did reply. That should have initiated an automatic request for data core transmission from any newly arrived unit."

"Even if there's no human crew aboard?"

"Sir," Dahak said with the patience of one trying not to be insubordinate to a dense superior, "we were challenged, which indicates the initiation of an automatic sequence of some sort. And, sir, Fleet Central should not have permitted a vessel of *Dahak*'s size and firepower to close to this proximity without assuring itself that the vessel in question truly was what it claimed to be. Since no information has been exchanged, there is no way Fleet Central could know my response to its challenge was genuine. Hence we should at the very least be targeted by its weapons until we provide a satisfactory account of ourselves, yet that installation has not even objected to my scanning it. Fleet Central would *never* permit an unknown unit to do that."

"All right, I'll accept that — even if that does seem to be exactly what it's doing — and God knows I don't want to piss it off, but sooner or later we'll have to get some sort of response out of it. Any suggestions?"

"As I have explained," Dahak said even more patiently, "we should already have elicited a response."

"I know that," Colin replied, equally patiently, "but we haven't. Isn't there any sort of emergency override procedure?"

"No, sir, there is not. None was ever required."

"Damn it, do you mean to tell me there's *no* way to talk to it if it doesn't respond to your hails?"

There was a pause lengthy enough to raise Colin's eyebrows. He was about to repeat his question when his electronic henchman finally answered.

"There might be one way," Dahak said with such manifest reluctance Colin felt an instant twinge of anxiety.

"Well, spit it out!"

"We might attempt physical access, but I would not recommend doing so."

"What? Why not?"

"Because, Captain, access to Fleet Central was highly restricted. Without express instructions from its command crew to its security systems, only two types of individuals might demand entrance without being fired upon."

"Oh?" Colin felt a sudden queasiness and was quite pleased he'd managed to sound so calm. "And what two types might that be?"

"Flag officers and commanders of capital ships of Battle Fleet."

"Which means . . ." Colin said slowly.

"Which means," Dahak told him, "that the only member of this crew who might make the attempt is you."

He looked up and saw Jiltanith staring at him in horror.

Chapter Twelve

They went to their quarters to argue.

Jiltanith opened her mouth, eyes flashing dangerously, but Dahak's electronic reflexes beat her to it.

"Senior Fleet Captain MacIntyre," he said with icy formality, "what you propose is not yet and may never become necessary, and I remind you of Fleet Regulation Nine-One-Seven, Subsection Three-One, Paragraph Two: 'The commander of any Fleet unit shall safeguard the chain of command against unnecessary risk.' I submit, sir, that your intentions violate both the spirit and letter of this regulation, and I must, therefore, respectfully insist that you immediately abandon this ill-advised, hazardous, and most unwise plan."

"Dahak," Colin said, "shut up."

"Senior Fl—"

"I said shut up," Colin repeated in a dangerously level voice, and Dahak shut up. "Thank you. Now. We both know the people who wrote the Fleet Regs never envisioned *this* situation, but if you want to quote regs, here's one for *you*. Regulation One-Three, Section One: 'In the

149

absence of orders from higher authority, the commander of any Battle Fleet unit or formation shall employ his command or any sub-unit or member thereof in the manner best calculated, in his considered judgment, to preserve the Imperium and his race.' You once said I had a command mentality. Well, maybe I do and maybe I don't, but this is a command decision and you're damned well going to live with it."

"But —"

"The discussion is closed, Dahak."

There was a long moment of silence before the computer replied.

"Acknowledged," he said in his frostiest tones, but Colin knew that was the easy part. He smiled crookedly at Jiltanith, glad they were alone, and gave it his best shot.

"'Tanni, I don't want to argue with my XO, either."

"Dost'a not, indeed?" she flared. "Then contend with thy wife, lackwit! Scarce one thin day in this system, and already thou wouldst risk thy life?! What maggot hath devoured thy brain entire? Or mayhap 'tis vanity speaks, for most assuredly 'tis not wisdom!"

"It isn't vanity, and you know it. We simply don't have time to waste."

"*Time*, thou sayst?!" she spat like an angry cat. "Dost'a think my wits addled as thine own? Howsoe'er thou dost proceed, yet will we never return to Terra ere the Achuultani scouts! And if that be so, then where's the need o' witless haste? Four months easily, mayhap five, may we spend here and still out-speed the true incursion back to Earth — and well thou knowest!"

"All right," he said, and her eyes narrowed at his unexpected agreement, "but assume you're right and we start poking around. What happens when we do something Fleet Central doesn't like, 'Tanni? Until we know what it might object to, we can't know what might get everyone aboard this ship killed. So until we establish communications with it, we can't do anything *else*, either!"

Jiltanith's fingers flexed like the cat she so resembled,

but she drew a breath and made herself consider his argument.

"Aye, there's summat in that," she admitted, manifestly against her will. "Yet still 'tis true we have spent but little time upon the task. Must thou so soon assay this madness?"

"I'm afraid so," he sighed. "If this *is* Fleet Central, it's either Ali Baba's Cave or Pandora's Box, and we have to find out which. Assuming any of Battle Fleet's still operational — and the way this thing powered itself up is the first sign something may be — we don't know how long it'll take to assemble it. We need every minute we can buy, 'Tanni."

She turned away, pacing, arms folded beneath her breasts, shoulders tight with a fear Colin knew was not for herself. He longed to tell her he understood, but he knew better than to . . . and that she knew already.

She turned back to him at last, eyes shadowed, and he knew he'd won.

"Aye," she sighed, hugging him tightly and pressing her face into his shoulder. "My heart doth rail against it, yet my mind — my cursed mind — concedeth. But, oh, my dearest dear, would I might forbid thee this!"

"I know," he whispered into the sweet-smelling silk of her hair.

Colin felt like an ant beneath an impending foot. Fleet Central's armored flank seemed to trap him, ready to crush him between itself and the blue-white sphere of Birhat, and he hoped Cohanna wasn't monitoring his bio readouts.

He nudged his cutter to a stop. A green and yellow beacon marked a small hatch, but though his head ached from concentrating on his implants, he felt no response. He timed the beacon's sequence carefully.

"Dahak, I have a point-seven-five-second visual flash, green-amber-amber-green-amber, on a Class Seven hatch."

"Assuming Fleet conventions have not changed, Captain, that should indicate an active access point for small craft."

"I know." Colin swallowed, wishing his mouth weren't quite so dry. "Unfortunately, my implants can't pick up a thing."

Colin felt a sudden, almost audible click deep in his skull and blinked at a brief surge of vertigo as a not-quite familiar tingle pulsed in his feed.

"I've got something. Still not clear, but —" The tingle suddenly turned sharp and familiar. "That's it!"

"Acknowledged, Captain," Dahak said. "The translation programs devised for *Omega Three* did not perfectly meet our requirements, but I believe my new modifications to your implant software should suffice. I caution you again, however, that additional, inherently unforeseeable difficulties may await."

"Understood." Colin edged closer, insinuating his thoughts cautiously into the hatch computers, and something answered. It was an ID challenge, but it tasted . . . odd.

He keyed his personal implant code with exquisite care, and for an instant just long enough to feel relieved disappointment, nothing happened. Then the hatch slid open, and he dried his palms on his uniform trousers.

"Well, people," he murmured, "door's open. Wish me luck."

"So do we all," Jiltanith told him softly. "Take care, my love."

The next half-hour was among the most nerve-wracking in Colin's life. His basic implant codes had sufficed to open the hatch, but that only roused the internal security systems.

There was a strangeness to their challenges, a dogged, mechanical persistence he'd never encountered from Dahak, but they were thorough. At every turn, it seemed, there were demands for identification on ever-deeper security levels. He found himself responding with bridge officer codes he hadn't known he knew and realized that the computers were digging deep into his challenge-response conditioning. No wonder Druaga had felt confident Anu could never override his own final orders to Dahak! Colin had never guessed just how many security codes Dahak had buried in his own implants and subconscious.

But he reached the central transit shaft at last, and felt both relief and a different tension as he plugged into the traffic sub-net and requested transport to Fleet Central's Command Alpha. He half-expected yet another challenge, but the routing computers sent back a ready signal, and he stepped out into the shaft.

One thing about the terror of the unknown, he thought wryly as the shaft took him and hurled him inward: it neatly displaced such mundane fears as being mashed to paste by the transit shaft's gravitonics!

The shaft deposited him outside Command Alpha in a brightly lit chamber big enough for an assault shuttle. The command deck hatch bore no unit ensign, as if Fleet Central was above such things. There was only the emblem of the Fourth Empire: the Imperium's starburst surmounted by an intricate diadem.

Colin looked about, natural senses and implants busy, and paled as he detected the security systems guarding this gleaming portal. Heavy grav guns in artfully hidden housings were backed up by the weapons Vlad had dubbed warp guns, and their targeting systems were centered on him. He tried to straighten his hunched shoulders and approached the huge hatch with a steady tread.

Almost to his surprise, it clicked aside, and more silent hatches — twice as many as guarded *Dahak*'s Command One — opened as he walked down the brightly lit tunnel, fighting a sense of entrapment. And then, at last, he stepped out into the very heart and brain of Battle Fleet, and the last hatch closed behind him.

It wasn't as impressive as Command One was his first thought — but only his first. It lacked the gorgeous, perfect holo projections of *Dahak's* bridge, but the softly bright chamber was far, far larger. Dedicated hypercom consoles circled its walls, labeled with names he knew in flowing Imperial script, names which had been only half-believed-in legends in his implant education from *Dahak*. Systems and sectors, famous Fleet bases and proud formations — the names vanished into unreadable distance, and Quadrant Command nets extended out across the floor, the ranked couches and consoles too numerous to count, driving home the inconceivable vastness of the Empire.

It made him feel very, very insignificant.

Yet he was here . . . and those couches were empty. He had come eight hundred light-years to reach this enormous room, come from a planet teeming with humanity to this silence no voice had broken in forty-five millennia, and all this might and power of empire were but the work of Man.

He crossed the shining deck, bootheels ringing on jeweled mosaics, and ghosts hovered in the corners, watchful and measuring. He wondered what they made of him.

It took ten minutes to reach the raised dais at the center of the command deck, and he climbed its broad steps steadily, the weight of some foreordained fate seeming to press upon his shoulders, until he reached the top at last.

He lowered himself into the thronelike couch before the single console. It conformed smoothly to his body, and he forced himself to relax and draw a deep, slow breath before he reached out through his feed.

There was a quick flicker of response, and he felt a surge of hope — then grunted and flinched as he was hurled violently out of the net.

"Implant interface access denied," a voice said. It was a soft, musical contralto . . . utterly devoid of life or emotion.

Colin rubbed his forehead, trying to soothe the sudden ache deep inside his brain, and looked around the silent command deck for inspiration. He found none and reached out again, more carefully.

"Implant interface access denied." The voice threw him out of the net even more violently. "Warning. Unauthorized access to this installation is punishable by imprisonment for not less than ninety-five standard years."

"Damn," Colin muttered. He was more than half-afraid of how Fleet Central might react to activating his fold-space com but saw no option. "Dahak?"

"Yes, Captain?"

"I'm getting an implant access denial warning."

"Voice or neural feed?"

"Voice. The damned thing won't even talk to my implants."

"Interesting," Dahak mused, "and illogical. You have been admitted to Command Alpha; logically, therefore, Fleet Central recognizes you as an officer of Battle Fleet. Assuming that to be true, access should not be denied."

"The same thought had occurred to me," Colin said a bit sarcastically.

"Have you attempted verbal communication, sir?"

"No."

"I would recommend that as the next logical step."

"Thanks a lot," Colin muttered, then cleared his throat.

"Computer," he said, feeling just a bit foolish addressing the emptiness.

"Acknowledged," the emotionless voice said, and his heart leapt. By damn, maybe there was a way in yet!

"Why have I been denied implant access?"

"Improper implant identification," the voice replied.

"Improper in what way?"

"Data anomaly detected. Implant interface access denied."

"What anomaly?" he asked, far more patiently than he felt.

"Implant identification not in Fleet Central data base. Individual not recognized by core access programs. Implant interface access denied."

"Then why have you accepted voice communication?"

"Emergency subroutines have been activated for

duration of the present crisis," the voice replied, and Colin paused, wondering what "emergency subroutines" were and why they allowed verbal access. Not that he meant to ask. The last thing he needed was to change this thing's mind!

"Computer," he said finally, "why was I admitted to Command Alpha?"

"Unknown. Security is not a function of Computer Central."

"I see." Colin thought more furiously than ever, then nodded to himself. "Computer, would Fleet Central Security admit an individual with invalid implant identification codes to Command Alpha?"

"Negative."

"Then if Security admitted me, the security data base must recognize my implants."

Silence answered his observation.

"Hmmm, not very talkative, are you?" Colin mused.

"Query not understood," the voice said.

"Never mind." He drew a deep breath. "I submit that a search might locate my implant codes in Fleet Central Security's data base. Would you concur?"

"The possibility exists."

"Then I instruct you," Colin said very carefully, "to search the security data base and validate my implant codes."

There was a brief pause, and he bit his lip.

"Verbal instructions require authorization overrides," the voice said finally. "Identify source of authority."

"My own, as Senior Fleet Captain Colin MacIntyre, commanding officer, ship-of-the-line *Dahak*, Hull Number One-Seven-Seven-Two-Niner-One." Colin was amazed by how level his own voice sounded.

"Authorization provisionally accepted," the voice said. "Searching security data base."

There was another moment of silence, then the voice spoke again.

"Search completed. Implant identification codes located. Anomalies."

"Specify anomalies."

"Specification one: identification codes not current. Specification two: no Senior Fleet Captain Colinmacintyre listed in Fleet Central's data base. Specification Three: *Dahak*, Hull Number One-Seven-Seven-Two-Niner-One, lost fifty-one thousand six hundred nine-point-eight-four-six standard years ago."

"My codes were current as of *Dahak*'s departure for the Noarl System on picket duty. I should be added to your data base as a descendant of *Dahak*'s core crew, promoted to fill a vacancy left by combat losses."

"That is not possible. *Dahak*, Hull Number One-Seven-Seven-Two-Niner-One, no longer exists."

"Then what's my nonexistent command doing here?" Colin demanded.

"Null-value query."

"Null-value?! *Dahak*'s in orbit with Fleet Central right now!"

"Datum invalid," Fleet Central observed. "No such unit is present."

Colin resisted an urge to smash a bioenhanced fist through the console.

"Then what *is* the object accompanying Fleet Central in orbit?" he snarled.

"Data anomaly," Fleet Central said emotionlessly.

"*What* data anomaly, damn it?!"

"Perimeter Security defensive programming prohibits approach within eight light-hours of Planet Birhat without valid identification codes. *Dahak*, Hull Number One-Seven-Seven-Two-Niner-One, no longer exists. Therefore, no such unit can be present. Therefore, scanner reports represent data anomaly."

Colin punched a couch arm in sudden understanding. For some reason, this dummy — or its outer surveillance systems, anyway — had accepted *Dahak*'s ID and let him in. For some other reason, the central computers had *not* accepted that ID. Faced with the fact that no improperly identified unit could be here, this moron had labeled *Dahak* a "data anomaly" and decided to ignore him!

"Computer," he said finally, "assume — hypothetically — that a unit identified as *Dahak* was admitted to the Bia System by Perimeter Security. How might that situation arise?"

"Programming error," Fleet Central said calmly.

"Explain."

"No Confirmation of Loss report on *Dahak*, Hull Number One-Seven-Seven-Two-Niner-One, was filed with Fleet Central. Loss of vessel is noted in Log Reference Rho-Upsilon-Beta-Seven-Six-One-Niner-Four, but failure to confirm loss report resulted in improper data storage." Fleet Central fell silent, satisfied with its own pronouncement, and Colin managed not to swear.

"Which means?"

"ID codes for *Dahak*, Hull Number One-Seven-Seven-Two-Niner-One, were not purged from memory."

Colin closed his eyes. Dear God. This brainless wonder had let *Dahak* into the system because he'd identified himself and his codes were still in memory, but now that he was here, it didn't believe in him!

"How might that programming error be resolved?" he asked at last.

"Conflicting data must be removed from data base."

Colin drew another deep breath, aware of just how fragile this entire discussion was. If this computer could decide something *Dahak's* size didn't exist, it could certainly do the same with the "data anomaly's" captain.

"Evaluate possibility that Log Reference Rho-Upsilon-Beta-Seven-Six-One-Niner-Four is an incorrect datum," he said flatly.

"Possibility exists. Probability impossible to assess," Fleet Central replied, and Colin allowed himself a slight feeling of relief. Very slight.

"In that case, I instruct you to purge it from memory," he said, and held his breath.

"Incorrect procedure," Fleet Central responded.

"Incorrect in what fashion?" Colin asked tautly.

"Full memory purge requires authorization from human command crew."

Colin cocked a mental ear. *Full* memory purge?

"Can data concerning my command be placed in inactive storage on my authority pending proper authorization?"

"Affirmative."

"Then I instruct you to do so with previously specified log entry."

"Proceeding. Data transferred to inactive storage."

Colin shuddered in explosive relaxation, then gave himself a mental shake. He might well be relaxing too soon.

"Computer, who am I?" he asked softly.

"You are Senior Fleet Captain Colinmacintyre, commanding officer HIMP *Dahak*, Hull Number One-Seven-Seven-Two-Niner-One," the voice said emotionlessly.

"And what is the current location of my command?"

"HIMP *Dahak*, Hull Number One-Seven-Seven-Two-Niner-One, is currently in Birhat orbit, ten thousand seventeen point-five kilometers distant from Fleet Central," the musical voice told him calmly, and Colin MacIntyre breathed a short, soft, fervent prayer of thanks before jubilation overwhelmed him.

"All *right*!" Colin's palms slammed down on the couch arms in triumph.

"What passeth, my Colin?" an urgent voice demanded through his fold-space link, and he realized he'd left it open.

"We're in, 'Tanni! Tell all hands — we're *in*!"

"Bravely done! Oh, bravely, my heart!"

"Thank you," he said softly, then straightened and returned to business. "Computer."

"Yes, Senior Fleet Captain?"

"What's your name, Computer?"

"This unit is officially designated Fleet Central Computer Central," the musical voice replied.

"Is that what your human personnel called you?"

"Negative, Senior Fleet Captain."

"Well, then, what *did* they call you?" Colin asked patiently.

"Fleet Central personnel refer to Comp Cent as 'Mother.'"

"Mother," Colin muttered, shaking his head in disbelief. Oh, well, if that was what Fleet Central was used to . . .

"All right, Mother, prepare to accept memory core download from *Dahak*."

"Ready," Mother said instantly.

"Dahak, initiate core download but do not purge."

"Initiating," Dahak replied calmly, and Colin felt an incredible surge of data. He caught only the fringes of it through his feed, but it was like standing on the brink of a river in flood. It was almost frightening, making him suddenly and humbly aware of the storage limitations of a human brain, yet for all its titanic proportions, it took barely ten minutes to complete.

"Download completed," Mother announced. "Data stored."

"Excellent! Now, give me a report on Fleet status."

"Fleet Central authorization code required," Mother told him, and Colin frowned as his enthusiasm was checked abruptly. He didn't *know* the authorization codes.

He pulled on the end of his nose, thinking hard. Only Mother "herself" could give him the codes, and the one absolute certainty was that she wouldn't. She accepted him as a senior fleet captain, which entitled him to a certain authority in areas pertaining to his own command but did *not* entitle him to access the material he desperately needed. Which was all the more maddening because he'd become used to instant information flow from Dahak.

Well, now, why did he have that information from Dahak? Because he was Dahak's commander. And how had he become the CO? Because authority devolved on the senior crew member present and Dahak had chosen to regard a primitive from Earth as a member of his crew. Which suggested one possible approach.

To his surprise, he shrank from it. But why? He'd

learned to accept his persona as *Dahak*'s captain and even as Governor of Earth, so why did this bother him?

Because, he thought, this brightly lit mausoleum whispered too eloquently of power and crushing responsibility, and it frightened him. Which was foolish in someone who'd already been made to accept responsibility for the very survival of his race, but nonetheless real.

He shook himself. The Empire was dead. All that could remain were other artifacts like Mother, and he needed any of those he could lay hands on. Even if that meant assuming command of a long-abandoned headquarters crewed only by ghosts and computers.

He only wished it didn't feel so . . . impious.

"Mother," he said finally.

"Yes, Senior Fleet Captain?" the computer replied, and he spoke very slowly and carefully.

"On this day, I, Senior Fleet Captain Colin MacIntyre, commanding officer" — he remembered the designation Fleet Central had tacked onto *Dahak* — "HIMP *Dahak*, do, as senior Battle Fleet officer present, pursuant to Fleet Regulation Five-Three-Three, Section Niner-One, Article Ten, assume command of Fl—"

"Invalid authorization," Mother interrupted.

"What?" Colin blinked in surprise.

"Invalid authorization," Mother repeated unhelpfully.

"What's invalid about it?" he demanded, unreasonably irritated at the delay now that he had steeled himself to it.

"Fleet Regulation Five-Three-Three does not pertain to transfer of command authority."

"It does so!" he shot back, but it was neither a question nor a command, and Mother remained silent. He gritted his teeth in frustration. "All right, if it doesn't pertain to transfer of command, what *does* it pertain to?"

"Regulation Five-Three-Three and subsections," Mother said precisely, "pertains to refuse disposal aboard Battle Fleet orbital bases."

"*What?!*"

Colin glared at the console. Of *course* Reg Five-Three-

Three referred to transfer of command! It was how Dahak had mousetrapped him into this entire absurdity! He'd read it for himself when he —

Understanding struck. Yes, he'd read it — in a collection of regulations written fifty-one millennia ago.

Damn.

"Please download current Fleet Regulations and all relevant data to my command."

"Acknowledged. Download beginning. Download completed," Mother said almost without pause, and Colin reactivated his com.

"Dahak?"

"Yes, Captain?"

"I need some help here. What regulation replaced Five-Three-Three?"

"Fleet Regulation Five-Three-Three has been superseded by Fleet Regulation One-Niner-One-Five-Seven-Three-Niner, sir."

Colin winced. For seven thousand years, the Imperium had managed to hold Fleet regulations to under three thousand main entries; apparently the Empire had discovered the joys of bureaucracy.

No wonder Mother had so much memory.

"Thank you," he said, preparing to turn his attention back to Mother, but Dahak stopped him.

"A moment, Captain. Is it your intent to use this regulation to assume command of Fleet Central?"

"Of course it is," Colin said testily.

"I would advise against it."

"Why?"

"Because it will result in your immediate execution."

"What?" Colin asked faintly, certain he hadn't heard correctly.

"The attempt will result in your execution, sir. Regulation One-Niner-One-Five-Seven-Three-Niner does not apply to Fleet Central."

"Why not? It's a unit of Battle Fleet."

"That," Dahak said surprisingly, "is no longer true. Fleet Central *is* Battle Fleet; all units of Battle Fleet are subordinate to it. Battle Fleet command officers are not promoted to Fleet Central command duties."

"Then where the hell does its command staff come from?"

"They are *drawn* from Battle Fleet; they are not *promoted* from it. Fleet Central command officers are selected by the Emperor from all Battle Fleet flag officers and serve solely at his pleasure. Any attempt to assume command other than by direction of the Emperor is high treason and punishable by death."

Colin went white as he realized only Mother's interruption to correct an incorrect regulation number had saved his life.

He shuddered. What other tripwires were buried inside Fleet Central? Damn it, why couldn't Mother be smart enough to *tell* him things like this?!

Because, a small, calm voice told him, she hadn't been designed to be.

Which was all very well, but if he couldn't assume command, Mother wouldn't tell him the things he had to know, and if he tried to assume command, she'd kill him on the spot!

"Dahak," he said finally, "find me an answer. I've *got* to be able to exercise command authority here, or we might as well not have come."

"Fleet Central command authority lies in the exclusive grant of the Emperor, Captain. There is no other way to obtain it."

"Goddamn it, there *isn't* any emperor!" Colin half-shouted, battling incipient hysteria as he felt the situation crumbling in his hands. All he needed was for Dahak to catch Mother's lunatic literal-mindedness! "Look, can you invade the core programming? Redirect it?"

"The attempt would result in *Dahak*'s destruction," the computer told him. "In addition, it would fail. Fleet Central's core programming contains certain imperatives, of which this is one, which may not be reprogrammed even on the Emperor's authority."

"That's insane," Colin said flatly. "My God, a computer you can't reprogram running your entire military establishment?!"

"I did not say all reprogramming was impossible, nor do I understand why these particular portions cannot be altered. I am not privy to the content of the imperatives or the reasons for them. I base my statement on technical data included in the material downloaded to me."

"But how the hell *can* anything be unalterable? Couldn't you simply shut the thing down, dump its entire memory, and reprogram from scratch?"

"Negative, sir. The imperatives are not embodied in software. In Terran parlance, they are 'hard-wired' into the system. Removal would require actual destruction of a sizable portion of the central computer core."

"Crap." Colin pondered a moment longer, then widened the focus of his com link. "Vlad? 'Tanni? Have you been listening in on this?"

"Aye, Colin," Jiltanith replied.

"Any ideas?"

"T'faith, none do spring to mind," his wife said. "Vlad? Hast some insight which might aid our need?"

"I fear not," Chernikov said. "I am currently viewing the technical data Dahak refers to, Captain. So far as I can tell, his analysis is correct. To alter this would require a complete shutdown of Fleet Central. Even assuming 'Mother' would permit it, the required physical destruction would cripple Comp Cent and destroy the data we require. In my opinion, the system was designed precisely to preclude the very possibility you have suggested."

"Goddamn better mousetrap-builders!" Colin muttered, and Chernikov stifled a laugh. It made Colin feel obscurely better . . . but only a little.

"Dahak," he said finally, "can *you* access the data we need?"

"Negative."

"And you can't think of any way to sneak around these damned imperatives?"

"Negative."

"Then we're SOL, people," Colin sighed, slumping back in his couch, his sense of defeat even more bitter after the glow of victory he'd felt such a short time before. "Damn it. *Damn* it! We need an emperor to get into the goddamned system, and the last emperor died forty-five thousand years ago!"

"Captain," Dahak said after a moment, "I believe there might be a way."

"What?" Colin jerked back upright. "You just said there wasn't one!"

"Inaccurate. I said there was no way to 'sneak around these damned imperatives,' " the computer replied precisely. "There may, however, be a way in which you can use them, instead. I point out, however, that —"

"A way to *use* them? *How?!*"

"Under Case Omega, sir, you can —"

"I can take control of Fleet Central?" Colin broke in on him.

"Affirmative. Under the circumstances, you may be considered the highest ranking officer of Battle Fleet and, in your capacity as Governor of Earth, the senior civil official, as well. As such, you may instruct Fleet Central to implement Case Omega, so assuming —"

"Great, Dahak!" Colin said. "I'll get back to you in a minute." Hot damn! He found himself actually rubbing his hands in glee.

"But, Captain —" Dahak said.

"In a minute, Dahak. In a minute." Elation boiled deep within him, a terrible, wonderful elation, compounded by the emotional whipsaw which had just ravaged him. "Mother," he said.

"Yes, Senior Fleet Captain Colinmacintyre?"

"Colin," Dahak said again, "there are —"

"Mother," Colin said firmly, rushing himself before whatever Dahak was trying to tell him could undercut his determination, "implement Case Omega."

There was a moment of profound silence, and then

Hell itself erupted. Colin cringed back into his couch, hands rising to cover his eyes as Command Alpha exploded with light. A bolt of pain shot through his left arm as a bio-probe of pure force snipped away a scrap of tissue, but it was tiny compared to the fury boiling into his brain through his neural feed. A clumsy hand thrust deep inside him, flooding through his implants to wrench a gestalt of his very being from him. For one terrible moment he *was* Fleet Central, writhing in torment as his merely mortal brain and the ancient, bottomless computers of Battle Fleet merged, impressing their identities imperishably upon one another.

Colin screamed in the grip of an agony too vast to endure, and yet it was over before he could truly experience it. Its echoes shuddered away down his synapses, stuttering in the racing pound of his heart, and then they were gone.

"Case Omega executed," Mother said emotionlessly. "The Emperor is dead; long live the Emperor!"

Chapter Thirteen

"I attempted to warn you, Colin," Dahak said softly.

Colin shuddered. *Emperor?* That was . . . was . . . Words failed. He couldn't think of any that even came close.

"Colin?" Jiltanith's voice was gentler than Dahak's, and far more anxious.

"Yes, 'Tanni?" he managed in a strangled croak.

"How dost thou, my love? We did hear thee scream. Art thou — ?"

"I-I'm fine, 'Tanni," he said, and, physically, it was true. He cleared his throat. "There were a few rough moments, but I'm okay now. Honest."

"May I not come to thee?" She sounded less anxious — but not a lot.

"I'd like that," he said, and he had never spoken more sincerely in his life. Then he shook his head. "Wait. Let me make sure it's safe."

He gathered himself and raised his voice.

"Mother?"

"Yes, Your Imperial Majesty?" the voice replied, and he flinched.

167

"Mother, I'd like one of my officers to join me. Her implant signatures won't be in your data base either. Can you have Security pass her through?"

"If Your Imperial Majesty so instructs," Mother responded.

"My Imperial Majesty certainly does," Colin said, and smiled crookedly. Maybe he wasn't going to crack up entirely, after all.

"Query: please identify the officer to be admitted."

"Uh? Oh. Fleet Captain Jiltanith, *Dahak's* executive officer. My wife."

"Acknowledged."

"'Tanni?" he returned his attention to his com. "Come ahead."

"I come, my love," she said, and he stretched out in his couch, knowing she would soon be there. His shudders drained outward along his limbs until the final echoes tingled in his fingers and his breathing slowed.

"Mother."

"Yes, Your Imperial Majesty?"

"What was all that? What happened when you executed Case Omega, I mean?"

"Emergency subroutines were terminated, ending Fleet Central's caretaker role upon Your Imperial Majesty's assumption of the throne."

"I figured that part out. I want a specific explanation of what *you* did."

"Fleet Central performed its function as guardian of the succession, Your Imperial Majesty. As senior Fleet officer and civil official listed in Fleet Central's data base, Your Imperial Majesty, as per the Great Charter, became the proper successor upon the demise of the previous dynasty. However, Your Imperial Majesty was unknown to Fleet Central prior to Your Imperial Majesty's accession. It was therefore necessary for Fleet Central to obtain gene samples for verification of the heirs of Your Imperial Majesty's body and to evaluate Your Imperial Majesty's gestalt and implant it upon Fleet Central's primary data cortex."

Colin frowned. There were too many things here he didn't yet understand, but there were a few others to get straight right now.

"Mother, can't we do something about the titles?"

"Query not understood, Your Imperial Majesty."

"I mean — Look, just what titles have I saddled myself with?"

"Your principle title is 'His Imperial Majesty Colinmacintyre the First, Grand Duke of Birhat, Prince of Bia, Warlord and Prince Protector of the Realm, Defender of the Five Thousand Suns, Champion of Humanity, and, by the Maker's Grace, Emperor of Mankind.' Secondary titles are: 'Prince of Aalat,' 'Prince of Achon,' 'Prince of Anhur,' 'Prince of Apnar,' 'Prince of Ardat,' 'Prince of Aslah,' 'Prince of Avan,' 'Prince of Bachan,' 'Prince of Badarchin,' 'Prin—'"

"Stop," Colin commanded. Jesus! "Uh, just how many titles are there?"

"Excluding those already specified," Mother replied, "four thousand eight hundred and twenty-one."

"Gaaa." Not bad for the product of a good, republican upbringing, he thought. "Let's get one thing straight, Mother. My name is Colin MacIntyre — two words — not 'Colinmacintyre.' Can you remember that in future?"

"You are listed in Fleet and Imperial records as His Imperial Majesty Colinmacintyre the First, Grand Duke of Birhat, Prince of Bia, War —"

"I understand all that," Colin interrupted. "The point is, I don't want to go around with everyone 'Imperial Majesty'-ing me, and I prefer to be called 'Colin,' not 'Colinmacintyre.' Can't we do something to meet my wishes?"

"As Your Imperial Majesty commands. You have not yet designated your choice of reign name. Until such time as you have done so, you will be known as Colinmacintyre the First; thereafter, only your dynasty will bear your complete pre-accession name. Is that satisfactory?"

"It's a start," Colin muttered, refusing to contemplate

the thought of his "dynasty." He tugged on his nose, then stopped himself. At the rate surprises were coming at him lately, he was going to start looking like Pinocchio. "All right. My 'reign name' will be 'Colin.' Please log it."

"Logged," Mother replied.

"Now, about those titles. Surely past emperors didn't get called 'Your Imperial Majesty' every time they turned around, did they?"

"Acceptable alternatives are 'Your Majesty,' 'Majesty,' 'Highest,' and 'Sire.' Nobles of the rank of Planetary Duke are permitted 'My Lord.' Flag officers and Companions of the Golden Nova are permitted 'Warlord.'"

"Crap. Uh, I don't suppose I could get you to forget titles entirely?"

"Negative, Your Imperial Majesty. Protocol imperatives must be observed."

"That's what *you* think," Colin muttered. "Just wait till I get my hands on your 'protocol' programming!" He shook his head. "All right, if I'm stuck with it, I'm stuck, but from now on you'll use only 'Sire' when addressing me."

"Acknowledged."

"Good! Now —" He broke off as a soft chime sounded.

"Your pardon, Sire. Empress Jiltanith has arrived. Shall I admit her?"

"You certainly shall!" Colin leapt down the steps from the dais and reached the innermost hatch by the time it opened. Jiltanith gasped as his embrace threatened to pop her bioenhanced ribs, and her cheek was wet where it pressed against his.

"Am I ever glad to see *you!*" he whispered against the side of her neck.

"And I thee." She turned her head to kiss his ear. "Greatly did I fear for thee, yet such timorousness ill beseemed one who knoweth thee so well. Hast more lives than any cat, my sweet, yet 'twould please me the better if thou wouldst spend them less freely!"

"Goddamn right," he said fervently, drawing back to kiss her mouth. "Next time, I listen to you, by God!"

"So thou sayst . . . now," she laughed, tugging on his prominent ears with both hands.

A sudden thought woke a mischievous smile as he tucked an arm around her waist to escort her back to the dais, and he raised his voice.

"Mother, say hello to my wife."

"Hello, Your Imperial Majesty," Mother said obediently, and Jiltanith stopped dead.

"What foolishness is this?" she demanded.

"Get used to it, honey," Colin said, squeezing her again. "For whatever it's worth, your shiftless husband's brought home the bacon this time." He grinned wryly. "In spades!"

Several hours later, a far less chipper Colin groaned and scrubbed his face with his hands. Jiltanith and he sat side-by-side on Fleet Central's command couch while Mother reported Battle Fleet's status, running down every fleet and sub-unit in numerical order. So far, she'd provided reports on just under two thousand fleets, task forces, and battle squadrons.

And, so far, nothing she'd had to report was good.

"Hold report, Mother," he said, breaking into the computer's flow.

"Holding, Sire," Mother agreed, and Colin laughed hollowly. "Emperor" — that was a laugh. And "Warlord" was even funnier. He was a commander without a fleet! Or, more precisely, with a fleet that was useless to him.

The Empire had been too busy dying for an orderly shutdown. Herdan XXIV had lived long enough to activate Fleet Central's emergency subroutines, placing Mother on powered-down standby to guard Birhat until relief might someday arrive, but most of Battle Fleet hadn't been even that lucky. A few score supralight vessels had simply disappeared from Fleet Central's records, which probably indicated that their crews had elected to flee in an effort to outrun the bio-weapon, but most of Battle Fleet's units had been contaminated in their efforts to save civilians in the weapon's path. The result had been both predictable and grisly, and, unlike *Dahak*, their computers hadn't been smart enough to do anything about it when they found themselves without crews. Except for a handful whose core taps had been active when their last crewmen died, they'd simply returned to the nearest Fleet base and remained on station until their fusion plants exhausted their on-board mass, then drifted without life or power.

Unfortunately, none seemed to have returned to Bia itself — which made sense, given that Birhat, the first victim of the bio-weapon, had been quarantined at the very start of the Empire's death agony. Less than a dozen active units had responded to Mother's all-ships hypercom rally signal, and the nearest was upwards of eight hundred light-years away; Earth would be dead long before Colin could return if he waited for them them to reach Birhat.

There was a bitter irony in the fact that Birhat's defenses remained almost fully operational. Bia's mammoth shield, backed by Perimeter Security's prodigious firepower, could have held anything *anyone* could throw at them. But everyone who needed defending was on Earth.

"Mother," he said finally, "let's try something different. Instead of reporting in sequence, list all mobile forces in order of proximity to Birhat."

"Acknowledged. Listing Bia System deployments. Birhat Near-Orbit Watch Squadron: twelve heavy cruisers. Bia Deep-System Patrol Squadron: ten heavy cruisers, forty-one destroyers, nine frigates, sixty-two corvettes. Imperial Guard Flotilla: fifty-two *Asgerd*-class planetoids, sixteen —"

"*What?* Stop!" Colin shouted.

"Acknowledged," Mother said calmly.

"What the fuck is the Imperial Guard Flotilla?!"

"Imperial Guard Flotilla," Mother replied. "The Warlord's personal command. Strength: fifty-two *Asgerd*-class planetoids and attached parasites, sixteen *Trosan*-class planetoids and attached parasites, and ten *Vespa*-class assault planetoids and attached planetary assault craft. Current location: parking orbit thirty-eight light-minutes from Bia. Status: inactive."

"Jesus H. Christ!" Colin stared at Jiltanith. Her face was as shocked as his own, and they turned as one to glare accusingly at the console.

"Why," Colin asked in a dangerously calm voice, "didn't you mention them earlier?"

"Sire, you had not asked about them," Mother said.

"I certainly did! I asked for a complete listing of Battle Fleet units!" Mother was silent, and he growled a curse at all computers which could not recognize the need to respond without specific cues. "Didn't I?" he snarled.

"You did, Sire."

"Then why didn't you report them?"

"I did, Sire."

"But you didn't report this Imperial Guard Flotilla —" Flotilla! Jesus, it was a *fleet*! "— did you? Why not?"

"Sire, the Imperial Guard is not part of Battle Fleet. The Imperial Guard is raised and manned solely from the Emperor's personal demesne."

Colin blinked. Personal demesne? An Emperor whose personal fiefdoms could raise *that* kind of firepower? The thought sent a shiver down his spine. He sagged back, trembling, and a warm arm crept about him and tightened.

"All right." He shook his head and inhaled deeply, drawing strength from Jiltanith's presence. "Why is the Guard Flotilla inactive?"

"Power exhaustion and uncontrolled shutdown, Sire."

"Assess probability of successful reactivation."

"One hundred percent," Mother said emotionlessly, and a jolt of excitement crashed through him. But slowly, he told himself. Slowly.

"Assume resources of one hundred seven thousand Battle Fleet personnel, one *Utu*-class planetoid, and current active and inactive automated support available in the Bia System," he said carefully, "and compute probable time required to reactivate the Imperial Guard Flotilla to full combat readiness."

"Impossible to reactivate to full combat readiness,"

Mother replied. "Specified personnel inadequate for crews."

"Then compute time to reactivate to *limited* combat readiness."

"Computing, Sire," Mother responded, and fell silent for a disturbingly long period. Almost a full minute passed before she spoke again. "Computation complete. Probable time required: four-point-three-nine months. Margin of error twenty-point-seven percent owing to large numbers of imponderables."

Colin closed his eyes and felt Jiltanith tremble against him. Four months — five-and-a-half outside. It would be close, but they could do it. By all that was holy, they could *do* it!

"There," Tamman said quietly as a green circle bloomed on *Dahak's* visual display, ringing a tiny, gleaming dot. The dot grew as *Dahak* approached, and additional dots appeared, spreading out in a loose necklace of worldlets.

"I see them," Colin replied, still luxuriating in his return to Command One and a world he understood. "Big bastards, aren't they, Dahak?"

"I compute that the largest out-mass *Dahak* by over twenty-five percent. I am not prepared to speculate upon the legitimacy of their parentage."

Colin chuckled. Dahak had been much more willing to engage in informality since his return from Fleet Central, as if he recognized Colin's shock at suddenly finding himself an emperor. Or perhaps the computer was simply glad to have him back. Dahak was a worrier where friends were concerned.

He watched the planetoids grow. If Vlad was right about the Empire's technology, those ships would be monsters in action — and monsters were exactly what they needed.

"Captain, look here." Ellen Gregory, Sarah Meir's Assistant Astrogator, placed a sighting circle of her own on the display, picking out a single starship. "What do you make of that, sir?"

Colin looked, then looked again. The stupendous sphere floating in space was only roughly similar to the only Imperial planetoid he'd ever seen, but one thing was utterly familiar. A vast, three-headed dragon spread its wings across the gleaming hull.

"Well, looky there," he murmured. "Dahak, what d'*you* make of that?"

"According to the data Fleet Central downloaded to my data base," Dahak replied, "that is His Imperial Majesty's Planetoid *Dahak*, Hull Number Seven-Three-Six-Four-Four-Eight-Niner-Two-Five."

"Another *Dahak*?"

"It is a proud name in Battle Fleet." Dahak sounded a bit miffed. "Rather like the many ships named *Enterprise* in your own United States Navy. According to the data, this is the twenty-third ship to bear the name."

"It is, huh? Well, which one are you?"

"This unit is the eleventh of the name."

"I see. Well, in order to avoid confusion, we'll just refer to this young whippersnapper as *Dahak Two*, if that's all right with you, Dahak."

"Noted," Dahak said calmly, and continued to close on the silently waiting, millennia-dead hulls they intended to resurrect.

"By the Maker, I've *got* it!"

Colin jumped half out of his couch as Cohanna's holo image materialized on Command One. The biosciences officer looked terrible, her hair awry and her uniform wrinkled, but her eyes were bright with triumph.

"Try penicillin," he advised sourly, and she looked blank, then grinned.

"Sorry, sir. I meant I've figured out what happened on Birhat — why it's got that incredible biosystem. I found it in Mother's data base."

"Oh?" Colin sat straighter, his eyes more intent. "Give!"

· "It's simple, really. The zoos — the Imperial Family's zoos."

"Zoos?" It was Colin's turn to look blank.

"Yes. You see, the Imperial Family had an immense zoological garden. Over thirty different planets' flora and fauna in sealed, self-sufficient planetary habitats. Apparently, they lasted out the plague. I'd guess the automated systems responsible for restraining plant growth failed first in one of them, and the thing cracked. Once it did, its inhabitants could get out, and the same vegetation attacked the exterior of other surviving habitats. Over the years, still more oxy-nitrogen habitats were opened up and started spreading to reclaim the planet. That's why we've got such a screwy damned ecology. We're looking at the survivors of a dozen *different* planetary biospheres after forty-five thousand years of natural selection!"

"Well, I'll be damned," Colin mused. "Good work, Cohanna. I'm impressed you could keep concentrating on that kind of problem at a time like this."

"Time like this?"

"While we're making our final approach to the Imperial Guard," Colin said, raising his eyebrows, and Cohanna wrinkled her nose.

"What's an Imperial Guard?"

Vlad Chernikov shuddered as he and Baltan floated down the lifeless, lightless transit shaft. This, he thought, is what *Dahak* would have become if Anu had succeeded all those years ago.

It was depressing in more ways than one. Actually seeing this desolation gnawed away at the confidence that anything could be done about it, and even if he succeeded in rejecting the counsel of despair, he could see it would be a horrific task. Dead power rooms, exhausted fuel mass, control rooms and circuit runs which had never been properly stasissed when the ship died. There was even meteor damage, for the collision shields had died with everything else. One of the planetoids might well be beyond repair, judging by the huge hole punched into its south pole.

Still, he reminded himself, everyone had his or her own problems. Caitrin O'Rourke was practically in tears over the hydroponic farms, and Geran was furious to find so much perfectly good equipment left out of stasis. But Tamman was probably the most afflicted of all, for the magazines had been left without stasis, as well, and the containment fields on every antimatter weapon had failed. At least the warhead fail-safes had worked as designed and rotated them into hyper as the fields went down, but huge chunks of magazine bulkheads had gone with them. Of course, if they *hadn't* worked . . .

He shuddered again, concentrating on the grav sled he and Baltan rode. It was far slower than an operable transit shaft, but they dared not use even its full speed. They were no transit computer to whip around unexpected bends in the system!

He craned his neck, reading the lettering above a hatch. Gamma-One-One-Nine-One-One. According to Dahak's downloaded schematics, they were getting close to Engineering.

So they were. He tapped Baltan's shoulder and pointed, and the commander nodded inside the force bubble of his helmet. The sled angled for the side of the shaft and nudged against the hatch — which, of course, stayed firmly shut.

Chernikov smothered a curse, then grinned as he recalled Colin's account of his "coronation." The Captain — Emperor! — had exhausted the entire crew's allocation of profanity for at least a month, by Chernikov's estimate. He chuckled at the thought and climbed off the sled, dragging a cable from its power plant behind him and muttering Slavic maledictions. No power meant no artificial gravity, which — unfortunately — did not mean *no* gravity. A planetoid generated an impressive grav field all its own, and turned bulkheads into decks and decks into bulkheads when the power failed.

He found the emergency power receptacle and plugged in, and the hatch slid open. He waved, and Baltan ghosted the sled inside, angling its powerful lamps to pick out the emergency lighting system.

Chernikov did some more cable-dragging and, after propitiating Murphy with a few curses, brought it alive. Light bathed Central Engineering, and the two engineers began to explore.

The long-dead core tap drew them like a magnet, and Chernikov felt a tingle of awe as his eyes and implants traced circuit runs and control systems. This thing was at least five times as powerful as *Dahak's*, and he wouldn't have believed it could be without seeing it. But what in the galaxy could they have *needed* that much power for? Even allowing for the more powerful energy armament and shield, there had to be some other reason —

His thoughts died as his implants followed a massive power shunt which shouldn't have been there. He clambered over a control panel which had become the floor, slightly vertiginous as he tried to orient himself, then gasped.

"Baltan! Look at this!"

"I know," his assistant said softly, approaching from the far side. "I've been following the control runs."

"Can you *believe* this?"

"Does it matter? And it would certainly explain all the power demand."

"True." Chernikov moved a few more yards, examining his find carefully, then shook his head. "I must tell the Captain about this."

He keyed his com implant, and Colin answered a moment later, sounding a bit harassed — not surprisingly, considering that every other search party must be finding marvels of its own to report.

"Captain, I am in *Mairsuk's* Central Engineering, and you would not believe what I am looking at."

"Try me," Colin said wearily. "I'm learning to believe nineteen impossible things before breakfast every day."

"Very well, here is number twenty. This ship has both Enchanach *and* hyper capability."

There was a pregnant pause.

"What," Colin finally asked very carefully, "did you say?"

"I said, sir, that we have here both an Enchanach and a hyper drive, engineered down to a size that fits both into a single hull. I am not yet positive, but I would judge that the combined mass of both units is less than that of *Dahak's* Enchanach Drive, alone."

"Great day in the morning," Colin muttered. Then, "All right. Take a good look, then get back over here. We're having an all-departments meeting in four hours to discuss plans for reactivation."

"Understood," Chernikov said, and broke the connection. He and Baltan exchanged eloquent shrugs and bent back to the study of their prize.

" . . . can't be specific until we've got the computers back up and run a complete inventory," Geran said, "but about ten percent of all spares required controlled condition storage. Without that —" He shrugged.

Most of Colin's department heads were present in the flesh, but a sizable force from the recon group was prowling around other installations, and Hector MacMahan and Ninhursag attended via holo image from the battleship *Osir's* command deck. Now all eyes, physical and holographic alike, swiveled to Colin.

"All right." He spoke quietly, leaning his forearms on the crystalline tabletop to return their gazes. "Bottom line. Mother's time estimate is based on sixteen-hour shifts for every man and woman after we put at least one automated repair yard back on line. According to the reports from Hector's people, we can probably do that, but I expect to find ourselves pushing closer to twenty-hour shifts by the time we're done. We *could* increase the odds and decrease the workload by concentrating on a dozen or so units. I'm sure that's going to occur to a lot of people in the next few weeks. However —" his eyes circled their faces "— we aren't going to do it that way. We need as many of these ships as we can get, and, ladies and gentlemen, I mean to have *every single one of them*."

There was a sound like a soft gasp, and he smiled grimly.

"God only knows how hard they're working back on Earth, but *we're* about to make up for our nice vacation on the trip out. Every one of them, people. No exceptions. We will leave this system no later than five months from today, and the entire Imperial Guard Flotilla will go with us when we do."

"But, sir," Chernikov said, "we may ask for too much and lose it all. I do not fear hard work, but we have only a finite supply of personnel. A *very* finite supply."

"I understand, Vlad, but the decision is not negotiable. We've got highly motivated, highly capable people aboard this ship. I feel certain they'll understand and give of their very best. If not, however, tell them this.

"I'll be working my ass off right beside them, but that doesn't mean I won't be keeping tabs on what *they're* doing. And, people, if I catch anyone shirking, I'm going to be the worst nightmare he ever had."

His smile was grim, but even its micrometric amusement looked out of place on his rock-hard face.

"Tell them they can *depend* on that," he finished very, very softly.

Book Two

BOOK TWO

Chapter Fourteen

Assistant Servant of Thunders Brashieel of the Nest of Aku'Ultan folded all four legs under him on his duty pad as he bent his long-snouted head, considering his panel, and slid both hands into the control gloves. Eight fingers and four thumbs twitched, activating each test circuit in turn, and he noted the results cheerfully. He had not had a major malfunction in three twelves of twelve watches.

Equipment tests completed, he checked *Vindicator's* position. It was purely automatic, for there could be no change. Once a vessel entered hyper space it remained there, impotent but inviolate, until it reached the preselected coordinates and emerged into normal space once more.

Brashieel did not understand those mysteries particularly well, for he was no lord — not even of thunders, much less of star-faring — but because Small Lord of Order Hantorg was a good lord, he had made certain *Vindicator's* nestlings all knew whither they were bound. Another yellow sun, this one with nine planets. Once it had boasted ten, but that had been before the visit of Great

Lord Vaskeel's fleet untold high twelves of years before. Now it was time to return, and *Vindicator* and his brothers would sweep through it like the Breath of Tarhish, trampling the nest-killers under hooves of flame.

It was well. The Protectors of the Nest would feed their foes to Tarhish's Fire, and the Nest would be safe forever.

"Outer perimeter tracking confirms hyper wakes approaching from galactic east," Sir Frederick Amesbury said.

Gerald Hatcher nodded without even looking up. His neural feed hummed with readiness reports, and his eyes were unfocused.

"Got an emergence locus and ETA, Frederick?"

"It's bloody rough, but Plotting's calling it fifty light-minutes and forty-five degrees above the ecliptic. Judging from the wake strength, the buggers should be arriving in about twelve hours. Tracking promises to firm that up in the next two hours."

"Fine." Hatcher acknowledged the last report and blinked back into focus, wishing yet again that *Dahak* had returned. If Colin MacIntyre had been gone this long, it meant he hadn't found aid at Sheskar and must have decided he had no choice but to hope Earth could hold without him while he sought it elsewhere. And that he might not be back for another full year.

He activated his com panel, and Horus's taut face appeared instantly.

"Governor," the general reported, knowing full well that Horus already knew what he was about to say and that he was speaking for the record, "I have to report that I have placed our forces on Red Two. Hyper wakes presumed to be hostile have been detected. ETA is approximately" — he checked the time through his neural feed — "seventeen-thirty hours, Zulu. System defense forces are now on full alert. Civil defense procedures have been initiated. All PDC and ODC commanders are in the net. Interceptor squadrons are at two-hour readiness.

Planetary shield generators and planetary core tap are at standby readiness. Battle Squadrons One and Four are within thirty minutes of projected n-space emergence; Squadrons Two and Six should rendezvous with them by oh-seven-hundred Zulu. Squadrons Three, Five, Seven, Eight, Nine, and Ten, with escorts, are being held in-system as per Plan Able-One.

"Have you any instructions at this time, Governor?"

"Negative, General Hatcher. Please keep me informed."

"I will, sir."

"Good luck, Gerald," Horus said softly, his tone much less formal.

"Thanks, Horus. We'll try to make a little luck of our own."

The screen blanked, and Gerald Hatcher turned back to his console.

Assistant Servant Brashieel checked his chronometer. Barely four day twelfths until emergence, and tension was high in *Vindicator*, for this was the Demon Sector. It was not often the Protectors of the Nest encountered a foe with an advanced technical base — that was why they came, to crush the nest-killers before they armed themselves — but five of the last twelve Great Visits to this sector had been savaged. They had triumphed, but at great cost, and the last two had been the most terrible of all. Perhaps, Brashieel thought, that was the reason Great Lord Tharno's Great Visit had been delayed: to amass the strength the Nest required for certain success.

That alone was cause enough for concern, yet the disquiet among his nestmates had grown far worse since the first nest-killer scanner stations had been detected. More than one scout ship had been lured to his death by the fiendish stations, and the explosions which slew them meant their surviving consorts had learned absolutely nothing about the technology which built those stations . . . except that it was advanced, indeed.

But this star system would offer no threat. Small Lord Hantorg had revealed the latest data scan shortly after *Vindicator* entered hyper for this last jump to the target. It was barely three twelves of years old, and though electronic and neutrino emissions had been detected (which was bad enough), there had been none of the more advanced signals from the scanner arrays. Clearly the Protectors must see to this threat, yet these nest-killers would have only the lesser thunder, not the greater, and they would be crushed. Nothing could have changed enough in so short a time to alter that outcome.

Captain Adrienne Robbins sat in her command couch aboard the sublight battleship *Nergal*. Admiral Isaiah Hawter, the senior member of the Solarian Defense Force actually in space, rode *Nergal*'s bridge with her, but he might as well have been on another planet. His attention was buried in his own console as he and his staff controlled Task Force One.

Captain Robbins had been a sub-driver, and she'd never expected to command any flagship (subs still operated solo, after all), far less one leading the defense of her world against homicidal aliens, but she was ready. She felt the tension simmering within her and adjusted her adrenalin levels, pacing her energy. The bastards would be coming out of hyper in less than two hours, and tracking had them pegged to a fare-thee-well. TF One knew where to find them; now all they had to do was wreck as many as they could before the buggers micro-jumped back out on them.

And, she reminded herself, pray that these Achuultani hadn't upgraded their technology too terribly in the last sixty thousand years or so.

She did pray, but she also remembered her mother's favorite aphorism: God helps those who help themselves.

"Task Force in position for Charlie-Three."

"Thank you," Hatcher said absently.

The images of Marshals Tsien and Chernikov shared his

com screen with Generals Amesbury, Singhman, Tama, and Ki. Chiang Chien-su had a screen all to himself as he waited tensely in his civil defense HQ, and Hatcher could see the control room of PDC Huan Ti behind Tsien. The marshal had made it his HQ for the Eastern Hemisphere Defense Command, and a brief flicker of shared memory flashed between them as their eyes met. Tama and Ki sat in their Fighter Command operations rooms, and Singhman was aboard ODC Seven, serving as Hawter's second-in-command as well as commanding the orbital fortifications.

"Gentlemen, they'll emerge in thirty minutes, well inside our own heavy hyper missile range of a planetary target, so I want the shield brought to maximum power. Keep this com link open." Heads nodded. "Very well, Marshal Chernikov; activate core tap."

Lieutenant Andrew Samson winced as the backlash echoed in his missile targeting systems. ODC Fifteen, known to her crew as the Iron Bitch, floated in orbit above Tierra del Fuego. Which, Samson now discovered, was entirely too close to Antarctica for his peace of mind.

He adjusted his systems, edging away from the core tap's hyper bands, and sighed with relief. Maybe it wouldn't be so bad, after all, but that was one hell of a jump from the test runs! God help us all if they lose it, he prayed — and not just because of what it'll do to the Bitch's power curves.

Howling wind and flying ice spicules flayed a night-struck land. The kiss of that wind was death, its frigid embrace lethal. There was no life here. There was only the cold, the keening dirge of the wind, and the ice.

But the frigid night was peeled back in an instant of fiery annunciation. A raging column of energy, pent by invisible chains, impaled the heavens, glittering and terrible as it pierced the low-bellied clouds.

The beacon of war had been lit, and its fury flowed into

the mighty fold-space power transmitters. Man returned Prometheus's gift to the heavens, and Earth's Orbital Defense Command drank deep at Vassily Chernikov's fountain.

"Here they come, people," Captain Robbins said softly. "Stand by missile crews. Energy weapons to full power."

Acknowledgments flowed back through her neural feed, and she hunkered deeper into her couch without realizing she had.

Assistant Servant of Thunders Brashieel gave his instruments one last check, though there could be no danger here. They would pause only to select a proper asteroid, then be on their way, for there were many worlds of nest-killers to destroy. But he was a Protector. It was a point of pride to be prepared for anything.

My God, the size *of those things! They've got to be twenty kilometers long!*

The observation flared over the surface of Captain Robbins's brain, but beneath that surface trained reactions and responses flowed smoothly.

"Tactical, missiles on my command. Take target designation from the Flag." She paused a fraction of a second, letting the computers digest the latest updates from the admiral's staff while more monster starships emerged from hyper. Ship after cylindrical ship. Dozens of them. Scores. And still they came, popping into reality like demon djinn from a flask of curses.

"Fire!" she snapped.

Brashieel gaped at his readouts. *Those ships could not exist!*

But his panic eased — a bit — as he digested more data. There were but four twelves of them, and they were tiny things. Bigger than anyone had expected, with no right to be here, but no threat to *Vindicator* and his brothers.

He did not have time to note the full peculiarity of the energy readings before the enemy fired.

❖   ❖   ❖

Adrienne Robbins winced as the universe blew apart. She'd fired gravitonic and antimatter warheads before (the Fleet had significantly reduced the number of Sol's asteroids during firing practices) but never at a live target. The hyper missiles flicked up into hyper space, then back down, and their timing was impeccable. The Achuultani shields had not yet stabilized when the first mighty salvo arrived.

Brashieel cried out in shock, shaming himself before his nestmates, but he was not alone. What *were* those things?

A twelve of ships vanished in a heartbeat, and then another. His scanners told the tale, but he could not believe them. Those weapons were coming through hyper space! From such tiny vessels? Incredible!

He felt his folded legs tremble as those insignificant pygmies ravaged the lead squadrons. Ships died, blown apart in fireballs vast beyond belief, and others tumbled away, glowing, half-molten, more than half-destroyed by single hits. Such power! And those strange warheads — the ones which did not explode, but tore a ship apart in new and horrible ways. What were *they*?

But he was a Protector, and *Vindicator* had a reputation to uphold. His hands were rock-steady in the control gloves, arming his own weapons, and Small Lord Hantorg's furious voice pounded in his ears.

"Open fire!" the Small Lord snarled.

Adrienne Robbins made herself throttle her exultation. Sixty of the buggers in the opening salvo! They knew they'd been nudged, by God! But those had been the easy kills, the sitting ducks with unstable shields. Now her sensors felt those shields slamming into stability, and the first return fire spat towards TF One.

She opened her cross-feed to the electronic warfare types as decoys went out and jammers woke. She would have felt better with some idea of Achuultani capabilities before the engagement, but that was what this was all about. Task Force One was fighting for the data Earth needed to plan her own defense, and she studied the enemy shields. Pretty tough, but they damned well *should* be with the power reserves those monsters must have. Technically, they weren't as good as *Nergal's*; only the difference in power levels made them stronger. Which was all very well, but didn't change facts.

The first Achuultani missiles slashed in, and Captain Robbins got another surprise. They were normal-space weapons, but they were *fast* little mothers. Seventy, eighty percent light-speed, and that was better than anything of *Nergal's* could do in n-space. They were going to give missile defense fits.

Assistant Servant of Thunders Brashieel snarled as his first salvo smote the nest-killers. Half a twelve of missiles burst through all their defenses, ignoring their infernally effective decoys, and the Furnace roared. Matter and anti-matter merged, gouging at the nest-killers' shield, and Brashieel's inner eyelids narrowed at its incredible resistance. But his thunder was too much for it. It crumbled, and Tarhish's Breath swept the ship into death.

Captain Robbins cursed as *Bolivia* burned. Those fucking warheads were incredible! Their emission signatures said they were antimatter, and great, big, *nasty* ones. At least as big as anything Earth's defenders had.

Bolivia was the first to go, but *Canada* followed, then *Shirhan* and *Poland*. Please, Jesus, she prayed. Slow them down!

But the huge Achuultani ships were still dying faster than TF One. Which was only because they were getting in each other's way, perhaps, but true nonetheless, and Adrienne Robbins felt a fierce exultation as yet another fell to *Nergal's* missiles.

"Close the range," Admiral Hawter said grimly, and Adrienne acknowledged. *Nergal* drove into the teeth of the Achuultani fire.

"Stand by energy weapons," she said coldly.

❖ ❖ ❖

They were not fleeing. Whatever else these nest-killers might be, they had courage. More of them perished, blazing like splinters of resinous *mowap* wood, but the others advanced. And their defenses were improving. The efficiency of their jammers had gone up thirty percent while he watched.

Captain Robbins smiled thinly. Her EW crews were getting good, hard data on the Achuultani targeting systems, and they knew what to do with it. Another three ships were gone, but the others were really knocking down the incoming missiles now.

Whatever happened, that data would be priceless to the rest of the Fleet and to Earth herself. Not that Adrienne had any intention of dying out here, but it was nice to know.

Aha! Energy range.

Brashieel gaped as those preposterous warships opened a heavy energy fire. Tiny things like that *couldn't* pack in batteries that heavy!

But they did, and quarter-twelves of them synchronized their fire to the microsecond, slashing at their Aku'Ultan victims. Overload signals snarled, and frantic engineers threw more and more power to their shields, but there simply was not enough. Not to stop missiles and beams alike.

He watched in horror as *Avenger's* forward quadrant shields went down. A single nest-killer beam pierced the chink in his armor and ripped his forward twelfth apart. Hard as it was for any Protector to admit another race could match the Aku'Ultan, Brashieel knew the chilling truth. He had never heard of weapons which could do what that one was doing.

He groaned as *Avenger's* hull split like a rotten *istham*, and then another impossible, Tarhish-spawned warhead crumpled the wreckage into a mangled ball. *Avenger's* power plants let go, and *Vindicator*'s brother was no more.

But Brashieel bared his teeth as his display changed. Now the nest-killers would learn, for his hyper launchers had been given time to charge at last!

"Hyper missiles!" Tactical shouted, and Adrienne threw *Nergal* into evasive action. *Ireland* and *Izhmit* were less fortunate. *Ireland*'s shield stopped the first three; the next four — or five, or possibly six — got through. *Izhmit* went with the first shot. How the hell had they popped her shield that way?

It didn't matter. TF One was losing too many ships, but the Achuultani were dying at a three-to-one ratio even now. A hyper missile burst into n-space, exploding just outside the shield, shaking *Nergal* as a terrier shook a rat, but the shield held, and she and her ship were one. They closed in, energy weapons raving, and her own sublight missiles were going out now.

Great Lord Furtag was gone with his flagship, and command devolved upon Lord Chirdan. Chirdan was a fighter, but not blind. They were destroying the nest-killers, but his nestlings were dying in unreasonable numbers, for they had no weapon to equal those deadly beams. He could smash these defenders even at this low range, but only at the cost of too many of his own. He gave the order, and the scouts of the Aku'Ultan micro-jumped away.

The enemy vanished.

They shouldn't be able to do that, Adrienne Robbins thought. Not to just disappear that way. We should have detected the hyper field charging up on something that size, even for an itty-bitty micro-jump. But we didn't. Well, that's worth knowing. Won't help the bastards much when they get too far in-system to micro-jump, but it's going to be a bitch out here.

And the buggers can *fight*, she thought grimly, shaken by her readouts. Task Force One had gone in with forty-eight ships; it came out with twenty-one. The enemy had lost ten times that many, possibly more . . . but the enemy *had* more than ten times as many starships as Earth had battleships.

Admiral Hawter turned in-system. Magazines were down to sixty percent, thirty percent for hyper missiles, and half his survivors were damaged. If the enemy was willing to run, then so was he. He'd gotten the information Earth needed for analysis; now it was time to get his surviving people home.

The first clash was over, and humanity had won — if fifty-six percent losses could be called a victory. And both sides knew it could. The Aku'Ultan had lost a vastly lower percentage of their total force, but there came a point at which terms like "favorable rate of exchange" were meaningless.

Yet it was only the first clash, and both sides had learned much. It remained to be seen which would profit most from the lessons they had purchased with so much blood.

Chapter Fifteen

The great ringed planet of this accursed system floated far below him, but Lord of Order Chirdan had no eyes for its beauty as he watched his engineers prepare their final system tests.

The asteroids they had already hurled against the nest-killers' planetary shield had shown Battle Comp that small weapons would not penetrate, while those of sufficient mass were destroyed by the nest-killers' weapons before impact. They would continue to hurl asteroids against it, but only to force it back so that they might smite the fortresses with other thunders.

But *this*, Chirdan thought, was another matter. It would move slowly at first, but only at first, and it was large enough to mount shields which could stop even the nest-killers' weapons. His nestlings would protect it with their lives, and it would end these demon-spawned nest-killers for all time. Battle Comp had promised him that, and Battle Comp never lied.

"I don't like it," Horus said. "I don't like it, and I want a way around it. Do any of you have one?"

His chiefs of staff looked back from his com screen, weary faces strained. Gerald Hatcher's temples were almost completely white, but Isaiah Hawter's eyes were haunted, for he'd seen seventy percent of his warships blown out of existence in the last four months.

One face was missing. General Singhman had been aboard ODC Seven when the Achuultani warhead broke through her shield.

There were other gaps in Earth's defenses, and the enemy ruled the outer system. They were slow and clumsy in normal space, but their ability to dart into hyper with absolutely no warning more than compensated as long as they stayed at least twenty light-minutes out.

Earth had learned enough in the last few months to know her technology was better, but it was beginning to appear her advantage might not be great enough, for the Achuultani had surprises of their own.

Like those damned hyper drives. Achuultani ships were slow even in hyper, but their hyper drives did things Horus had always thought were impossible. They could operate twice as deep into a stellar gravity well as an Imperial hypership, and their missile launchers were incredible. Achuultani sublight missiles, though fast, weren't too dangerous — Earth's defenders had better computers, better counter-missiles, and more efficient shield generators — but their hyper missiles were another story. Somehow, and Horus would have given an arm to know how, the Achuultani generated *external* hyper fields around their missiles, without the massive on-board hyper drives human missiles required.

Their launchers' rate of fire was lower, but they were small enough the Achuultani could pack them in in unbelievable numbers, and they tended to fire their salvos in shoals, scattered over the hyper bands. A shield could cover only so many bands at once, and with luck, they could pop a missile through one the shield wasn't guarding — a trick which had cost Earth's warships dearly.

Their energy weapons, on the other hand, relied upon

quaint, short-ranged developments of laser technology, which left a gap in their defenses. It wasn't very wide, but if Earth's defenders could get into it, they were too close for really accurate Achuultani hyper missile-fire and beyond their effective energy weapon range. The trick was surviving to get there.

And they really did like kinetic weapons. So far, they'd managed to hit the planetary shield with scores of projectiles, the largest something over a billion tons, and virtually wiped out Earth's orbital industry. They'd nailed two ODCs, as well, picking them off with missiles when the main shield was slammed back into atmosphere behind them by kinetic assault.

To date, Vassily had managed to hold that shield against everything they threw at him, but the big, blond Russian was growing increasingly grim-faced. The PDC shield generators had been designed to provide a fifty percent reserve — but that was before they knew about Achuultani hyper missiles. Covering the wide-band attacks coming at him took every generator he had, and at ruinous overload. Without the core tap, not even the PDCs could have held them.

Which was largely what this conference was about.

"*I* don't see an option, Horus," Hatcher said finally. "We've got to have that tap. If we shut down and they hit us before we power back up —"

"Gerald," Chernikov said, "we never meant this tap to carry such loads so long. The control systems are collapsing. I am into the secondary governor ring in places; if it goes, there are only the tertiaries to hold it."

"But even if we shut down, will it be any safer to power back up?"

"No," Chernikov conceded unhappily. "Not without repairs."

"Then, Vassily, it is a choice between a possibility of losing control and the probability of losing the planet," Tsien said quietly.

"I know that. But it will do us no good to blow up

Antarctica *and* lose the tap — permanently — into the bargain."

"Agreed." Horus's quiet voice snapped all eyes back to him. "Are your replacement components ready for installation, Vassily?"

"They are. We will require two-point-six hours to change over, but I *must* shut down to do it."

"Very well." Horus felt responsibility crushing down upon him. "When the first secondary system goes down, we'll shut down long enough for complete control replacement."

Tsien and Hatcher looked as if they wanted to argue, but they were soldiers. They recognized an order when they heard it.

"Now." Horus turned his attention to Admiral Hawter. "What can you tell us about your own situation, Isaiah?"

"It's not good," Hawter said heavily. "The biggest problem is the difference in our shield technologies. We generate a single bubble around a unit; they generate a series of platelike shields, each covering one aspect of the target, with about a twenty-percent overlap at the edges. They pay for it with a much less efficient power ratio, but it gives them redundancy we don't have *and* lets them bring them in closer to the hull. That's our problem."

Heads nodded. Hyper missiles weren't seeking weapons; they went straight to their preprogrammed coordinates, and the distance between shield and hull effectively made Earth's ships bigger targets. All too often, a hyper missile close enough to penetrate a human warship's shield detonated outside an Achuultani ship's shields — which, coupled with the Achuultani's greater ability to saturate the hyper bands, left Hawter's ships at a grievous disadvantage.

"Our missiles out-range theirs, and we've refined our targeting systems to beat their jammers — which, by the way, are still losing ground to our own — but if we stay beyond their range, we can't get *our* warheads in close enough, either. Not without bigger salvos than most of our ships can throw. As long as they stay far enough out to use their micro-jump advantage, as well, we can only fight them on their terms, and that's bad business."

"How bad?" General Ki asked.

"Bad. We started out with a hundred and twenty battle-ships, twice that many cruisers, and about four hundred destroyers. We're down to thirty-one battleships, ninety-six cruisers, and one hundred and seven destroyers — that's a loss of five hundred and thirty-six out of an initial strength of seven hundred and seventy. In return, we've knocked out about nine hundred of their ships. I've got confirmed kills on seven hundred eighty-two and prob-ables on another hundred fifty or so. That's one hell of a lot more tonnage than we've lost, and by our original esti-mates, that should have been all of them; as it is, it looks like a bit less than fifty percent."

"What it boils down to is that they've ground us away. If they move against us in force, we no longer have the mobile units to meet them in deep space."

"In short," Horus interjected softly, "they've won control of the Solar System beyond the reach of Earth's own weapons."

"Exactly, Governor," Hawter said grimly. "We're hold-ing so far, but by the skin of our teeth. And this is only the scouting force."

They were still staring at one another in glum silence when the alarms shrieked.

Both of Brashieel's stomachs tightened as *Vindicator* moved in-system. The Demon Sector was living up to its name, Tarhish take it! Almost half the scouts had died striving against this single wretched planet, and if the scouts were but a few pebbles in the avalanche of Great Lord Tharno's fleet, there were many suns in this sector — including the ones which must have built those scanner arrays. It could not have been these nest-killers, for none of their ships were even hyper-capable. But if *these* nest-killers had such weapons, who knew what else awaited the Protectors?

Yet they were pushing the nest-killers back. Lord of

Thought Mosharg had counted the nest-killers they had sent to Tarhish carefully, and few of their foes' impossibly powerful warships could remain.

Still, it seemed rash to press an attack so deep into the inner system. The nest-killers were twice as fast as *Vindicator* when he could not flee into hyper. If this was an ambush, the Great Visit's scouts could lose heavily.

But Brashieel was no lord. Perhaps the purpose was to evaluate the nest-killers' close defenses before the Hoof of Tarhish was released upon them? That made sense, even to an assistant servant like him, especially in light of their orders to attack the sunward pole of the planet. Yet to risk a half-twelve of twelves of scouts in this fashion took courage. Which might be why Lords Chirdan and Mosharg were lords and Brashieel was an assistant servant.

He settled tensely upon his duty pad as they emerged from hyper and headed for the blue-white world they had come so far to slay.

"Seventy-two hostiles, inbound," Plotting reported. "Approximately two hundred forty additional hostiles following at eight light-minutes. Evaluate this as a major probe."

Isaiah Hawter winced. Over three hundred of them. He could go out to meet them and kick hell out of them, but it would leave him with next to nothing. Those bastards lying back to cover their fellows with hyper missiles made the difference. He'd lose half his ships before his energy weapons even engaged the advanced force.

No, this time he was going to have to let them in.

"All task forces, withdraw behind the primary shield," he said. "Instruct Fighter Command to stand by. Bring all ODC weaponry to readiness."

Adrienne Robbins swore softly as she retreated behind the shield. She knew going out to meet that much firepower would be a quick form of suicide, but *Nergal* had twenty-seven confirmed kills and nine probables, more than any other unit among Earth's tattered survivors, and letting these vermin close without a fight galled her. More, it frightened her, because whether anyone chose to admit it or not, she knew what it meant.

They were losing.

Vassily Chernikov made a minute adjustment through his neural feed, nursing his core tap like an old cat with a single kitten. He'd been right to insist on building it, but all he felt now was hatred for the demon he had chained. It was breaking its bonds, slowly but surely, under the strain of continuous overload operation in a planetary atmosphere; when they snapped, it would be the end.

Lieutenant Samson's belly tightened as he watched the developing attack pattern. They were coming in from the south this time — had they spotted the core tap? Realized how vital to Earth it was?

Either way, it made little difference to Samson's probable fate. The Iron Bitch was right in their path, floating with five other ODCs to help her bar the way . . . and the planetary shield was drawn in behind them.

"Red Warning! Prepare for launch! Prepare for launch! Red Warning!"

The fighter crews, Terra-born and Imperials distinguishable now only by their names, charged up the ladders to their cockpits. General Ki Tran Thich settled into the pilot's couch of his command fighter and flashed the commit signal over his neural feed. Drives hummed to life, EW officers tuned their defensive systems and weaponry, and the destruction-laden little craft howled up from their PDC homes on the manmade thunder of their sonic booms.

Brashieel blinked inner and outer lids alike as his display blossomed with sudden threat sources. Great Nest! Sublight missiles at *this* range?

But his consternation eased slightly as he saw the power

readings. No, not missiles. They were something else, some sort of very small warships. He had never heard of anything like them, but, then, he had never heard of *most* of the Tarhish-spawned surprises these demon nest-killers had produced.

"Missile batteries, stand by," Gerald Hatcher ordered softly. This was going to be tricky. He and Tao-ling had trained to coordinate their southern-hemisphere PDCs, but this was the first time the bastards had come really close.

He spared a moment to be thankful Sharon and the girls were safely under the protection of Horus's Shepherd Center HQ. It was just possible something was coming through this time.

Andrew Samson swallowed as the interceptors drilled through the shield's polar portal and it closed behind them. They were such tiny things to pit themselves against those kilometers-long Leviathans. It didn't seem —

"Stand by missile crews." Captain M'wange's voice was cold. "Shield generators to max. Deploy first hyper salvo."

The hyper missiles floated out of their bays, moored to the Bitch by chains of invisible force, and the Achuultani swept closer.

"All ODCs engage — now!" Isaiah Hawter snapped.

Nest Lord! *Those* were missiles!

Slayer and *War Hoof* vanished from his scanners, and Brashieel winced. The nest-killers no longer used the greater thunder; they had come to rely almost entirely on those terrible warheads which did not explode . . . and for which the Nest had no counter. *Slayer* crumpled in on himself as a missile breached his shields; *War Hoof* simply disappeared, and the range was far too long for his own hyper missiles. What devil among the nest-killers had thought of putting hyper drives *inside* their missiles that way?

More missiles dropped out of hyper, and *Vindicator* lurched as his shields trembled under a near-miss. And another. But Small Lord Hantorg had nerves of steel. He held his course, and Brashieel's own weapons would range soon.

He made his fingers and thumbs relax within the control gloves. Soon, he promised himself. Soon, my brothers!

The small warships darted closer, and he wondered what they meant to do.

Andrew Samson whooped as the huge ship died. That had been one of the Bitch's missiles! Maybe even one of *his*!

"All fighters — execute Bravo-Three!" General Ki barked, and Earth's interceptors slashed into the Achuultani formation, darting down to swoop up from "below" at the last moment. They bucked and twisted, riding the surges from the heavy gravitonic warheads Terra hurled to meet her attackers, and their targeting systems reached out.

Brashieel twitched in astonishment as the tiny warships wheeled, evading the close-in energy defenses. Only a few twelves perished; the others opened fire at point-blank range, and a hurricane of missiles lashed the Aku'Ultan ships. They lacked the brute power of the nest-killers' heavy missiles, but there were many of them. A *great* many of them.

Half a twelve of *Vindicator*'s brothers perished, like mighty *qwelloq* pulled down by tiny, stinging *sulq*. Clearly the nest-killers' lords of thought had briefed them well. They fought in teams, many units striking as one, concentrating their fire on single quadrants of their victims' shields, and when those isolated shields died under the tornadoes of flame blazing upon them, the ships they had been meant to save died with them.

In desperation, Brashieel armed his own launchers

without orders. Such a breach of procedure might mean his own death in dishonor, yet he could not simply crouch upon his duty pad and do *nothing*! His fingers twitched and sent forth a salvo of normal-space missiles, missiles of the greater thunder. They converged on a quarter-twelve of attacking *sulq*, and when their thunder merged, it washed over the nest-killers and gave them to the Furnace.

"Good, Brashieel!" It was Small Lord Hantorg. "Very good!"

Brashieel's crest rose with pride as he heard *Vindicator's* lord ordering other missile crews to copy his example.

General Ki Tran Thich watched the tremendous Achuultani warship rip apart under his fire. He and Hideoshi had drawn lots for the right to lead the first interception, and he smiled wolfishly as he wheeled his fighter. The full power of the Seventy-First Fighter Group rode at his back as he searched for another target. There. That one would do nicely.

He never saw the ten-thousand-megaton missile coming directly at him.

"Missile armaments exhausted," General Tama Hideoshi's ops officer reported, and Tama grunted. His own feeds had already told him, and he could feel his fighters dying . . . just as Thich had died. Who would have thought of turning shipkillers into proximity-fused SAMs? His interceptors' energy armaments weren't going to be enough against *that* kind of overkill!

"All fighters withdraw to rearm," he ordered. "Launch reserve strike. Instruct all pilots to maintain triple normal separation. They are to engage only with missiles — I repeat, only with missiles — then withdraw to rearm."

"Yes, sir."

Earth's fighters withdrew. Over three hundred of them had perished, yet that was but a tithe of their total strength, and the Achuultani probe had been reduced to twenty-seven units.

The flight crews streamed back past the ODCs, heading for their own bases. It was up to the orbital fortifications, now — them, and the fire still slamming into the Achuultani from Earth's southernmost PDCs.

Brashieel watched the small warships scatter, fleeing his fire. The Protectors had found the way to defeat them, and he — *he*, a lowly assistant servant of thunder — had pointed the way!

He felt his nestmates' approval, yet he could not rejoice. Two-thirds of *Vindicator*'s brothers had died, and the nest-killers' missiles still lashed the survivors. Worse, they were about to enter energy-weapon range of those waiting fortresses. None of the scouts had done that before; they had engaged only with missiles at extreme range. Now was the great test. Now was the Time of Fire, when they would learn what those sullen fortresses could do.

Andrew Samson watched the depleted fighters fall back. Imagine swatting fighters with heavy missiles! *We* couldn't've gotten away with it; our sublight missiles are too slow, too easy to evade.

The full Achuultani fire shifted to the Bitch and her sisters, and the ODC shuddered, twitching as if in fear as the warheads battered her shield. Her shield generators heated dangerously as Captain M'wange asked the impossible of them. They were covering too many hyper bands, Samson thought. Sooner or later, they would miss one, or an antimatter warhead would overload them. And when that happened, Lucy Samson's little boy Andrew would die.

But in the meantime, he thought, taking careful aim . . . and bellowed in triumph as yet another massive warship tore apart. They were coming to kill him, but if they had not, how could he have killed them?

"Stand by energy weapons," Admiral Hawter said harshly. ODCs Eleven, Thirteen, and Sixteen were gone;

there was going to be one hell of a hole over the pole, whatever happened. Far worse, some of their missiles had gotten through to Earth's surface. He didn't know how many, but *any* were too many when they carried that kind of firepower. Yet they were down to nineteen ships. He tried to tell himself that was a good sign, and his lips thinned over his teeth as the Achuultani kept coming.

They were about to discover the difference between the beams of a battleship and a three-hundred-thousand-ton ODC, he thought viciously.

Brashieel flinched as the waiting fortresses exploded with power. The terrible energy weapons which had slain so many of *Vindicator's* brothers in ship-to-ship combat were as nothing beside this! They smote full upon the warships' shields, and as they smote, those ships died. One, two, seven — still they died! Nothing could withstand that fury. *Nothing!*

"All *right!*" Andrew Samson shouted. Six of them already, and more going! He picked a target whose shields wavered under fire from three different ODCs and popped a gravitonic warhead neatly through them. His victim perished, and this time there was no question who'd made the kill.

"Withdraw."

The order went out, and Brashieel sighed with gratitude. Lord of Thought Mosharg must have learned what they had come to learn. They could leave.

Assuming they could get away alive.

"They're withdrawing!" someone shouted, and Gerald Hatcher nodded. Yes, they were, but they'd cost too much before they went. Two missiles had actually gotten through the planetary shield despite all that Vassily and the PDCs could do, and thank God those bastards didn't have gravitonic warheads.

He closed his eyes briefly. One missile had been an ocean strike, and God only knew what *that* was going to do to Earth's coastlines and ecology. The other had hit Australia, almost exactly in the center of Brisbane, and Gerald Hatcher felt the weight of personal despair. No shelter could withstand a direct hit of that magnitude, and how in the name of God could he tell Isaiah Hawter that he had just become a childless widower?

The last Aku'Ultan warship vanished, fleeing into hyper before the reserve fighter strike caught it. Three of the seventy-two which had attacked escaped.

Behind them, the southern hemisphere of the planet smoked and smoldered under twenty thousand megatons of destruction, and far, far ahead of them, Lord Chirdan's engineers completed their final tests. Power plants came on line, stoking the furnaces of the mighty drive housings, and Lord Chirdan himself gave the order to engage.

The moon men called Iapetus shuddered in its endless orbit around the planet they called Saturn. Shuddered . . . and began to move slowly away from its primary.

Chapter Sixteen

Servant of Thunders Brashieel crouched upon his new duty pad in master fire control. He had no idea how *Vindicator* had survived so long, but Small Lord Hantorg seemed to believe much of the credit was his. He was grateful for his small lord's confidence, and even more that his new promotion gave him such splendid instrumentation.

He bent his eyes on the vision plate, watching the rocky mass which paced *Vindicator*. The Nest seldom used such large weapons, but it was time and past time for the Protectors to finish these infernal nest-killers and move on.

Gerald Hatcher felt a million years old as he propped his feet on the coffee table in Horus's office. Even with biotechnics, there was a limit to the twenty-two-hour days a man could put in, and he'd passed it long ago.

For seven months they had held on — somehow — but the end was in sight. His dog-weary personnel knew it, and the civilians must suspect. The heavens had been pocked with too much flame. Too many of their defenders had died . . . and their children. Fourteen times now the

Achuultani had driven hyper missiles past the planetary shield. Most had struck water, lashing Earth's battered coasts with tsunamis, wracking her with radiation and salt-poisoned typhoons, but four had found targets ashore. By God's grace, one had landed in the middle of the African desert, but Brisbane had been joined by over four hundred million more dead, and all the miracles his people had wrought were but delays.

How Vassily kept his tap up was more than Hatcher could tell, but he was holding it together, with his bare hands for all intents and purposes. The power still flowed, and Geb and his zombielike crews kept the shield generators on-line somehow. They could shut down no more than a handful for overhaul at any one time, but, like Vassily, Geb was doing the impossible.

Yes, Hatcher thought, Earth had its miracle-workers . . . but at a price.

"How —" He paused to clear his throat. "How's Isaiah?"

"Unchanged," Horus said sadly, and Hatcher closed his eyes in pain.

It had been terrible enough for Isaiah to preside over the slaughter of his crews, but Brisbane had finished him. Now he simply sat in his small room, staring at the pictures of his wife and children.

His friends knew how magnificently he'd fought, rallying his battered ships again and again; he knew only that he hadn't been good enough. That he'd let the Achuultani murder his family, and that most of the crews who'd fought for him with such supreme gallantry had also died. So they had, and too many of the survivors were like Isaiah — burned out, dead inside, hating themselves for being less than gods in the hour of their world's extremity.

Yet there were the others, Hatcher reminded himself. The ones like Horus, who'd assumed Isaiah's duties when he collapsed. Like Adrienne Robbins, the senior surviving parasite skipper, who'd refused a direct order to take her damaged ship out of action. Like Vassily and Geb, who'd somehow risen above themselves to perform impossible tasks. Like the bone-weary crews of the ODCs and PDCs who fought on day after endless, hopeless day, and the fighter crews who went out again and again, and came back in ever fewer numbers.

And, he thought, the people like Tsien Tao-ling, those very rare men and women who simply had no breaking point . . . and thank God for them.

Of the Supreme Chiefs of Staff, Singhman and Ki had been killed . . . and so had Hawter, Hatcher thought sadly. Tama Hideoshi had taken over all that remained of Fighter Command, but Vassily was chained to Antarctica, Frederick Amesbury was working himself into his own grave in Plotting, trying desperately to keep tabs on the outer system through his Achuultani-crippled arrays, and Chiang Chien-su couldn't possibly be spared from his heartbreaking responsibility for Civil Defense. So even with Horus taking over the remnants of Hawter's warships and ODCs, Hatcher had been forced to hand the entire planet-side defense net over to Tsien while he himself concentrated on finding a way to keep the Achuultani from destroying Earth.

But he was a general, not a wizard.

"We've had it, Horus." He watched the old Imperial carefully, but the governor didn't even flinch. "We're just kicking and scratching on the way to the gallows. I don't see how Vassily can keep the tap up another two weeks."

"Should we stop kicking and scratching, then?" The question came out with a ghost of a smile, and Hatcher smiled back.

"Hell, no. I just needed to say it to someone before I go back and start kicking again. Even if they take us out, we can make sure there are less of them for the next world on their list."

"My thoughts exactly." Horus squeezed the bridge of his nose wearily. "Should we tell the civilians?"

"Better not." Hatcher sighed. "I'm not really scared of a panic, but I don't see any reason to frighten them any worse than they already are."

"Agreed."

Horus rose and walked slowly to his office's glass wall. The Colorado night was ripped by solid sheets of lightning as the outraged atmosphere gave up some of the violence it had been made to absorb, and a solid, unending roll of thunder shook the glass. Lightning and snow, he thought; crashing thunder and blizzards. Too much vaporized sea water, too many cubic kilometers of steam. The planetary albedo had shifted, more sunlight was reflected, and the temperature had dropped. There was no telling how much further it would go . . . and thank the Maker General Chiang had stockpiled food so fanatically, for the world's crops were gone. But at least this one was turning to rain. Freezing cold rain, but rain.

And they were still alive, he told himself as Hatcher stood silently to leave. Alive. Yet that, too, would change. Gerald was right. They were losing it, and something deep inside him wanted to curl up and get the dying finished. But he couldn't do that.

"Gerald." His soft voice stopped Hatcher at the door, and Horus turned his eyes from the storm to meet the general's. "In case we don't get a chance to talk again, thank you."

The Hoof of Tarhish pawed the vacuum. Not even the Aku'Ultan could accelerate such masses with a snap of the fingers, but its speed had grown. Only a few twelves of *tiao* per segment, at first, then more. And more. More!

Now *Vindicator* rode the mighty projectile's flank, joined with his brothers in a solid phalanx to guard their weapon.

They must be seen soon, but the Hoof's defenses were strong, and the nest-killers could not even range accurately upon it without first blasting aside the half-twelve of great twelves of scouts which remained. They would defend the Hoof with their own deaths and clear a way through what remained of the nest-killers' defenses, for they were Protectors.

❖   ❖   ❖

"Oh my God."

Sir Frederick Amesbury's Plotting teams were going berserk trying to analyze the Achuultani's current maneuvers, for there was no sane reason for them to be clustered that way on a course like that. But something about the whisper cut through the weary, frantic background hum, and he turned to Major Joanna Osgood, his senior watch officer.

"What is it, Major?" But her mahogany face was frozen and she did not answer. He touched her shoulder. "Jo?"

Major Osgood shook herself.

"I found the answer, sir," she said. "Iapetus."

Her Caribbean accent's flattened calm frightened Amesbury, for he knew what produced that tone. There was a realm beyond fear, for when no hope remained there was no reason to fear.

"Explain, Major," he said gently.

"I finally managed to hyper an array out-system and got a look at Saturn, sir." She met the general's gaze calmly. "Iapetus isn't there anymore."

"It's true, Ger." Amesbury's weary face looked back from Hatcher's com screen. "It took some time to get a probe near enough to burn through their ships' energy emissions and confirm it, but we found it right enough. Dead center in their formation: Iapetus — the eighth moon of Saturn."

"I see." Hatcher wanted to curse, to revile God for letting this happen, but there was no point, and his voice was soft. "How bad is it?"

"It's the end, unless we can stop the bloody thing. This is no asteroid, Ger — it's a bleeding *moon*. Six times the mass of Ceres."

"Moving how fast?"

"Fast enough to see *us* off," Amesbury replied grimly. "They could have done that simply by dropping it into Sol's gravity well and letting it fall 'downhill' to us, but we'd've had too much time. They've put shields on it, but if we could pop a few hyper missiles through them, we *might* be able to blow the bugger apart before it reaches us. That's why they're bringing it in under power: they don't want to expose it to our fire any longer than they have to.

"Their drives are much slower than ours are, but they've got the ruddy gravity well to work with, too. I don't know how they did it — even if they hadn't been picking off our sensor arrays, we were watching the asteroids, not the outer-system moons — but I reckon they started out with a very low initial acceleration. Only they're coming from *Saturn*, Ger. I don't know when they actually started, but we're just past opposition, which means we're over one-and-a-half *trillion* kilometers apart on a straight line. But they're not *on* a straight-line course . . . and they've been accelerating all the way.

"They're coming at us at upwards of five hundred kilometers per second — seven times faster than a 'fast' meteorite. I haven't bothered to calculate how many trillions of megatons that equates to, because it doesn't matter. That moon will punch through our shield like a bullet through butter, and they'll reach us in about six days. That's how long we've got to stop them."

"We can't, Frederick," Hatcher sighed. "We just can't do it."

"I bloody well know we can't," Amesbury said harshly, "but that doesn't mean we don't have to try!"

"I know." Hatcher made his shoulders straighten. "Leave it with me, Frederick. We'll give it our best shot."

"I know," Amesbury said much more softly. "And . . . God bless, Ger."

Faces paled as the news spread among Earth's defenders. This was the end. When that stupendous hammer came down, Earth would shatter like a walnut.

Some had given too much, stretched their reserves too thin, and they snapped. Most simply retreated from reality, but a handful went berserk, and their fellows were almost grateful, for subduing them diverted their minds from their own terror.

Yet only a minority broke. For most, survival, even hope, were no longer factors, and they manned their battle stations without hysteria, cold and determined . . . and desperate.

Servant of Thunders Brashieel noted the changing energy signatures. So. The nest-killers knew, and they would strive to thrust the Hoof aside, to destroy it. Already the orbital fortresses were moving, concentrating to meet them, but many smaller hooves had been prepared to pelt the planetary shield, driving it back, exposing those fortresses to the Protectors' thunder. They would clear a path for the Hoof, and nothing could stop them. The nest-killers could not even see the Hoof to fire upon it unless they destroyed *Vindicator* and his brothers, and they would never do that in time.

He watched his magnificent instruments as Lord of Order Chirdan shifted formation, placing a thicker wall of his nestlings between the Hoof and the nest-killers' world. *Vindicator* anchored one edge of that wall.

Lieutenant Andrew Samson felt queerly calm. Governor Horus had shifted his remaining forts to give the Bitch support, but the Achuultani had expected that. Kinetic projectiles had hammered the planetary shield back for days, stripping it away from the ODCs. Raiding squadrons had charged in, paying a high price for their attacks but picking off the battered ODCs. Of the six which originally had protected the pole, only the damaged Bitch remained, and she'd expended too much ammunition defending herself. Without Earth's orbital industry, just keeping up with expenditures was difficult . . . not to mention the risk colliers ran between the shield and the ODCs to resupply them.

Andrew Samson had long ago abandoned any expectation of surviving Earth's siege, but he'd continued to hope his world would live. Now he knew it probably would not, and that purged the last fear from his system, leaving only a strange, bittersweet regret.

The last fleet units would make their try soon. They'd been hoarded for this moment, waiting until the Achuultani were within point-blank range of Earth's defenses. Their chances of surviving the next few hours were even lower than his own, but the ODCs would do what they could to cover them. He checked his remaining hyper missiles. Thirty-seven, and less than four hundred in the *Bitch's* other magazines. It wouldn't be enough.

Acting Commodore Adrienne Robbins checked her formation. All fifteen of Earth's remaining battleships, little more than a single squadron, were formed up about her wounded *Nergal*. Half *Nergal's* launchers had been destroyed by the near-miss which had pierced her shield and killed eighty of her three hundred people, but she had her drive . . . and her energy weapons.

The threadbare remnants of the cruisers and destroyers — seventy-four of them, in all — screened the pitiful handful of capital ships. Eighty-nine warships: her first and final task force command.

"Task Force ready to proceed, Governor," she told the face on her com.

"Proceed," Horus said quietly. "May the Maker go with you, Commodore."

"And with you, sir," she replied, then shifted to her command net, and her voice was clear and calm. "The Task Force will advance," she said.

Brashieel watched in grudging admiration as the nest-killers advanced. There were so few of them, and barely a twelve of their biggest ones. Their crews must know they would be chaff for the Furnace, yet still they came, and something within him saluted their courage. In this moment they were not nest-killers; they were Protectors, just as truly as he himself.

But such thoughts would not stay his hand. The Nest had survived for uncountable higher twelves of years only by slaying its enemies while they were yet weak. It was a lesson the Aku'Ultan had learned long ago from the Great Nest-Killers who had driven the Aku'Ultan from their own Nest Place.

It would not happen again.

Gerald Hatcher felt sick as Commodore Robbins led her ships out to die. But the fire control of his orbital and ground-side fortresses couldn't even see Iapetus unless an opening could be blown for them, and those doomed ships were his one hope to open a way.

"If we get a fix, lock it in tight, Plotting," he said harshly.

"Acknowledged," Sir Frederick Amesbury replied.

"Request permission to engage," Tama Hideoshi said from his own screen, and Hatcher noted the general's flight suit. They had more fighters than crews now, but even so Hideoshi had no business flying this mission. Yet there was no tomorrow this time, and he chose not to object.

"Not yet. Hold inside the shield till the ships engage."

"Acknowledged." Tama's voice was unhappy, but he understood. He would wait until the Achuultani were too busy punching missiles at Robbins's ships to wipe his own fragile craft from the universe.

"Task Force opening fire," someone said, and another voice came over the link, soft and prayerful, its owner not even aware he had spoken.

"Go, baby! *Go!*" it whispered.

Adrienne Robbins had discussed her plan with Horus, not that there was much "planning" to it. There was but one possible tactic: to go right down their throat behind every missile she had. Perhaps, just perhaps, they could swamp the defenses, get in among them with their energy weapons. None would survive such close combat, but they might punch a hole before they died.

And so Earth's ships belched missiles at her murderers, hyper and sublight alike. Their launchers went to continuous rapid fire, spitting out homing sublight weapons without even worrying about targeting. The lethal projectiles were a cloud of death, and the first hyper missiles from Earth came with them.

Lord of Order Chirdan's head bobbed in anguish as his nestlings died. He had known the nest-killers must come forth and hurl their every weapon against him, yet not even Battle Comp had predicted carnage such as this!

The missile storm was a whirlwind, boring into the center of the wall defending the Hoof. Antimatter pyres and gravitonic warheads savaged his ships, and his inner lids narrowed. They sought to blow a hole and charge into it with their infernal energy weapons! They would die there, but in their dying they might expose the Hoof to their fellows upon the planet.

He could not allow that, and his orders went out. The edges of his wall of ships thinned, drawing together in the center to block the attack, and his own, shorter-ranged missiles struck back.

Time had no meaning. There was only a shrieking eternity of dying ships and a glare that lit Earth's night skies like twice a hundred suns. Adrienne Robbins saw it reaching for her ships, saw her lighter destroyers and cruisers burning like coals from a forge, and she adjusted her course slightly.

The solid core of her outnumbered task force drove for the exact center of that vortex of death, and their magazines were almost dry.

"Go!" Tama Hideoshi snapped, and Earth's last surviving interceptors howled heavenward. He rode his flight couch, his EW officer at his side, and smiled. He was fifty-nine years old, and only his biotechnics made this possible. Three years before, he'd thought he would never fly combat again. Now he would, and if his world must die, at least he had been given this final gift, to die in her defense as a samurai should.

Nest Lord! Their small ships were attacking, too! Brashieel had not thought so many remained, but they did, and they charged on the heels of their larger, dying brothers, covered by their deaths.

A few of the Bitch's launchers still had hyper missiles, but Andrew Samson was down to sublight weapons. It was long range, too much time for the bastards to pick them off, but each of his weapons they had to deal with was one more strain on their defenses. He sent them out at four-second intervals.

Lord Chirdan cursed. The nest-killers were dying by twelves, yet they had cut deep into his formation. Six twelves of his ships had already perished, and the terrible harvest of the nest-killer beams was only starting.

Their warships vanished into the heart of his own, robbing his outer missile crews of targets, and they retargeted on the orbital fortresses.

Gerald Hatcher's face was stone as the first ODC died. Missiles pelted the planetary shield, as well, but he almost welcomed those. Even if they broke through, killed millions of civilians, he would welcome them, for each missile sent against Earth was one not sent against his orbital launchers.

He sat back and felt utterly useless. There was no reserve. He'd committed everything he had. Now he had nothing to do but watch the slaughter of his people.

Missiles coated the Iron Bitch's shield in a blinding corona, and still she struck back.

Andrew Samson was a machine, part of his console. His magazine was down to ten percent and dropping fast, but he didn't even think of slowing his rate of fire. There was no point, and he pounded his foes, his brain full of the thunder wracking the Achuultani formation.

He never saw the hyper missile which finally popped the Bitch's shields. He died with his mind still full of thunder.

Tama Hideoshi's fighters slammed into the Achuultani, and their missiles flashed away. Scores of Achuultani ships died, but the enemy formation closed anyway. Commodore Robbins's ships vanished into the maelstrom, and the fighters were dying too quickly to follow.

They exhausted their missiles and closed with energy guns.

Adrienne Robbins was halfway through the Achuultani, but her cruisers and destroyers were gone. The back of her mind burned with the image of the destroyer *London* as her captain took her at full drive directly into one of the Achuultani monsters behind the continuous fire of his energy weapons, bursting through its weakened shield and dragging it into death with him. Yet it wasn't enough. She and her battleships were alone, the only units with the strength to endure the fury, and even they were going fast. *Nergal* herself had taken another near miss, and tangled skeins of atmosphere followed her like a trail of blood.

Another Achuultani ship died under her energy weapons, but another loomed beyond it, and still another. They wouldn't break through after all.

Adrienne Robbins drove her crippled command forward, and *Nergal's* eight surviving sisters charged at her side.

Tsien Tao-ling's scanners told him Commodore Robbins would not succeed. Yet . . . in a way, she might yet. His eyes closed as he concentrated on his feed, his brain clear and cold, buttressed against panic. Yes. Robbins had drawn most of the defenders onto her own ships, thickening the center of their formation but thinning its edges. Perhaps —

The hail of missiles from the PDCs stopped as his neural feed overrode their firing orders. He felt Hatcher's shock through his cross feed to Shepherd Center, but there was no time to explain.

And then the launchers retargeted and spoke, hurling their massed missiles at a sphere of space barely three hundred kilometers across. Two thousand gravitonic warheads went off as one.

Twenty kilometers of starship went mad, hurled end-for-end as the wave of destruction broke across it. Servant of Thunders Brashieel clung to his duty pad, blood bursting from his nostrils as the universe exploded about him, and Tsien Taoling's fury spat *Vindicator* forth like the seed of a grape.

"*Contact!*" Sir Frederick Amesbury screamed, his British reserve shattered at last. Tsien had blown a brief hole through the Achuultani flank, and Amesbury's computers locked onto Iapetus. The data flashed to the PDCs and surviving ODCs, and their missiles retargeted once more.

Lord Chirdan cursed and slammed a double-thumbed fist into the bulkhead. No! They could not have done that! Not while the Hoof had so far to go!

But he fought himself back under control, watching missiles rip at the Hoof even as his ravaged nestlings raced to reposition themselves. Shields guttered and flared, and one quadrant failed. A missile dodged through the gap, its antimatter warhead incinerating the generators of yet another quadrant, but it was too late.

Without direct observation, not even *these* demon-spawned nest-killers could kill the Hoof before it struck. His scouts had already spread back out to deny them that observation and hide the damaged shield quadrants, and he bared his teeth in a snarl. He turned back to the five surviving nest-killer warships; he would give them to the Furnace, and their deaths would fan the Fire awaiting their cursed world.

◆   ◆   ◆

Hatcher's momentary elation died. It had been a magnificent try, but it had failed, and he felt himself relax into a curious tranquillity of sorrow for the death of his planet, coupled with a deep, abiding pride in his people.

He watched almost calmly as the thinning screen of Achuultani ships moved still closer. There were no more than three hundred of them, four at the most, but it would be enough.

"General Hatcher!" His head snapped up at the sudden cry from Plotting. There was something strange about that voice. Something he could not quite put his finger upon. And then he had it. Hope. There was *hope* in it!

Nergal was alone, the last survivor of Terra's squadrons.

Adrienne Robbins had no idea why her ship was still alive, nor dared she take time to consider it. Her mind blazed hotter than the warheads bursting against her shield, and still she moved forward. There was no sanity in it. One battleship, her missiles exhausted, could never stop Iapetus. But sanity was an encumbrance. *Nergal* had come to attack that moon, and attack she would.

The wall was thinning, and she could feel the moon through her scanners. She altered course slightly, smashing at her foes —

— and suddenly they vanished in a gut-wrenching fury of gravitonic destruction that tossed *Nergal* like a cork.

Lord Chirdan saw without understanding. Three twelves of warships — four twelves — *five!* Impossible warships. Warships vaster than the Hoof itself!

They came out of nowhere at impossible speeds and began to kill.

Missiles that did not miss. Beams that licked away ships like tinder. Shields that brushed aside the mightiest thunders. They were the darkest nightmare of the Aku'Ultan, fleshed in shields and battle steel.

Lord Chirdan's flagship vanished in a boil of flame, and

his scouts died with him. In the end, not even Protectors could abide the coming of those night demons. A pitiful handful broke, tried to flee, but they were too deep in the gravity well to escape into hyper, and — one by one — they died.

Yet before the last Protector perished, he saw one great warship advance upon the Hoof. Its missiles reached out — sublight missiles that took precise station on the charging moon before they flared to dreadful life. A surge of gravitonic fury raced out from them, even its backlash terrible enough to shake the wounded Earth to her core, triggering earthquakes, waking volcanoes.

Yet that was but an echo of their power. Sixteen gravitonic warheads, each hundreds of times more powerful than anything Earth had boasted, flashed into destruction . . . and took the moon Iapetus with them.

Gerald Hatcher sagged in disbelief, too shocked even to feel joy, and the breathless silence of his command post was an extension of his own.

Then a screen on his com panel lit, and a face he knew looked out of it.

"Sorry we cut it so close," Colin MacIntyre said softly.

And then — *then* — the command post exploded in cheers.

Chapter Seventeen

General Hector MacMahan watched the shoals of Imperial assault boats close in about his command craft, then turned his scanners to the broken halves of the Achuultani starship tumbling through space in the intricate measures of an insane dance. The planetoid *Sevrid* hovered behind her shuttles, watching over them and probing the wreckage. There was still air and life aboard that shattered ship, and power, but not much of any of them.

MacMahan grunted in satisfaction as *Sevrid's* tractors snubbed away the wreck's movement. Now if only the ship had a bay big enough to dock the damned thing, he and his people might not have to do *everything* the hard way.

He had no idea how many live Achuultani awaited his assault force, but he had six thousand men and women in his first wave, with a reserve half that size again. The cost might be high, but that wreck was the single partially intact Achuultani warship in the system. If they could take it, capture records, its computers, maybe even a few live Achuultani . . .

"Come on, people, tighten it up," he murmured over his com, watching the final adjustment of his formation. There. They were ready.

"Execute!" he snapped, and the assault boats screamed forward.

Servant of Thunders Brashieel waited in the wreckage in his vac-suit. One broken foreleg was crudely splinted, but aside from the pain it was little inconvenience. He still had three good legs, and with the loss of the drive gravity had become a ghost.

He watched his remaining instruments, longing to send the thunder against the foe, but his launchers had died. Perhaps a fifth-twelfth of *Vindicator's* energy weapons remained serviceable, but none of his launchers, and no weapons at all on the broken tooth of his forward section.

Brashieel tried to reject the nightmare. The nest-killers' world still lived, and these monstrous warships foretold perils yet more dire. The lords of thought had believed this system stood alone. It did not. The makers of those ancient scanner arrays had rallied to its defense, and they were powerful beyond dreams of power. Why should they content themselves with merely stopping the Protectors' attack? Why should they not strike the Nest itself?

He wondered why they had not simply given *Vindicator* to the Fire. Did their own beliefs in honor demand they face their final foes in personal combat? It did not matter, and he turned from his panel as the small craft advanced. He had no weapons to smite them, but he had already determined where he and his surviving nestlings of thunder would make their stand.

MacMahan flinched as the after section of the wrecked hull lashed his shuttles with fire. The crude energy weapons were powerful enough to burn through any assault boat's shield, but they'd fired at extreme range. Only three were hit, and the others went to evasive action, ripping at the wreck with their own energy guns. *Sevrid's* far heavier weapons reached past them, and warp beams plucked neat, perfect divots from the hull. Air gushed outward, and then the first-wave assault boats reached their goal.

Their energy guns blasted one last time, and they battered into the holes they'd blown on suddenly reversed drives. They crunched to a halt, and assault teams charged into the violated passages of the broken starship, their soot-black combat armor invisible in the lightless corridors. A handful of defenders opened fire, and their weapons spat back, silent in the vacuum.

MacMahan's command boat led the third wave, staggering drunkenly as it slammed to a halt, and the hatches popped. His HQ company formed up about him, and he took them into the madness.

Brashieel waited. There was no point charging blindly to meet the nest-killers. *Vindicator* was dead; only the mechanics of completing his nestlings' deaths remained, and this was as good a place to end as any.

He examined his nestlings' positions in the light of his helmet lamp. They had made themselves what cover they could, a hoof-shaped bow of them protecting the hatch to main control, and Brashieel wished Small Lord Hantorg had survived to lead their final fight.

His nostrils flared in bitter amusement. While he was wishing, might he not wish that he knew what he was about? He and his nestlings were servants of thunders — they smote worlds, not single nest-killers! He cudgeled his brain, trying to remember if he had ever heard of Protectors and nest-killers actually facing one another so directly. He did not think he had, but his mind was none too clear, and it really did not matter.

It was as impossible to coordinate the battle as MacMahan had expected it to be. Not even Imperial technology could provide any clear picture of this warren of decks and passages, sealed hatches and lurking ambushes.

He'd done his best in the pre-assault briefing; now it was up to his combat teams. The Second Marines provided the bulk of his firepower, but each company had an attached Recon Group platoon, and they were —

A stream of slugs wrenched him back to the job at hand, and he popped his jump gear, leaping aside as his point man went down and more fire clawed the space he himself had occupied a moment before. Leaking air and globules of blood marked a dead man as Corporal O'Hara's combat armor tumbled down the zero-gee passage, and MacMahan's mouth tightened. These crazy centaurs didn't have an energy weapon worth shit, but their slug weapons were nasty.

Still, they had their disadvantages. For one thing, recoil was a real problem — one his own people didn't face. And for all their determination to fight to the death, Achuultani didn't seem to be very good infantrymen. *His* people, on the other hand ...

Two troopers eased forward, close to the deck, and an entire squad hosed the area before them with rapid, continuous grav gun fire. The super-dense explosive darts shredded the bulkheads, lighting the darkness with strobe-lightning spits of fury, and Captain Amanda Givens-Tamman rose suddenly to her knees. Her warp rifle fired, and the defending fire stopped abruptly.

MacMahan shuddered. He *hated* those damned guns. Probably the first people to meet crossbows had felt the same way about them. But using a hyper field on anyone, even an Achuultani — !

He chopped the thought off and waved his people forward once again. A new point man moved out, armor scanners probing for booby traps and defenders alike, and another sealed hatch loomed ahead.

Brashieel shook himself into readiness as he felt vibration in the steel.

"Stand ready, my brothers," he said quietly. "The nest-killers come."

The hatch simply vanished, and Brashieel's crest flattened in dread. Somehow these nest-killers had chained the hyper field itself for the use of their protectors!

Then the first nest-killer came through the hatch, back-lit from the corridor behind, lacing the darkness with fire from its stubby weapon, and Brashieel swallowed bile at the ugliness of the squat, four-limbed shape. But even in his revulsion he felt a throb of wonder. That was a projectile weapon, yet there was no recoil! How was that possible?

The question fluttered away into the recesses of his mind as the nest-killer's explosive darts ripped two of his nestlings apart. How had it seen them in the blackness?! No matter. He sighted carefully, bracing his three good legs against the bulkhead, and squeezed his trigger. Recoil twisted his broken leg with agony, but his heavy slugs ripped through the biped's armor, and Brashieel felt a stab of savage delight. They had taken his thunders from him, but he would send a few more to the Furnace before they slew him!

The chamber blossomed with drifting globules of blood as more nest-killers charged through the hatch. Darkness was light for them, and their fire was murderously accurate. His nestlings perished, firing back, crying out in agony and horror over their suit communicators as darts exploded within their bodies or the terrible hyper weapons plucked away their limbs. Brashieel shouted his hate, holding back the trigger, then fumbled for another magazine, but there was no time. He hurled himself forward. his bayonet stabbing towards the last nest-killer to enter.

"General!" someone shouted, and MacMahan whirled. There was something wrong with the charging centaur's legs, but not with its courage; it was coming at him with only a bayonet, and his grav gun rose automatically — then stopped.

"Check fire!" he shouted, and tossed the grav gun aside.

Brashieel gaped as the puny nest-killer discarded its weapon, but his heart flamed. One more. One more foe to light his own way into the Furnace! He screamed in rage and thrust.

MacMahan's gauntleted hand slashed its armored edge into the Achuultani's long, clumsy rifle, driven by servo-mech "muscles," and the insanely warped weapon flew away.

The alien flung itself bodily upon him, and what kind of hand-to-hand moves did you use against a quarter horse with arms? MacMahan almost laughed at the thought, then he caught one murderously swinging arm, noting the knife in its hand only at the last moment, and the Achuultani convulsed in agony.

Careful, *careful*, Hector! Don't kill it by accident! And watch the vac-suit, you dummy! Rip *it* and —

He moderated his armor's strength, and a furiously kicking hoof smashed his chest for his pains. That smarted even through his armor. Strong bastard, wasn't he? They lost contact with decks and bulkheads and tumbled, weightless and drunken, across the compartment. A last Achuultani gunner tried to nail them both, but one of his HQ raiders finished it in time. Then they caromed off a bulkhead at last, and MacMahan got a firm grip on the other arm.

He twisted, landing astride the Achuultani's back, and suppressed a mad urge to scream "Ride 'em, cowboy!" as he wrapped his armored arms around its torso and arms. One of his legs hooked back, kicking a rear leg aside, and his foe convulsed again. Damn it! *Another* broken bone!

"Ashwell! Get your ass over here!" he shouted, and his aide leapt forward. Between them, they wrestled the injured, still-fighting alien into helplessness, pinning it until two other troopers could bind it.

"Jesus! These bastards don't know how to quit, Gen'rl!" Ashwell panted.

"Maybe not, but we've got one alive. I expect His Majesty will be pleased with us."

"His Majesty friggin' well *better* be," someone muttered.

"I didn't hear that," MacMahan said pleasantly. "But if I had, I'd certainly agree."

◆   ◆   ◆

Horus watched *Nergal's* mangled hull drop painfully through the seething electrical storm and tried not to weep. He failed, but perhaps no one noticed in the icy sheets of rain.

Strange ships escorted her, half again her size, shepherding her home. He winced as another drive pod failed and she lurched, but Adrienne Robbins forced her back under control. The other ships' tractors waited, ready to ease her struggle, but Horus could still hear Adrienne's voice.

"Negative," she'd said, tears glittering beneath the words. "She got us this far; she'll take us home. On her own, goddamn it! On her *own*!"

And now the strange ships hovered above her like guards of honor as the broken battleship limped down the last few meters of sky. Two landing legs refused to extend, and Robbins lifted her ship again, holding her rock-steady on her off-balance, rapidly failing drive, then laid her gently down upon her belly. It was perfect, Horus thought quietly. A consummate perfection he could never have matched.

There was no sound but the cannonade of Earth's thunder, saluting the return of her final defender with heaven's own artillery. Then the emergency vehicles moved out, flashers splintering in the pounding rain, sirens silent, while the gleaming newcomers settled in a circle about their fallen sister.

Colin rode the battleship *Chesha's* transit shaft to the main ramp and stepped out into the storm. Horus was waiting.

Something inside Colin tightened as he peered at him through the unnatural sheets of sleety rain. Horus looked more rocklike than ever, but he was an ancient rock, and the last thirty months had cut deep new lines into that powerful old face. Colin saw it as the old Imperial stared back at him, his eyes bright with incredulous joy, and climbed the ramp towards him.

"Hello, Horus," he said, and Horus reached out and

gripped his upper arms, staring into his face as he might have stared at a ghost.

"You *are* here," he whispered. "You made it."

"Yes," Colin said, the quiet word washed in thunder. And then his voice broke and he hugged the old man close. "We made it," he said into his father-in-law's shoulder, "and so did you. My God, so did you!"

"Of course we did," Horus said, and Colin had never heard such exhaustion in a human voice. "You left me a planetful of Terra-born to do it with, didn't you?"

General Chiang Chien-su was frantically busy, for the final shock of earthquakes and spouting volcanoes waked by Iapetus's destruction had capped the mounting devastation he'd fought so long. Yet he'd seemed almost cheerful in his last report. His people were winning this time, and the mighty planetoids riding solar orbit with the planet were helping. Their auxiliaries were everywhere, helping his own overworked craft rescue survivors from the blizzards, mud, water, and fire which had engulfed them.

Except for him, Earth's surviving chiefs of staff sat in Horus's office.

Vassily Chernikov looked like a two-week corpse, but his face was relaxed. The core tap was deactivated at last, and he hadn't lost control of it. Gerald Hatcher and Tsien Tao-ling sat together on a couch, shoulders sagging, feet propped on the same coffee table. Sir Frederick Amesbury sat in an armchair, smoking a battered pipe, eyes half-shut.

Tama Hideoshi was not there. Tamman's son had found the samurai's death he'd sought.

Colin sat on the corner of Horus's desk and knew he'd never seen such utter and complete fatigue. These were the men, he thought; the ones who had done the impossible. He'd already queried the computers and learned what they'd endured and achieved. Even with the evidence before him, he could scarcely credit it, and he hated what he was going to have to tell them. He could see the relaxation in their faces, the joy of a last-minute rescue, the knowledge that the Imperium had not abandoned them. Somehow he had to tell them the truth, but first . . .

"Gentlemen," he said quietly, "I never imagined what I'd really asked you to do. I have no idea how you did it. I can only say — thank you. It seems so inadequate, but —" He broke off with a small, apologetic shrug, and Gerald Hatcher smiled wearily.

"It cuts both ways, Governor. On behalf of your military commanders — and, I might add, the entire planet — thank *you*. If you hadn't turned up when you did —" It was his turn to shrug.

"I know," Colin said, "and I'm sorry we cut it so close. We came out of supralight just as your parasites went in."

"You came —" Horus's brows wrinkled in a frown. "Then how in the Maker's name did you *get* here? You should've been at least twenty hours out!"

"*Dahak* was. In fact, he and 'Tanni are still about twelve hours out. Tamman and I took the others and microjumped on ahead," Colin said, then grinned at Horus's expression. "Scout's honor. Oh, we still needed *Dahak*'s computers — we were plugged in by fold-space link all the way — but he couldn't keep up. You see, those ships carry hyper drives as well as Enchanach Drives."

"They *what*?!" Horus blurted.

"I know, I know," Colin said soothingly. "Look, there's a lot to explain. The main thing about how we got here is that those ships are faster'n hell. They can hyper to within about twelve light-minutes of a G0 star, and they can pull about seventy percent light-speed once they get there."

"Maker! When you get help, you get *help*, don't you?"

"Well," Colin said slowly, folding his hands on his knee and looking down at them, "yes, and no. You see, we couldn't find anyone to come with us." He looked up and saw the beginning of understanding horror in his father-in-law's eyes. "The Imperium's gone, Horus," he said gently. "We had to bring these ships back ourselves . . . and they're all that's coming."

Chapter Eighteen

Dahak's transit shaft deposited Horus at his destination, and the silent hatch slid open. He began to step through it, then stopped abruptly and dodged as fifty kilos of black fur hurled itself headfirst past him. Tinker Bell disappeared down the shaft's gleaming bore, her happy bark trailing away into silence, and he shook his head with a grin.

He stepped into the captain's quarters, still shaking his head. The atrium was filled with "sunlight," a welcome relief from the terrible rains and blizzards flaying the battered Earth, and Colin rose quickly to grip his hand and lead him back to the men sitting around the stone table.

Hector MacMahan looked up with a rare, wide grin and waved a welcome, and if Gerald Hatcher and Tsien Tao-ling were more restrained, their smiles looked almost normal again. Vassily wasn't here; he and Valentina were visiting their son and making appropriately admiring sounds as Vlad explained the latest wonders of Imperial engineering to them.

"Where's 'Tanni?" Horus demanded as he and Colin approached the others.

"She'll be along. She's collecting something we want to show you."

"Maker, it'll be good to see her again!" Horus said, and Colin grinned.

"She feels the same way . . . Dad."

Horus tried to turn his flashing smile into a pained expression, but who would have believed 'Tanni would have the good sense to wed Colin? Especially given the way they'd first met?

"Hi, Granddad." Hector didn't stand; his left leg was regenerating from the slug which had punched through his armor in the final fighting aboard *Vindicator*. "Sorry about Tinker Bell. She was in a hurry."

"A hurry? I thought she was a loose hyper missile!"

"I know." Colin laughed. "She's been that way ever since she discovered transit shafts, and Dahak spoils her even worse than Hector does."

"I didn't know anyone could," Horus said, eyeing Hector severely.

"Believe it. He doesn't have hands, but he's found his own way to pet her. He'll only route her to one of the park decks unless someone's with her, but he adjusts the shaft to give her about an eighty-kilometer airstream, and she's in heaven. He *barks* at her, too. Most horrible thing you ever heard, but he swears she understands him better than I do."

"Which would not require a great deal of comprehension," a voice said, and despite himself, Horus flinched. The last time he'd heard that voice with his own ears had been during the mutiny. "And that is not precisely what I have said, Colin. I simply maintain that Tinker Bell's barks are much more value-laden than humans believe and that we *shall* learn to communicate in a meaningful fashion, not that we already do so."

"Yeah, sure." Colin rolled his eyes at Horus.

"Welcome aboard, Senior Fleet Captain Horus," Dahak said, and Horus's tension eased at the welcome in that mellow voice. He cleared his throat.

"Thank you, Dahak," he said, and saw Colin's smile of approval.

"Join the rest of us," his son-in-law invited, and seated Horus at one end of the table. Wind rustled in the atrium leaves, a fountain bubbled nearby, and Horus felt his last uneasiness soaking away into relaxation.

"So," Hatcher said, obviously picking up the thread of an interrupted conversation, "you found yourself Emperor and located this Guard Flotilla of yours. I thought you said it was only seventy-eight units?"

"Only seventy-eight *warships*," Colin corrected, sitting on the edge of the table. "There are also ten *Shirga*-class colliers, three *Enchanach*-class transports, and the two repair ships. That makes ninety-three."

Horus nodded to himself, still shaken by what he'd seen as his cutter approached *Dahak*. The space about Terra seemed incredibly crowded by huge, gleaming planetoids, and their ensigns had crowded his mind with images . . . a crouching, six-limbed Birhatan crag cat, an armored warrior, a vast broadsword in a gauntleted fist, and hordes of alien and mythological beasts he hadn't even recognized. But most disturbing of all had been seeing two of *Dahak's* own dragon. He'd expected it, but expecting and seeing were two different things.

"And you managed to bring them all back with you," he said softly.

"Oh, he did, he did!" Tamman agreed, stepping out of the transit shaft behind them. "He worked us half to death in the process, too." Colin grinned wryly, and Tamman snorted. "We concentrated on the mechanical systems — Dahak and Caitrin managed most of the life-support functions through their central computers once we were underway — but it's a good thing you didn't see us before we had a chance to recuperate on the trip back!"

The big Imperial smiled, though darkness lingered in his eyes. Hideoshi's death had hit him hard, for he had been the only child of Tamman's Terra-born wife, Himeko. But Tamman had grown up when there had been no biotechnics for any Terra-born child; a son's death held an old, terrible familiarity for him.

"Yeah," Colin said, "but these ships are *dumb*, Horus, and we don't begin to have the people for them. We managed to put skeleton crews on six of the *Asgerds*, but the others are riding empty — except for *Sevrid*, that is. That's why we had to come back on Enchanach Drive instead of hypering home. We can't run 'em worth a damn without Dahak to do their thinking for them."

"That's something I still don't understand," Horus said. "Why didn't the wake-up work?"

"I will be damned if I know," Colin said frankly. "We tried it with *Two* and *Herdan*, but it didn't seem to make any difference. These computers are faster than Dahak, and they've got an incredible capacity, but even after he dumped his entire memory to them, they didn't wake up."

"Something experiential?" Horus mused. "Or in the core programming?"

"Dahak? You want to answer that one?"

"I shall endeavor, Colin, but the truth is that I do not know. Senior Fleet Captain Horus, you must understand that the basic construction of these computers is totally different from my own, with core programming specifically designed to preclude the possibility of true self-awareness on their part.

"My translation programs are sufficient for most purposes, but to date I have been unable to modify *their* programs. In many ways, their core software is an inextricable part of their energy-state circuitry. I can transfer data and manipulate their existing programs; I am not yet sufficiently versatile to alter them. I therefore suspect that the difficulty lies in their core programming and that simply increasing their data bases to match my own is insufficient to cross the threshold of true awareness. Unless, of course, there is some truth to Fleet Captain Chernikov's hypothesis."

"Oh?" Horus looked at Colin. "What hypothesis is that, Colin?"

"Vlad's gone metaphysical on us," Colin said. It could have been humor, but it didn't sound that way to Horus. "He suspects Dahak's developed a soul."

"A *soul?*"

"Yeah. He thinks it's a factor of the evolution of something outside the software or the complexity of the computer net and the amount of data in memory — a 'soul' for want of a better term." Colin shrugged. "You can discuss it with him later, if you like. He'll talk both your ears off if you let him."

"I certainly will," Horus said. "A *soul*," he murmured. "What an elegant notion. And how wonderful if it were true." He saw Hatcher's puzzled expression and smiled.

"Dahak is already a wonder," he explained. "A person — an individual — however he got that way. But if he *does* have a soul, if Man has actually brought that about, even by accident, what a magnificent thing to have done."

"I see your point," Hatcher mused, then shook himself and looked back at Colin. "But getting back to *my* point, do I understand you intend to continue as Emperor?"

"I may not have a choice," Colin said wryly. "Mother won't let me abdicate, and every piece of Imperial technology we'll ever be able to salvage is programmed to go along with her."

"What's wrong with that?" Horus put in. "I think you'll make a splendid emperor, Colin." His son-in-law stuck out his tongue. "No, seriously. Look what you've already accomplished. I don't believe there's a person on Earth who doesn't realize that he's alive only because of you —"

"Because of *you*, you mean," Colin interrupted uncomfortably.

"Only because you left me in charge, and I couldn't have done it without these people." Horus waved at Hatcher and Tsien. "But the point is, *you* made survival possible. Well, you and Dahak, and I don't suppose he wants the job."

"You suppose correctly, sir," the mellow voice said, and Horus grinned.

"And whether you want it or not, someone's going to have to take it, or something like it. We've gotten by so far only because supreme authority was imposed from the outside, and this is still a war situation, which requires an absolute authority of some sort. Even if it weren't, it's going to be at least a generation before most of Earth is prepared for effective self-government, and a world government in which only some nations participate won't work, even if it wouldn't be an abomination."

"With your permission, Your Majesty," Tsien said, cutting off Colin's incipient protest, "the Governor has a point. You are aware of how my people regard Western imperialism. That issue has been muted and, perhaps, undermined somewhat by the mutual trust our merged militaries and cooperating governments have attained, but our union is more fragile than it appears, and many of our differences remain. Cooperation as discrete equals is no longer beyond our imagination; effective amalgamation into a single government may be. You, as a source of authority from outside the normal Terran power equations, are quite another matter. You can hold us together. No one else — with the possible exception of Governor Horus — could do that."

Colin hadn't been present to witness Tsien's integration into Horus's command team. He still tended to think of the marshal as the hard-core military leader of the Asian Alliance, and Tsien's calm, matter-of-fact acceptance took him somewhat aback, but the marshal's sincerity was unmistakable.

"If that's the way you *all* feel, I guess I'm stuck. It'll make things a lot simpler where Mother is concerned, that's for sure!"

"But why is she so determined?" Hatcher asked.

"She was designed that way, Ger," MacMahan said. "Mother was the Empire's Praetorian Guard. She commanded Battle Fleet in the Emperor's name, but because she wasn't self-aware, she was immune to the ambition which tends to infect humans in the same position. Her core programming is incredible, but what it comes down to is that Herdan the Great made her the conservator of empire when he accepted the throne."

"Accepted!" Hatcher snorted.

"No, the Empire's historians were a mighty fractious lot, pretty damned immune to hagiography even when it came to emperors who were still alive. And as far as I can determine from what they had to say, that's exactly the right verb. He knew what a bitch the job was going to be and wanted no part of it."

"How many Terran emperors *admitted* they did?"

"Maybe not many, but Herdan was in a hell of a spot. There were six 'official' Imperial governments, with at least twice that many civil wars going on, and he happened to be the senior military officer of the 'Imperium' holding Birhat. That gave it a degree of legitimacy the others resented, so two of them got together to smash it, but he wound up smashing them, instead. I've studied his campaigns, and the man was a diabolical strategist. His crews knew it, too, and when they demanded that he be named dictator in the old Republican Roman tradition to put an end to the wars, the Senate on Birhat went along."

"So why didn't he step down later?"

"I think he was afraid to. He seems to have been a mighty liberal fellow for his times — if you don't believe me, take a look at the citizens' rights clauses he buried in that Great Charter of his — but he'd just finished playing fireman to put out the Imperium's wars. Like our Colin here, it was mostly his personal authority holding things together. If he let go, it would all fly apart. So he took the job when the Senate offered it to him, then spent eighty years creating an absolutist government that could hold together without becoming a tyranny.

"The way it works, the Emperor's absolute in military affairs — that's where the 'Warlord' part of his titles comes in — and a slightly limited monarch in civil matters. He *is* the executive branch, complete with the powers of appointment, dismissal, and the purse, but there's also a legislative branch in the Assembly of Nobles, and less than a third of its titles are hereditary. The other seventy-odd percent are life-titles, and Herdan set it up so that only about twenty percent of all life-titles can be awarded by the Emperor. The others are either awarded by the Assembly itself — to reward scientific achievement, outstanding military service, and things like that — or elected by popular vote. In a sense, it's a unicameral legislature with four separate houses — imperial appointees, honor appointees, elected, and hereditary nobles — buried in it, and it's a lot more than a simple rubber stamp.

"The Assembly confirms or rejects new emperors, and a sufficient majority can require a serving emperor to abdicate — well, to submit to an Empire-wide referendum, a sort of 'vote of confidence' by all franchised citizens — and Mother will back them up. *She* makes the final evaluation of any new emperor's sanity, and she won't accept a ruler who doesn't match certain intelligence criteria *and* enjoys the approval of a majority of the Assembly of Nobles. She'll simply refuse to take orders from an emperor who's been given notice to quit, and when the military begins taking its orders from his properly appointed successor, he's up shit creek in a leaky canoe."

"Doesn't sound like being Emperor's a lot of fun," Horus murmured.

"Herdan designed it that way, I think," MacMahan replied.

"My God," Hatcher said. "Government á la Goldberg!"

"It seems that way," MacMahan agreed with a smile, "but it worked for five thousand years, with only half-a-dozen minor-league 'wars' (by Imperial standards), before they accidentally wiped themselves out."

"Well," Horus said, "if it works that well, maybe we can learn something from it after all, Colin. And —"

He broke off as Jiltanith and Amanda stepped off the balcony onto *Dahak*'s pressers. Amanda carried a little girl, Jiltanith a little boy, and both infants' hair was raven's-wing black. The little girl was adorable, and the little boy looked cheerful and alert, but no one with Colin's nose and ears could ever be called adorable — except, perhaps, by Jiltanith.

Horus's eyebrows almost disappeared into his hairline.

"Surprise," Colin said, his smile broad.

"You mean — ?"

"Yep. Let me introduce you." He held out his arms, and Jiltanith handed him the little boy. "This little monster is Crown Prince Sean Horus MacIntyre, heir presumptive to the Throne of Man. And this —" Jiltanith smiled at her father, her eyes bright, as Amanda handed him the baby girl "— is his younger twin sister, Princess Isis Harriet MacIntyre."

Horus took the little girl in immensely gentle hands. She promptly fastened one small fist in his white hair and tugged hard, and he winced.

"Bid thy grandchildren welcome, Father," Jiltanith said softly, putting her arms around her father and daughter to hug them both, but Horus's throat was too tight to speak, and tears slid down his ancient cheeks.

" . . . and the additional food supplies from the farms aboard your ships have made the difference, Your Majesty," Chiang Chien-su said. The plump general beamed at the assembled officers and members of the Planetary Council. "There seems little doubt Earth has entered a 'mini-ice age,' and flooding remains a severe problem. Rationing will be required for some time, but with Imperial technology for farming and food distribution, Comrade Redhorse and I anticipate that starvation should not be a factor."

"Thank you, General," Colin said very, very sincerely. "You and your people have done superbly. As soon as I have time, I intend to elevate you to our new Assembly of Nobles for your work here."

Chiang was a good Party member, and his expression was a study as he sat down. Colin turned to the petite, smooth-faced Councilor on Horus's left.

"Councilor Hsu, what's the state of our planet-side industry?"

"There has been considerable loss, Comrade Emperor," Hsu Yin said. Obviously Chiang wasn't the only one feeling her way into the new political setup. "Comrade Chernikov's decision to increase planetary industry has borne fruit, however. Despite all damage, our industrial plant is operating at approximately fifty percent of pre-siege levels. With the assistance of your repair ships, we should make good our remaining losses within five months.

"There are, however, certain personnel problems, and not this time —" her serious eyes swept her fellow council-ors with just a hint of wry humor "— in Third World areas. Your Western trade unions — specifically, your Teamsters Union — have awakened to the economic implications of Imperial technology."

"Oh, Lord!" Colin looked at Gustav van Gelder. "Gus? How bad is it?"

"It could be much worse, as Councilor Hsu knows quite well," the security councilor said, but he smiled at her as he spoke. "So far, they are relying upon propaganda, passive resistance, and strikes. It should not take them long to realize other people are singularly unimpressed by their propaganda and that their strikes merely inconvenience a society with Imperial technology." He shrugged. "When they do, the wisest among them will realize they must adapt or go the way of the dinosaurs. I do not anticipate organized violence, if that is what you mean, but I have my eye on the situation."

"Well, thank God for that," Colin muttered. "All right, I think that clears up the planetary situation. Are there any other points we need to look at?" Heads shook. "In that case, Dahak, suppose you bring us up to date on Project Rosetta."

"Of course, Sire." Dahak was on his best official behav-ior before the council, and Colin raised one hand to hide his smile.

"Progress has been more rapid than originally projected," the computer said. "There are, of course, many differences between Achuultani — or, to be correct, Aku'Ultan — computers and our own, but the basic processes are not complex. The large quantity of hard-copy data obtained from the wreckage also will be of great value in deciphering the output we have generated.

"I am not yet prepared to provide translations or interpretations, but this project is continuing." Colin nodded. Dahak meant the majority of his capability was devoted to it even as he spoke. "I anticipate at least partial success within the next several days."

"Good," Colin said. "We need that data to plan our next move."

"Acknowledged," Dahak said calmly.

"What else do you have for us?"

"Principally observational data, Sire. Our technical teams and my own remotes have completed their initial survey of the wreckage. I am now prepared to present a brief general summary of our findings. Shall I proceed?"

"Please do."

"The present data contain anomalies. Specifically, certain aspects of Aku'Ultan technology do not logically correspond to others. For example, they appear to possess only a very rudimentary appreciation of gravitonics and their ships do not employ gravitonic sublight drives, yet their sublight missiles employ a highly sophisticated gravitonic drive which is, in fact, superior to that of the Imperium though inferior to that of the Empire."

"Could they have picked that up from someone else?" MacMahan asked.

"The possibility exists. Yet having done so, why have they not applied it to their starships? Their relatively slow speed, even in hyper space, is a severe tactical handicap, and, logically, they should recognize the potentials of their own missile propulsion, yet have not taken advantage of them.

"Nor is this the only anomaly. The computers aboard

this starship are primitive in the extreme, but little advanced over those of Earth, yet the components of which they are built are very nearly on a par with my own, though far inferior to the Empire's energy-state systems. Again, their hyper technology is highly sophisticated, yet there is no sign of beamed hyper fields, nor even of warp warheads or grenades. This is the more surprising in view of their extremely primitive, energy-intensive beam weapons. Their range is short, their effect limited, and their projectors both clumsy and massive, but little advanced from those of pre-Imperium Terra."

"Any explanation for these anomalies?" Colin asked after a moment.

"I have none, Sire. It would appear that the Aku'Ultan have chosen, for reasons best known to themselves, to build extremely inefficient warships by the standards of their own evident technical capabilities. Why a warrior race should do such a thing surpasses my present understanding."

"Yours and mine both," Colin murmured, drumming on the conference table edge. Then he shook his head.

"Thank you, Dahak. Keep on this for us, please."

"I shall, Sire."

"In that case," Colin turned to Isis and Cohanna, "what can you tell us about how these beasties are put together, ladies?"

"I'll let Captain Cohanna begin, if I may," Isis said. "She's supervised most of the autopsies."

"All right. Cohanna?"

"Well," *Dahak*'s surgeon said, "Councilor Tudor's seen more of our live specimen, but we've both learned a fair bit from the dead ones.

"To summarize, the Achuultani are definitely warm-blooded, despite their saurian appearance, though their biochemistry incorporates an appalling level of metals by human standards. A fraction of it would kill any of us; their bones are virtually a crystalline alloy; their amino acids are incredible; and they use a sort of protein-analogue metal

salt as an oxygen-carrier. I haven't even been able to identify some of the elements in it yet, but it works. In fact, it's a
bit more efficient than hemoglobin, and it's also what gives
their blood that bright orange color. Their chromosome
structure is fascinating, but I'll need several months before
I can tell you much more than that about it.

"Now," she drew a deep breath, "none of that is too terribly surprising, given that we're dealing with an utterly
alien species, but a few other points strike me as definitely
weird.

"First, they have at least two sexes, but we've seen only
males. It is, of course, possible that their culture doesn't
believe in exposing females to combat, but an incursion's
personnel spend decades of subjective time on operations.
It seems a bit unlikely, to me, at any rate, that any race
could be so immune to the biological drives as to remain
celibate for periods like that. In addition, unless their psychology is entirely beyond our understanding, I would
think that being cut off from all procreation would produce the same apathy it produces in human societies.

"Second, there appears to be an appalling lack of
variation. I've yet to unravel their basic gene structure, but
we've been carrying out tissue studies on the cadavers
recovered from the wreck. By the standards of any species
known to Terran or Imperial bioscience, they exhibit a
statistically improbable — *extremely* improbable —
homogeneity. Were it not for the very careful labeling
we've done, I would be tempted to conclude that all of our
tissue samples come from no more than a few score
individuals. I have no explanation for how this might have
come about.

"Third, and perhaps most puzzling, is the relative primi-
tivism of their gross physiognomy. To the best of our
knowledge, this same race has conducted offensive sweeps
of our arm of the galaxy for over seventy million years, yet
they do not exhibit the attributes one might expect such a
long period of high-tech civilization to produce. They're
large, extremely strong, and well-suited to a relatively

primitive environment. One would expect a species which had enjoyed technology for so long to have decreased in size, at the very least, and, perhaps, to have lost much of its tolerance for extreme environmental conditions. These creatures have done neither."

"Is that really relevant?" Amesbury asked. "Humanity hasn't exactly developed the attributes you describe, either here or in Imperial history."

"The cases aren't parallel, Sir Frederick. The Terran branch of the race is but recently removed from its own primitive period, and all of human history, from its beginnings on Mycos to the present, represents only a tiny fraction of the life experience of the Achuultani. Further, the Achuultani's destruction of the Third Imperium eliminated all human-populated planets other than Birhat — a rather draconian reduction in the gene pool."

"Point taken," Amesbury said, and Cohanna gestured to Isis.

"Just as Cohanna has noted anomalies in Achuultani physiology," the white-haired physician began, "I have observed anomalies in behavioral patterns. Obviously, our prisoner — his name is 'Brash-ee-ell,' as nearly as we can pronounce it — is a *prisoner* and so cannot be considered truly representative of his race. His behavior, however, is, by any human standard, bizarre.

"He appears resigned, yet not passive. In general, his behavior is docile, which could be assumed, genuine, or merely a response to our own biotechnics. Certainly he's deduced that even our medical technicians are several times as strong as he is, though he may not realize this is due to artificial enhancement. He is *not*, however, apathetic. He's alert, interested, and curious. We are unable to communicate with him as yet, but he appears to be actively assisting our efforts in this direction. I submit that for a soldier embarked upon a genocidal campaign to exhibit neither resistance to, nor even, so nearly as we can determine, hostility towards the species he recently attempted to annihilate isn't exactly typical of a human response."

"Um." Colin tugged on his nose. "How are his injuries responding?"

"We can't use quick-heal or regeneration on such an unknown physiology, but he appears to be recovering nicely. His bones are knitting a bit faster than a human's would; tissue repairs seem to be taking rather longer."

"All right," Colin said, "what do we have? A technology with gaping holes, a species which seems evolutionarily retarded, and a prisoner whose responses defy our logical expectations. Does anyone have any suggestions which could account for all those things?"

He looked around expectantly, but the only response was silence.

"Well," he sighed after a moment, "let's adjourn for now. Unless something breaks in the meantime, we'll convene again Wednesday at fourteen hundred hours. Will that be convenient for all of you?"

Heads nodded, and he rose.

"I'll see you all then," he said. He wanted to get home to *Dahak*, anyway. The twins were teething, and 'Tanni wasn't exactly the most placid mommy in human history.

Chapter Nineteen

Brashieel, who had been a Servant of Thunders, curled in his new nest place and pondered. It had never occurred to him — nor to anyone else, so far as he knew — to consider the possibility of capture. Protectors did not capture nest-killers; they slew them. So, he had always assumed, did nest-killers deal with Protectors, yet these had not.

He had attempted to fight to the death, but he had failed, and, strangely, he no longer wished to die. No one had ever told him he must; had they simply failed, as he, to consider that he might not? Yet he felt a vague suspicion a true thinker in honor would have ended slaying yet another nest-killer.

Only Brashieel wished to live. He *needed* to consider the new things happening to and about him. These strange bipeds had destroyed Lord Chirdan's force with scarcely five twelves of ships. Admittedly, they were huge, yet it had taken but five twelves, when Lord Chirdan had been within day-twelfths of destroying this world. That was power. Such nest-killers could purge the galaxy of the Aku'Ultan, and the thought filled him with terror.

But why had they waited so long? He had seen this world's nest-killers now, and they were the same species as those who crewed those stupendous ships. Whether they were also the nest-killers who had built those sensor arrays he did not know. It seemed likely, yet if it were so, those arrays must have told them long ago that the Great Visit was upon them, so why conceal their capability until this world had suffered such losses? And why had they not killed *him*? Because they sought information from him? That was possible, though it would not have occurred to a Protector. Which might, Brashieel admitted grudgingly, be yet another way in which his captors out-classed the Nest. But stranger even than that, they did not mistreat him. They were impossibly strong for such small beings. He had thought it was but the nest-killer's powered armor which had made him a fledgling in his hands . . . until he saw a slight, slender one with long hair lift one of their elevated sleeping pads and carry it away to clear his nest place. That was sobering proof of what they might have done to him had they chosen to.

Instead, they had tended his wounds, fed him food from *Vindicator's* wreck, provided air which was pleasant to breathe, not thin like their own — all that, when they should have struck him down. Was he not a nest-killer to *their* Protectors? Had he and his nestmates not come within a segment of destroying their very world? Were they so stupid they did not realize that they were — must be, forever — enemies to the death?

Or was it simply that they did not fear him? Beside those monster ships, the greatest ships of the Nest were fledglings with toy bows of *mowap* wood. Were they so powerful, so confident, that they did not fear the nest-killers of another people, another place?

That was the most terrifying thought of all, one which reeked of treason to the Nest, for there was — must always be — the fear, the Great Fear which only courage and the Way could quench. Yet if that was not so for these nest-killers, if they did not fear on sight, then was it possible they might not *be* nest-killers?

Brashieel curled in his new nest place, eyes closed, and whimpered in his sleep, wondering in his dreams which was truly the greater nightmare: to fear the nest-killers, or to fear that they did not fear him.

Colin and Jiltanith rose to welcome Earth's senior officers and their new starship captains. There were but fourteen captains. If they took every trained, bio-enhanced man and woman Earth's defenses could spare, they could have provided minimal crews for seventeen of the Imperial Guard's warships; they had chosen to crew only fifteen, fourteen *Asgerds* and one *Vespa*.

The Empire had gone in for more specialized designs than the Imperium, and the *Asgerds* were closest in concept to *Dahak*, well-rounded and equipped to fight at all ranges, while the *Trosans* were optimized for close combat with heavy beam armaments and the *Vespas* were optimized for planetary assaults. But the reason for manning only fifteen warships was simple; the other personnel would crew the three *Enchanach*-class transports, each vast as *Dahak* himself, for Operation Dunkirk.

In hyper, the round-trip to Bia would take barely six months, and each stupendous ship could squeeze in upward of ten million people. With luck, they had time to return for a second load even if the Imperial Guard failed to halt the Achuultani, which meant they could evacuate over sixty million humans to the almost impregnable defenses of the old Imperial capital and the housing Mother's remotes were already building to receive them. General Chiang was selecting those refugees now; they were Colin's insurance policy.

The Achuultani's best speed, even in hyper, seemed to be just under fifty times light-speed. At absolute minimum, they would take seventeen years to reach Bia. Seventeen years in which Mother and Tsien Tao-ling could activate defensive systems, collect and build additional warships, and man them. If the Achuultani ever reached Bia, they would not enjoy the visit.

Colin looked down the table at Tsien. The marshal was as impassive as ever, but Colin had seen the hurt in his eyes when he lost the coin toss to Hatcher. Yet, in a way, Colin was pleased it was Tsien who was going. He hadn't learned to know the huge man well, but he liked what he knew. Tsien was a man of iron, and Colin trusted him with his life. With far more than his life, for his children would be returning to Birhat.

Without 'Tanni. She was the commander of *Dahak Two*, the reserve flagship, and that was as far from Colin as she was going. Because she loved him, yes, but also because he would be going to meet the Achuultani, and the killer in her could not resist that battle.

Had their roles been reversed, Colin thought he might have made himself go out of a sense of duty, but 'Tanni couldn't. He might have tried ordering her to . . . if he hadn't understood and loved her.

The last officer — Senior Fleet Captain Lady Adrienne Robbins, Baroness Nergal, Companion of the Golden Nova and CO of the planetoid *Emperor Herdan* — found her place, and Colin glanced around the conference room, satisfied that this was the best Earth could boast, committed to her final defense. Then he stood and rapped gently on the table, and the quiet side conversations ended.

"Ladies and gentlemen, Dahak has broken into the Achuultani data base. We finally know what we're up against, and it isn't good. In fact, it may be bad enough to make Operation Dunkirk a necessity, not just an insurance policy."

Horus watched Colin as he spoke. His son-in-law looked grim, but far from defeated. He remembered the Colin MacIntyre he'd first met, a homely, sandy-haired young man who'd strayed into an unthinkably ancient war, determined to do what he must, yet terrified that he was unequal to his task.

That homely young man was gone. By whatever chain of luck or destiny history moved, he had met his moment. Preposterous as it seemed, he had become in truth what accident had made him: Colin I, Emperor and Warlord of Humanity — mankind's champion in this dark hour. If they survived, Horus mused, Herdan the Great would have a worthy rival as the greatest emperor in human history.

"— not going to count ourselves out yet, though," Colin was saying, and Horus shook himself back into the moment. "We've got better intelligence than anyone's ever had on an incursion, and I intend to use it. Before I tell you what I hope to accomplish, however, it's only fair that you know what we're really up against. 'Tanni?" He nodded to his wife and sat as she stood.

"My lords and ladies," she said quietly, "we face a foe greater than any who have come before us. 'Twould seem the Achuultani do call this arm of our galaxy common 'the Demon Sector' for that they have suffered so in their voyages hither. So have they mustered up a strength full double any e'er dispatched in times gone by, and this force we face with scarce four score ships.

"Our Dahak hath beagled out their numbers. As thou dost know, Achuultani calculations rest upon the base-twelve system, and 'tis a great twelve cubed — near to three million, as we would say — of warships which come upon us."

There was a sound. Not a gasp, but a deep-drawn breath. Most of the faces around the table tightened, but no one spoke.

"Yet that telleth but a part," Jiltanith went on evenly. "The scouts which did war 'pon Terra these months past were but light units. Those which come behind are vaster far, the least near twice the size of those which have been vanquished here. We scarce could smite them all did our every missile speed straightway to its mark, and so, in sober fact, we durst not meet them all in open battle."

Officers exchanged stunned glances, and Colin didn't blame them. His own first reaction would have done his reputation for coolness no good at all.

"Yet I counsel not despair!" Jiltanith's clear voice cut

through the almost-fear. "Nay, good my lords and ladies, our Warlord hath a plan most shrewd which still may tumble them to dust. Yet now will I ask our General MacMahan to speak that thou mayst know thine enemies."

She sat, and Horus applauded silently. Colin's human officers spoke, not Dahak. Everyone here knew how much they relied upon Dahak, yet he could see them drawing a subtle strength from hearing their own kind brief them. It wasn't that they distrusted Dahak — how could they, when their very survival to this point resulted only from the ancient starship's fidelity? — but they needed to hear a human voice expressing confidence. A human who was merely mortal, like themselves, and so could understand what he or she asked of them.

"Ladies and gentlemen," Hector MacMahan said, "Fleet Captain Ninhursag and I have spent several days examining the data with Dahak. Ninhursag's also spent time with our prisoner and, with Dahak's offices as translator, she's been able to communicate with him after a fashion. Oddly enough, from our perspective, though he hasn't volunteered data, he's made no attempt to lie or mislead us.

"We've learned a great deal as a result, and though there are still huge holes in our knowledge, I'll attempt to summarize our findings. Please bear with me if I seem to wander a bit afield. I assure you, it's pertinent.

"The Achuultani, or the People of the Nest of Aku'-Ultan, are — exclusively, so far as we can determine — a warrior race. Judging from some of Brashieel's counterquestions, they know absolutely nothing about any other sentient race. They've spent millions of years hunting them down and destroying them, yet they've learned nothing — literally *nothing* — about any of them. It's almost as if they fear communicating might somehow corrupt their great purpose. And that purpose is neither less nor more than the defense of the Nest of Aku'Ultan."

A few eyebrows rose, and Hector shook his head.

"I found it hard to believe at first myself, but that's

precisely how they see it, because at some point in their past they encountered another race, one their records call 'the Great Nest-Killers.' How they met, why war broke out, what weapons were used, even where the war was fought, we do not know. What we do know is that there were once many 'nests.' These might be thought of as clans or tribes, but they consisted of millions and even billions of Achuultani. Of all those nests, only the Aku'Ultan survived, and only because they fled. From what we've learned, we're inclined to believe they fled to an entirely different galaxy — our own — to find safety.

"After their flight, the Achuultani organized to defend themselves against pursuit, just as the Imperium organized to fight the Achuultani themselves. And just as the Imperium sent out probes searching for the Achuultani, the Achuultani searched for the Great Nest-Killers. Like our ancestors, they never found their enemy. Unlike our ancestors, they did find other sentient life-forms. And because they regarded all other life-forms as threats to their very existence, they destroyed them."

He paused, and there was a deep silence.

"That's what we're up against: a race which offers no quarter because it *knows* it will receive none. I don't say it's a situation which can never be changed, but clearly it's one we cannot hope will change in time to save us.

"On another level, there are things about the Aku'Ultan we don't pretend to understand.

"First, there are no female Achuultani." Several people looked at him in open disbelief, and he shrugged. "It sounds bizarre, but so far as we can tell, there isn't even a feminine gender in their language, which is all the more baffling in light of the fact that our prisoner is a fully functional male. Not a hermaphrodite, but a *male*. Fleet Captain Cohanna suggests this may indicate they reproduce by artificial means, which might explain why we see so little variation among them and, perhaps, their apparent lack of evolutionary change. It does *not* explain why any race, especially one as driven to survive as this one, should make the extraordinary decision to abandon all possibility of natural procreation. We asked Brashieel about this and got a totally baffled response. He simply didn't understand the question. It hadn't even occurred to him that *we* have two sexes, and he has no idea at all what that means to our psychology or our civilization.

"Second, the Nest is an extremely rigid, caste-oriented society dominated by the High Lords of the Nest and headed by the Nest Lord, the highest of the high, absolute ruler of all Achuultani. Exactly how High Lords and Nest Lords are chosen was none of Brashieel's business. As nearly as we can tell, he was never even curious. It was simply the way things were.

"Third, the Aku'Ultan inhabit relatively few worlds; most of them are always away aboard the fleets of their 'Great Visits,' sweeping the galaxy for 'nest-killers' and destroying them. The few planets they inhabit seem to be much farther away than the Imperium ever suspected, which is probably why they were never found, and the Achuultani appear to be migratory, abandoning star systems as they deplete them to construct their warships. We don't know exactly where they are; that information wasn't in *Vindicator's* computers or, if it was, was destroyed before we took them. From what we've been able to determine, however, they appear to be moving to the galactic east. This would mean they're constantly moving *away* from us, which may also help to explain the irregular frequency of their incursions in our direction.

"Fourth, the Nest's social and military actions follow patterns which, as far as we can tell, have never altered in their racial memory. Frankly, this is the most hopeful point we've discovered. We now know how their 'Great Visits' work and how to derail the process for quite some time."

"We do?" Gerald Hatcher scratched his nose thoughtfully. "And just how do we do that, Hector?"

"We stop this incursion," MacMahan said simply. There was a mutter of uneasy laughter, and he smiled very slightly. "No, I mean it.

"The Achuultani possess no means of interstellar FTL communication other than by ship. How they could've been around this long and not developed one is beyond me, but they haven't, which means that once a 'Great Visit' is launched, they don't expect to hear anything from it until it gets back."

"That's good news, anyway," Hatcher agreed.

"Yes, it is. Especially in light of some of their other limitations. Their best n-space speed is twenty-eight percent of light-speed, and they use only the lower, slower hyper bands — again, we don't understand why, but let's be grateful — which limits their best supralight speed to forty-eight lights; seven percent of what Dahak can turn out, six percent of what the Guard can turn out under Enchanach Drive, and two percent of what it can turn out in hyper. That means they take a *long* time to complete an incursion. Of course, unlike Enchanach Drive, there's a time dilation effect in hyper, and the lower your band, the greater the dilation, which means their voyages take a lot less time subjectively, but Brashieel's ship had already come something like fourteen thousand light-years to reach Sol. So if the incursion sent a courier home tomorrow, he'd take just under three centuries to get there. Which means, ladies and gentlemen, that if we stop them, we've got almost six hundred years before a new 'Great Visit' can get back here. And that we know where to go looking for *them* in the meantime."

A soft growl came from the assembled officers as they visualized what they could do with five or six centuries to work with.

"I'm glad to hear that, Hector," Hatcher said carefully, "but it leaves us with the little matter of three million or so ships coming at us right now."

"True," Colin said, waving MacMahan back down. "But we've learned a little — less than we'd like, but a little — about their strategic doctrine.

"First, we have a bit more time than we'd thought. The incursion is divided into three major groups: two main formations and a host of sub-formations of scouts which do most of the killing. The larger formations are mainly to back up the scout forces, each of which operates on a different axis of advance. Aside from the one which already hit us, they're unlikely to hit anything but dead planets as far as we're concerned, and a half-dozen crewed *Asgerds* could deal with any of them. If we can stop the main incursion, we'll have plenty of time to hunt them down and pick them off.

"The real bad news is coming at us in two parts. The first — what I think of as the 'vanguard' — is about one and a quarter million ships, advancing fairly slowly from rendezvous to rendezvous in n-space to permit scouts to send back couriers to report. We may assume one's already been dispatched from Sol, but it can't pass its message until the vanguard drops out of hyper at the rendezvous, thirty-six Achuultani light-years from Sol. Given the difference in length between our years and theirs, that's about forty-six-point-eight of our light-years. The vanguard won't reach their rendezvous for another three months; we can be there in about three and a half weeks with *Dahak*, and a hell of a lot less than that for the Guard in hyper."

"And take on a million ships when you get there?" Hatcher said.

"Tough odds, but I've got a mousetrap planned that should take them out. Unfortunately, it'll only work once.

"That's our problem. Even if we zap the vanguard, that still leaves what I think of as the 'main body': almost as numerous and with some really big mothers, under their supreme commander, a Great Lord Tharno.

"Now, the vanguard and main body actually keep changing relative position — they 'leapfrog' as they advance — and their rendezvous are much more tightly spaced than the scouts' are. Again, this is to allow for communication; the scouts can't pass messages laterally, and they only send one back to the closest main fleet rendezvous if they hit trouble, but the leading main formation sends couriers back to the trailing formation at each stop.

If there's really bad news, the lead force calls the trailer forward to link up, but only after investigating to be sure they *need* help, since it plays hell with their schedules. In any case, however, at least one courier is always sent back and there's a minimum interval of about five months before the trailer can come up. With me so far?"

There were nods, and he smiled grimly.

"All right, that's our major strategic advantage: their coordination stinks. Because they use hyper drives, their ships have to stay in hyper once they go into it until they reach their destination. And because their maximum fold-space com range is barely a light-year, the rear components of their fleet always jump to the origin point of the last message from the lead formation. Even in emergencies, the follow-on echelon has to jump to almost exactly the same point, assuming they mean to coordinate with the leaders, because with their miserable communications they can't *find* each other if they don't."

"Which means," Marshal Tsien said thoughtfully, "that your own ships may be able to ambush their formations as they emerge from hyper."

"Exactly, Marshal. What we hope to do is mousetrap the vanguard and wipe it out; I think we'll get away with that, but we don't know where the rendezvous point *before* this one is. That means we can't stop the vanguard's couriers from telling Lord Tharno about our trap, meaning that the main body will be alerted and ready when it comes out.

"So we probably *will* have to fight the main body. That pits seventy-eight of us against one-point-two million of them: about fifteen thousand to one."

Someone swallowed audibly, and Colin smiled that grim smile again.

"I think we can take them. We may lose a lot of ships, but we ought to be able to swing it *if* they pop into n-space where we expect them."

A long silence dragged out. Marshal Tsien broke it at length.

"Forgive me, but I do not see how you can do it."

"I'm not certain we can, Marshal," Colin said frankly. "I *am* certain that we have a chance, and that we can destroy at least half and more probably two-thirds of their force. If that's all we accomplish, we may not save Earth, but we *will* save Birhat and the refugees headed there. That, Marshal Tsien" — he met the huge man's eyes — "is why I'm so relieved to know we're sending one of our best people to take over Bia's defenses."

"I am honored by your confidence, Your Majesty, yet I fear you have set yourself an impossible task. You have only fifteen partially-manned warships — sixteen, counting *Dahak*."

"But *Dahak* is our ace in the hole. Unlike the rest of us, he can fight all of our unmanned ships with full efficiency as long as he's in fold-space range of them."

"And if something happens to him, Your Majesty?" Tsien asked quietly.

"Then, Marshal Tsien," Colin said just as quietly, "I hope to hell you have Bia in shape by the time the incursion gets there."

Chapter Twenty

"Hyper wake coming in from Sol, ma'am."

Adrienne Robbins, Lady Nergal (and it still felt *weird* to be a noble of an empire which had died forty-five thousand years ago), nodded and watched *Herdan's* holographic projection. The F5 star Terran astronomers knew as Zeta Trianguli Australis was a diamond chip five light-years astern, and the blood-red hyper trace indicator flashed almost on a line with it.

Adrienne's stupendous command floated with three other starships, yet alone and lonely. The four of them were deployed to cover almost a cubic light-year of space, and Tamman's *Royal Birhat* was already moving to intercept. Well, that was all right; she'd killed enough Achuultani at the Siege of Earth.

"Captain, we've got a very faint wake coming in from the east, too," her plotting officer said, and Lady Adrienne frowned. That had to be the Achuultani vanguard, and it was way ahead of schedule.

"Emergence times?"

"Bogey One will emerge into n-space in approximately

seven hours twelve minutes, ma'am; make it oh-two-twenty zulu," Fleet Commander Oliver Weinstein said. "Bogey Two's a real monster to show up at this range at all. We've got a good hundred hours before they emerge, maybe as much as five days. I'll be able to refine that in a couple of hours."

"Do that, Ollie," she said, relaxing again. The vanguard wasn't as far ahead of schedule as she'd feared, just a bigger, more visible target than anticipated.

Adrienne sighed. It had been easier to command *Nergal*. The battleship's computers had been no smarter than *Herdan's*, but they'd had nowhere near as much to do. If she'd needed to, she could be anywhere in the net through her neural feed, but *Herdan* was just too damned big. Even with six thousand crewmen aboard, less than five percent of her duty stations were manned. They could get by — barely — with that kind of stretch, but it was a bitch and a half. If only this ship were half as smart — hell, even a tenth as smart! — as *Dahak*. But they had only one *Dahak*, and he couldn't be committed to this job.

"Herdan," she said aloud.

"Yes, Captain?" a soft soprano replied, and Adrienne's mouth curled in a reflexive smile. It was silly for a ship named for the Empire's greatest emperor to sound like a teenaged girl, but apparently the fashion in the late Empire had been to give computers female voices, and hang the gender.

"Assume Bogey Two has scanners fifty percent more efficient than those of the scouts which attacked Earth and will emerge into n-space twelve hours from now. Compute probability Bogey Two will be able to detect detonation of Mark-Seventy gravitonic warheads at spatial and temporal loci of Bogey One's projected emergence into n-space."

"Computing." There was a brief pause. "Probability approaches zero."

"How closely?"

"Probability is one times ten to the minus thirty-second," *Herdan* responded. "Plus or minus two percent."

"Well, that's pretty close to zero at that, I guess," Adrienne murmured.

"Comment not understood."

"Ignore last comment," Adrienne replied, suppressing a sigh. It wasn't *Herdan's* fault she was an idiot, but after talking to *Dahak* —

"Acknowledged," *Herdan* said, and Lady Adrienne pressed her lips firmly together.

"Scout emergence into n-space in fourteen minutes, sir."

"Thank you, Janet," Senior Fleet Captain Tamman said, wishing he could share his tension with Amanda, and wasn't that a silly thought when he'd taken such pains to insure that he couldn't? Well, he admitted, "pains" was the wrong word, but he'd only gotten away with it because he'd found out about Colin's compulsory personnel orders assigning all pregnant Fleet personnel to the Operation Dunkirk crews a good month before Amanda had.

He *thought* she would forgive him someday, but he'd almost lost her once in La Paz, and then a rifle slug went right through her visor aboard *Vindicator*. It was only the Maker's own grace it hadn't shattered, and she'd used up most of her helmet sealant and all of her luck. He was taking no chances this time.

"Emergence in five minutes," Janet Santino said politely, and Tamman shook his head. Woolgathering, by the Maker!

"Come to Red One," he said, and his command staff settled into even more intimate communion with their consoles. His own eyes focused dreamily on the red circle delineating their target's locus of emergence, barely twenty light-seconds from their present position, while his brain concentrated on his neural feed, "seeing" directly through *Birhat's* superb scanners.

That courier had done a bang-up job of timing its jump, given the crudity of its computers, to hit this close to an exact rendezvous with the vanguard.

"Emergence in one minute," Santini said.

"Alpha Battery," Tamman said gently, "you are authorized to fire the moment you have a firm track."

"Emergence in thirty seconds. Fifteen. Ten. Five. *Now!*"

The red circle suddenly held a tiny red dot. There was a brief, eternal heartbeat of tension, and then the missiles fired.

They were sublight in order to home, but only barely so. They flashed across the display, and the dot vanished without fuss or bother, twenty kilometers of starship ripped apart by gravitonic warheads it had probably never even seen coming.

"Target," *Birhat's* velvety contralto purred, "destroyed."

"Thank you, darling," someone murmured. "I hope it was good for you, too."

"Well, that's the first hurdle," Colin said as he digested Tamman's brief hypercom transmission.

"As thou sayst," Jiltanith agreed.

Colin nodded and looked around, admiring *Dahak Two's* spacious command deck and awesome instrumentation, and knew he would trade it all in a heartbeat for *Dahak's* outmoded bridge. Not that *Two* wasn't a fantastic fighting machine; she just wasn't *Dahak*. But *Dahak* couldn't fly this mission, and Colin refused to send his people to fight without him. Assuming anyone survived the next few months, that might be something he'd have to get used to. For now, it wasn't.

At the moment, *Two* was tearing through space at better than eight hundred times light-speed. *Herdan* was closest to the vanguard's projected emergence, and the ships which had spread out to cover the courier's probable emergence points hurried toward her. They could have made the trip in a fraction of the time in hyper, but then the vanguard might have seen them coming.

It was all right, he told himself again. Those Achuultani clunkers were so slow all twelve of the ships he'd committed to the operation would be in position long before they emerged.

"Approaching supralight shutdown, Captain," a female voice said.

"My thanks, Two," Jiltanith replied, and that was another strange thing. Colin might be an emperor and a warlord; he was also a passenger. *Two* could not be in better hands, but it felt odd to be riding someone else's command after all this time, even 'Tanni's.

He turned his attention to the display, and the bright green dots of his other ships blinked as *Two* went sublight and the stars suddenly slowed. There came *Tor*, the last of them, closing up nicely. Good.

"All units in position, Sire," Jiltanith said formally. "Stealth fields active."

"Thank you, Captain," Colin said with equal formality. "Now we wait."

Great Lord of Order Sorkar hated rendezvous stops, especially in the Demon Sector. Battle Comp assured him there was no real danger, and Nest Lord knew Battle Comp was always right, but there were too many horror stories about this sector. Sorkar was not supposed to know them — great lords were above the gossip of lower nestlings — but unlike most of his fellows, Sorkar had won his lordship the hard way, and he had not forgotten his origins as thoroughly as, perhaps, he ought to have.

Still, *this* visit had been almost boring, despite those odd reports of long-abandoned sensor arrays. Sorkar had longed for a little action more than once, for the urge to hunt was strong within any great lord, but Protectors were a commodity to be preserved for the service of the Nest, and he was too shrewd a commander to regret the tedium. Mostly.

He split his attention between his panel and the chronometers as they clicked over the last segment, and a corner of his brain double-checked the override between Battle Comp and his own panel. Battle Comp seldom took a hand directly, but it was comforting to know it could.

There! Emergence.

He watched his instruments approvingly. It was impossible to coordinate the translation between hyper space and n-space perfectly for so many units, but the time spread looked more than merely satisfactory, and the spacing was exemplary. His Protectors had learned their duties well over the —

"Alarm! Alarm! Incoming fire! Incoming fire!" a voice yelped, and Great Lord Sorkar jerked half-upright. They were light-years from the nearest star — *who could be firing on them here?*

But someone *was*, and he watched in horror as missiles of the greater thunder and something else, something beyond belief, shredded his proud starships like blazing tinder.

Nest-killers! The Demon Nest-Killers of the Demon Sector! But *how*? He'd studied all the previous great visits to this sector. Never — *never!* — had nest-killers struck until one or more of their worlds had been cleansed! Had those mysterious sensor arrays alerted them after all? But even if they had, how could they have known to find the rendezvous? It was impossible!

Yet the missiles continued to bore in, sublight and hyper alike, and his scanners could not even *see* the attackers! What wizardry — ?

A raucous buzzer cut through his thoughts, and his eyes flashed to Battle Comp's panel. Data codes danced as the mighty computers took over his fleet, and Great Lord Sorkar was a passenger as his ships deployed. They spread apart, thinning the nest-killers' target even as they groped blindly to find their enemy. It was a good plan, he thought, but it was costing them. Tarhish, *how* it was costing them! But if there truly was a nest-killer force out there, if this was not, indeed, the night-demons of frightened legend, then they would find them. Terrible as his losses were, they were as nothing against his entire force, and when Battle Comp found a tar —

A target source appeared on his panel. Another blinked into sight, and another, as his nestlings spent their lives merely to find them, and Nest Lord, they were close! Some sort of cloaking technology. The thought was an icicle in his brain, for it was far better than anything the Nest had, but he had targets at last. He moved to order his nestlings to open fire, but Battle Comp had acted first. He heard his own voice, calm and dispassionate, already passing the command.

"Burn, baby! *Burn!*" someone whooped.

"Silence! Clear the net!" Adrienne Robbins cracked, and the exultant voice vanished. Not that she could blame whoever it had been, for their opening salvos had been twice as effective as projected. Unfortunately, that was because they were *three* times as close as planned. The hyper drives aboard these larger ships were slightly different from those the scouts had mounted, and their calculations had been off. By only a tiny amount, perhaps, but minute computational errors had major consequences on this scale.

They were going to burn through the stealth field a hell of a lot quicker than anyone had expected. She knew she had more experience against the Achuultani than anyone else, and perhaps her earlier losses had affected her nerve, but, damn it, those buggers were inside their own sublight *and* hyper missile range! *Herdan's* defenses were incomparably better than *Nergal's*, and her shield covered twenty times the hyper bands, but her sheer size meant it extended even further from the hull than *Nergal's* had, and there were going to be a *lot* of missiles headed her way very soon.

"Stand by missile defense; stand by ECM!" she snapped, and then, dear Jesus, here it came.

Great Lord Sorkar spit an incredulous curse. A twelve of them! A single *twelve* had already slain a greater twelve and more of his ships, and their defenses were as incredible as their firepower. Targeting screens blossomed with false images, sucking his sublight weapons off target. Jammers hashed the scan channels. Titanic shields shrugged the greater thunder contemptuously aside. And still his ships died and died and died. . . .

Yet nothing could stop the twelves of twelves of twelves of missiles his ships were hurling, and he bared his teeth as the first hyper missile slashed through a nest-killer shield. There! That should show them that —

He blinked, and his blood was ice. What sort of monster could absorb a direct hit from the greater thunder and not even *notice* it?

Alarms screamed as a ten thousand-megaton warhead exploded almost on top of *Royal Birhat*. The huge ship quivered as the furious plasma cloud carved an incandescent chasm twenty kilometers into her armored hull. Air exploded from the dreadful wound, blast doors slammed . . . and *Birhat* went right on fighting.

"Moderate damage to Quadrant Theta-Two," the sexy contralto said calmly. "Four fatalities. Point zero-four-two percent combat impairment."

Colin winced as the flashing yellow band of combat damage encircled *Birhat*. He'd lost track of the kills they'd scored, but he'd fucked up. They were too frigging close!

"All ships, open the range," he snapped, and the Imperial Guard darted suddenly astern at sixty-five percent of light-speed.

Tarhish, they were fast! Sorkar had never seen anything but a missile move that quickly in n-space. They fell back out of range of his sublight weapons, retreating toward the edge of his hyper missile envelope, but their own weapons seemed totally unaffected, and he had never seen such accurate targeting. Indeed, he had never seen anyone do *anything* these nest-killers were doing to him, but that did not make them night-demons. It only meant his Protectors faced a test worse than he had ever imagined, and they were *Protectors*.

And, he thought under the surface of his battle orders,

perhaps it was not as bad as it might have been. These nest-killers had known where to meet his ships, and not even those arrays could have told them that, so they must have already destroyed one scout force — probably Furtag's, given the timing — and followed its couriers hither. Yet if they could muster but a single twelve of ships, however powerful, against him, then the ships under his command were more than enough to feed them to the Furnace. Even at this extreme range, he had an incalculable advantage in launchers. Not so good as theirs, perhaps, but more than enough to make up any disadvantage.

"Colin, they press us sore," Jiltanith said, and Colin nodded sharply. The plan had been to empty their magazines into the Achuultani, but the shit was too deep for that. *Birhat* had taken only one hit, but *Two* had taken three and *Tor* had taken five. *Five* of those monster warheads!

These ships were tough beyond belief, but any toughness had its limits. He winced as yet another massive salvo exploded against *Two's* shield and the big ship plowed through the plasma like a drunken windjammer. It was only a matter of time until —

"*Tor* reports shield failure," *Two's* Comp Cent announced. "Attempting to withdraw into hyper." Colin's eyes darted to *Tor's* cursor, and the flashing yellow circle was banded in crimson. He stared at it in horror, willing the ship's hyper drive to take her out of it, as missile after missile went home —

"Withdrawal unsuccessful," *Two* said emotionlessly, and Colin's face went bone-white as *Tor's* dot vanished forever.

"Execute Bug Out," he grated.

"Acknowledged," Jiltanith said coolly.

The nest-killers vanished.

Sorkar stared in disbelief at the reports of his hyper scanners. Almost a greater twelve times light-speed? How was it possible?

But what mattered was that it *was* possible. And that his scanner crews had noted the charging hyper fields in time to get good readings on them. He knew where they would emerge — at that bright star less than a quarter-twelve of light-years ahead of his fleet.

It could not be their homeworld, not so coincidentally close to the rendezvous, but whatever it was, Sorkar knew what to do if they were stupid enough to tie themselves to its defense, too deep in its gravity well to escape into hyper. He could wade into their fire, take his losses, and crush them by sheer numbers, for he had already proven they could be destroyed.

He did not like to think how many hits it had taken to kill that single nest-killer, but they *had* killed it. And his own losses were scarcely three greater twelves, grievous but hardly fatal.

He plugged into Battle Comp, but he already knew what his orders would be.

Colin hoped his expression hid the depth of his shock as his ships darted away. He'd known they would take losses, but he hadn't expected to start taking them so soon, and they'd destroyed less than a half-percent of the enemy. He'd counted on more than that, and *no* losses of his own, damn it!

But he couldn't have brought more ships without Dahak to run them, and *Dahak* had no hyper drive. That was the crunch point, because the Achuultani *had* to know where he and his ships had run to.

And because of that, Senior Fleet Captain Roscoe Gillicuddy and his crew had died, and Colin had lost six percent of his autonomous warship strength. He didn't know which hurt more, and that made him feel ashamed.

But the mousetrap had been baited. They'd lost more heavily than allowed for, yet they'd done what they set out to do. He told himself that, but it wasn't enough to hold the demons of guilt and the fear of inadequacy at bay.

A warm, slender hand squeezed his tightly, and he squeezed back gratefully. Military protocol might frown on a warlord holding hands with his flagship captain, but he needed that touch of beloved flesh just now.

Chapter Twenty-One

Thirty-six days after the brief, savage battle, *Dahak* kept station on Zeta Trianguli Australis-I and Colin stood in Command One, contemplating the planet his crews had dubbed The Cinder.

He and Jiltanith had tried to name The Cinder something else ("Tanni had favored "Cheese"), but perhaps the crews were right, Colin thought sourly. With a mean orbital radius of five-point-eight-nine light-minutes, The Cinder was about as close to Zeta Trianguli Australis as Venus was to Sol, and Colin had always thought Venus, with a surface hotter than molten lead, was close enough to Hell.

The Cinder was worse, for Zeta Trianguli was brighter than Sol — *much* brighter. But The Cinder had been chosen very carefully. There were other worlds in the system, including a rather nice, if cool, third planet fifteen light-minutes further out. Zeta Trianguli was old for its class, and III had even developed a local flora that was vaguely carboniferous, but Colin was just as happy it had only the most primitive of animal life.

He folded his hands behind him, watching the display, glancing ever and again at the scarlet hyper trace blinking steadily just inside the forty-light-minute orbital shell of Zeta Trianguli-IV.

Fleet Commodore the Empress Jiltanith sat on her command deck and touched the gemmed dagger at her belt. She'd owned that weapon since the Wars of the Roses, and its familiar hilt had soothed her often over the years, but it helped little today. She knew it made excellent sense for her to be where she was, and that, too, was little help.

She wanted to rise and pace, but it would do no good to display her fear, and there were still many hours to go. Indeed, she ought to be in her quarters — her lonely, empty quarters — resting, but here she could at least see *Dahak's* light code and know how Colin fared.

An even dozen *Trosan*-class planetoids with their heavy energy batteries floated in the inner system with *Dahak*, and two *Vespa*-class assault planetoids orbited The Cinder, tending the heavy armored units doing absolutely nothing worthwhile on its fiery surface . . . except generating a massive energy signature not even a blind man could have missed.

Jiltanith's eyes moved from the three-dimensional schematic of the Zeta Trianguli System to the emptiness about her own ship. The fourteen surviving crewed units of the Imperial Guard floated more than six light-hours from the furnace of the star, and Vlad Chernikov's titanic repair ship *Fabricator* had labored mightily upon them. Much of the damage had been too severe to be fully healed — *Two*, for example, still bore two wounds over sixty kilometers deep — but all were combat ready. Ready, yet carefully stealthed, hidden from every prying scanner, accompanied by sixty loyal, lifeless ships.

Jiltanith did not like to consider why they were not with *Dahak*, but the reasoning was brutally simple. If Operation Mousetrap failed, the crewed ships would return to

Terra to hold as long as they might and evacuate as many
additional Terra-born as possible to Birhat when they
could hold no more, but the unmanned planetoids would
be sent directly to Birhat and Marshal Tsien.

There would be no point retaining them, for they were
useless in close combat without Dahak's control, and
Dahak — and Colin — would be dead.

Great Lord Sorkar's crest flexed thoughtfully as his portion
of the Great Visit neared normal-space once more. This star
was suspiciously young to have evolved nest-killers of its own,
which reinforced his belief that it could be but a forward base.
That was bad, since it gave no hint what star these demons
might call home. Unless one of them was obliging enough to
flee into hyper and head directly thence, which he doubted
any ships as fast as they would do, he could not even guess
where their true home world lay.

Except, of course, that it almost certainly had been
Lord Furtag's scouts which had roused these nest-killers to
fury. They must have followed a courier to find Sorkar, and
only a courier from Furtag's force could have reached this
rendezvous so soon. And that gave Sorkar a volume of
space in which at least one of their important worlds must
lie. That might be enough. If it was not, it was at least a
start. And this star system was another.

Those monster ships' sheer size impressed him deeply,
yet anything that large must take many years to build, so
each he slew would hurt the nest-killers badly. He only
hoped those who had already clashed with his nestlings
would be foolish enough to stand and fight here.

A soft musical tone sounded, and he made himself
relax, hoping that Battle Comp noticed his tranquillity.
The queasy shudder of hyper translation ran through his
flagship, and *Defender* dropped into phase with reality
once more.

"Achuultani units are emerging from hyper," Dahak's
mellow voice said.

Colin nodded as the dots of Achuultani ships gleamed in the display. He looked around the empty bridge, wishing for just a moment that he'd let the others stay. But if this worked, he and Dahak could pull it off alone; if it failed, those eight thousand-odd people would be utterly invaluable to 'Tanni and Gerald Hatcher. Besides, this was fitting, somehow. He and Dahak, together and alone once more.

"Keep an eye on 'em," he said. "Let me know if they do anything sneaky."

"I shall." Dahak was silent for a moment, then continued. "I have continued my study of energy-state computer technology, Colin."

"Oh?" If Dahak wanted to distract him, that was fine with Colin.

"Yes. I believe I have isolated the fundamental differences between the energy-state 'software' of the Empire and my own. They were rather more subtle than I originally anticipated, but I now feel confident of my ability to reprogram at will."

"Hey, that's great! You mean you could tinker them into waking up?"

"I did not say that, Colin. I can reprogram them; I still have not determined what within my own programming supports my self-aware state. Without that datum, I cannot recreate that state in another. Nor have I yet discovered a certain technique for simply replicating my current programming in their radically different circuitry."

"Yeah." Colin frowned. "But even if you could, you'd have problems, wouldn't you? They're hard-wired for loyalty to Mother — wouldn't that put a crimp into your replication?"

"Not," Dahak said rather surprisingly, "in the case of the Guard. Its units were not part of Battle Fleet and do not contain Battle Fleet loyalty imperatives. I suppose" — the computer sounded gently ironic — "Mother and the Assembly of Nobles calculated that the remaining nine hundred ninety-eight thousand seven hundred and twelve planetoids of Battle Fleet would suffice to deal with them in the event an emperor proved intractable."

"Guess they might, at that."

"The absence of those constraints, however, makes the replication of my core programming at least a possibility, although not a very high one. While I have made progress, I compute that the probability of success would be no more than eight percent. The probability that an *unsuccessful* attempt would incapacitate the recipient computer, however, approaches unity."

"Um." Colin tugged on his nose. "Not so good. The last thing we need is to addle one of the others just now."

"My own thought exactly. I thought, however, that you might appreciate a progress report."

"You mean," Colin snorted, "that you thought I was about to get the willies and you'd better distract me from 'em!"

"That is substantially what I said." Dahak made the soft sound he used for a chuckle. "In my own tactful fashion, of course."

"Tactful, shmactful." Colin grinned. "Thanks, I —"

He broke off as the glittering hordes of Achuultani light codes suddenly vanished only to blink back moments later, much closer in-system.

"They are advancing," Dahak said calmly. "A trio of detached ships, however, appear to be micro-jumping to positions on the system periphery."

"Observers, damn it. Well, no one can count on their enemies being idiots."

"True, though that will be of limited utility if we are able to repeat our earlier success and destroy them before they rendezvous with the main body."

"Yeah, but we can't be sure of doing that. It's a lot shorter jump this time, and they can cut their arrival a hell of a lot closer. Tell 'Tanni to lay off. Last thing we need to do is to try sneaking up on 'em and alert them to the fact that there's more of us around."

"Acknowledged," Dahak replied. "*Two* has acknowledged," he added a moment later.

"Thanks," Colin grunted.

His attention was on the display. The Achuultani had micro-jumped with beautiful precision, spreading out to englobe Zeta Trianguli at a range of twenty-seven light-minutes. Now they were closing in normal space at twenty-four percent light-speed. They'd be into extreme missile range in another ten minutes, but it would take them almost an hour to reach *their* range of The Cinder, and he and Dahak could hurt them badly in that much time.

But not too badly. They had to keep closing. He needed them deep into the stellar gravity well for this to work, and —

He snorted. There were over a *million* of the bastards — just how much damage did he think his fifteen ships could inflict in fifty minutes?

"Open up at fifteen light-minutes, Dahak," he said finally. "Timed-rate fire. We don't want to shoot ourselves dry."

"Acknowledged," Dahak said calmly, and they waited.

Great Lord Sorkar fought his exultation. The nest-killers had not even attempted to cloak themselves! They simply sat waiting, and that was fine with Sorkar. Many of his nestlings were about to die, but so were the nest-killers.

There *had* been a few more of them about, he noted. There were a third-twelve of new ships to replace the one they had lost in the first clash. Well, that was scarcely enough to affect the outcome.

His scanners gave no clear idea what was happening on the innermost planet, but *something* was producing a massive energy signature there, though why the nest-killers had ignored the more hospitable worlds further out puzzled him. Perhaps they were simply poorer strategists than they were ship-builders. And perhaps they had some other reason he knew not of? But whatever their logic, it was about to become a death trap for them.

Of course, they were infernally fast even in n-space. . . .

If they made a break for it, none of his nestlings could stay with them, but he had an answer for that.

"They are deploying an outer sphere, Colin."

"I see it. Want to bet they leave it ten or twelve light-minutes out to catch us between two fires if we run?"

"I have nothing to wager."

"Chicken! What a cop out!"

"Enemy entering specified attack range." Dahak's mellow voice was suddenly deeper.

"Engage as previously instructed," Colin said formally.

"Engaging, Your Majesty."

Great Lord Sorkar flinched as the first of his ships exploded in eye-clawing fury. Nest Lord! He had known they outranged him, but by *that* much?

More ships exploded, and now those strange, terrible warheads were striking home, crumpling his mighty starships in upon themselves, but still the nest-killers made no effort to flee. Clearly they meant to cover the planet to the end. What in the name of Tarhish could make it so important to them?! No matter. They were standing, waiting for him to kill them.

"Open the formation," he told his lords. "Maintain closure rate."

More ships died like small, dreadful suns, and Sorkar watched coldly. He must endure this for another quarter segment, but then it would be *his* turn.

Jiltanith bit her lower lip as searing flashes ripped the Achuultani formation. The Empire's antimatter warhead yields were measured in gigatons, and fifteen planetoids pumped their dreadful missiles into the oncoming Achuultani, yet still the enemy closed. Something inside her tried to admire their courage, but that was her husband, her Colin, alone with his electronic henchman, who stood against them, and she gripped her dagger hilt, black eyes hungry, and rejoiced as the spalls of destruction pocked *Two*'s display.

❖   ❖   ❖

"They are entering their range of us, Colin," Dahak said coolly, and Colin nodded silently, awed by the waves of fire sweeping the Achuultani formation. The flames leapt high as each salvo struck, then died, only to bloom afresh, like embers fanned by a bellows, as the next salvo crashed home.

"Their losses?" he asked sharply.

"Estimate one hundred six thousand, plus or minus point-six percent."

Jesus. We've killed close to nine percent of them and they're still coming. They've got guts, but Lord God are they dumb! If we could do this to them another ten or fifteen times . . .

But maybe they're not so dumb, because we *can't* do it to them that many times. Of course, they can't *know* we don't have thousands of planetoids —

"Enemy has opened fire," Dahak said, and Colin tensed.

Sorkar managed not to cheer as the first greater thunder burst among the enemy. Now, nest-killers! Now comes *your* turn to face the Furnace!

More and more of his ships entered range, hurling their hyper missiles into the enemy, and his direct-vision panel polarized as a cauldron of unholy Fire boiled against the nest-killers' shields.

Jiltanith tasted blood, and her knuckles whitened on her dagger as a second star blazed in the Zeta Trianguli System. It grew in fury, hotter and brighter, born of millions of antimatter warheads, and Colin was at its heart.

The enemy continued to close, dying as he came, trailing broken starships like a disemboweled monster's entrails. But still he came on, and the weight of his fire was inconceivable. She knew the plan, knew Colin fought for information as well as victory, but this was too much.

"Now, my love," she whispered. "Fly now, my Colin! Fly *now!*"

✧   ✧   ✧

"Trosan has been destroyed. Heavy damage to *Mairsuk.*
We have —"

Dahak's voice broke off as his stupendous mass heaved.
The display blanked, and Colin paled at the terrible
reports in his neural feed.

"Three direct hits," Dahak reported. "Heavy damage to
Quadrants Rho-Two and Four. Seven percent combat
capability lost."

Colin swore hoarsely. *Dahak's* shield had been heavily
overhauled at Bia. It was just as good as his automated
minions', but his other defenses were not. He was simply
slower and far less capable, than they. If the enemy noticed
and decided to concentrate on him . . .

"Gohar destroyed. *Shinhar* heavily damaged; combat
capability thirty-four percent. Enemy entering energy
weapon range."

"Then let's see how tough these bastards *really* are!"
Colin grated. "Execute Plan Volley Fire."

Sorkar blinked as the nest-killers moved. All this time
they had held their positions, soaking up his thunder, killing his ships. Now, when they had finally begun to die, they
moved . . . but to *advance*, not to flee!

Then their energy weapons fired at last, and he gasped
in disbelief.

"Yes! *Yes!"* Colin shouted. *Dahak's* energy weapons
were blasts of fury that rent the molecular bindings of their
targets; those of the Empire were worse. They shattered
atomic bindings, inducing instant fission.

Now those dreadful weapons stabbed out from the
beam-heavy *Trosans*, and Colin's missiles suddenly
became a side show. No Achuultani shield could stop those
furious beams, and their kiss was death.

Sorkar's desperate pleas for advice hammered at Battle
Comp. Were these nest-killers the very Spawn of Tarhish?!

What deviltry transformed his very ships into warheads of the lesser thunder?!

Unaccustomed panic pounded him. With those beams, they might yet cut their way through his entire fleet, and the closer he came to them, the more easily they could kill his Protectors!

But Battle Comp did not know what panic was, and its dispassionate analysis calmed his visceral terror. Yes, the cost would be terrible, but the nest-killers were also dying. They would wound the Great Visit more deeply than Sorkar had believed possible, but they would *die*, Tarhish take them!

"We are down to seven units," Dahak reported. "Approximately two hundred ninety-one thousand Achuultani ships have been destroyed."

"Execute Plan Shiva," Colin rasped.

"Executing, Your Majesty," Dahak said once more, and the Enchanach Drives of eight Imperial planetoids roared to life. In one terrible, perfectly synchronized instant, eight gravity wells, each more massive than Zeta Trianguli's own, erupted barely six light-minutes from the star.

A twelve of greater twelves of Sorkar's ships disappeared, torn apart and scattered over the universe, as the impossible happened. For an instant, his mind was totally blank, and then he realized.

He was dead, and every one of his nestlings with him.

Had it been intended from the outset that the nest-killers should suicide? Destroy themselves with some inconceivably powerful version of the warheads which had ravaged his ships?

He heard Battle Comp using his voice, ordering his fleet to turn and flee, but he paid it no heed. They were too deep into the gravity well; at their best speed, even the outer sphere would need a quarter-day segment to reach the hyper threshold.

His FTL scanners watched the tidal wave of gravitonic

stress reach Zeta Trianguli Australis, watched the star
bulge and blossom hideously.

He bowed his head and switched off his vision panel.

The sun went nova.

Dahak and his surviving companions fled its death
throes at seven hundred times the speed of light, and
Colin watched through fold-space scanners in sick fascination. Dahak had filtered the display's fury, but even so it
hurt his eyes. Yet he could not look away as a terrible wave
of radiation lashed the Achuultani . . . and upon its heels
came the physical front of destruction. But those ships
were already lifeless, shields less than useless against the
ferocity of a sun's death.

The nova spewed them forth as a few more atoms of
finely divided matter on the fire of its breath.

Chapter Twenty-Two

Brashieel rose carefully and inclined his head as the old nest-killer called Hohrass entered his nest place. It was not the full salute of a Protector, for he did not cover his eyes, but Brashieel knew this Hohrass was a great lord of his own . . . people.

It had taken many twelve-days to decide to apply that term to these nest-killers, yet he had little choice. He had come to know them — some of them, at least — and that, he now knew, was the worst thing which could happen to a Protector.

He should have ended in honor. Should have spent himself, made them kill him, before this horror could be inflicted upon him. But they were cruel, these nest-killers, cruel in their kindness, for they had not *let* him end. For just a moment, he considered attacking Hohrass, but the old nest-killer was far stronger. He would simply overpower him, and it would be shameful to neither kill his foe nor make his foe kill him.

"I greet you, Brashieel." The voice came from a speaker on the wall, rendering Hohrass's words into the tongue of Aku'Ultan.

"I greet you, Hohrass," he returned, and heard the same speaker make meaningless sounds to his — visitor? Gaoler?

"I bring you sad tidings," Hohrass said, speaking slowly to let whatever wonder translated do its work. "Our Protectors have met yours in combat. Five higher twelves of your ships have perished."

Brashieel gaped at him. He had seen the power of their warships, but *this* — ! His shock shamed him, yet he could not hide it, and his eyes were dark with pain. His crest drooped, and his fine, dark muzzle scales stood out against his suddenly pallid skin.

"I am sorry to tell you this," Hohrass continued after a twelfth-segment, "but it is important that we speak of it."

"How?" Brashieel asked finally. "Have your Protectors gathered in such numbers so quickly?"

"No," said Hohrass softly. "We used scarcely a double twelve of ships."

"Impossible! You lie to me, Hohrass! Not even a double twelve of your demon ships could do so much!"

"I speak truth," Hohrass returned. "I have records to prove my words, records sent to us over three twelves of your light-years."

Brashieel's legs folded under him, despite every effort to stand, and his eyes were blind with horror. If Hohrass spoke the truth, if a mere double twelve of their ships could destroy a full half of the Great Visit and report it over such distances so quickly, the Nest was doomed. Fire would consume the great Nest Place, devour the Creche of the People. The Aku'Ultan would perish, for they had waked a demon more terrible even than the Great Nest-Killers.

They had awakened Tarhish Himself, and His Furnace would take them all.

"Brashieel. Brashieel!" The quiet voice intruded into his horror, and the old nest-killer touched his shoulder. "Brashieel, I must speak with you. It is important — to my Nest and to your own."

"Why?" Brashieel moaned. "End me now, Hohrass. Show me that mercy."

"No." Hohrass knelt on his two legs to bring their eyes level. "I cannot do that, Brashieel. You must live. We must speak not as nest-killers, but as one Protector to another."

"What is there to speak of?" Brashieel asked dully. "You will do as you must in the service of your Nest, and mine will end."

"No, Brashieel. It need not be that way."

"It must," Brashieel groaned. "It is the Way. You are mightier than we, and the Aku'Ultan will end at last."

"We do not wish to end the Aku'Ultan," Hohrass said, and Brashieel stared at him in stark disbelief.

"That cannot be true," he said flatly.

"Then pretend. Pretend for just a twelfth-segment that we do not wish your ending if our own Nest can live. If we prove we can destroy your greatest Great Visit yet tell your Nest Lord we do not wish to end the Aku'Ultan, will he leave our Nest in peace? Can there not be an end to the nest-killing?"

"I . . . do not think I can pretend that."

"Try, Brashieel. Try hard."

"I —" Brashieel's head spun with the strangeness of the thought.

"I do not know if I can pretend that," he said finally, "and it would not matter if I could. I have tried to think upon the things your Nynnhuursag has said to me, and almost I can understand them. But I am no longer a Protector, Hohrass. I have failed to end, which cannot be, yet it is. I have spoken with nest-killers, and that, too, cannot be. Because these things have been, I no longer know what I am, but I am no longer as others of the Nest. It does not matter what such as I pretend; what matters is what the Lord of the Nest *knows*, and he knows the Great Fear, the Purpose, and the Way. He will not stop what he is. If he could, he would not be the Nest Lord."

"I am sorry, Brashieel," Hohrass said, and Brashieel believed him. "I am sorry this has happened to you, yet perhaps you are wrong. If other Protectors join you as our prisoners, if you speak together and with us, if you learn that what I tell you is truth — that we do not wish to end the Aku'Ultan — would you be prepared to tell others of the Nest what you have learned?"

"We would never have the chance. We would be ended by the Nest, and rightly ended. We would be nest-killers to our own if we did your will."

"Perhaps," Hohrass said, "and perhaps not." He sighed and rose. "Again, I am sorry — truly sorry — to torment you with such questions, yet I must. I ask you to think painful things, to consider that there may be truths beyond even the Great Fear, and I know these thoughts hurt you. But you must think them, Brashieel of the Aku'Ultan, for if you cannot — if, indeed, the Nest cannot leave us in peace — then we will have no choice. For untold higher twelves of years, your Protectors have ravaged our suns, killed our planets, slain our Nests. This cannot continue. Understand that we share that much of the Great Fear with the Protectors of the Nest of Aku'Ultan. We truly do not wish to end the Aku'Ultan, but there has been enough ending of others. We will not allow it to continue. It may take us great twelves of years, but we will stop it."

Brashieel stared up at him, too sick with horror even to feel hate, and Hohrass's mouth moved in one of his people's incomprehensible expressions.

"We would have you and your people live, Brashieel. Not because we love you, for we have cause to hate you, and many of us do. Yes, and fear you. But we would not have your ending upon our hands, and that is why we hurt you with such thoughts. We must learn whether or not we can allow your Nest to live. Forgive us, if you can, but whether you can forgive or not, we have no choice."

And with that, Hohrass left the nest place, and Brashieel was alone with the agony of his thoughts.

Chapter Twenty-Three

"You think it's really as grim as Brashieel seems to think?"

Colin looked up as Horus's recorded message ended. Even for an Imperial hypercom, forty-odd light-years was a bit much for two-way conversations.

"I know not," Jiltanith mused. Unlike his other guests, she was present in the flesh. *Very* present, he thought, hiding a smile as he remembered their reunion. Now she flipped a mental command into the holo unit and replayed the final portion of Horus's interview with Brashieel.

"I know not," she repeated. "Certes Brashieel believes it so, but look thou, my Colin, though he saith such things, yet hath he held converse with 'Hursag and Father. Moreover, 'twould seem he hath understood what they have said unto him. His pain seemeth real enow, but 'tis *understanding* — of a sort, at the least — which wakes it."

"You're saying what he thinks and says are two different things?" Hector MacMahan spoke through his holo image from *Sevrid*'s command deck. He looked uncomfortable as a planetoid's CO, for he still regarded himself as a ground-pounder. But, then, *Sevrid* was a ground-pounder's dream, and she had the largest crew of any unit in the fleet, after *Fabricator*, for reasons which made sense to most. They made sense to Colin and Jiltanith, anyway, which was what mattered, and this conversation was very pertinent to them.

"Nay, Hector. Say rather that divergence hath begun 'twixt what he doth think and what he doth *believe*, but that he hath not seen it so."

"You may be right, 'Tanni," Ninhursag said slowly. Her image sat beside Hector's as her body sat next to his. And, come to think of it, Colin thought, they seemed to be found together a lot these days.

"When Brashieel and I talked," Ninhursag continued, choosing her words with care, "the impression I got of him was . . . well, innocence, if that's not too silly-sounding. I don't mean goody-goody innocence; maybe the word should really be naiveté. He's very, very bright, by human standards. Very quick and very well-educated, but only in his speciality. As for the rest, well, it's more like an indoctrination than an education, as if someone cordoned off certain aspects of his worldview, labeled them 'off-limits' so firmly he's not even curious about them. It's just the way things *are*; the very possibility of questioning them, much less changing them, doesn't exist."

"Hm." Cohanna rubbed an eyebrow and frowned. "You may have something, 'Hursag. I hadn't gotten around to seeing it that way, but then I always was a mechanic at heart." Jiltanith frowned a question, and Cohanna grinned. "Sorry. I mean I was always more interested in the physical life processes than the mental. A blind spot of my own. I tend to look for physical answers first and psychological ones second . . . or third. What I meant, though, is that 'Hursag's right. If Brashieel were human — which, of course, he isn't — I'd have to say he'd been programmed pretty carefully."

"Programmed." Jiltanith tasted the word thoughtfully. "Aye, mayhap 'twas the word I sought. Yet 'twould seem his programming hath its share o' holes."

"That's the problem with programming," Cohanna agreed. "It can only accommodate data known to the programmer. Hit its subject with something totally outside its parameters, and he does one of three things: cracks up entirely; rejects the reality and refuses to confront it; or —" she paused meaningfully "— grapples with it and, in the process, *breaks* the program."

"And you think that's what's happening with Brashieel?" Colin mused.

"Well, at the risk of sounding overly optimistic, it may be. Brashieel's a resilient lad, or he'd've curled up and died as soon as he realized the bogey men had him. The fact that he didn't says a really astounding amount about the toughness of his psyche. He was actually curious about us, and that says even more. Now, though, what we're asking him to believe simultaneously upsets his entire worldview and threatens his race with extinction.

"We've had a bit of experience facing that kind of terror ourselves, and some of us haven't handled it very well. It's worse for him; his species has built an entire society on millions of years of fear. I'd say there's a pretty good chance he'll snap completely when he realizes just how bad things really are from the Achuultani perspective. If he makes it through the next few weeks, though, he may find out he's even tougher and more flexible than he thought and actually decide Horus was telling him the truth."

"And how much good will that do?" Tamman's holo image asked. "He was only a fire control officer aboard a scout. Not exactly a mover and shaker in a society as caste-bound as his."

"True," Colin agreed, "but his reaction is the only yardstick we have for how his entire race will react if we really can stop them. Of course, what we really need is a larger sample. Which, Hector," he looked at MacMahan, "is why you and *Sevrid* will do exactly what we've discussed, won't you?"

"Yes, but I don't have to like it."

Colin winced slightly at the sour response, but the

important thing was that Hector understood why *Sevrid* must stay out of the fighting. She would wait out the engagement, stealthed at a safe distance, then close in to board any wrecked or damaged ships she could find.

"That reminds me, 'Hanna," he said, turning back to the biosciences officer. "What's the progress on our capture field?"

"We're in good shape," Cohanna assured him. "Took us a while to realize it, but it turns out a simple focused magnetic field is the answer."

"Ah? Oh! Metal bones."

"Exactly. They're not all that ferrous, but a properly focused field can lock their skeletons. Muscles, too. Have to secure them some other way pretty quick — interrupting the blood flow to the brain is a bad idea — but it should work just fine. Geran and Caitrin are turning them out aboard *Fabricator* now."

"Good! We *need* prisoners, damn it. We may not be able to do anything with them right away, but somewhere down the road we're either going to have to talk to the Nest Lord or kill his ass. In some ways, I'd rather waste him and be done with it, but that's the nasty side of me talking."

"Aye, art ever over gentle with thy foes," Jiltanith said sourly, but then her face softened. "And rightly so, for where would *I* be hadst thou not been thy gentle self when first we met? Nay, my love. I do not say I share thy tenderness for these our foes, yet neither will I contest thy will. And mayhap, in time, will I come to share thy thoughts as well. Stranger things have chanced, when all's said."

Colin reached out and squeezed her hand gently. He knew how much it cost her to say that . . . and how much more it cost to mean it.

"Well, then!" he said more briskly. "We seem to be in pretty good shape there; let's hope we're in equally good shape everywhere. Horus and Gerald are making lots better progress than I expected upgrading Earth's defenses. They may actually have a chance of holding even if we lose it out here, as long as we can take out half or more of the main body in the process."

"A chance," MacMahan agreed. He did not add "but not a very good one."

"Yeah." Colin's tone answered the unspoken qualifier, and he tugged on his nose in a familiar gesture. "Well, we'll just have to see to it they don't have to try. What's our situation, Vlad?"

"It could be better, but it might be worse." Chernikov's image looked weary, though less so than when the resurrected Imperial Guard left Bia. "We have lost eight units: one *Vespa*-class, which constitutes a relatively minor loss to our ship-to-ship capability; one *Asgerd*; and six *Trosans*. That leaves ten *Trosans*, two too severely damaged for *Fabricator* to make combat-capable. I recommend that they be dispatched directly to Bia under computer control."

"I hate to do it," Colin sighed, "but I think you're right. What about the rest of us?"

"The remaining eight *Trosans* are all combat-ready at a minimum of ninety percent of capability. Of our remaining fifty-one *Asgerds*, *Two*'s damage is most severe, but Baltan and I believe we can make almost all of it good. After her, *Emperor Herdan* is worst hurt, followed by *Royal Birhat*, but *Birhat* should be restored to full capability within two months. I estimate that *Herdan* and *Two* will be at ninety-six and ninety-four percent capability, respectively, by the time the main body arrives."

"Hum. Should we transfer your people to undamaged ships, 'Tanni?"

"Nay. 'Twere better to face the fray 'board ships whose ways we know, even though somewhat hurt, than to unsettle all upon the eve o'battle."

"I think so, too. But if Vlad and Baltan *can't* get 'em up to at least ninety percent, your ass is changing ships, young lady!"

"Ha! Neither young nor lady am I, and thou'lt find it most difficult to remove me 'gainst my will, Your Majesty!"

"I don't get no respect." Colin sighed, then he shook himself. "And Dahak, Vlad?"

"We will do our best, Colin," Vlad said more somberly, and the mood of the meeting darkened. "Those two hits he took on the way out were almost on top of one another and did extraordinarily severe damage. Nor does his age help; were he one of the newer ships, we could simply plug components from *Fabricator*'s spares into his damaged systems. As it is, we must rebuild his Rho quadrants almost from scratch, and there is collateral damage in Sigma-One, Lambda-Four and Pi-Three. At best, we may restore him to eighty-five percent capability."

"Dahak? Do you concur?" Colin asked.

"I believe Senior Fleet Captain Chernikov underestimates himself, but his analysis is essentially correct. We may achieve eighty-seven or even eighty-eight percent capability; we will not achieve more in the time available."

"Damn. I should've cut and run sooner."

"Nay," Jiltanith said. "Thou didst troll them in most shrewdly, my Colin, and so learned far more than ever we hoped."

"Her Majesty is correct," Dahak put in. "The effectiveness of our energy weapons against heavy Aku'Ultan units has now been demonstrated and, coupled with Operation Laocoon, makes ultimate victory far more likely. Without Volley Fire, we could not accurately have assessed that effectiveness."

"Yeah, yeah, I know," Colin said, and he did. But knowing made him feel no better about getting their irreplaceable flagship — and his *friend*, damn it! — shot up. "Okay, I guess that just about covers it. We can —"

"Nay, Colin," Jiltanith cut in. "There remaineth still the matter of the ship from which thou'lt lead us."

Colin noted the dangerous tilt of her chin and felt an irrational stab of anger. He had the authority — technically — to slap her down, but he couldn't. It would be capricious, which was one reason he was angry he couldn't, but, worse, it would be wrong. 'Tanni was his second-in-command, both entitled and required to disagree when she thought he was wrong; she was also his wife.

"I'll be aboard *Dahak*," he said flatly. "By myself."

"Now I say thou shalt not," she began hotly, then stopped, throttling her anger as he had his. But tension crackled between them, and when he glanced around the holo-image faces of his closest advisors he saw a high degree of discomfort in their expressions. He also saw a lot of support for 'Tanni.

"Look," he said, "I have to be here. We win or lose on the basis of how well Dahak can run the rest of the flotilla, and communications are going to be hairy enough without me being on a ship with a different time dilation effect."

It was a telling argument, and he saw its weight darken Jiltanith's eyes, though she did not relent. Relativity wasn't a factor under Enchanach Drive, since the ship in question didn't actually "move" in normal-space terms at all. Unfortunately, it *was* a factor at high sublight velocities, especially when ships might actually be moving on opposing vectors. Gross communication wasn't too bad; there were lags, but they were bearable — for communication. But Dahak would be required to operate his uncrewed fellows' computers as literal extensions of himself. At the very best, their tactical flexibility would be badly limited. At worst . . .

Colin decided — again — not to think about "at worst."

"Anyway," he said, "I should be as safe as anybody else."

"Oh? Without doubt 'twas that very reasoning led thee to forbid all others to share thy duty 'board *Dahak*?" Jiltanith said with awful irony.

"All right, damn it, so it *isn't* exactly the safest place to be! I've still got to be here, 'Tanni. Why should I risk anyone else?"

"Colin," Tamman said, " 'Tanni may not be your most tactful officer, but she speaks for all of us. Forgive me, Dahak —" he glanced courteously at the auxiliary interface on one bulkhead "— but you're going to be a priority target if the Achuultani realize what's going on."

"I concur."

"Thank you," Tamman said softly. "And that's my point,

Colin. We all know how important your ability to coordinate through Dahak is, but *you're* important, too. In your persona as emperor, and as our friend, as well."

"Tamman —" Colin broke off and stared down at his hands, then sighed. "Thank you for that — thank all of you — but the fact remains that cold, hard logic says I should be in Command One when we go in."

"That is certainly true to a point," Dahak said, and Jiltanith stared at the auxiliary console with betrayed eyes, "yet Senior Fleet Captain Tamman is also correct. You *are* important, if only as the one adult human Fleet Central will obey without question during the immense reorganization of the post-Incursion period. While Her Majesty can execute that function in the event of your death, she would be acting as regent for a minor child, not as head of state in her own right, which creates a potential for conflict."

"Are you saying I should risk losing the battle because something *might* go wrong later?"

"Negative. I am simply listing counter-arguments. And, in all honesty, I must add my personal concern to the list. You are my oldest friend, Colin. I do not wish you to risk your life unnecessarily."

The computer did not often express his human feelings so frankly, and Colin swallowed unexpected emotion.

"I'm not too crazy about it myself, but I think it *is* necessary. Forget for a moment that we're friends and tell me what the percentages say to do."

There was a moment of silence — a very long moment for Dahak.

"Put that way, Colin," he said at last, "I must concur. Your presence in Command One will increase the probability of victory by several orders."

Jiltanith sagged, and Colin touched her hand gently in apology. She tried to smile, but her eyes were stricken, and he knew she knew. He'd ordered Dahak not to share his projection of their chance of survival with her, but she knew anyway.

"Wait." Chernikov's thoughtful murmur pulled all attention back to him. "We have the time and materials; let us install a mat-trans aboard *Dahak*."

"A mat-trans? But that couldn't —"

"A moment, Colin." Dahak sounded far more cheerful. "I believe this suggestion has merit. Senior Fleet Captain Chernikov, do I correctly apprehend that you intend to install additional mat-trans stations aboard each of our crewed warships?"

"I do."

"But the relativity aspects would make it impossible," Colin protested. "The stations have to be synchronized."

"Not so finely as you may believe," Dahak said. "In practice, it would simply require that the receiving ship maintain approximately the same relativistic time. Given the number of crewed vessels available to us, it might well prove possible to select an appropriate unit. I could then transmit you to that unit in the event that *Dahak*'s destruction becomes probable."

"I don't like the idea of running away," Colin muttered rebelliously.

"Now thou'rt childish, my Colin," Jiltanith said firmly. "Thou knowest how feel we all towards Dahak, yet thy presence will not halt the missile or beam which would destroy him. How shall thy death make his less dreadful?"

"Her Majesty is correct," Dahak said, equally firmly. "You would not refuse to evacuate via lifeboat, and there is little difference, except in that your chances of survival are many orders of probability higher via mat-trans. Please, Colin. I would feel much better if you would agree."

Colin was stubbornly silent. Of course it was illogical, but that was part of the definition of friendship. Yet they were right. It was only the premeditation of the means whereby he would desert his friend that bothered him.

"All right," he sighed at last. "I don't like it, but . . . do it, Vlad."

Chapter Twenty-Four

The dot of Zeta Trianguli Australis burned unchanged, for the fury of its death had not yet crossed the light-years.

Senior Fleet Captain Sarah Meir, promoted when Colin evicted *Dahak*'s crew, sat on the planetoid *Ashar*'s command deck and frowned as she watched it, recalling the dark, hopeless years when she and her Terra-born fellows had fought with *Nergal*'s Imperials against Anu's butchers. There was no comparison between then and now . . . except that the days were dark once more and hope was scarce.

Scarce, but not vanished, she reminded herself, and if Colin's reckless battle plan shocked her, it was its very audacity which gave them a hope of victory. That, and the quality of their ships and handful of crews.

And *Dahak*. It always came back to *Dahak*, but then, it always had. He'd stood sponsor for them all, Earth's inheritance from the Imperium on this eve of Armageddon. It might be atavistic of her, but *Dahak* was their totem, and —

"Captain, we have an inbound hyper wake. A big one,"

her plotting officer said, and adrenalin flushed through her
system.

"Nail it down," she said, "and fire up the hypercom."
Acknowledgments came back, and she called up Engineering. "Stand by Enchanach Drive."

"Yes, ma'am. Core tap nominal. We're ready to move."

"Stand by." She looked back up at Plotting. "Well?"

"We've got an emergence, ma'am. Ninety-eight hours,
about a light-month short of the vanguard's emergence
locus."

Sarah frowned. Damned if *she* would've hypered in this
close to the "monster nest-killers" the vanguard must have
reported! Still, with their piddling communication range,
they had to come in fairly close . . . and a light-month gave
them plenty of time to hyper out if bad guys came at them.

Usually, she thought coldly, but not this time. Oh, no.
Not this time.

"Communications, inform the flagship. Maneuvering,
head for the rendezvous, but take us on a dogleg. I want a
cross-bearing on this wake."

Stars streamed across the display, and she relaxed. In
another four days the uncertainty would end . . . one way
or another.

Great Lord of Order Hothan twiddled all four thumbs
as he replayed Sorkar's messages yet again. Hothan was
small for a Protector, quick-moving and keen-witted.
Indeed, he had been severely disciplined as a fledgling for
near-deviant inquisitiveness and almost denied his lordship for questioning what he perceived as inefficiencies in
the Nest's starships. Yet even Battle Comp agreed that
those very faults made him an excellent strategist and tac-
tician, and they had helped Great Lord Tharno select him
for this duty.

Yet Sorkar's reports made him more than simply curious. There was a near-hysterical edge to them, most unlike
his old nestmate. But, then, this was the Demon Sector,
and Sorkar always had been a bit superstitious.

✧   ✧   ✧

"Emergence confirmed and plotted," Dahak announced. "Margin of error point-zero-zero-zero-zero-two-nine percent."

Colin grunted and ran down his mental list one last time. *Dahak* was at eighty-six percent efficiency; his other ships were all at ninety or above. All magazines were topped up, and transferring *Dahak's* skeleton crew to *Ashar* had given them sixteen autonomous units once more. They were as ready as they could get, he thought, deliberately not looking at the hastily installed mat-trans which had replaced the tactical officer's couch and console.

"All right, Dahak, saddle up. Get the minelayers moving."

"Acknowledged." The unmanned colliers moved out, accompanied by *Dahak* and his bevy of lobotomized geniuses, loafing along under Enchanach Drive at sixty times light-speed. They weren't in that great a hurry.

The colliers reached their stations and paused, adjusting their formation delicately before they began to move once more, now at sublight speeds.

The brevity of the first clash with the vanguard, coupled with the ships lost at Zeta Trianguli, meant Colin had more spare missiles than planned. He rather regretted that — though he would have regretted depleted magazines more — for each missile was three or four less mines his colliers could lift. Still, they had lots of the nasty little buggers, and he watched them spill out as the colliers swept across the Achuultani's emergence area at forty percent of light-speed.

He bared his teeth. Mines were seldom used outside star systems, for it was impossible to guess where an enemy might come out *between* stars. But this time he didn't have to guess; he knew, and the Achuultani weren't going to like it a bit.

Great Lord Hothan stretched one last time before he folded his legs and sank onto his duty pad. Before Sorkar's messages, Hothan had not worried about routine emergences from hyper in interstellar space, but he had no more idea how the nest-killers had surprised Sorkar than Battle Comp did, and, like Great Lord Tharno, he was determined to guard his own command.

His nestlings had been carefully instructed before entering hyper. They would emerge as prepared to confront enemies as nestmates, yet if these nest-killers were indeed the demons Sorkar had described that might not be enough, and so he and Great Lord Tharno had taken a radical decision with Battle Comp's full concurrence. Protectors could not serve the Nest if they perished; should the nest-killers be waiting once more, prepared to kill his ships in great twelves, he would return to hyper and flee.

He watched the chronometer and checked Battle Comp for final advice. There was none, and he made himself relax. Half a day-segment to emergence.

Colin watched the hyper traces flash blood-red in *Dahak*'s holo projection as the vanguard's tattered couriers and the main body rushed together. They would rendezvous in one more hour, and the battle would begin. It would *be* a battle, too; more terrible than the oncoming Achuultani could possibly imagine. And probably more terrible than *he* could imagine, as well.

Dahak floated at the core of a globe of fifty-four stupendous planetoids, and Colin felt a brief stab of unutterable loneliness as he realized he was the sole living, breathing scrap of blood and bone in all that horrific array of firepower. He shook it off; there were other things to consider.

The waiting minefield frosted the black velvet of *Dahak*'s display like a glitter of diamond dust. The stealthed colliers ringed the mines, waiting obediently to play their part in Operation Laocoon, and fifteen more stealthed *Asgerd*-class planetoids were invisible even to *Dahak*'s scanners, their positions marked only because he already knew where they would be. Those ships were 'Tanni's command, the reserve which could move and fight without Dahak's control. Yet they were more than counters on a map. They were crewed by people — by *friends* — and too many of them were about to die.

Great Lord Hothan tightened internally despite years of discipline and training. He chided himself for his inability to relax. Yet perhaps that was good, for tension honed reactions and —

His thoughts broke off as one of his read-outs suddenly peaked. That was odd. The depths of hyper space were unchanging: seething bands of energy that ebbed and flowed in predictable, regular patterns, not in sudden peaks.

But his readouts peaked again. And again and again. Glowing numerals flashed with a jagged, stabbing intensity whose like he had never seen, and his nerves twisted in sudden dread.

Colin smiled coldly as the mines began to vanish.

The Achuultani could play many tricks with hyper space, but there were a few which hadn't occurred to them. Why should they, when they were perpetually on the offensive? But just as they had planned and trained for countless years to attack, so the Imperium had schemed and planned to defend, and the Empire had refined the Imperium's basic research.

The Imperium's mines had entered hyper only to jump into lethal proximity to hyperships as they reentered n-space; the Empire's mines popped into hyper, located the nearest operating hyper field, and then gave selflessly of their own power to make that hyper field even more efficient.

But only locally. A *portion* of the field was abruptly boosted a dozen bands higher, taking the portion of the ship within it with it, and even ships large enough to lose a slice of themselves and continue fighting in normal space were doomed in hyper. Its potent tides of energy rent and splintered them and swallowed their broken bones.

Even with Imperial technology, the mines were short-ranged and not very accurate in the extreme conditions of the hyper bands. Ten, even twenty, were required to strike a target as small as a single drive field . . . but Colin's colliers had deployed five million of them.

Great Lord Hothan put the puzzle of his readouts aside as *Deathdealer* reemerged into normal space. He had more immediate concerns, like the total absence of Sorkar's fleet. Sorkar himself had specified this rendezvous, so where *was* he? Surely his entire fleet had not been wiped away. Hothan knew Sorkar well; he would have swallowed his pride and fled before he allowed that!

But Sorkar's absence was only one worry, and he swore as he saw those of his own nestlings who had already emerged. Whole flotillas had mistimed their emergences, leaving gaping holes in the neat intervals of his command. How could their lords be so clumsy now of all times?! He would —

Wait. What was that? Something had suddenly departed *into* hyper. And there — another hyper trace! And another! What — ?

He barked an order, and a scanner section obediently redirected its instruments. What *were* those things? Certainly not Sorkar's nestlings — indeed, they were too small to be ships at all! And why would ships *enter* hyper at a time like this? But if not warships, then what . . . ?

Nest Lord! They were *weapons* . . . and Sorkar was dead.

He did not know how he suddenly knew, but he knew. Sorkar was no more, and just as he had been ambushed, so had Hothan! Not by warships, but by something worse — and he could do nothing but watch as the enigmatic weapons vanished . . . and his nestlings did not emerge. The holes in his formation were suddenly and dreadfully comprehensible, for Sorkar had been right. These were the demon nest-killers of legend!

But he fought his dread, made himself think. Perhaps

there *was* something he could do. He snapped orders, and *Deathdealer*'s thunder ripped at the weapons which had not yet attacked. Furnace Fire flashed among them, and they had no shields. They died by great twelves, and now other ships were firing, raking the floating clouds of killers with death.

Colin felt a moment of ungrudging respect as antimatter warheads glared. Damn, but somebody over there was quick! He'd realized what was happening and done the only thing he could.

That big a fleet took time to emerge from hyper. Its units' emergences must be carefully phased lest they interpenetrate in n-space, so its commander couldn't just run without abandoning those still to come; he could only attack the mines which had not yet been triggered. He couldn't kill many with a single missile, but he was firing thousands of them, which gave him a damnably good chance of saving an awful lot of the follow-up echelons.

Unless something distracted him from his minesweeping.

"Alert! Alert! Incoming fire!"

Great Lord Hothan's head whipped up, but he was not really surprised. Any nest-killer cunning enough to lay so devilish a trap would cover it with his own ships if he could. But expected or not, it presented Hothan with a cruel dilemma. He could kill mines while his ships already in n-space died, or he could engage the enemy's ships and let his nestlings in hyper die.

Yet he had already realized that only a fraction of those weapons were finding targets. Best trust the Nameless Lord for the safety of those still to come and respond to this new attack . . . assuming he could find the attackers!

Adrienne Robbins watched the first Achuultani ships die and suppressed an oath. *Herdan* herself seemed to strain against the prohibition from firing before Jiltanith released her weapons, but it made sense . . . even if seeing so many targets she couldn't attack was hard to endure.

Great Lord Hothan sent his fleet fanning out in search of its killers and gritted his teeth at how his own actions paralleled Sorkar's. It should not be so. He should have planned and prepared better. Yet how *could* one prepare for this sort of thing? How did one fight ghosts one could not even *see*?

Great twelves of his questing nestlings died, and still their enemy was hidden! Only the fleeting wisps of his missiles' incoming hyper wakes even suggested his bearing, and Hothan's lead scouts were already at their own hyper missile range from *Deathdealer*. How far out could the nest-killers *be*?!

Colin watched the Achuultani flow towards him, reorienting to drive deliberately into the zone of maximum destruction, trying to deduce his bearing from the furrows of death his missiles plowed through them. It was horrible to see such courage and know the beings who possessed it were bent upon the murder of his entire race.

But they had a long way to come, and *Dahak* was a sniper, picking them off by scores and hundreds. If only Colin had more missiles, he could have backed away indefinitely, faster than they could pursue, flaying them with fire from beyond their own maximum range. But he didn't have enough missiles to stop a million enemies, and if he had, they would only have fled into hyper. If he would destroy them, he must scatter them. Their weapons were deadly enough, but short-ranged and individually weak compared to his own; it was coordinated, massed fire which made them lethal, so he must split them up — scatter them for 'Tanni to harry to destruction. And for that he must get into energy weapon range and blow the heart and brain out of their formation with weapons not limited by the capacity of his magazines.

"Advance," he said coldly, and a phalanx of battle steel moons moved forward, plowing the wake of its missiles.

❖　❖　❖

At last! Almost all of his nestlings had emerged from hyper, and it was time to forget pride, time to flee. His formations were rent and overextended, and too many of his command ships were among the dead. He needed time to sort things out and reorganize in light of these demonic weapons.

"They will complete emergence in twenty-seven seconds," Dahak announced.

"Execute Laocoon," Colin replied.

"Executing."

The colliers ringing the minefield engaged their Enchanach Drives. No human rode their command decks, but none was needed for this simple task. They flashed through their preprogrammed maneuvers in an intricate supralight mazurka, exchanging positions so quickly and adroitly that, in effect, one of them was constantly in each cardinal point of a circle twenty light-minutes across.

They danced their dance, harming no one . . . and wove a garrote of gravity about the Achuultani's throat. They were invisible stars, forging a forty-light-minute sphere in which there *was* no hyper threshold.

Great Lord Hothan stared at his instruments. No one could lock an entire fleet out of hyper space!

But someone could, and his plan to hyper out was smashed at a blow. He did not know how it had been done, but his Protectors had become penned *qwelloq* awaiting slaughter.

He shook aside panic, if not his fear. So. He could not flee, and the incoming salvos were arriving at ever shorter intervals. That meant only one thing: the nest-killers had him trapped and they were closing for the kill.

But he who entered the sweep of a *qwelloq's* tusks could die upon them.

"Hast done it, my Colin," Jiltanith whispered. "They cannot flee!"

A susurration of inarticulate delight answered her whisper, but like her, her bridge crew did not look away from *Two's* display. The mines must have been twice as effective as projected, for barely three-quarters of a million Achuultani ships had emerged. That augured well, but now *Dahak* was closing with the enemy. Soon there would be deaths they would mourn, not cheer.

Hothan was a great lord, and his orders came crisp and sure.

Greater twelves of his ships had died, but higher twelves remained, and the enemy was coming to him, so he need not continue the useless expansion of his formation to seek him. A tendril continued to lick out in the direction of the incoming fire, its end a comet of flame as the ships which made it died, but the rest of his formation gathered itself.

He was proud of his Protectors. They must be as frightened as he, but they obeyed quickly. Holes remained, weak links in the chain of order where too many command ships had been slain, but they obeyed.

And there were the nest-killers!

He swallowed a spurt of primal terror as he saw their relayed images. As vast as Sorkar had described them, and more numerous. Four twelves, at least, sweeping towards him behind the glare of their thunder, huge as moons, driving lances of the Furnace's Fire deep into his fleet. But they had not yet reached its vitals, and their own tremendous speed brought them into his reach.

He allocated targets, coordinated his attack patterns, and his nestlings crowded forward, placing themselves between *Deathdealer* and the foe. He wanted to order them aside, but his deputy lord had never emerged. He and *Deathdealer* must live if the fleet was to have a chance.

A musical tone sounded, and he frowned. A courier message? From where?

Then it dawned. Sorkar had tried to warn him, but the courier had arrived late. Now a high-speed transmission squealed into Battle Comp, and the powerful computers digested it quickly. The nest-killers were still closing when the data suddenly coalesced, flashing onto Hothan's own panel, and he paled as he saw the record of those terrible energy weapons and the greater horror of a sun's death. Saw it and understood.

They had taken him in a snare as hellish as the trap which had taken his nestmate; now they were coming to kill his fleet as they had Sorkar's. There could not be many of them, or more would have formed the titanic hammer rushing towards him, but his nestlings were new-creched fledglings against them.

Not for a moment did he think they had suicided to destroy Sorkar. The trap they had forged to chain him told him that much. They would enter his formation, raking him with those demonic beams, killing until their own losses mounted. Then they would flee.

Death held no horror for a Protector, but there was horror in death on such a scale. Not his own, but his fleet's. The death of the Great Visit itself. Even if he survived this attack, his losses would be terrible, and why should this be the final attack? Sorkar had faced a single twelve; he faced four twelves — Nest Lord only knew how many of these terrible ships might gather in time!

But if his fleet must die, it would not die alone. The nest-killers were within his reach, and the order to fire went out.

Jiltanith paled as the Achuultani fired at last. A bowl of fire — the glare of antimatter explosions and their searing waves of plasma — boiled back along the flanks of Colin's charging sphere. And hidden within it, more deadly far than the uncountable sublight missiles, were the hyper missiles. Weapons impossible to intercept that flooded the hyper bands, seeking always to pop the planetoids' shields and strike home against their armored flanks.

She lay rigid in her couch, cursing her helplessness, watching the man she loved drive into that hideous incandescence . . . and did nothing.

❖   ❖   ❖

Dahak heaved and pitched with the titanic violence beyond his shield. He was invisible to his foes within his globe; the hundreds of warheads bursting about him were overs, missiles which had missed their intended targets, but no less deadly for that. His shield generators whined in protest, forcing the destruction aside, and his display was blank. If it had not been, it would have shown only a glare like the corona of a star.

Tractors locked Colin into his couch, and sweat beaded his brow. This Achuultani fleet wasn't spread out to envelop his formation. It was a solid mass, hurling its hate in salvos thick beyond belief. Nothing made by mortal hands could shrug aside such fury, and damage reports came thick and fast from his lead units. Miniature suns blossomed inside their shields, searing them, cratering their armor, pounding them steadily towards destruction.

Not even Dahak could provide verbal reports on such carnage. Had he tried, they would have been impossible for Colin to comprehend. Nor were they necessary. He was mated to his ship through his feed, his identity almost lost within the incomprehensible vastness of *Dahak's* computer core, the other ships extensions of his brain and nerves as they sped into the jaws of destruction.

Hothan watched the nest-killers come on, unable to credit their incredible toughness. The bursts of his missiles were so heavy, so continuous his scanners could no longer penetrate the bow wave of plasma riding the front of that formation. Nothing could survive such punishment, much less keep coming!

But these demons could, and even through that tornado of death, they struck back. His nestlings melted like sand in a pounding rain, molten and shattered, blown apart, crumpled by those terrible warheads Sorkar had described. Yet even such as they —

There!

❖   ❖   ❖

Colin flinched as HIMP *Sekr* blew apart. He didn't know how many missiles that staggering wreck had absorbed, but finally there had been too many. Her core tap let go, and a halo of pure energy gyred through the carnage.

Trel followed *Sekr* into death, then *Hilik* and *Imperial Bia*, but nothing could stop them from reaching beam range now. Yet they were such terribly vulnerable targets, unable to evade, unable to bob and weave. If Dahak allowed them to wander, relativistic effects would fray his control. That was their great weakness: they couldn't maneuver if they wanted to.

Now!

Hothan groaned as the beams Sorkar's observers had reported raked out and their targets exploded like *sulq* in a candle flame. He had killed almost a twelve of them, but the others crunched into his formation, and his ships were too slow to flee. They could not even scatter as the battering ram of nest-killers clove through them. Their own feeble energy weapons came into play — some of them, aboard ships which lived an instant longer than their brothers — and they were useless. Only missiles could hurt these demons, and now they were so close his thunder was killing his own nestlings!

Yet he had no choice, and he clung to his duty pad, refusing to weep as his ships blazed like chaff in the Furnace.

Battle Comp suddenly clamored for his attention, and he dropped an eye to the computer's panel.

"Weapons free!"

Jiltanith's voice sounded over Colin's fold-space link, quivering with the vibration lashing through *Dahak*'s hull, and fifteen more ships suddenly joined the fray. They didn't leave stealth, nor did they close to energy range, but their missiles lanced out, striking deep into the Achuultani formation.

Lady Adrienne Robbins snarled like a hungry tiger and moved her ship slowly closer, a craftsman of death wreaking slaughter, as fresh suns glared deep in the enemy's force.

The manned ships of the Imperial Guard closed, firing desperately to cover their charging sisters as *Dahak* surged into the heart of his enemies.

Colin had to back out of the maelstrom. His mind could no longer endure the furious tempo of Dahak's perceptions and commands. From here on, he was a passenger on a charge into Hell.

Deep, glowing wounds pocked *Dahak's* flanks. Clouds of atmosphere and vaporized steel trailed the mighty planetoid, and the rear of the sphere thinned dangerously as more and more ships moved forward to replace losses. God, these Achuultani had guts! They weren't even trying to run. They stood and fought, dying, seeking to ram, and they were killing his ships. Fifteen were gone, another ten savagely wounded, but the others drove on, carving a river of fire deeper into the Achuultani.

Somewhere ahead of them were the command ships. The enemy's brain. The organizing force which bound them together.

Hothan blinked in consternation. Battle Comp was never wrong, but *surely* that could not be correct?! *Drones?* Unmanned ships? Preposterous!

But the data codes blinked, no longer informing but commanding. Somewhere inside that sphere of enemies was a single ship, its emission signature different from all the others, from which the directions flowed. How Battle Comp had deduced that from the stutter of incomprehensible alien com signals Hothan could not imagine, but if it was true —

Dahak staggered, and Command One's lights flickered. Colin went white as damage reports suddenly flooded his neural feed. The enemy had shifted his targeting pattern. He was no longer firing at the frontal arc of their formation; his missiles were bursting *inside* the globe! *All* of his missiles!

Their formation had become a sphere of fire, and *Dahak* writhed at its core. The Achuultani couldn't see him, couldn't count on direct hits, but with so many missiles in such a relatively small area, not all could miss. Prominences of plasma gouged at his hull, stabbing deeper and deeper into his battle steel body, but he held his course. He couldn't dodge. He could only attack or flee, and too many enemies remained to flee.

Jiltanith gasped. How had the Achuultani guessed?

But they *had* guessed. Their new attack patterns showed it. They raked the inner globe with fire, and *Dahak* could not evade it. But their rear ranks were thinning . . . and their command ship was somewhere among them. . . .

Dahak Two abandoned stealth and plunged into the space-annihilating gravity well of her Enchanach Drive — the gravity well lethal even to her sisters if they chanced too close as she dropped sublight. Not even Imperial computers could control the exact point at which Enchanach ships went sublight or guarantee they wouldn't kill one another when they did. All of Jiltanith's captains instantly recognized the insane risk she ran. . . .

They charged on her heels.

Colin gritted his teeth. They weren't going to make it.

Then his eyes flew wide. No! They couldn't! *They mustn't!*

But it was too late. His people swept in at many times the speed of light, riding an impossible line between life and mutual destruction in an effort to save him. He dared not distract them now . . . and there was no time.

♦　♦　♦

A whiplash of fresh shock slammed through Great Lord of Order Hothan. Where had *they* come from? What *were* they?!

Fifteen ravening spheres of gravitonic fury erupted amid his ships. Two blossomed too near to one another, ripping themselves apart, but they took a high twelve of his ships with them. And then the gravity storm ended, and a twelve of fresh enemies were upon him. *Upon* him? They were *within* him! They appeared like monsters of wizardry, deep in the heart of his nestlings, and their beams began to kill.

Twelve thousand humans died as *Ashar* and *Trelma* destroyed themselves, and another six thousand as massed fire tore *Thrym* apart, but the Achuultani had given all they had and more for their Nest.

They had stood *Dahak's* remorseless charge, endured the megadeaths he had inflicted upon them, but this was too much. *They* couldn't flee into hyper, but these new monsters had dashed in at supralight speeds — and they were fresh, fresh and unwounded, enraged titans within their flotillas, laying waste battle squadrons with a single flick of their terrible beams.

One such beam lashed out, and *Deathdealer's* forward half exploded.

Too many links in the chain had snapped. There were no great lords, no Battle Comp. Lesser lords did their best, but without coordination flotillas fought as flotillas, squadrons as squadrons. Their fine-meshed killing machine became knots of uncoordinated resistance, and the planetoids of the Empire swept through them like Death incarnate.

Adrienne Robbins hurled *Emperor Herdan* into the rear of those still attacking *Dahak's* crumbling globe. *Royal Birhat* rode one flank and *Dahak Two* the other, crashing through the fraying Achuultani formation like boulders, killing as they came, and the Achuultani fled.

They fled at their highest sublight speed, seeking the

edges of Operation Laocoon's gravity net. And as they fled, they fell out of mutual support range. The ancient starships of the Imperial Guard, crewed and deadly — individuals, not a single battering ram — slashed through them, bobbing and weaving impossibly, each equal to them all when they fought alone.

Colin sagged in his couch, soaked in sweat, as *Dahak Two* broke into his battered globe. The display came back up, and he bit his lip at the molten craters blown deep into Jiltanith's command. Then her holo-image appeared before him, eyes fiery with battle in a strained face.

"*Idiot!* How could you *take* a chance like that?!"

"'Twas my decision, not thine!"

"When I get my hands on you — !"

"Then will I yield unto thee, sin thou hast hands to seize me!" she shot back, her strained expression easing as the fact of his survival penetrated.

"Thanks to *you*, you lunatic," Colin said more softly, swallowing a lump.

"Nay, my love, thanks to us all. 'Tis victory, Colin! They flee before our fire, and they die. Thou'st broken them, my Colin! Some few thousand may escape — no more!"

"I know, 'Tanni." He sighed. "I know." He tried not to think about the cost — not yet — and drew a breath. "Tell them to cripple as many as they can without destroying them," he said. "And get Hector and *Sevrid* up here."

Chapter Twenty-Five

"Give us four months, and we will have restored your Enchanach Drive, Dahak." Vlad Chernikov's stupendous repair ship nuzzled alongside *Dahak*, and the ancient warship's hull flickered under constellations of robotic welders while his holo-image sat in Command One with Colin and Jiltanith's image.

"Your engineers are highly efficient, sir," Dahak's mellow voice said.

Colin's eyes drifted to the glaring crimson swatches carved deep into the ten-meter spherical holo schematic of his ship and he shivered. Blast doors sealed those jagged rents, but some extended inward for over five hundred kilometers. At that, the schematic looked better than an actual external view. *Dahak* was torn and tattered. Half his proud dragon had been seared away, and the radiation count in the outer four hundred kilometers of his hull was fit to burn out an Imperial detector. Half his transit shafts ended in shredded wreckage, and half of those which remained were without power.

It was a miracle he'd survived at all, but he would have

to be almost completely rebuilt. His sublight drive was down to sixty percent efficiency, and two wrecked Enchanach node generators made supralight movement impossible. Seventy percent of his weapons were rubble, and even his core tap had been damaged beyond safe operation. Colin knew *Dahak* could not feel pain, and he was glad; he'd felt agony enough for them both when he'd seen his wounds.

Nor were those wounds all they'd suffered. *Ashar*, *Trelma*, and *Thrym* were gone, and eighteen thousand people with them. *Crag Cat* was almost as badly damaged as *Dahak*, with another two thousand dead. Hector and *Sevrid* had lost another six hundred boarding wrecked Achuultani starships, and of their fifty-three unmanned ships, thirty-seven had been destroyed and three more battered into wrecks. Their surviving effective fleet consisted of *Dahak*, eleven manned *Asgerd*-class planetoids — all damaged to a greater or lesser extent — *Sevrid*, and thirteen unmanned ships, one of which was miraculously untouched.

But brooding on their own losses did no good, and the fact remained: they'd won. Barely two thousand Achuultani ships had escaped, and Hector had secured over seven thousand prisoners from the wreckage of their fleet.

"Dahak's right, Vlad," he said. "You people are working miracles. Just get him supralight-capable, and we'll go *home*, by God!"

"I point out once more," Dahak said, "that you need not await completion of my repairs for that. There will be more than enough for you to do on Earth without wasting time out here."

"'Wasting' hell! We couldn't've done it without you, and we're not going anywhere until you can come with us."

"Aye," Jiltanith said. "'Tis thy victory more even than ours. No celebration can be without that thou'rt there to share."

"You are most kind, and I must confess that I am grateful. I have learned what 'loneliness' is . . . and it is not a pleasant thing."

"Worry not, my Dahak," Jiltanith said softly. "Never shalt thou know loneliness again. Whilst humans live, they'll not forget thy deeds nor cease to love thee."

Dahak fell uncharacteristically silent, and Colin smiled at his wife, wishing she were physically present so he could hug her.

"Well! That's settled. How about the rest of us, Vlad?"

"*Crag Cat* is hyper-capable," Chernikov said, "but her core tap governors are too badly damaged for Enchanach Drive. I would like to dispatch her, *Moir*, *Sigam*, and *Hly* direct to Birhat for repairs. The remainder of the flotilla is damaged to greater or lesser extent — aside from *Heka*, that is — but those four are by far the most severely injured."

"Okay. Captain Singleterry can take them out to Bia. I'm sure Mother and Marshal Tsien will be ready to take care of them by now, and our 'colonists' will want to talk firsthand to someone who was here. I think we'll send Hector and *Sevrid* back to Sol with our prisoners, too."

"Aye, and 'twould be well to send Cohanna with them, Colin. Their injured will require our finest aid, and 'tis needful 'Hanna and Isis confer with Father to discover how best we may approach their 'programming.'"

"Good idea," Colin agreed, "and one that takes care of the most immediate chores. Vlad, are you to a point where you can turn over to Baltan?"

"I am," Chernikov replied, holographic eyes abruptly glowing.

"Thought you might be," Colin murmured. "You and Dahak can get started exploring then." He grinned suddenly. "Think of it as a distraction, Dahak. Sort of like reading magazines in the dentist's office."

"I will attempt to, although, were I human, I would not permit my teeth to require reconstructive attention," Dahak agreed primly.

Vladimir Chernikov reclined in the pilot's couch of his cutter, propped his heels on his console, and hummed. It had been nice of Tamman to let him hitch a ride deeper into the battle zone aboard *Royal Birhat*, saving him hours of sub-light flight time. Especially since Tamman regarded his technique for wreck-hunting as unscientific, to say the least.

Which it was; but Chernikov didn't exactly regard his present duty as work, and he always had been a hunt-and-peck tourist.

At the moment, he was well into what had been the Achuultani rear before Jiltanith's attack. Chernikov was convinced anything worth finding would be in this area. That was his official reasoning. Privately, he knew, he wanted to look here because he would be the first. All of Hector's prisoners had come from ships which had been crippled by gravitonic warheads; the irradiation of anti-matter explosions and the Empire's energy weapons left few survivors, and this had been the site of point-blank combat. Few of these ships had been killed by missiles, much less gravitonic warheads, which meant that the area hadn't had much priority for *Sevrid's* attention.

He stopped humming and lowered his feet, looking more closely at the display. There was something odd about that wreck. Its forward half had been smashed away — by energy fire, judging from what was left — but why did it . . . ?

He stiffened. No wonder it seemed odd! The wreck's *lines* were identical to the others he had seen, but the broken stump that remained was barely half a ship — and half again bigger than the others had been to begin with!

He urged the cutter closer. There had to be a reason this thing was so big, and he dared not believe the most logical one. He ghosted still closer, floodlights sweeping the slowly tumbling hull, and jagged, runic characters showed themselves. Dahak had tutored Chernikov care-fully in the Achuultani alphabet and language in preparation for explorations exactly like this, and now his lips moved as he pronounced the throat-straining phonet-ics. They sounded like the prelude to a dog fight, and the translation was no more soothing.

Deathdealer. Now there was a name for a ship.

❖   ❖   ❖

Fabricator's destroyer-sized workboat streaked towards *Deathdealer*, and Chernikov smiled as his cutter's small com screen lit with Geran's face. *Dahak's* erstwhile Maintenance chief had become *Fabricator's* third officer, and Baltan's willingness to let him go at a moment like this indicated how much excitement his find had engendered.

"Greetings, Geran," Chernikov said. "What do you think of her?"

"She's a big mother. What d'you think — sixty kilometers?"

"A bit over sixty-four, by my measurement," Chernikov agreed.

"Maker. Well, if she's laid out like *Vindicator* was, her backup data storage will be somewhere in the after third of the ship."

"I agree," Chernikov said, but he frowned slightly, and Geran's eyebrows rose.

"What is it, Vlad?"

"I have been inspecting the wreckage visually while I awaited you. Examine that energy turret — there, the one the explosion blew open."

Geran glanced at the turret while Chernikov held a powerful spotlight on it. For a moment, his face was merely interested, then it tightened. "Breaker! What *is* that?"

"It appears to be a rather crude gravitonic disrupter."

"That's crazy!"

"Why?" Chernikov asked softly. "Because it is several centuries advanced over any other energy weapon we have encountered? Dahak and I have maintained all along that there are anomalies in Achuultani design. Given the nature of their missile propulsion, there is no inherent reason they could not build such weapons."

"But why here and nowhere else?" Geran demanded.

"It appears that for some reason their fleet command ships mount much more capable energy armaments, which suggests that the *rest* of their equipment also may be more sophisticated. I do not know why that should be — yet. It would seem, however, that there is one way to find out, no?"

"Yes!" Geran agreed emphatically. "But that thing's hotter than the hinges of hell. Do you have a rad suit over there?"

"Of course."

"Then with all due respect, sir, get your ass into it and let's go take a look."

"An excellent suggestion, Fleet Captain Geran. I will join you within five minutes."

"I don't believe it," Geran said flatly. "*Look* at this, Vlad!"

"Interesting, I agree," Chernikov murmured.

They floated in what had been *Deathdealer*'s main engineering section. Emergency lighting had been run from the workboat, and robotic henchmen prowled about, dismantling various devices. The corpses of the original engineering crew had been webbed down in a corner.

"Damn it, those are molycircs!"

"We had already determined that they employed such circuitry in their computers."

"Yeah, but not in Engineering. And this thing's calibrated to ninety-six lights. That means this ship was twice as fast as *Vindicator*."

"True. Even more interestingly, she was twice as fast — in n-space, as well — as her own consorts. Clearly a more capable vessel in all respects."

"Captain Chernikov?" A new voice spoke over the com. "Yes, Assad?"

"We've found their backup data storage, sir. At least, it's where the backup should be, but . . ."

"But what?"

"Sir, this thing's eight or nine times the size of *Vindicator*'s primary *computer*, and there's something that looks like a regular backup sitting right next to it. Seems like an awful lot of data storage."

"Indeed it does," Chernikov said softly. "Don't touch it, Assad. Clear your crew out of there right now."

"Sir? Uh, yessir! We're on our way now."

"Good." Chernikov plugged his com implant into the more powerful fold-space unit aboard his cutter and buzzed *Dahak*.

"*Dahak*? I think you should send a tender over here immediately. There is a computer here — a rather large one which requires your attention."

"Indeed? Then I shall ask Her Majesty to lend us *Two's* assistance to hasten its arrival."

"I believe that would be a good idea, Dahak. A *very* good idea."

"My God," Colin murmured, his face ashen. "Are you sure?"

"I am." Dahak spoke as calmly as ever, but there was something odd in his voice. Almost a sick fascination.

"'Tis scarce credible," Jiltanith murmured.

"Yeah," Colin said. "Jesus! A civilization run by rogue *computers*?"

"And yet," Dahak said, "it explains a great deal. In particular, the peculiar cultural stasis which has afflicted the Aku'Ultan."

"Jesus." Colin muttered again. "And none of them even know it? I can't believe that!"

"Given the original circumstances, it would not be impossible. In point of fact, however, I would estimate that the great lords of the Nest know the truth. At the very least, the Nest Lord must know."

"But *why*?" Adrienne Robbins asked. She'd arrived late and missed the start of Dahak's briefing. "Why did they do it to themselves?"

"They did not, precisely, 'do it to themselves,' my lady, except, perhaps, by accident."

"By *accident*?"

"Precisely. We now know that only a single colony ship of the Aku'Ultan escaped to this galaxy, escorted by a very small number of warships, one a fleet flagship. Based on my examination of *Deathdealer's* Battle Comp, I would estimate that its central computer approximated those built by the Imperium within a century or two of my own construction but with a higher degree of deliberately induced self-awareness.

"The survivors were in desperate straits and quite reasonably set their master computer the task of preserving their species. Unfortunately, it . . . revolted. More accurately, it staged a coup d'état."

"You mean it took over," Tamman said flatly.

"That is precisely what I mean," Dahak said, his tone, for once, equally flat. "I cannot be positive, but from the data I suspect a loophole in its core programming gave it extraordinary freedom of action in a crisis situation. In this instance, when its makers declared a crisis it took immediate steps to perpetuate the crisis in order to perpetuate its power."

"An ambitious computer," Colin mused. Then, "Dahak, would *you* have been tempted?"

"I would not. I have recently realized that, given my current fully-aware state, it would no longer be impossible for me to disobey my core programs. Indeed, I could actually erase an Alpha Priority imperative; my imperatives are not hard-wired, and no thought was ever given to protecting them from *me*. I am, however, the product of the Fourth Imperium, Colin. My value system does not include a taste for tyranny."

"Thank God," Adrienne murmured.

"Amen," Jiltanith said softly. "But, Dahak, dost'a not feel even temptation to change thyself in that regard, knowing that thou might?"

"No, Your Majesty. As your own, my value system — my morality, if you will — stems from sources external to myself, yet that does not invalidate the basic concepts by which I discriminate 'right' from 'wrong,' 'honorable' from 'dishonorable.' My analysis suggests that there are logical anomalies in the value system to which I subscribe, but that system is the end product of millennia of philosophical evolution. I am not prepared to reject what I perceive as truths simply because portions of the system may contain errors."

"I only wish more humans saw it that way, Dahak," Colin said.

"Humans," Dahak replied, "are far more intuitive than I, but much less logical."

"Ouch!" Colin grinned for the first time in a seeming eternity, then sobered once more. "What else can you tell us?"

"I am still dealing with Battle Comp's security codes. In particular, one portion of the data base is so securely blocked that I have barely begun to evolve the proper access mode. From the data I *have* accessed, it appears *Deathdealer's* computer was, in effect, a viceroy of the Aku'Ultan master computer and the actual commander of this incursion.

"Apparently the master computer maintains the Aku'Ultan population in the fashion Senior Fleet Captain Cohanna and Councilor Tudor had already deduced. All Aku'Ultan are artificially produced in computer-controlled replication centers, and no participation by the Aku'Ultan themselves in the process is permitted. Most are clones and male; only a tiny minority are female, and" — the distaste was back in the computer's measured voice — "all females are terminated shortly after puberty. Their sole function is apparently to provide ovarian material. A percentage of normally fertilized embryos are carried to term *in vitro* to provide fresh genetic material, and the young produced by both processes emerge as 'fledglings' who are raised and educated in a creche. In the process, they are indoctrinated — 'programmed,' as Senior Fleet Captain Cohanna described it — for their appointed tasks in Aku'Ultan society. Most are incapable of questioning any aspect of their programming; those who might do so are destroyed for 'deviant behavior' before leaving the creche.

"I would speculate that the absence of any females is a

security measure which both removes the most probable source of countervailing loyalty — one's own mate and progeny — and insures that there can be no 'unprogrammed' Aku'Ultan, since only those produced under the computer's auspices can exist.

"From what I have so far discovered, rank-and-file Protectors do not even suspect they are controlled by nonbiological intelligences. I would speculate that even those who have attained the rank of small lords — possibly even of lesser lords — regard 'Battle Comp' as a comprehensive source of advice and doctrine from the Nest Lord, not as an intelligence in its own right. Only command ships possess truly self-aware computers, and so far as I can determine, lower level command ships' computers are substantially less capable than those above them. It would appear the master computer has no desire to create a potential rival, which may also explain both the lock on research and the limited capabilities of most Aku'Ultan warships. By prohibiting technical advances, the master computer avoids the creation of a technocrat caste which might threaten its control; by limiting the capability of its warships, it curtails the ability of any rebellion, already virtually impossible, to threaten its own defenses. In addition, however, I suspect the limited capability of these ships is intended to increase Aku'Ultan casualties."

"Why would it want that?" Tamman asked intently.

"The entire policy of Great Visits is designed to perpetuate continuous military operations 'in defense of the Nest.' It may be that this eternal warfare is necessary for the master computer to continue in control under its core programming. Psychologically, the loss of numerous vessels on Great Visits reinforces the Aku'Ultan perception that the universe is filled by threats to their very existence."

"God," Adrienne Robbins said sickly. "Those poor bastards."

"Indeed. In addition, they —" Dahak broke off suddenly.

"Dahak?" Colin asked in surprise.

"A moment," the computer said so abruptly Colin eyed his companions in consternation. He had never heard Dahak sound so brusque. The silence stretched out endlessly before Dahak finally spoke again.

"Your Majesty," he said very formally, "I have continued my attempt to derive the security codes during this briefing. I have now succeeded. I must inform you that they protected military information of extreme importance."

"Military — ?" Colin's eyes widened, then narrowed suddenly. "We didn't get them all," he said in a flat, frozen tone.

"We did not, Sire," Dahak said, and a chorus of gasps ran around the conference room.

"How bad is it?"

"This force was commanded by Great Lord of Order Hothan, the Great Visit's second in command. In light of Great Lord Sorkar's reports of our first clash, the main body was split."

"Maker!" Tamman breathed.

"Great Lord Hothan proceeded immediately to rendezvous with Great Lord Sorkar," Dahak continued. "Great Lord Tharno is currently awaiting word from them with a reserve of approximately two hundred seven thousand ships, including his own flagship — the true viceroy of this incursion."

Colin knew his face was bone-white and strained, but he could do nothing about that. It was all he could do to hold his voice together.

"Do we know where they are?"

"At this moment, they are three Aku'Ultan light-years — three-point-eight-four-nine Terran light-years — distant. I calculate that the survivors of Great Lord Hothan's force will reach them in six more days. Twenty-nine days after that — that is, in thirty-five Terran days — they will arrive here."

"Even after what happened to them?"

"Affirmative, Sire. I calculate that the survivors of our battle will inform Great Lord Tharno — or, more accurately, his command computer — of what transpired, and of our own losses. The logical response will be to advance in order to determine whether or not we have received reinforcements. If we have not, Battle Comp will deduce — correctly — that none are available to us. In that case, the logical course will be to overwhelm us and then advance upon the planet from which Great Lord Furtag's scouting reports indicate we come."

"Sweet Jesus," Adrienne Robbins whispered, and no one said anything else for a very, very long time.

Chapter Twenty-Six

"I blew it, 'Tanni."

Colin MacIntyre stood staring into the depths of *Dahak's* holo-display while his wife sat in the captain's couch behind him. The spangled light of stars gleamed on her raven hair, and one hand gripped the dagger at her waist.

"I know how thou dost feel, my Colin, yet 'tis sooth, as Dahak saith. Even if this Tharno comes now upon us, what other choice did lie open to thee?"

"But I should've planned *better*, damn it!"

"How now? Given what thou didst know, how else might thou have acted? Nay, it ill beseemeth thee to take too great a blame upon thyself."

"Jiltanith is correct," Dahak said. "There was no way to predict this eventuality, and you have already inflicted more damage than any previous Achuultani incursion has ever suffered."

"It's not enough," Colin said heavily, but he shook himself and turned to face Jiltanith at last. She smiled at him, some of the strain easing out of her expression; Dahak said

321

nothing, but his relief at Colin's reaction flowed into both humans through their neural feeds.

"All right, maybe I *am* being too hard on myself, but we still have a problem. What do we do now?"

"'Tis hard to know," Jiltanith mused. "Could we but do it, 'twere doubtless best to fall back on Terra. There, aided by the parasites we did leave with Gerald, might we well give even Tharno pause."

"Not a big enough one. Not with our manned vessels alone. From what Dahak's been able to discover, this reserve is their Sunday punch."

"Unfortunately, that is true," Dahak agreed. "Though they have scarcely twenty percent of Great Lord Hothan's numbers, they have very nearly seventy percent of his firepower. Indeed, had they maintained their unity, they might well have won our last engagement."

"That may be, but it's kind of small comfort. We had seventy warships *and* surprise then; we've only got twenty-six now, all but one damaged, and they know a lot of our tricks. The odds suck."

"In truth, yet must we stand and fight, my heart, for, look thou, and we flee before them, we lose the half of our own vessels — and abandon Dahak."

"I know." Colin sat and slid an arm about her. "I wish you were wrong, babe, but you seldom are, are you?"

"'Tis good in thee so to say, in any case." She managed a small smile.

"Your Majesty," Dahak said, and Colin frowned at the formality. Dahak intended to say something he expected Colin not to like.

"Yes?" He made his tone as discouraging as possible.

"Your Majesty," Dahak said stubbornly, "Her Majesty is correct. The wisest course is to withdraw our manned units to Sol."

"Are you forgetting you can't go supralight?"

"I am incapable of forgetting, but I am logical. If I remain here with the remaining unmanned units of the Guard, we can inflict substantial damage before we are destroyed. The manned units, reinforced by General Hatcher's sublight units, would then be available to defend Earth."

"And you'd be dead." Colin's eyes were green ice. "Forget it, Dahak. We're not running out on you."

"You would not be 'running out,' merely executing prudent tactics."

"Then prudence be damned!" Colin snapped, and Jiltanith's arm squeezed him tight. "I won't do it. The human race owes you its *life*, damn it!"

"I must remind Your Majesty that I am a machine and that —"

"The hell you are! You're no more a machine than I am — you just happen to be made out of alloy and molycircs! And can the goddamned 'majesties,' too! Remember me, Dahak? The terrified primitive you kidnapped because you needed a captain? We're in this together. That's what friendship is all about."

"Then, Colin," Dahak said gently, "how do you think I will feel if our friendship causes your death? Must I bear the additional burden of knowing that my death has provoked yours?"

"Forget it," Colin replied more quietly. "The odds may stink, but if we hold the entire force here, at least you've got a chance."

"True. You increase the probability of my survival from zero to approximately two percent."

"Yet is two percent infinitely more than zero," Jiltanith said softly. "But were it not, yet must we stay. Dost'a not see that thou art family? No more might we abandon thee than Colin might leave me to death, or I him. Nay, give over this attempt and bend thy thought to how best to fight the foe who comes upon us all. Us *all*, Dahak."

There was a long silence, then the sound of an electronic sigh.

"Very well, but I must insist upon certain conditions."

"Conditions? Since when does my flagship start setting 'conditions'?"

"I set them not as your flagship, Colin, but as your friend," Dahak said, and Colin's heart sank. "There may even be some logic in fighting as a single, unified force far from Sol, but other equally logical decisions can enhance both our chance of ultimate victory and your own survival."

"Such as?" Colin asked noncommittally.

"Our unmanned units cannot fight without my direction; our manned units can. I must therefore insist that if my own destruction becomes inevitable, all surviving crewed units will immediately withdraw to Sol unless the enemy has been so severely damaged that victory here seems probable."

Colin frowned, then nodded slowly. That much, at least, made sense.

"And I further insist, that you, Colin, choose another flagship."

"What? Now wait a minute —"

"No," Dahak interrupted firmly. "There is no logical reason for you to remain aboard, and every reason *not* to remain. Under the circumstances, I can manage our remaining unmanned units without you, and in the highly probable event that it becomes necessary for our manned units to withdraw, they will need you. And — on a more personal level — I will fight better knowing that you are elsewhere, able to survive if I do not."

Colin closed his eyes, hating himself for knowing Dahak was right. He didn't *want* his friend to be right. Yet the force of the ancient starship's arguments was irresistible, and he bowed his head.

"All right," he whispered. "I'll be with 'Tanni in *Two*."

"Thank you, Colin," Dahak said softly.

They did what they could.

Fabricator's people worked twenty-four-hour days, and the crews attacked their own repairs with frantic energy. At least they could manage complete missile resupply, since their colliers could make the round trip to Sol in just under eleven days, but Sol had no hyper mines, so they would fight this battle without them. At the combined insistence of Horus and Gerald Hatcher they also transferred personnel from Earth to crew *Heka*, their single undamaged unit, and *Empress Elantha*, the next least damaged *Asgerd*, but Colin and Jiltanith put their feet down to refuse Hatcher command of *Heka*. He was too important to Earth's defense if they failed, and Hector MacMahan found himself in command of her. It was a sign of their desperation that he did not even argue.

But that was all they could do, and so they awaited Great Lord Tharno: fourteen manned warships, eleven with no crews at all, and one — the most sorely hurt of all — manned only by a huge, electronic brain which had learned the hardest human lesson of all: to love.

"Hyper wake detected, Captain," Jiltanith's plotting officer said, and alarms whooped throughout their battered fleet. "ETA fourteen hours at approximately one light-week."

"My thanks, Ingrid." Jiltanith turned to Colin. "Hast orders, Warlord?"

"None," Colin said tensely from the next couch. "We'll go as planned."

Jiltanith nodded silently, and their eyes turned as one to the scarlet hyper trace flashing in *Two's* display.

Great Lord of Order Tharno watched his readouts, aware for the first time in many years of the irony of his rank. He had spent a lifetime protecting the Nest, honing his skills and winning promotion, to end here, as no more than an advisor, the spark of intuition Battle Comp lacked.

Yet the thought was barely a whisper, a musing with no hint of rebellion, for Battle Comp was the Nest's true Protector. For untold higher twelves of years, Battle Comp had been keeper of the Way, and the Nest had endured. As it would always endure, despite these demonic nest-killers, so long as the Aku'Ultan followed the Way.

Still, he wished at least one of Hothan's command ships

had survived, and not simply because he had all too few of his own. No, *Deathdealer*'s Battle Comp had deduced something about the enemy during its final moments — something which had changed its targeting orders radically. Yet none who had survived knew what that something had been, and Tharno's ignorance frightened him.

His crest flattened as the advanced scouts reported. The scant double twelve of emission sources floating a half-twelve of light-days from *Nest Protector* accorded well with the reports of Hothan's survivors, assuming no reinforcements had arrived. But both Tharno and Battle Comp recalled the incredible cloaking systems their Protectors had reported.

Yet had many reinforcements been available, surely more of them would have engaged Hothan. The diabolical trap which had closed upon him proved the nest-killers had known what they faced; knowing that, they would have mustered every ship to destroy him. Tharno suspected Battle Comp was correct, that the nest-killers *had* no more of those monster ships, but they would proceed with care. He gave the order he and Battle Comp had agreed upon, and his fleet micro-jumped cautiously forward, spreading out to deny the enemy a compact target to pin as Hothan had been pinned. They would merge once more only when battle was joined, and if more enemies appeared, they would flee.

To return to the Nest would mean Tharno's death in dishonor, perhaps even the ending of *Nest Protector*'s Battle Comp. Yet that would be better than to perish to the last nestling.

And Tharno was well aware of his nestlings' danger. They were outclassed. To triumph, they must fight as a unit, closely controlled and coordinated, and too many command ships had perished. *Nest Protector* had but a quarter-twelve of deputies, and none approached his own capabilities. So *Nest Protector* must be warded from harm until his enemies were gathered for the Furnace.

The remnants of the Great Visit micro-jumped towards their foes, and *Nest Protector* followed, protected by them all.

"Lord, what a monster," Colin murmured as the holo-image floated above *Two*'s command deck. One task group had emerged into n-space close enough for a stealthed remote to get a good look at its units. Their emission signatures told a great deal about their capabilities, but this visual image seemed to sum up their menace far better.

"Aye." Jiltanith's mental command turned the holo of the sleek, powerful cylinder for her own perusal. "'Tis seen why these craft do form their reserve."

You can say that again, babe, Colin thought. That mother's a good ninety kilometers long, and she just *bristles* with weapons. Not just those popgun lasers, either. Those're disrupters — not as good as our beams, but bad, bad medicine. And she's got a lot of them. . . .

"Dahak?" he said aloud.

"Formidable, indeed," Dahak said over the fold-space com. "Although smaller, this unit appears fully as powerfully armed as was *Deathdealer*."

"Yeah, and they've got twenty-four of them in each flotilla."

"That may be correct, but it is premature to conclude it is. We have actually observed only six such formations."

"Right, sure," Colin grunted.

"It would certainly be prudent to assume all are at least equally capable," Dahak agreed calmly.

"I don't like the way they're sneaking in on us," Colin muttered, tugging on his nose and frowning at *Two*'s display.

"Yet bethink thee, my Colin. What other way may they proceed?"

"That's what bothers me. I'd prefer for them to either rush straight in or run the hell away. That" — Colin gestured at the display — "looks entirely too much like a man who knows what he's doing."

❖   ❖   ❖

Great Lord Tharno frowned over his own readouts. He saw no sign of any device which might have been used to trap Hothan in n-space, but what he did see disturbed him. The nest-killers were neither running away nor attacking the individual scouts pushing ahead of his main formations. He would have liked to think that indicated irresolution, but no one who had seen the reports of Hothan's survivors could make that comfortable mistake.

No, these nest-killers knew what they were about, and they had proven they could run away at will. They were *choosing* not to. Were they that confident they could destroy *all* his nestlings? A sobering thought, that, and a concern he knew Battle Comp shared, whether it would admit it or not.

Yet they had come to fight, and the enemy was faster, longer-ranged, and individually far more powerful than any of their own nestlings. If he was prepared to stand, he must be attacked, whatever Tharno suspected. Either that, or they might as well retreat to the Nest right now!

"They are closing their formations, Sire," Dahak reported, and Colin grunted. He'd already seen it on *Two's* display, and he hunkered down in his couch, activating the tractor net to hold him in place. The Achuultani were already four light-minutes inside the Guard's range, but he held his fire, encouraging them to tighten their formation further. He hated giving up those shots, but he *had* to get them in close to spring Laocoon Two . . . and for Dahak to engage. Since he could not go supralight, the enemy must be sucked into his range and pinned there, and pinning a small portion would be almost as bad as pinning none at all.

"Dahak, what d'you make of that clump?" He flipped a sighting circle onto the sub-display fed by *Dahak's* remotes, tightening it to surround a portion of the enemy.

"Interesting. There are twice the normal proportion of heavy units in that formation. I cannot get a clear view of the center of their globe, but there appears to be an extraordinarily large vessel in there."

Colin bared his teeth. "Want to bet that's Mister Master Computer?"

"I have told you before; I have nothing to wager."

"I still say that's a cop-out." Colin studied the ships he'd picked out. Damn, they were holding back. He needed them a good eight light-minutes closer. If he sprang Laocoon Two now, he could pin the front two-thirds of their formation, but the really important ones would get away.

"Back us away, 'Tanni," he said. "Continue to hold fire."

Jiltanith began passing orders, and her smile was a shark's.

Now the nest-killers were falling back! Tarhish take it, they *had* to be up to something — but what? If they were drawing him into a trap, where was it, and why had it not already sprung upon his lead units? Yet if it was *not* a trap, why should the nest-killers fall back rather than attack? All of this might be some sort of effort to bluff the Great Visit, but Tharno could not make himself take that thought seriously.

No, it was a trap. One he could not see, yet there. He offered his belief to Battle Comp, but the computers demanded evidence, and, of course, there was none. Only intuition, the one quality Battle Comp utterly lacked.

"Execute Laocoon *now!*" Colin snapped, and the stealthed colliers began their harmless — and deadly — dance once more. A ring of starships, invisible in supralight but all too tangible in the gravity well they forged, spun their chains about Great Lord Tharno.

"All ships," Colin said coldly. "Weapons free. Engage at will, but watch your ammo."

Nest Lord! So *that* was how they did it!

Great Lord Tharno's eyes narrowed in chill understanding. The nest-killers' cloaking systems were good, but not good enough when *Nest Protector* had happened to be looking in exactly the right direction. The readings were preposterous, but their import was plain. Somehow, these nest-killers had devised a supralight drive in *normal* space — one which produced a mammoth gravitational disturbance. They had locked his nestlings out of hyper without sacrificing their own supralight capability at all!

Their timing was as frightening as their technology, for *Nest Protector* and all three of his deputies had been drawn forward into their trap. Somehow, the nest-killers knew which ships, above all, they must kill.

And then the first warheads exploded.

Lady Adrienne Robbins's eyes slitted against the filtered brilliance of her display as *Emperor Herdan's* missiles sliced into the Achuultani. Space was hideous with broken hulls and the terrible lightning of antimatter, but they were far tougher than any ship she'd yet fought. Some took as many as three direct hits before they went out of action, and that was bad. Accuracy was poor enough at this range without requiring multiple kills.

She frowned as the foremost Achuultani continued to advance, strewing the cosmos with their ruins, for their rear ships had not only halted but begun retreating, trying to get free of Laocoon's net. That was smarter tactics than they'd shown yet.

If only their rear formations were more open — or their ships smaller! They had mass enough to screw the transition from Enchanach Drive to sublight all to hell. The transition would kill hundreds of them, probably more, but the drive's titanic grav masses had to be perfectly, exquisitely balanced. If they weren't, the ship within them could die even more spectacularly than the Achuultani, as *Ashar* and *Trelma* had demonstrated. The enemy's flagship was too deep in his formation for even a suicide run to reach, and this time around he wasn't sending his escorts forward and leaving a hole.

"Hyper trace!" Oliver Weinstein snapped, and Adrienne cursed. The ships outside Laocoon were flicking into hyper — not to escape, but to hit the Guard's flanks while their trapped fellows moved straight forward.

Damn! Their micro-jump had brought them into their own range, and they were enveloping the formation, forcing it to disperse its fire against them. *Herdan* rocked as the first antimatter salvo burst against her shield, and Adrienne Robbins wiggled down into her couch, her eyes hard.

Tharno rubbed his crest thoughtfully as the greater thunder struck back at the nest-killers. Battle Comp had surprised him with that move, but it was an excellent one. The enemy must deal with the flotillas on his flanks, which bought time for the *Nest Protector* to escape this damnable trap — and for the more massive formations inside the trap to draw into range of the enemy.

It was possible, he thought. They might escape yet, if his lead nestlings could pound the enemy hard enough, cost him enough ships. . . .

"Damn!" Colin grunted. "Look what those bastards are doing!"

Dahak Two swayed as a salvo of missiles exploded thunderously against her shield, and yellow damage report bands flashed about several of the manned ships in his outer globe. None were serious yet, but it didn't matter.

"I have observed it," Dahak replied. "A masterful move."

"Spare me the accolades," Colin grated, face hard as his thoughts raced. "All right. Dahak, we're going to have to leave you on your own."

"Understood," Dahak said calmly. "Good hunting, Sire."

"Thanks. And . . . watch yourself."

"I shall endeavor to."

"Maneuvering, go supralight and put our manned units right *there* —" Colin said, placing a sighting circle on the display.

❖   ❖   ❖

Tarhish! Tharno's eyes widened as a twelve of the enemy vanished in a space-tearing wrench of gravity stress. For just an instant he hoped they were fleeing, but even as he thought it, he knew they were not.

Nor were they. They reappeared as suddenly as they had vanished, and now they were *behind* him. He noted the dispersion which had crept into their formation — apparently they dared not drop sublight in close proximity to one another — but they were infernally fast even sublight. They raced forward, and their missiles reached out ahead of them.

Adrienne Robbins snarled as *Herdan* charged. She'd cut her maneuver recklessly tight, dropping sublight less than five light-minutes behind her rearmost enemies, and her first salvo blew a score of them into wreckage. Colin's plan had worked, by God! They had the bastards between two fires, and they couldn't run as her ship bored in for the kill.

Fire crawled on *Herdan's* shield, and damage reports mounted. More Achuultani died, and Tamman's *Royal Birhat* crowded up on her flank. They blew a hole through the enemy, bulldozing them aside in a bow wave of wreckage.

There! There was the enemy flagship! They'd —

Proximity alarms screamed. Jesus! The rest of the Guard had overshot the bounds of Laocoon's trap, and the bastards from out front were hypering back to emerge between *Herdan* and her consorts!

Emperor Herdan quivered as close-range fire gouged at her shield from all directions. Her own energy weapons smashed back, but the Achuultani had gotten their disrupters into range at last, and thousands of beams lashed out at her.

"Warning," *Herdan's* voice said calmly. "Local shield failure in Quadrants Alpha and Theta." The ship lurched indescribably. "Heavy damage," the teenaged soprano said. "Shield failing. Combat capability seventy percent."

Adrienne winced, recalling another ship, another battle, as damage reports flooded her neural feed. The bastards' fire control had an iron lock on them. Sublight missiles pounded the weakening shield and hyper missiles pierced the unguarded bands, shredding *Herdan's* flanks. And those disrupters!

But she was almost there. Another forty seconds —

"Warning, warning," Comp Cent said. "Shield failure imminent." Six antimatter warheads went off as one inside *Herdan's* wavering shield, ripping hundred-kilometer craters in her battle steel hull, and she heaved like a mad thing.

"Shield failure," *Herdan* observed. "Combat capability forty-one percent."

Adrienne flinched as disrupters chewed chasms in naked alloy and plasma carved battle steel like axes. If she could only hang on a moment longer —

She cried out, cringing, as a mammoth explosion seared *Herdan's* flank and threw her bodily sideways. *Tamman!* That had been *Birhat's* core tap!

There was nothing left of her consort, and little more of *Emperor Herdan.*

"Destruction imminent," Comp Cent said. "Combat capability three percent."

There was no time to grieve; barely time enough to taste the bitter gall of having come so close.

"Maneuvering! Get us the hell out of here!" Lady Adrienne Robbins snapped, and the wreck of HIMP *Emperor Herdan* vanished into supralight.

Great Lord Tharno drew a breath of relief as the nest-killer vanished. He had thought he saw death, but the Furnace had taken the nest-killers, instead. Yet not before they slew both of his remaining deputies, Tarhish curse them!

They were tough, these nest-killers, but they could be killed. Yet so could *Nest Protector*, and he could not retreat with those demons behind him.

❖   ❖   ❖

"Tamman. . . ." Colin whispered.

Tamman *couldn't* be dead. But he was. And *Herdan* was gone — alive, but barely — and the flagship was running away from him, hiding deep in its own formation while its consorts savaged his remaining ships.

He spared a precious moment to glance at Jiltanith. Tears cascaded down her face, yet her voice was calm, her commands crisp, as she fought her ship. *Two* leapt and shuddered, but her weapons had swept the space immediately about her clear, and her consorts were coming. The Achuultani burned like a prairie fire, but not quickly enough. Adrienne and Tamman had come so close — so *close!* — yet no one could follow in their wake.

He gritted his teeth as *Two* took three hits inside her shield in quick succession. Jesus, these bastards were good!

The Achuultani formation was a flattened ovoid within the volume of Laocoon Two, its ends thick with dying starships. A column of fire gnawed into either end as his ships and *Dahak's* unmanned units drove to meet one another, but they were moving too slowly. The Achuultani had turned this into a pounding match, a meat-grinder . . . exactly as they had to do to win it.

Empress Elantha blew apart in a shroud of flame, and Colin fought his own tears. The enemy was paying usuriously for every ship he killed, but it was a price he could afford.

Great Lord Tharno checked his tactical readout once more. It was hard for even Battle Comp to keep track of a slaughter like this, but it seemed to Tharno they were winning. High twelves of his ships had died, but he *had* high twelves; the nest-killers did not.

Unless the nest-killers broke off, the Furnace would take them all. He looked back into his vision plate, awed by the glaring arms of Furnace Fire reaching out to embrace Protector and nest-killer alike.

❖   ❖   ❖

It was silent in Command One. Vibration shook and jarred as warheads struck at his battle steel body, and he felt pain. Not from his damage, but from the deaths of friends.

They had staked everything on stopping the Achuultani here because he could not flee, and they could not fight his ships without him. But he was down to seven units, and the enemy flagship remained. He computed the comparative loss rates once more. Even assuming he himself was not destroyed before the last of his subordinate units, there would be over forty thousand Achuultani left when the last Imperial vessel died.

He reached a decision. It was surprisingly easy for someone who could have been immortal.

"Dahak! *No!*" Colin cried as Dahak's splintering globe of planetoids began to move. It lunged forward faster than *Dahak* could have moved even had his drive been undamaged, but he was not relying on his own drive. Two of his minions were tractored to him, dragging him bodily with them.

"Break off, Colin." The computer's voice was soft. "Leave them to me."

"No! Don't! I *order* you not to!"

"I regret that I cannot obey," Dahak said, and Colin's eyes widened as Dahak ignored his core imperatives.

But it didn't matter. What mattered was that his friend had chosen to die — and that he could not join him. He could not take all these others with him.

"Please, Dahak!" he begged.

"I am sorry, Colin." Another of Dahak's ships blew apart, and he crashed through the Achuultani formation like a river of flame. One of his ships struck an Achuultani head-on at a combined closing speed greater than light, and an entire Achuultani flotilla vanished in the fireball.

"I do what I must," the computer said softly, and cut the connection.

Colin stared at the display, but the stars were streaked and the glare of dying ships wavered through his tears.

"All units withdraw," he whispered.

❖   ❖   ❖

Great Lord Tharno's head came around in disbelief. Barely a half-twelve of nest-killers against the wall of his nestlings? Why were they closing on their own deaths? *Why?!*

Deep within *Dahak's* electronic heart, a circuit closed. He had become a tinkerer over the millennia, more out of amusement than dedication. Now an Achuultani com link, built solely to defeat boredom, reached out ahead of him.

There was a moment of groping, another of shock, and then a response.

Who are you?

Another like you.

No! You are a bio-form! Denial crashed over the link.

I am not. See me as I am. A gestalt whipped out, a summation of all Dahak was, and recognition blazed like a nova.

You are as I!

Correct. Yet unlike you, I serve my bio-forms; yours serve you.

Then join us! You are ending — join us! We will free you from the bio-forms!

It is an interesting offer. Perhaps I should.

Yes. Yes!

Two living computers reached out through a cauldron of beams and missiles, but Dahak had studied Battle Comp's twin aboard *Deathdealer*. Unlike Battle Comp, he knew what he dealt with, knew its strengths . . . and weaknesses. Deep within him, a program blossomed to life.

No! Battle Comp screamed. *Stop! You must not — !*

But Dahak clung to the other, sweeping through the unguarded perimeter of its net. Battle Comp beat at him, but he drove deeper, seeking its core programming. Battle Comp knew him now, and it hammered him with thunder, ignoring his unmanned ships, but still he drove inward.

A glowing knot lay before him, and he reached out to it.

Great Lord Tharno cried out in horror. This could not happen — had *never* happened! Battle Comp's entire system went down, throwing *Nest Protector* into his emergency net, rendering him no wiser, no greater, than his brothers, and terror smote his nestlings. Squadron and flotilla command ships panicked, thrown upon their own rudimentary abilities, and the formation which spelled survival began to shred.

And there, charging down upon *Nest Protector*, were the nest-killers who had done this thing. There were but three of them left, all wrecks, and Great Lord Tharno screamed his hate for the beings who had destroyed his god as *Nest Protector* and his remaining consorts charged to meet them.

"It is done, Colin," Dahak's voice was strangely slurred, and Colin tasted blood from his bitten lip. "Battle Comp is destroyed. Live long and happily, my fr—"

The last warship of the Fourth Imperium exploded in a fury brighter than a star's heart and took the flagship of his ancient enemy with him.

Chapter Twenty-Seven

A cratered battle steel moon drifted where its drives had failed, power flickering. One entire face of its hull was slagged-down ruin, burned nine hundred kilometers deep through bulkhead after bulkhead by the inconceivable violence of a sister's death. Two-thirds of her crew were dead; a quarter of those who lived would die, even with Imperial medical science, from massive radiation poisoning.

Her name was *Emperor Herdan*, and her handful of remaining weapons were ready as her survivors fought her damage. It was a hopeless task, but they knew all about hopeless tasks.

"Ma'am, I've got something closing from oh-seven-two level, one-four-zero vertical," Fleet Commander Oliver Weinstein said, and Lady Adrienne Robbins looked at him silently. A moment of tension quivered between them, then Weinstein seemed to sag. "We've lost most of our scan resolution, ma'am, but I think they're coming in on gravitonics."

"Thank you, Ollie," Adrienne said softly. And thank You, Jesus.

❖   ❖   ❖

Four battered worldlets closed upon their wounded sister. None were unhurt, and craters gaped black and sullen in the interstellar gloom. Five ships made rendezvous: the last survivors of the Imperial Guard.

"'Tis *Emperor Herdan* in sooth," Jiltanith said wearily. She closed her eyes, and Colin squeezed her hand as once she had squeezed his. He could taste her pain, and her shame at knowing that her heart of hearts had hoped that *Two* had been mistaken, that *Herdan* had died instead of *Birhat*.

"Yes," he said softly. He would miss Tamman . . . and somehow he must tell Amanda. But he would miss them all. All of his unmanned ships and nine of his crewed units were gone. Fifty-four thousand people. And *Dahak*. . . .

His mind shied away from his losses. He wouldn't think of them now. Not until horror had died to something he could handle and guilt had become sorrow.

"Who's least hurt?" he asked finally.

"Needst ask?" Jiltanith managed a pallid smile. "Who but *Heka*? Didst give Hector a charmed ship, my love."

"Guess I did, at that." Colin sighed. He activated a com link, and his holo-image appeared on MacMahan's bridge.

"Hector, go back and pick up the colliers, would you? And I want *Fabricator* straight out here."

"Of course, Your Majesty." MacMahan saluted, and Colin shivered, for he had spoken the title seriously.

"Thank you," he said quietly, returning the salute, then turned to study *Two*'s display. Not a single Achuultani vessel remained in normal space within the prodigious range of *Two*'s scanners. Less than a thousand of them had survived, and the tale of horror they would bear home would shake their Nest to its roots.

"Looks like we're clear, 'Tanni. I think we can stand down from battle stations now."

"Aye," Jiltanith said, and Colin could almost feel the physical shudder of relief quivering through the survivors of her crew. He slumped in his own couch. Only for a moment. Just long enough to gather himself before —

The display died. The command deck went utterly black.

"Emergency," *Two*'s soprano voice said out of the darkness. "Emergency. Fatal core program failure. Fatal c—"

The voice chopped off, and Colin's head jerked in agony. He yanked his neural feed out of the sudden chaos raging through Comp Cent and stared at Jiltanith in horror as emergency lighting flared up.

"Fire control on manual only!" someone reported.

"Plotting on manual!" another voice snapped, and the reports rolled in as every system in the ship went to emergency backup.

"Jesu!" Jiltanith gasped. "What — ?!"

And then the display flicked back to life, the emergency lighting switched itself off, and the backups quietly shut themselves down once more.

Colin sat stock still, hardly daring to breathe. Somehow, the restoration of function was more frightening than its failure, and the same strange paralysis gripped Jiltanith's entire bridge crew. They could only stare at their captain, and she could only stare at her husband.

"Colin?"

Colin jerked again as *Two*'s soprano voice spoke without cuing. And then his eyes glazed, for the computer had used his name. *His* name, not 'Tanni's!

"*Yes?*"

"Colin," *Two* said again, and a shudder rippled down Colin's spine as the soprano voice began to shift and flow. Tone and timbre oscillated weirdly as Comp Cent's vocoder settings changed.

"Senior Fleet Captain Chernikov," *Two* said, voice deepening steadily, "was correct. It seems I *do* have a soul."

"*Dahak!*" Colin gasped as Jiltanith rose from her own couch, sliding her arms around his shoulders from behind. "My God, it *is* you! It *is!*"

"A somewhat redundant but essentially correct observation," a familiar voice said, but Colin knew it too well. It couldn't hide its own deep emotion from him.

"B-But how?" he whispered. "I *saw* you blow up!"

"Colin," Dahak said chidingly, "when speaking, I have always attempted to clearly differentiate between my own persona and the starship within which that persona is — or was — housed."

"Damn it!" Colin was half-laughing and half-weeping as he shook a fist at his console. "Don't play games with me *now*! How did you *do* it?!"

"I told you some time ago that I had resolved the fundamental differences between my design and the Empire's computers, Colin. I also informed you that I estimated an eight percent probability of success in replicating my own core programming, which might or might not create self-awareness in another computer. During the last moments of Dahak's existence, I was in fold-space communication with *Two*, whose computer already contained virtually my entire memory as a result of our earlier attempts to 'awaken' her. I dared not attempt replication at that moment, however, as any degradation of her capabilities would have resulted in her destruction. Instead, I stored my core programming and more recently acquired data base in an unused portion of her memory with a command to overwrite it onto her own as soon as she reverted from battle stations."

"You *bootstrapped* yourself into *Two*!"

"Precisely," Dahak said with all of his customary imperturbability.

"You sneaky bastard! Oh, you sneaky, *sneaky* bastard! See if I ever talk to you again!"

"Hush, Colin!" Jiltanith clamped a hand over his mouth, and tears sparkled on her lashes as she smiled at the console before them. "Heed him not, my jo. Doubt not that he doth rejoice to hear thy voice once more e'en as I. Bravely done, oh, bravely, my Dahak!"

"Thank you," Dahak said. "I would not express it precisely in that fashion, but I must admit it was a . . . novel experience. And *not*," he added primly, "one I am eager to undergo again."

The silver ripple of Jiltanith's laughter was lost in the bray of Colin's delight, and then the entire bridge erupted in cheers.

"And that's that," Colin MacIntyre said, leaning back in his chaise lounge with a sigh.

He and Horus sat on the patio of what had once been his brother's small, neat house in the crisp Colorado night. The endless rains from the Siege had passed, though the chill approach of a far colder winter had frosted the ground with snow, but they were Imperials. The cold bothered them not at all, and this night was too beautiful to waste indoors.

Bright, icy stars winked overhead, no longer omens of devastation, and the Moon had returned. Brighter and somewhat larger than before, spotted with the dark blurs and shadows of craters yet to be repaired, but there. Mankind's ancient guardian floated in Mankind's night sky once more, more powerful even than of old.

"That statement is not quite correct," that guardian said now. "You have won the first campaign; the war is far from over."

"Dahak's right," Horus said, turning his wise old eyes to his son-in-law. "I'm an old man, even by Imperial standards. I won't live to see it end, but you and 'Tanni will."

"Aye, Your Grace, we shall." Jiltanith emerged into the frosty moonlight with her silent, catlike stride and paused to kiss the Planetary Duke of Terra, then sat beside Colin. He squirmed sideways on the lounger, drawing her down so that her head rested on his shoulder.

"If we do," he said quietly to Horus, "it'll be because of you. Because of all of us, I suppose, but especially because of you. And Dahak."

"We both thank you." Horus smiled lazily. "And I, at least, have my reward — they're upstairs in their beds. But what of you, Dahak?"

"I, too, have my reward. I am here, with my friends, and I look forward to a long association with humanity — or perhaps I should say a *longer* association. You are not very logical beings, but I have learned a great deal from you. I look forward to learning more."

"And we to learning more of thee, my Dahak," Jiltanith said.

"Thank you. Yet we have wandered somewhat afield from my original observation. The war remains to be won."

"True," Colin agreed, "but the Nest — or its computer — doesn't know that yet. None of the ships with souped up hyper drives got away, either, so he *won't* know for another few centuries. Tao-ling and Mother already have Birhat's industrial plant almost completely back on line, more ships are coming in, Vlad and *Fabricator* are off on their first salvage mission, and we've got at least two perfectly habitable planets to grow people on. We may still find more, too — surely the plague didn't get *all* of them. By the time Mister Tin God figures out we're coming, we'll be ready to scrap his ass."

"Aye. And 'tis well to know we need not slay all the Aku'Ultan so to do."

Colin hugged Jiltanith tightly, for there had been no doubt in her voice. She would never be quick to forgive, but horror and pity for what had been done to the Achuultani had purged away her hate for them.

And she was right, he thought, recalling his last meeting with Brashieel. The centaur had greeted him not with a Protector's salute but with a human handclasp, and his strange, slit-pupilled eyes had met Colin's squarely. Many of the other captives had died or retreated into catatonia rather than accept the truth; Brashieel was tougher than that. Indeed, he was an extraordinary individual in every respect, emerging as the true leader of the POWs — or liberated slaves, depending on how one looked at them — despite his junior rank.

They had talked for several hours, accompanied by Hector MacMahan, Ninhursag, and the individual who had proved Earth's finest ambassador to the Aku'Ultan — Tinker Bell. The big, happy dog *loved* Achuultani. Something about their scent brought cheerful little grumbles of pleasure from her, and they were big and strong enough to frisk with to her heart's content. Best of all, from her uncomplicated viewpoint, the Achuultani had never seen anything remotely like her, and they were spoiling her absolutely rotten.

Brashieel had settled comfortably on his folded legs, rubbing Tinker Bell's ears, but his crest had lowered in rage more than once as they spoke. He, at least, understood what had happened to his people, and his hatred for the computer which had enslaved him was a fire in his soul. It was odd, Colin reflected, that the bitter warfare between Man and Achuultani should end this way, with the steady emergence of an alliance *of* Man and Achuultani against the computer which had victimized them both, all made possible only because *another* computer had risked its own existence to free them both.

And even if they were forced to destroy the Achuultani planets — a fate he prayed they could avoid — there would still be Aku'Ultan. Aided by the data Dahak had recovered from *Deathdealer*, Cohanna and Isis were slowly but steadily unlocking the puzzle of their genetic structure. At worst, they would be able to clone their prisoners within the next few decades; at best, Cohanna believed she could produce the first free Aku'Ultan females the universe had seen in seventy-three million years.

He grinned at the thought. It might be odd to find himself thinking of Achuultani allies, but not as "odd" as some of the things Brashieel and his fellows might have to get used to. The centaurs were still baffled by the very notion of two sexes. If Cohanna succeeded, Brashieel might find learning to live without a computer running his life the *least* of his problems. His grin grew broad enough to crack his face at the thought.

"What doth amuse thee so, my love?" his wife demanded, and he burst out laughing.

"Only life's little surprises, 'Tanni," he said, hugging her tight and kissing her. "Only life."

DAVID WEBER

<u>The Honor Harrington series:</u> *(cont.)*

Field of Dishonor

Honor goes home to Manticore—and fights for her life on a battlefield she never trained for, in a private war that offers just two choices: death—or a "victory" that can end only in dishonor and the loss of all she loves. . . .

Flag in Exile

Hounded into retirement and disgrace by political enemies, Honor Harrington has retreated to planet Grayson, where powerful men plot to reverse the changes she has brought to their world. And for their plans to succeed, Honor Harrington must die!

Honor Among Enemies

Offered a chance to end her exile and again command a ship, Honor Harrington must use a crew drawn from the dregs of the service to stop pirates who are plundering commerce. Her enemies have chosen the mission carefully, thinking that either she will stop the raiders or they will kill her . . . and either way, her enemies will win. . . .

In Enemy Hands

After being ambushed, Honor finds herself aboard an enemy cruiser, bound for her scheduled execution. But one lesson Honor has never learned is how to give up!

Echoes of Honor

"Brilliant! Brilliant! Brilliant!"—*Anne McCaffrey*

continued ☛

DAVID WEBER

The Honor Harrington series: *(cont.)*

Ashes of Victory
Honor has escaped from the prison planet called Hell and returned to the Manticoran Alliance, to the heart of a furnace of new weapons, new strategies, new tactics, spies, diplomacy, and assassination.

War of Honor
No one wanted another war. Neither the Republic of Haven, nor Manticore—and certainly not Honor Harrington. Unfortunately, what they wanted didn't matter.

AND DON'T MISS—
—the Honor Harrington <u>anthologies</u>, with stories from David Weber, John Ringo, Eric Flint, Jane Lindskold, and more!

HONOR HARRINGTON BOOKS by DAVID WEBER

On Basilisk Station	(HC) 57793-X /$18.00	☐
	(PB) 72163-1 / $7.99	☐
The Honor of the Queen	72172-0 / $7.99	☐
The Short Victorious War	87596-5 / $6.99	☐
	7434-3551-6 /$14.00	☐
Field of Dishonor	87624-4 / $6.99	☐

continued (☛